# Dacia Wolf
## & the Prophecy

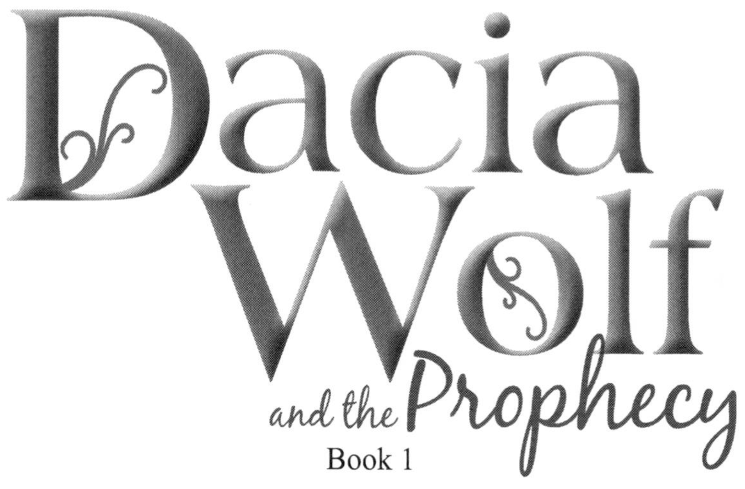


Book 1

Visit Mandi Oyster online at
www.MandiOyster.com

Facebook: https://www.facebook.com/MandiOysterAuthor
Instagram: https://www.instagram.com/mandioyster/

Cover Illustration by Mandi Oyster

Typography and formatting by Mandi Oyster

*This book is dedicated to my family:*
*my loving husband, Jeff, my soulmate and best friend;*
*my beautiful daughter, Jami, who believes she can stop the wind;*
*my mischievous son, Jesse, who fills my life with amusement;*
*and to my Dad and Mom, Jim and Vicki, the best parents*
*anyone could ask for.*

*I couldn't live without them.*

# Chapter 1

## *My Name Is Dacia Wolf, And This Is My Story*

Fire twirled and spun across my ceiling. I stared at the blue-green flames, dancing along my curtains, flickering down the walls. Behind them, a trail of blackened boards glowed red.

Mom and Dad told me what to do in a fire, but I was too scared to remember. I pulled Glacier, my teddy bear, closer to me and huddled beneath the covers. "Mommy. Daddy." My voice escaped as little more than a whisper. I closed my eyes, gathered my strength and shouted, "Mom! Dad!"

Smoke burned my nose and throat, making me cough so hard tears ran down my cheeks. The fire climbed my dresser. Snapping, blue sparks shot up to the ceiling.

The doorknob rattled, and I looked away from the flames. My parents stood in the hallway. Mom's hand covered her mouth. “Oh, Dacia, no.” She ran down the hall at the same time Dad ran into my room.

I reached my arms out to Dad and scooted to the edge of my bed. Flames shot up between us, pushing him back.

“Daddy!” I sucked in a lungful of smoke and coughed it back out. I stretched as far as I could reach. “Come back, Daddy!”

Mom screamed. She ran to my door, her face nuzzled against my brother’s. She held Jonathan out to Dad, then pulled him back against her. Tears ran down her cheeks. “Dear God, don’t take my baby. Please don’t take my baby.”

Dad looked over his shoulder at me. “We’re going to get you out of there, Angel. You’re going to be all right.” He grabbed Mom’s hand and pulled her down the hall.

I stared at the empty doorway. Tears filling my eyes, I buried my face in Glacier’s fur and whispered, “They left me.” I watched the door, waiting for them to come back to get me. I waited longer than any girl should have to wait.

Smoke filled my lungs. Coughing and spluttering, I hunched over Glacier to keep her safe. “It’s okay, Glacier. Don’t cry.”

Flames licked the end of my bed, popping and crackling as the fire crept to my comforter. Sweat ran from my forehead and dripped off my nose and chin. I whimpered as I sat up and pushed back against my headboard, clutching Glacier to my chest.

Red and blue lights flashed along my walls. My window burst in. Glass flew across the room, and a fireman stepped through the flames. He ran to my bed, lifted me up, climbed over the windowsill with me in his arms and carried me to the flashing lights.

Fresh air hit my face, carrying the smell of smoke away. It felt good not to cough with each breath.

"She needs a paramedic." The fireman's chest bounced against my ear when he talked. "Ozzie, bring the stretcher over here." I heard a clattering noise. Then the fireman said, "I'm gonna lay you down now, honey." He put me on a little bed with wheels. "This is Ozzie. He's going to make sure you're okay."

My lip trembled, and I started crying. "Please … please don't leave me and Glacier." I reached out to him. "Mommy and Daddy left me."

He patted my head and bent down. Black streaks marked his face. "I'll stay right here with you, but Ozzie needs to make sure you're not hurt."

Ozzie put me and the bed in an ambulance, and the fireman sat beside me, holding my hand as I clutched Glacier with the other. "I'm going to ask you some questions. Okay?"

I nodded while Ozzie put a band around my arm. Then he shined a flashlight in my eyes. "I need to put this on one of your fingers." He held a pincher thing up for me to see. "It's going to tell me how much oxygen is in your blood." His mustache wiggled when he talked.

I stuck my finger out, and it squeezed but not too hard.

The fireman asked, "What's your name?"

The thing on my arm tightened. "Dacia. What's yours?"

"Dale. How old are you?"

I looked at the thing on my finger. A green light flashed on it. "Six."

"How about your bear … Glacier?"

"She's six too."

"Wow, you guys are really brave for six."

I looked up at him and giggled. "We're not guys."

His smile reminded me of playing in the sprinkler. "No. No, you're ladies."

I covered my laugh with my hand. "Silly, we're girls."

"You sure are."

Ozzie took the band off my arm. "I'm going to make sure you don't have any burns now." He lifted my hair back and looked at my face. Then he pushed my sleeves up.

Dale pointed to my house while Ozzie checked me. "Can you tell me what happened in there?"

I shook my head. "Where are Mommy and Daddy? Where's Jonathan?"

He pointed to another ambulance with red and blue lights flashing. "Over there."

My eyes got really big, and my lip started shaking. "Are they okay?"

He turned away, and when he looked back, his eyes were shiny. He rubbed his face. "Can you answer me now?"

"Um." I looked around the ambulance, not wanting to tell him. "I forgot what you asked."

"What happened in there?" He pointed at my bedroom. "How did the fire start?"

I squeezed Glacier and whispered in her ear, "He looks nice, Glacier. Should I tell him?"

I watched the fireman while Glacier answered.

"She says I should tell you."

He nodded. "She's a smart bear."

"A monster was in my room, and I said get out, and he said no, and I said leave now, and he growled at me, and I threw fire at him." My voice started quiet and slow and got louder and faster.

Ozzie took the thing off my finger. "I need to give her oxygen now."

Dale held up his finger. "One more question." He looked at me again. "With matches?"

"No, silly, matches don't make blue and green fire." I wiggled my fingers at him. "My hands do."

# Chapter 2

## Twelve Years Later

Okay, I'll admit it. I was scared. No, not scared. I was terrified. I paced the floor. I sat down and crossed my legs. I uncrossed my legs and tapped my foot. I sprung to my feet and started pacing again.

The sign on my door listed my roommate as Samantha Waters, but that didn't tell me anything. *Is she nice? Will I like her? Will she like me?* I ran my fingers through my hair and walked to the window, longing to see a familiar car in the lot, but my parents, early birds to the core, had already come and gone.

On her way out, Mom had put her hand on my arm. "This will be easier for you if you don't have your father and me watching over your shoulder."

I looked to Dad for help, but I should've known better. "We'll just be in your way here."

"I went to kindergarten with the same kids I graduated with." Looking at the floor, I wrapped my arms around myself. "I don't know how to meet new people."

Mom pulled me into a hug. "You'll be fine," she said as she released me.

"We've got a long drive home, Angel." Dad gave me a quick, one-armed hug.

I rolled my eyes. "Not that far."

"Call if you need us." Mom waved and walked out the door.

*I need you now.*

I pushed off the windowsill and resumed pacing. Through the open door, I saw students and their parents lugging boxes to their rooms. If I were braver, I would offer to help. Instead, I stayed hidden, staring at the white walls, wondering what it would be like to have a roommate, hoping I could control my powers and seem like any other eighteen-year-old.

I glanced at my cell phone. No signal. I blew out a heavy sigh. *I guess that's what I get for going to school in the mountains.*

A woman's voice drifted through the door. "Now, Samantha, I'm sure everything will be fine."

I slumped into a chair and ran my hand through my hair. The time had come.

"I hope you're right," a nervous voice responded.

"Oh, this is it here." A heavy-set woman with short, auburn hair stepped into the room. "And, look. This must be your roommate, Day … How do you say your name, dear?"

"Day-sha," I said. Looking into her light brown eyes, my anxiety eased. She seemed like the type of person who never met a stranger.

She took a couple steps forward. "What a pretty name. I'm Deana Waters." She peeked over her shoulder. "And, what happened to my husband and daughter?"

"We're right behind you, Mother," a man said.

Deana put her hands on her hips and shook her head at the tall, balding man. "Now, do I really look like your mother?" she asked him before turning back to me. "Despite what he thinks, this is my husband, Wayne. Wayne, Dacia."

"Nice to meet you," Wayne said, extending his hand to me. His hand was etched by a lifetime of hard work and dwarfed mine. His hazel eyes were friendly and reassuring. "This is our daughter, Samantha."

A petite brunette lifted her hand in a timid wave. "Hi."

I returned her wave. "Would you like help carrying your stuff in?"

"That would be wonderful," Deana replied. "When we're finished, we're going to take Samantha to dinner in Althea. We'd love for you to join us."

I looked from Deana to Wayne to Samantha unsure what to say. My parents couldn't wait to get away from me. They hadn't taken me to a restaurant with them in years. *What would it be like to have a family that wasn't embarrassed by you, that didn't fear you?* "Oh … uh, that's okay."

"Oh, you must come along," she insisted. "We'd love to get to know you."

"Mom," Samantha said with a huff. "Maybe she has plans."

Deana turned to me as if the thought had never occurred to her. "Well, do you, dear?"

"No, ma'am."

"It's settled, then." Deana turned to Wayne. "Shall we?"

Samantha took in the room. One window faced the parking lot, and one looked toward Falcon Lake and the Snowfire mountains. There was a sink by the door with a mirror above it. Two loft beds hung on the wall with a desk under one and a TV under the other. The lavender carpet did not go with the two fuzzy chairs, one blue and one yellow. "Oh." She covered her mouth with her hand. "Those chairs are perfect. They look so comfy."

"They are," I agreed. "I named them Big Bird and Cookie Monster when I was little." My face flushed with the revelation.

Samantha's soft brown eyes lit up. "Cute!"

We carried Samantha's boxes and luggage in, then piled in her parents' SUV and rode to Althea. Phlox University sat above the small mountain town. Life came to Althea in the summer as tourists filled the streets, wanting to enjoy the clean mountain air and beautiful vistas. During the winter months, skiers took shelter in the various types of lodging, from the rustic cabins to elegant hotels, offered by the small town.

Wayne drove while Deana chatted. "Where are you from?"

"Bittersweet. It's about three hours west of here."

"What are your parents like?"

*How should I answer?* This isn't the kind of thing you get into with your brand-new roommate and her family. This is the kind of question therapists get rich off. I lifted my shoulders. "They're nice, still married."

"Do you have any brothers or sisters?"

"I had a brother." I tried not to dwell on my answer. "He died when he was two."

Samantha gasped. "That's terrible."

"I can't imagine losing a child." Deana wiped at her eyes. After a brief pause, she asked, "Have you decided on a major?"

"No."

Wayne never said a word, but he met my eyes in the mirror and gave me an encouraging smile.

"Do you have any hobbies?"

"Yeah—"

Samantha interrupted, "Mom. This is not the Spanish Inquisition. Give her a break."

"I'm sorry." She turned in her seat and flashed me a lopsided grin. "I just love making new friends."

I couldn't help smiling at her enthusiasm. "It's okay."

"Don't tell her it's okay." Wayne chuckled. "If she thinks it's okay, she'll never stop asking questions."

Wayne pulled into the parking lot at Rocky's Bar and Grille. "We're here, so further interrogations will have to wait."

Peanut shells littered the floor of the dimly lit restaurant. It smelled like steak and homemade bread. My stomach growled in response.

I would've been fine listening to Samantha and her parents talk through dinner, but it seemed Deana wanted to keep me actively involved.

"Do you have a boyfriend?" she asked around a bite of salad.

"No."

"Neither does Sammi. The two of you can go trolling for guys."

"Mo-om!" Samantha set her fork down and buried her face in her hands.

Deana shrugged and tilted her head. "I'm just saying."

Wayne shook his head. His eyes twinkled when he said, "Now, Deana, you know mothers aren't supposed to say trolling."

"No, she's not supposed to talk about guys." Samantha turned to me. "She always tries to set me up with the geeky ones."

"Oh, fine." Deana waved her hand as if clearing the subject from the air. "What about school? Are you a good student?"

"Uh … yeah." I fidgeted with my napkin.

"Oh, it's okay if you're not."

"No, I am."

"Sammi was valedictorian." Deana gave Samantha an award-winning smile.

"You don't have to brag," Samantha said. "But, I would die if I didn't get an A."

My lips curved up. "I know what you mean."

"Deana"—Wayne pointed at my plate—"you need to leave Dacia alone. She can't eat with you grilling her."

After we finished eating, our waitress returned to the table. "Can I get anything else for you?"

"No," Wayne said. "I think we're ready for the check."

"I'll be right back with that." She turned and walked off.

"I'll pay for mine," I said.

"No, you won't," Deana argued. "We invited you to dinner. We pay for our guests."

Heat blanketed my cheeks as I set my napkin on my plate. Not wanting anyone to notice, I stared down at it. "Thank you."

When we stepped out of Rocky's, the sunset cast a pink glow on the mountains, softening their edges. I wished I had a camera with me or better yet, my paints and a canvas. My fingers itched to hold a brush in them.

Judging by the silence on the ride back to campus, I assumed Deana ran out of questions for me. I glanced at Samantha and smiled. It was nice to have a clean slate with someone, to have the chance to be more than just a freak of nature for a change. Maybe if I could control my emotions and keep bad things from happening, I could make friends at Phlox University.

"Thanks for dinner," I told Wayne and Deana when they dropped us off at Wisteria Hall.

"No problem," Wayne replied. "After the badgering you went through, you deserved it."

I walked up to my room by myself. The walls were white with wisteria vines painted on them. White and purple-flecked tiles covered the floors.

Parents and students carrying boxes crowded the hallways. I dodged to avoid running into somebody coming out of a room and bumped into someone else instead.

"Watch where you're going," she said in a frosty voice. I turned to see a couple girls standing in the hall. Icy blue eyes glared at me.

"Sorry."

"Yeah, well, steer clear of me in the future."

"It's not a big deal, Cassandra," the other one said.

Cassandra flicked her long, black hair over her shoulder. "Yes, it is."

My stomach tightened. I needed to get away from her. "Don't worry. I'll do my best to stay away from you." I hurried down the hall, stepped into my room and slammed the door.

Moments later, Samantha came in. "I'm sorry about Mom. She's a people person and doesn't understand some people are shy."

"You don't have to apologize. Your parents are great."

She laughed. "Yeah, maybe, but my poor dad can't get a word in edgewise when she's around." She plopped down in Big Bird.

"I noticed." Silence grew between us, filling the room like a third person. Unable to stand it, I asked, "So, are any of your friends going here?"

"I have some acquaintances here but no close friends. How about you?"

"My best friend will be here tomorrow."

"Oh." Her eyes pulled down, and she rubbed the fuzzy, yellow fabric of the chair. "Why aren't you sharing a room?"

"Cody's a guy." My lips crept up in a smile. "There are no co-ed dorms here, and it would be kind of weird anyway." I hesitated a moment before asking, "So, uh, do you know somebody here named Cassandra?"

"No. Why?"

"I accidentally bumped into her. No big deal, right?" I flicked my palms up. "The halls are crowded, but she warned me to stay away from her."

"Sounds like a psycho."

# Chapter 3

## *Never Judge A Book By Its Cover*

I walk through thick fog, heading toward a diffused light. As I near it, the silence is broken by a shrill, terrified scream.

I don't think; I run toward the commotion. My feet thud against the pavement. I slow, wondering what I am running to. Movement in the bushes makes my heart race. I glance over my shoulder, but fog obscures my vision and distorts my surroundings. I strain, listening for anything to help me find the source of the scream.

Footsteps.

"Who's there?" My voice shakes. I stop. My breath is shallow, ragged. I turn in circles. Then I see them. Cold, hard, reptilian eyes. Evil permeates the air.

Fear tickles my neck, and my flesh shudders. Dread clutches my heart, and my breath is torn from my lungs.

I woke up with a jolt, sitting upright in bed. My heart raced, and I gasped for breath. I glanced at Samantha's bed to find her sound asleep. *At least I didn't scream.*

For the rest of the night, I tossed and turned. Sleep eluded me. I got up, dressed in blue jeans and a hunter green hoodie, pulled on my tennis shoes and went for a walk. I strolled across campus. Breathing in the crisp mountain air, tension released from my body.

The sun rose above the Snowfire Mountains. Pine trees covered the hillsides, growing sparser toward the tree line. The rugged cliffs were topped with snow from winters gone by. At the base, deciduous trees wore their stunning autumn dresses. They covered the campus and surrounded nearby Falcon Lake. As I took in the scenery, I felt more like myself.

I sat on a bench between the parking lot and the dorms. Several students came and went, but I only cared about one. Cody's blue Camaro pulled into the parking lot, and my heart danced. I jumped to my feet and jogged over to him.

Cody stepped out of his car and pulled on a purple and gold Bittersweet Lions hoodie. He stuffed his hands in his jeans pockets and waited for me. The wind tousled his blond hair. We had been friends since second grade, but I couldn't help admiring him.

I came to a stop in front of him, and he greeted me with a broad grin.

"Hey, where are your parents?" I asked.

"Britny's not feeling good, so I told them to stay and take care of her."

Standing this close to Cody, I had to look up to see his blue eyes. I could tell it bothered him to have to come on his own, but I knew he wouldn't want me to dwell on it. I rested my hand on his arm and said, "You're such a good brother."

Cody just stood there looking at me, one side of his mouth turned up in a mischievous grin.

"What?" I asked. "Do I have something on my face?"

"Besides the freckles?" He laughed, and it was contagious. "No, your eyes are really green today."

Heat rose up my neck and onto my face and ears. "Thanks." I twirled a red curl around my finger.

"Help me carry my stuff?" he asked.

"Sure."

We grabbed boxes and lugged them to Dracaena Hall, the men's dorm.

"Miss me?" he asked.

I bumped my hip into him playfully. "Of course."

Lines of tension branched from his eyes. "Seriously, though. Did anything happen?"

I shook my head.

"Good."

Over the years, Cody had taken a lot of crap for befriending me. His looks and athletic ability had always made him very popular, but the rest of his friends couldn't figure out why he spent time with me. When we were juniors in high school, I had asked him, "Why do you act like I'm special when everybody else treats me like the plague?"

"I feel drawn to you, Dacia. Like there's a connection between us." His blue eyes sparkled with sincerity. "Besides, somebody needs to watch your back."

"Hey, anybody in there?" Cody asked.

"Sorry, I was just reminiscing. Did you say something?"

He nodded his head at the door. "My room."

Cody turned the doorknob, but it was locked. "Crap." He knocked. "I hope he's in there."

A groggy guy wearing only boxers answered the door. "What?" He pushed his auburn hair off his forehead. He looked at the boxes, then at our faces. "You must be Cody Hawks. I'm Drew Crocus." He stood to the side to let us in. "And, you are?"

"Dacia Wolf."

"Your girlfriend's hot, dude." Drew held his hand up for a fist bump.

Cody hit it. "Yeah—" he let his gaze trail over me "—she is."

Warmth flooded my face. "And, right now, I think I could fill in for a stoplight."

"Sorry." Drew shrugged. "It's early. No filter."

I expected Cody to tell Drew our relationship was platonic, but he didn't. *Weird.*

We set our boxes down on his side of the room and went to get more.

"Well, that was awkward," I said.

Cody dragged his hand down his face. "You realize you have to get my approval before dating anyone, right?"

I expected his eyes to be light or a grin to spread across his face. His seriousness came as a surprise. "Nobody's gonna want to date me." I looked away from him. "I'm sure most people will avoid me by the end of the week."

"This isn't Bittersweet." He put his arm around my shoulders. "You get a second chance."

I stopped walking and stared off into the distance. The trees shivered in the light breeze. "I hope I can fit in." I pulled my fingers through my hair. "But, realistically, something will happen. I'll get angry or scared, and something will spontaneously combust or fly across the room. People will figure out it's me." My voice wasn't as strong as I hoped it would be. "You should separate yourself from me."

Cody lifted my chin, forcing me to look into his eyes. "I don't care what people think. You need me."

I couldn't deny that. His presence grounded me.

Cody was handing me boxes when I asked, "Do you really think I'm hot?"

His face turned bright red. He stared at me for a moment. "Haven't you ever looked in a mirror?"

I turned away from him to hide my embarrassment. "You're so sweet."

ஐ

My heart pounded, trying to free itself from my chest. I lay back on my pillow and closed my eyes. The yellow snake-like eyes from my nightmare stared back at me. They felt so real. I wiped sweat from my forehead and took a deep breath. *It's just a dream*, I told myself. *But it's been the same one for nine nights now.*

# Chapter 4

## Phlox University

Being a small, private college, Phlox University had an average class size of sixteen students. After the first two days, I realized this semester might be a little rough. Of the four classes I was taking, Cassandra was in three of them. Apparently, she was also undecided on her major.

Fortunately, Cody was in two of my classes, and Samantha was also in one of them. The class I looked forward to the most, though, was painting. Nobody I knew was in that class with me.

I didn't know what I did to offend Cassandra, but she made sure I knew she didn't like me. She glared at me. She pointed at me while talking to the two guys and girls who were with her most frequently.

I did my best to avoid her, to sit as far from her and her friends as possible. With the small classes, I couldn't get far enough away.

"What does she have against you anyway?" Samantha asked after we left advanced algebra. The only place we could find three seats together was right across the aisle from Cassandra and her friends.

"I have no idea," I said.

Cody stood back with his arms crossed, looking me up and down. "Jealousy."

I snorted, then covered my mouth. "Sorry. I don't think so. She's gorgeous."

Pushing my shoulder, Cody said, "But you're hot."

Samantha looked at us like we were nuts.

"According to Cody's roommate, I'm hot." I shrugged.

Tilting her head to the side, Samantha asked, "He just came out and said that?"

"His filter wasn't working," Cody said.

The walk from Kalmia Hall to Sedum Student Center only took a couple minutes. We went to the dining hall for lunch.

Just as I went to take a bite of my taco, a guy said, "Mind if I join you?"

Cody kicked a chair out. "Hey, Dan. Sit." Cody introduced us, and when Dan smiled, angels sighed.

"What are you lovely ladies doing with this guy anyway?" He hooked his thumb at Cody.

I pointed at my mouth to let him know I'd answer when my mouth wasn't full. "Sorry. He's my best friend." I pointed at Samantha. "She's my roommate. How do you know each other?"

"We shot some hoops yesterday," Dan said.

We talked longer than I expected. Finally, Samantha stood up and said, "I've got to go to class. See you later."

Dan looked at the clock. "Aw, crap. What class?"

"Accounting."

"Me, too." Dan picked up his tray. "I'll walk with you, if you don't mind."

Smiling, she said, "That'd be nice."

ꟈ

"Well, I met your buddy, Cassandra, today." Samantha plopped down in the desk chair. "She wanted to know if we knew each other before."

"Why would she care?" I asked.

Samantha rocked from side to side, not looking at me. "She warned me that you're dangerous."

"What?" I grasped the arms of the chair and planted my feet on the floor. "I bumped her. I said sorry. It was an accident." Heat rose inside me. I turned my chair so Samantha couldn't see my face. *How does she know? What does she know?*

"Dacia, I don't believe her." Her voice was soothing. "I've only known you a couple of days, but I … I think we could be great friends."

I spun the chair and smiled at her. "I think so, too. Thank God I didn't get stuck with her."

Samantha smiled back. “Just so you know, this means I’m trusting you not to kill me in my sleep.”

I tilted my head to the side and lifted my other shoulder. “I can’t make any promises.” I sighed. “But, I’ll try.”

# Chapter 5

## *Burning Books*

Standing in front of people talking had to be one of the worst forms of torture ever devised. In high school and college, they called it education. Maybe it wasn't as bad for other people as for me. However, when I stood in front of that many people, I got nervous. When I got nervous, things caught on fire or flew through the air.

If I'd ever met or heard of anybody else spontaneously combusting their peers' homework, maybe it wouldn't be such a big deal but, knowing what a freak I am, made things a little worse.

One week after classes had started, Professor Mantis scanned the room, searching for her first victim of the semester. Her long brown hair bounced against her shoulders as she strode across the floor. Her hazel eyes met mine. I looked away and willed her not to call my name. "Dacia, why don't you go first." It wasn't a question. I couldn't tell her no.

I ran my hand through my hair, grabbed my supplies and made my way down to her. I turned to face the class. "How to Paint an Apple."

"Louder, please," Professor Mantis said.

Resting my canvas on my shoulder, I began to paint the outline of an apple while explaining how to blend colors to make the painting come alive. Between brush strokes, I tried to make eye contact with Professor Mantis and each student. When my eyes met Cassandra Nightshade's, I swear I felt her hatred for me.

"Uh," I stammered. A slow burn made its way up my neck and onto my face. I pulled my eyes away from her glower. "You need to blend the colors together to keep the highlights and shadows from having hard edges."

My skin burned as if I had a high fever. I squeezed my paintbrush until it cracked. The sound of it snapping made me even more furious. *So I bumped into her. Did that give her the right to treat me like a pariah?*

The blood flowing through my veins burned like lava. Sweat dotted my forehead and the back of my neck. I needed to get out of the room, to get fresh air, but I was stuck on stage, the center of attention. I grabbed a new paintbrush and continued my speech. I glanced up. Cassandra's eyes narrowed on me, her lips curled in contempt.

A tiny, glowing ember dropped onto Cassandra's notebook. In the next breath, blue flames leapt from her desk. She jumped up, knocking her chair over with a loud crash. The canvas slipped from my fingers. For a moment, I saw fire dancing along my bedroom ceiling and walls, relentless in its approach.

"What is going on?" Professor Mantis turned to face my classmates. "Oh, dear." She pointed at a boy in the front row. "Mark, grab the fire extinguisher." She darted over to him, taking it from his hands. "Get out of here."

While she battled the fire, students scurried like rats from the room, knocking into each other in their panic. Cassandra stood in the hallway surrounded by friends. I tried not to look at her as I walked by, but her hand shot out, latching onto my arm. She stepped closer to me. Her eyes burned with hatred. "I'll get even with you for that, Freak."

"I-I don't know—"

"You can't blame her, Cassi," said a boy with white-blond hair. "She was in front of us all, giving her speech. It would've been impossible for her to do it."

She turned to face him, letting go of my arm as she did. "Bryce." Her voice was venomous. "Believe me. It. Was. Her."

His pale green eyes met mine, and he shrugged. I scurried away while he held her attention. I made my way to the library and sat down in a cubicle in the far corner.

*Why her books?* Resting my head in my hands, I tried to calm down. My shoulders hunched forward, the weight of my curse dragging them down. Most people hated being considered normal, but I'd give almost anything to feel that way. When I felt a hand on my shoulder, I nearly jumped out of my skin.

"Oops. Sorry to scare you," Cody said with a chuckle. "Guess you didn't hear me."

His blue eyes glimmered, and my heart skipped a beat. *Just friends,* I reminded myself.

"So … the fire." He knelt down beside me and rested his hands on my knees. "Yours?"

I lowered my head, not wanting to see his reaction. "Yep."

"No biggie. Nobody knows but me, and I won't tell."

A tear escaped from the corner of my eye. It raced down my cheek and dripped off my chin. "Cassandra knew. She told me she'd get even with me." Another tear followed.

His mouth opened, but nothing came out.

"I thought things would be better when I got out of Bittersweet. I thought I would be able to blend in here. Now, I'm not so sure." With my elbows on the desk and head in my hands, I whispered, "Samantha will find out. What will she think of me?"

"Hey, don't start feeling sorry for yourself," Cody said, his voice unexpectedly stern.

I felt like Cody'd sucker-punched me. He was supposed to be on my side. It was where he belonged, where he'd always been. "Why shouldn't I?"

"I like sunshine, and it'd be nice not to walk in rain."

I lifted my eyes to the ceiling and let out a long breath. "You're just jealous."

He raised his eyebrows. "Jealous?"

"Yeah, you wish your moods could change the weather."

"Darn right, I do." He pulled me to my feet and slung my backpack over his shoulder.

With every step we took toward class, I fought the urge to turn and flee. I didn't want to face Cassandra. I couldn't believe she, of all people, knew it was me. *How did she figure it out? How could she even guess? I was giving my speech, painting an apple when her books ignited. Why does she believe I did it? Does she know someone else like me?*

If not for Cody by my side, I never would have made it to the classroom, never would have climbed the stairs and sat in my seat, wouldn't have watched the door, waiting for Cassandra to stride in.

"Dacia, breathe." Cody threw his arm over the back of my chair. "Relax."

I shook my head. "Can't."

He pulled his arm away and ripped a piece of paper from his notebook. "Tic-Tac-Toe?"

I tore my focus away from the door and put an "X" in the upper left-hand corner. Three moves later, I said, "You let me win."

Cody shrugged. "It's working."

One move from winning the third game, the hair on my neck rose. Cassandra stood over me. Rage oozed from her. Through gritted teeth, she said, "You should have been drowned the day you were born."

My jaw tightened until it ached, and I curled my hands into fists. I pushed my chair back, but Cody wrapped his hand around my fist, rubbing his thumb over mine. At his touch, my tension began to diminish, loosening my muscles. Part of me wanted him to hold my hand forever, but the other part knew I couldn't do that to him. I couldn't take away his chance at a normal relationship, a normal life.

Cassandra looked from Cody's hand to his face and shook her head. "You could do so much better." She flipped her hair. "If you want to try, call me."

He squeezed my hand. "Nah, she's the best."

"What. Ever." She turned and stomped up the stairs.

Cody bent down and whispered. "You have to ignore her."

His breath brought goosebumps to my skin. I rubbed my arms. "Now, that's a power I'd love to have."

ꟗ

I sat in the crowded cafeteria. Utensils clanked against trays, students laughed and talked. I looked down at my grilled cheese, wondering if I should even try to eat it. I couldn't understand how Cassandra could hate me so much without even knowing me.

Samantha hadn't even sat down yet when she said, "I heard speech was exciting. Was that your class, Dacia?"

"Yeah." I lifted the top piece of bread off my sandwich and watched steam rise into the air. "I was giving my speech when Cassandra's book caught on fire."

"Wow." Her mouth hung open for a second. "What happened? Did you see?"

After years of covering for my powers, I'd gotten good at telling half-truths. It didn't feel right using them on Samantha, but what else could I do? If she knew what I was capable of she'd be terrified of me. Without looking at her, I answered, "I didn't see anybody do anything. I was even looking at her when it happened."

"So if you didn't see anyone else do it, did she start the fire herself?" Samantha asked just as Cody took a bite of his sandwich. "What's she saying?"

Cody swallowed his ham and cheese without chewing. "For some reason, she's blaming Dacia."

Samantha snorted. "She really is psycho, huh?"

# Chapter 6

## *Standing At A Crossroads*

The light for our voicemail flashed. Samantha picked the phone up and listened to the message. She fidgeted with her earring and walked in circles. A minute later, she hung up. "Dean Aspen wants to see you in her office. She's talking to everyone from your class this morning."

"Nice," I said without any inflection in my voice.

Samantha threw her bag over her shoulder. "I'll walk with you. It's on my way to Primrose."

"No, it's not."

She shrugged. "We have to walk outside to get to both of them."

I grabbed my stuff and followed her into the hall.

"Do you think you'll need that?" Samantha gestured to my backpack.

We stepped outside, and blinking back the light, I put my sunglasses on. "I'm hoping it'll go quickly, and I'll make it to my painting class." That's what I told Samantha, but I thought, *Is she really talking to everyone or just me? Does she know what I'm capable of? Will she expel me? Oh* ... I stopped walking and lowered my head. *What am I going to tell Mom and Dad?*

Shadows darkened the sidewalks. Grey clouds drifted overhead, clustering together and filling the sky until they blocked out the sun. I took my sunglasses off and put them on top of my head.

Samantha looked at the sky. "It wasn't supposed to rain today, was it?" She narrowed her eyes, tilted her head and turned to me. "Hey, are you okay? You're really pale."

"Just nervous." I tried to shoot her a reassuring smile, but it felt more like a grimace. I strolled forward, and she fell into step with me.

"You didn't do it. You didn't see who did." Samantha lifted her hands up and shrugged. "End of story. Right?"

*If only.* I let out a jittery sigh. "Yeah … but still. The Dean's office."

Samantha's voice lowered. "I know."

Walking across campus, I didn't take notice of anything: the mountain air, the birds singing, the herd of elk grazing in the pastures below the mountains, nothing. I was too concerned with what Dean Aspen might say, and how I would explain everything to her.

All too soon, we stood in front of Cacomistle Hall, a three-story, stone and timber building with Dean Aspen's office inside. My hand trembled as I reached for the door.

"You'll be fine." Samantha waved as she walked off. "See you after class," she called over her shoulder.

I took a deep breath and pushed the door open. Across from the seating area, a woman sat behind a desk. I walked up to her on shaking legs.

"Can I help you?" The plate on her desk said her name was Alicia Argali.

"Uh … yeah. I'm here …" I took a deep breath. "Sorry."

"Not a problem," she said politely.

Avoiding her eyes, for fear she would see my guilt, I focused on her spiky, bleached-blonde hair. "I'm Dacia Wolf. Dean Aspen is expecting me."

"Have a seat." She pointed a manicured finger at the leather couch and chairs that I had passed to get to her desk, then picked up the phone. "I'll let her know you're here."

I was too nervous to sit, but I sat. I felt like a kangaroo on a caffeine high; my leg drummed to a staccato beat against the stone tiles as I took in my surroundings. Timber columns formed a cathedral ceiling and large windows provided a spectacular view of the Snowfire Mountains. A stone fireplace filled the wall opposite the door.

"Miss Wolf, Dean Aspen will see you now."

I glanced around. No one was in the room but her and me. "Where?"

"Up the stairs, second door on the right."

"Thanks."

I climbed an open, rustic-looking staircase and stood in front of the door. I raised my fist to knock, then dropped it and wiped my palms on my jeans. Taking a deep breath, I lifted my hand. And the door opened.

"I thought you might be lost," said an older woman with gray streaks in her brown hair. She wore a tan pants suit with a sage silk blouse.

I struggled to breathe. *I'm not ready for this. I can't deal with a confrontation right now.* "No," I said, dropping my hand, "not lost, just really nervous."

The pictures I'd seen of Dean Aspen made her seem delicate. But, here, now, face to face, I didn't know why I'd thought that. Even though she was only a couple inches taller than me, I felt dwarfed by her. Maybe it was just nerves that made me feel so small, or maybe it was because she had the power to send me home.

She moved to the side and waved me in. "No need to be nervous. Come in and have a seat."

The room was massive. Two couches faced each other with a coffee table between them. A stone fireplace stood off to the side. A warm, inviting fire danced inside a hearth surrounded by floor-to-ceiling picture windows revealing the mountains. Bookcases lined the walls. Two doors interrupted the smooth wall across from me. One stood open, and judging from its contents, the room was an office. The other door remained closed.

I swallowed hard and sat. Dean Aspen perched on the couch opposite me. "Tell me about your class this morning."

She leaned forward with her elbow on her knee. Her chin rested on her thumb, and her index finger stretched along her cheek.

I ran my fingers through my hair. Noticing how bad they shook, I folded my hands in my lap. "There's not much to tell." I looked into her hazel eyes, willing her to believe me. "I was giving my speech and didn't see how it happened." I hated lying, hated that I had to do it to keep people from finding out the truth about me.

She tapped her finger against her cheek. Then sitting back, she said, "I interviewed Cassandra Nightshade first. She told me a slightly different version of this morning's episode."

My stomach did a cartwheel, and when it landed, it was tied in a thousand knots, each tightening with every breath I took. "Yeah." I rolled my eyes. "After class, she grabbed my arm and told me she knew I did it."

"And …"

"And." I unclasped my shaking hands and sat on them. "That's crazy. Isn't it? I can't imagine anyone else in there would blame me."

She lifted her shoulders. "For whatever reason, she does. Is there some animosity between the two of you?"

I shook my head. "I bumped into her … literally, the night I moved in here. I told her I was sorry, but …"

Understanding spread across the dean's face. "Some people have a tendency to blow things out of proportion."

I nodded my agreement. "Now every time I see her, she acts like I intentionally wronged her."

Her lips pressed together, and her forehead creased. "I know how teenage girls can be. Neither thinks they're the cause of the problem."

*How could she think that? I didn't start this. I don't even understand where Cassandra's hatred came from.* I clenched and unclenched my hands. "How could I have done it? I was standing in front of everyone."

Dean Aspen held her hand up. "I'm not suggesting you set her book on fire. She said that."

"I bumped her." Heat filled my stomach and spread through my veins. "I told her I was sorry. What more does she want?"

Dean Aspen's eyebrow lifted. "Maybe I need to have the two of you here together to work things out."

*That's all I need, to sit in a room with Cassandra. I'd be a ticking time bomb.* "If that's how you feel."

She looked at me like she expected me to say more.

I fidgeted and looked around the room. Finally, I looked her in the eyes. "What?"

She picked up her coffee mug and held it without taking a drink. "I think there's something you're not telling me."

*Of course, there is. Does she expect everyone to walk in here and spill their guts?* "Like what?"

She leaned forward. "You stood in front of the whole class and saw nothing. Nothing at all?"

A bitter laugh escaped from me.

"What?"

"Do you have any idea how many times I've thought that about teachers?" I shook my head. "Somehow most of them missed the kids pulling my hair and all the things they said and all the cheating."

Setting her cup back on the table, she said, "I'd like to think better of our teachers here."

I tugged my hand through my hair. "I'd like to think better of everyone, but how can you expect me to have seen everything while giving a speech while painting?"

Dean Aspen thrummed her fingers on the arm of the couch. "Cassandra said you were looking right at her when it happened."

Frustration built up inside of me. *Why is Cassandra's word gospel?* "What did the other students say?"

"I've only talked to the two of you so far."

I narrowed my eyes. "What about Mrs. Mantis? What did she say?"

The dean looked over my shoulder, avoiding my eyes. "She was taking notes and didn't see anything."

Another laugh. "And yet you think I should have." I clenched my teeth and sucked in a breath. This interrogation should've been over a long time ago. What was she trying to prove anyway? It was my word against Cassandra's, and the dean had no reason to believe I could've started the fire.

"I don't think you should have." She stared into my eyes. "I think you saw something or know what happened."

Fear and hopelessness clawed at my chest, fighting to escape. *How can I get out of this?* My leg bounced up and down. The room shook.

A low rumbling filled the room. Books shuddered and pictures pulled away from their hooks. I covered my ears, and Dean Aspen beamed like a lunatic.

She jumped up, clapped her hands together and let out a hearty laugh. "Crazy indeed."

The rumbling came to an abrupt stop when my tangled emotions turned into confusion. The only sounds in the room were the crackling of the fire and the thundering of my heart. Slouched down, I stared at the ceiling. Tears burned behind my eyes. I rubbed my hands over my face. "I'll pack my things." I swallowed to stop the wobble in my voice. "I can be out of here in a couple hours."

"Why would you want to do that?"

My eyebrows drew together. "I don't, but what choice do I have?"

"You can stay here." She sat next to me. "I can help you learn how to harness your power, to control it."

I wanted to say something, anything, but it was like I had just put a large spoonful of peanut butter in my mouth. I couldn't even begin to open it.

Dean Aspen put her hand on my shoulder. "This is not something you have to decide right now. Talk to your parents, your friends. Find out what they think. Then let me know what you want to do."

"Cody's the only one who understands." My voice was so soft, I wasn't sure if she heard me.

Her eyes widened a fraction. "Not your parents."

I shook my head.

"Talk to him. When you decide, give me a call."

Nothing about this felt right. Dean Aspen shouldn't have been comforting me and offering to help. She should have been afraid of me or at least amazed. I held my hand up. "Wait. What's going on? Why are you so happy about this?"

"I—"

Holding her in place with an icy stare, I stood up.

Her eyes widened.

"No, Cody's my best friend. He has been forever, but he was scared to death the first time he saw me do something like this." I pulled my hand through my curls. "Have you met someone like me before?"

"No."

"Then what?" I stood up and paced in front of the couch.

"I've heard about others like you."

I grabbed my stuff and ran out of her office, not stopping until I was outside, the fresh, clean scent of rain assaulted my nostrils, and the downpour washed away some of my anger.

*There's no one else like me.*

ꙮ

Cody slouched against his Camaro, waiting for me. I climbed into the passenger seat without as much as a hello. He got in and started the car. The radio blared. He reached over and turned it down, still on but too quiet to be distracting. "Where to?"

"Away."

He drove without saying anything. I watched the dense pine forest zip by.

Cody tapped on the wheel. "Well?"

I gazed out the window, not wanting to see his reaction. "Dean Aspen knows." Nothing but silence answered my confession. "She saw."

The car slowed down, and Cody pulled onto an overlook. A break in the trees left a view of meadows and a river flowing through the valley below. The vast scene made it seem like I could see the end of the world.

I turned to Cody. "Why are you stopping?"

He tilted his head to the side and let out a sigh. "This doesn't sound like a conversation we should have while I'm driving."

I chewed on my lip. "I needed privacy."

"Yeah. I get that." He turned the radio off. "You make it rain?"

I nodded.

"Stopped my basketball game but didn't last very long."

"Nah."

He ran his hands over the steering wheel. "So … not all bad."

The corners of my mouth lifted slightly. Nobody knew me like Cody. "Not all bad but …" I let out a troubled sigh. "It can't be good, can it?"

Cody squeezed my hand. "Start at the beginning."

With my head back against the seat, I took a deep breath and told him everything. He listened without interrupting.

"So where's the dilemma? Let her help you."

My eyes narrowed. "The dilemma. Really, you don't see it?" I tugged my fingers through my hair. "She knows what I can do."

"So do I." His voice was calm and even.

"So do Mom and Dad." I glared at Cody, daring him to say something.

He waved his hand in the air for me to continue.

"They can't stand to be around me. They're scared and in denial." I slumped forward, my head in my hands. "And I can't even blame them."

"Dacia." Cody's voice was a gentle caress. "The storm of the century won't help."

Ominous clouds rolled in, clashing against each other, creating lightning that spider-webbed through the sky. I got out of the car, slamming the door behind me and paced until the sky looked less foreboding.

Cody leaned against his car, his arms folded over his chest. "Don't overreact."

I shot him a dangerous look.

"Samantha needs to know."

"Why?"

"Really?" He walked over, hands in his pockets. "How do you want her to find out? With you in control or not?"

I kicked a rock, sending it soaring over the road and down the hill. "But, how am I supposed to tell her? She won't understand. No one does."

"I do," he said softly. "So does Dean Aspen."

I ran my hand through my hair. "She wasn't even scared."

"That's good isn't it?"

I took a long, slow breath. “No, it doesn’t make sense.”

He stepped closer to me and squeezed my shoulder. “It doesn’t scare me.”

“The first time?”

A humorless laugh escaped his lips. “Yeah, terrified.”

Pulling away from him, I stared off into the distance. “I don’t know if I can trust her. What if she wants to use me somehow?”

# Chapter 7

## Destinies And Prophecies

I sat in Dean Aspen's office, looking down at my hands, not knowing what to expect from her. "I don't know if I can trust you. You weren't scared. You weren't even surprised." I lifted my eyes to hers. "Nobody acts like that."

Dean Aspen had a faraway look in her eyes. "My grandfather was a man of faith. Not only did he have faith in God, he also had faith in our family's legacy. He believed some of us serve a higher purpose … that our paths have been shaped for us."

My face went blank. "Okaaay … My grandparents were religious too, but what does that have to do with anything?"

She smoothed her beige pants. "He told me I would meet someone like you, someone with powers, magic that was more than sleight of hand." She took a long, slow breath. "I thought I'd veered off my path, that my destiny was no longer mine to claim. I began to doubt my grandfather." She gestured toward me. "Now you're here. If my grandfather was right about this, then it all must be true. He told me my role in the prophecy was to train you."

I pushed my hands out in front of me, signaling for her to stop. "Hold on a minute. Prophecy?"

"Yes, we are part of a prophecy written long before either of us came to be. You, Dacia," she pointed at me a little too enthusiastically, "are destined to save the world."

I threw my head back and laughed. The sound lacked all traces of humor. "I don't think so. To be honest, I'm not even sure I'm destined to graduate from college. Yesterday, I felt destined to be expelled, but I've never felt destined to be great … to be a hero."

"I didn't anticipate your belief. However, I can help you." She stood up and paced in front of the couch. I counted her steps while trying to wrap my mind around what she was telling me. Three steps to the end, three steps back, then again.

She stopped. "If you decide to believe at some point, I can tell you more about the prophecy. If not, we can pretend I never mentioned it."

My elbows rested on my knees. I looked down at my hands, without blinking, until the shapes blurred into nothingness. "I don't know what to do."

"Let me help you."

I ran my hands over my face. "I don't know if I can."

Dean Aspen's eyebrows squished together. "Why not?"

"I never expected this. I never expected understanding, so I don't know if I can trust you." I looked into her hazel eyes, searching for any sign of deception, but in them, I only found reassurance. I took a deep breath, hoping I was making the right decision. "I never expected help, but I would be a fool to turn it down."

ꕥ

Cody waited on a bench outside Cacomistle Hall. His arms spread over the back, and his feet stretched out in front of him. His head tilted back, and his eyes closed. I walked over, shadowing him.

Without opening his eyes, he said, "What'd she say?"

"How did you know it was me?"

He lifted his head and looked at me with furrowed eyebrows. "Who else would it be?"

"Anybody." When he didn't respond, I plopped down beside him. "She believes we are part of a prophecy, and I'm supposed to save the world." I slumped against the bench and chewed my lower lip.

Cody nodded. "Cool."

"It's not cool." I smacked his arm and laughed. "The only other person who accepts me is a lunatic."

He shrugged. "If she can help, let her."

"I know. I told her I would, but … she believes in a prophecy. How can I take her seriously?"

Cody stood and stretched. The muscles in his arms flexed. I imagined his arms wrapped around me and then let out a sigh. *No, he deserves better.*

"One step at a time, Dacia."

"What?" It took me a second to remember what he was talking about. "Oh, yeah."

He reached his hand down and pulled me to my feet. "Maybe there's a reason you're the way you are. Maybe you have a destiny."

"Uh-huh. Sure."

"You never know."

ᘓ

I hide under Quartz Building's fire escape. The corrugated metal stairs wouldn't normally offer much shelter, but the dense fog makes it nearly impossible for me to see out. A smelly dumpster adds to my concealment.

My heart thunders, like the rumbling of timpani drums. I feel trapped. It takes all my restraint not to bolt.

I search the fog for the reason for my sudden, intense terror. *It can't just be my imagination.* I move forward, ready to make a break for my room. Then I see them; my breath catches in my throat. Two yellow, snake-like eyes search for me. I cower back into the corner. I haven't been spotted yet, but I can feel the creature penetrate my mind.

The creature moves closer. Encased in fog, I can't make out a face—just eyes surrounded by shadow. The beast invades my mind, reading my thoughts, using my eyes to see. A terrified scream pierces the still, night air. I glance around before realizing it came from me.

A low, growling voice fills the night. “This is the best your world has to offer, a scared little girl?” The air shakes with malevolent laughter. Just as the eyes peer into my hiding place, something grabs my shoulder.

My eyelids fluttered open. The light was on, and Samantha stood on my ladder. I sat up.

Samantha stifled a yawn. “You screamed.”

My hands shook as I pushed the hair out of my face. “Sorry.”

“Are you okay? You’re as white as a sheet. Do you need me to get you something?”

I shoved my sweat-soaked sheet away and took a deep breath. “I’ll be okay. It was just a dream.”

She rubbed the back of her neck. “You sure?”

“Yeah, why don’t you go back to sleep?” I fought to keep my voice calm. “I’m fine, really.”

“I’m here if you wanna talk about it.”

I pulled my lips into some semblance of a smile. “No.” I stretched and lay back down. “I’m going back to sleep, too. I’m sorry I woke you.”

My bravery wore off when Samantha turned off the light. I pulled the covers up to my chin and buried my face in Glacier’s fur, hiding from whatever monster my subconscious dug up for me to dream about.

# Chapter 8

## Laying Your Cards On The Table

Two days later, Samantha stood by the door. Her hand held the knob tight enough to make her tendons pop out. "You've been going to the dean's office every day." She turned to face me. "Why?"

I knew this question was coming, but I had hoped to avoid it until I came up with a way to tell her what I was capable of doing.

"You wouldn't believe me if I told you." I glanced at the clock on the wall. "I don't have time right now. How about we go to Falcon Lake with Cody after classes? I promise I'll tell you then."

She frowned at me before opening the door. "Sure. Whatever." We left our room together. Samantha fidgeted with her backpack. Finally, without looking at me, she said, "I know we haven't known each other very long, but you can trust me."

I put my hand on her shoulder. "I do, Samantha. I promise, I'll tell you everything after class."

"Whatever it is, it can't be that bad." The tension drained from her face.

A smirk pulled up one corner of my mouth. "We'll see."

Samantha headed off to her class, and I went to Cacomistle Hall. I trudged up to Dean Aspen's office and slouched on the couch with the best mountain view. Staring out at the snow-covered peaks, I tried to imagine what Samantha's reaction would be. It'd only been a few weeks, but I'd gotten used to having somebody other than Cody to talk to and share with. It would be nice to let her really know me, but could she handle that knowledge?

Dean Aspen sat across from me. "You seem a little down in the dumps today. Are you okay?"

An exaggerated sigh escaped my lips. "Samantha wants to know why I've been spending so much time here."

Dean Aspen lifted her mug to her lips. She had a way of processing everything I said before she responded, and right now, it was irritating.

"What are you going to tell her?"

My shoulder lifted in a half-hearted attempt at a shrug. "The truth. What else?" I hid my face in my hands. "Be prepared for her to ask for a new roommate."

"Do you really believe it will come to that?"

"Yeah, I do." I walked to the windows. "You and Cody are the only two people who have been able to handle knowing what I am."

"And what is that?"

I heard Dean Aspen's footsteps behind me, but I kept my back to her. "A freak of nature. A mistake. An anomaly."

"You don't think you're gifted, talented, blessed?" Her surprise was obvious.

I turned to face her. My voice, when it came out, was small. "No. This is a curse, not a blessing."

Her eyebrows pulled down. "It's clouding up again. I thought it was supposed to be sunny today." Shrugging, she walked back over to the couches. "I think we should try to decide what you would like to accomplish."

"I don't know, Dean."

"Why don't you call me Sarah when we're alone? Sometimes it's nice to remember I have an actual name."

I stopped pacing for a moment. My head tilted to the side. "Sure, I can do that." I took four steps toward the window. "I know it doesn't always seem like it, but I don't like being a negative person. I consider myself a realist." I took four steps away, turning to go back. "Anyway, to be honest with you, I don't know how you can help me."

Sarah picked up her cup off the coffee table and rested it on her knee. "If you let me, I think I can help you control your powers. I think the first step would be for you to tell me what causes you to misuse them most often."

"It only happens when my emotions get out of whack." I pointed out the window. "Like that. Those clouds rolled in when I told you how I feel. When I'm angry, things start flying through the air or catching on fire."

Sarah stared at the clouds with her head cocked.

*What is she thinking?*

Finally, she looked at me and jerked her thumb toward the window. "You have the power to change the weather?"

"Yup."

"Wow." Sarah shook her head and took a drink of her coffee. When she spoke again, it was without the awe in her voice. "My grandfather left me a couple journals. There is some information in them about how to train you. It will take some time, but to start with, I'll teach you some relaxation techniques to use when you feel your control slipping."

"Usually, by the time I realize my temper is becoming an issue, it's too late."

She tapped her finger against her chin. "Maybe working on relaxing will help with your awareness. We can try different techniques and figure out which works best for you."

"If you could do that for me, things would be much better."

"There are so many of them: yoga, tai chi, autogenic relaxation, visualization." She smiled like a six-year-old on Christmas morning. "The list goes on."

"I don't know anything about any of them, so it's up to you."

She nodded. "We'll start Tuesday."

I stood to leave but changed my mind and instead asked, "What makes you believe any of this?"

Her eyes looked far away. "For the last several years, I have been a Doubting Thomas. Before that, I knew Grandfather wouldn't lead me astray."

"So after years of questioning, you suddenly have no doubts?" I rubbed my face. This was too much. It was too much of a coincidence that I ended up at a college with somebody nutty enough to not be afraid of me. But to have somebody with prior knowledge of my powers was too good to be true. *Should I trust her?* "Just because you met me."

"Not exactly." She set her mug on the table. "I began to doubt the prophecy, but I've always known there was more in the world than most imagine. I have seen magical, wonderful things that have helped me believe."

I found myself leaning forward. Curiosity had gotten the best of me. "Like what?"

She stepped over and put her hand on my arm. "There are creatures in this world beyond what you could ever imagine. People are just so busy and so sure they know what's going on that they don't take notice. When somebody does, they are thought of as crazy, and these mystical creatures sigh in relief, knowing their secrets are safe for another day."

Sarah looked at her watch. "Now, I have a meeting to attend, so that will have to be a subject for a different day."

ꝏ

"How are you going to tell her?" Cody asked.

I plopped down on Cookie Monster. "I don't know. She's going to think I'm nuts." I got up and walked to our little refrigerator. "Do you want something to drink?" I pulled out a pop for myself.

"Sure. Water."

"Maybe we should stay here." I tossed a bottle to him. "I don't want anybody to overhear me."

Cody opened his water and took a swig. "Whatever you need. We can order pizza."

We turned on the TV. I tried to numb my mind, but all I could think about was telling Samantha. I thought about the people who'd found out in the past and how fast they ran. All of them were scared of me now. *She's going to run from here and never look back.*

The jiggle of the key in the doorknob sent my heart plummeting to my toes and the air whooshing from my lungs.

Cody knelt down on the floor in front of me and rested his hands on mine. "Breathe, Dacia. It's all right. Even if she can't accept it, you've got me. I won't abandon you."

"I know you won't, Code." I squeezed his fingers.

Samantha opened the door. "Hey, guys. Give me a few minutes, and we can head out."

Cody stood up. "We're going to order pizza and stay here … more privacy."

"Oh." Samantha set her stuff down and sat on Big Bird. "So … uh, what's going on? This sounds serious."

Cody sat on the arm of my chair and rested his hand on my shoulder. I drew strength from his touch. I couldn't watch Samantha. I didn't want to see her reaction. "We haven't known each other very long."

"Yeah …"

I lowered my head and took a deep breath. “Remember the day Cassandra’s books caught on fire?”

“Uh, yeah.” She looked at me like a third eye had opened up on my forehead. “It’s the most exciting thing that’s happened here. What about it?”

Cody stood up, and my chair rocked back. “Can Dacia trust you?”

Samantha looked from me to him. “What’s this about?”

“Can. She. Trust. You?” he asked again with more force.

“Yes, she can.”

Cody plopped down on the arm of my chair, bringing the rocking to a stop. “Go ahead then.”

“I did it.” I covered my face with my hands.

“Did what?”

“Set her books on fire.”

Samantha laughed, a strange humorless sound. “Sure. How? You were on the stage, nowhere near her.”

“I didn’t mean to, but sometimes I have trouble controlling my emotions. I’m not …” I swallowed over a lump in my throat. “I’m not normal.”

She looked from me to Cody. “I don’t know what you’re saying.” She tilted her head to the side.

Cody squeezed my shoulder. “Let me.”

I nodded.

“Dacia has powers.” Even though he was talking to Samantha, he never took his eyes off mine. “I guess that’s the word for what she can do. When she gets overemotional, it rains.” He pointed at the window. “It’s clouding up now. If she's angry, things fly through the air or catch on fire. Dean Aspen is helping her learn control."

"Um … okaaay. Sure." A hollow laugh penetrated the air. "You had me going for a minute." She slid her eyes from my face to Cody's. "So what's really going on?"

"It's the truth." I heard the desperation in my voice and hoped she did, too.

She twirled her bracelet around her wrist. "Yeah, well I suppose it could happen." She forced a smile at us. "According to Mom, I can breathe fire when I want."

I ran my fingers through my hair. "I knew you wouldn't believe me."

"Okay." She threw her arms up and stood. "So make me believe … show me."

I clenched my jaw. *Now she's really going to think I'm lying.* "I can't."

"You can't …" Samantha's voice was a challenge. "Why not?"

"I don't have that kind of control."

"So let me get this straight. You have these mysterious"—she wiggled her fingers in the air—"powers, but you have no control of them. Is that right?"

"Basically."

Samantha crossed her arms over her chest and pinned Cody with a steely gaze. "Besides the clouds—which I don't see how you can be sure Dacia is responsible for—have you seen these powers manifested?"

He returned the same hard look. "Yeah, I have, and … well, the first time it was scary as hell."

"Funny … very funny. Do you really think this is amusing? Because I sure don't."

Cody pulled himself up and stepped toward her. "No, it's not funny. It's Dacia's life. Believe it or not, it's the way it is."

"It's fine." The words scratched my throat.

Samantha turned her piercing gaze on me. "It's not fine. We haven't known each other long enough for the two of you to gang up on me. It's one thing to joke around but another to keep going." She pointed her finger at me. "I thought you were my friend."

"I am."

"Then stop yanking my chain!"

My gut twisted, and I dug my fingernails into the chair. "I. Am. Not. Yanking. Your. Chain."

Even with my hands clenched, I felt them shaking, felt myself losing control. The walls trembled, and Samantha's backpack wobbled before falling over and spilling its contents. The TV shuddered on its stand. Samantha's eyes widened, and her hand covered her mouth.

Cody stood in front of me and held my eyes with his. "Calm down, Dacia." His fingers brushed my cheek. The tenderness of his touch released some of my tension.

Samantha looked at the door, then back at Cody and me. "I think I need a minute."

I thought my heart would break when the door closed, but it didn't. Instead, I felt hollow.

Cody stared at the door long after Samantha pulled it shut. "I didn't see that coming." He looked down at me. "I'm sorry."

"I knew this would happen." My voice was flat and lifeless. Cody blurred through my unshed tears. "But, I hoped it wouldn't."

"She wasn't screaming." He shrugged. "Could be a good sign."

"You know there's not always a pot of gold at the end of the rainbow, don't you?" I stared out the window for a moment, then added, "Sometimes there isn't even a rainbow."

Cody reached his hand down to me. "There's always the possibility of a rainbow." He lifted me to my feet. "Let's get some fresh air."

When Cody opened the door, Samantha fell back into his arms and let out a scream of surprise. Red tinged her cheeks as she tried to right herself.

Cody helped her back to her feet. "You didn't make it very far."

"No." Samantha tucked a lock of hair behind her ear. "I just needed a second."

Relief slammed into my chest, making me stumble. I bent forward and rested my hands on my knees. "So you're okay with this?"

"Uh … well …"

Samantha walked around us and plopped down hard enough to rock the chair. "No, I can't wrap my mind around this. There's got to be some logical explanation, something that makes sense."

"There isn't." I wiped my hands on my jeans. "Believe me, I wish there was. I wish there were other people like me, so I didn't feel so alone all the time."

Her eyes searched Cody's face, then mine as if she looked for some sign of deception. "Okay, so you set Cassandra's books on fire. What does that have to do with Dean Aspen?"

My hands pulled through my hair, catching at the ends. "When she talked to me Tuesday, she caught a glimpse of my powers."

Samantha's fingers went up to her mouth to cover her gasp. "Oh, no."

"Oh, yeah." I shook my head. "And, she was excited."

"She was?"

"Yeah, she thinks I'm part of a prophecy."

Her mouth fell open, and she stared at me. "So … Dean Aspen is crazy?"

A small laugh escaped my lips. "It kinda seems that way."

Cody crossed his arms over his chest. His posture was stiff, imposing. His voice was hard. "You, Dean Aspen and I are the only ones who know what Dacia can do. Cassandra is just guessing."

Samantha swallowed. "Okay."

"It needs to stay that way."

She glared at Cody, then turned to me. "Dacia, you can call your guard dog off. I'm not going to tell anyone."

Cody rubbed his hands together. "So that's done. What kinda pizza we gettin'?"

# Chapter 9

## *Truth Hurts*

Cassandra sashayed into speech class flanked by three cronies. Bryce stood on the left. A girl with auburn hair and dark-rimmed glasses covered her right side. While a wiry guy with dark hair walked up behind her. From the corner of my eye, I watched them climb the stairs. When Cassandra neared my desk, she stumbled and dumped her cappuccino in my lap. I jumped up and wiped at my burning legs. The smell of the coffee made my stomach turn. My jeans dripped steaming liquid. But that was nothing compared to the beast raging inside me.

"Oh, my gosh. Are you okay?" Cassandra's hand shot up to cover her mouth. "I am so sorry."

To somebody sitting nearby, I'm sure she sounded sincere, but the laughter in her eyes sent a spark of fury shooting through me. I grabbed my papers and shoved them in my backpack. *I wonder if I can change my schedule. If she keeps antagonizing me, she's going to end up in the hospital or worse.*

"Why'd you do that?" the girl with Cassandra asked.

Cassandra shot her a nasty look. "Not now, Vanessa."

I took a deep breath. *Just get out of here, Dacia.* I started to push past them, but my anger won out. Through clenched teeth, I asked, "What did I ever do to you?"

Cassandra stood inches from me, her eyes slicing into mine. "You were born. Isn't that enough?"

My jaw floundered. "Wh-what?"

"You heard me."

I stumbled backward. People avoided me, feared me even, but her intense hatred surprised me. I turned and charged out of the room, my face hot with humiliation, my body vibrating with anger.

The wind howled through the trees as I walked back to my dorm room. Storm clouds rolled across the sky. *Breathe.* The first drops of rain fell with my tears. *How can a stranger hate me so much?* I wondered as I pulled my door open. I grabbed new clothes and went to take a shower.

Hot water pounded on my shoulders, easing the tension from my body. I stood under the steady stream until I felt reinvigorated.

ꟸ

By the time I got to English Literature, the storm had blown over. I sat beside Cody with my head down, doodling in the margins of my notebook. I didn't want to see Cassandra walk into class. I didn't want to see the haughty look on her face.

"People are wondering about these storms," Cody said. "Something happen?"

My pencil stopped mid-stroke. "After Cassandra dumped her cappuccino on me, she told me why she hates me."

He wrapped his arm around my shoulders but said nothing.

I sucked in a deep breath and whispered, "I was born."

"Don't let her get to you, Dacia." Cody rubbed my arm. "She's not worth it."

"Maybe." I resumed my drawing. The eyes from my nightmares took shape. I turned my pencil over and erased all traces of them.

Cody squeezed my shoulder, then stood up. I turned to see what was going on, just as he told Cassandra, "Stay away from Dacia."

Cassandra's voice was sweet innocence. "It was an accident."

"She told the little princess she was sorry." The dark undercurrent in Bryce's tone made me shiver. His green eyes simmered.

I shook my head and whispered, "We all know it wasn't an accident."

Cody slammed his fist down on the desk behind him. "It ends now."

"Sure, blondie," Cassandra said as she pushed past Cody, "whatever."

ഗ

I walk alone. A burning need pushes me. My pace quickens against my will. The glow from the streetlights can't penetrate the dense fog, but it doesn't slow me down. A scream cuts through the still night air. I pause, wanting to turn around. Instead, I sprint toward the sound. Stopping, my hand covers my mouth, holding in my own panicked cry. A crumpled body lies on the sidewalk.

I can't tell if it's a man or a woman. I don't know if the person is living or dead. I want to turn away, but I can't. I need to see who it is. I need to help. I glance around before I creep toward the body.

An owl hoots, and my heart jumps into my throat. I close my eyes and gather my wits. I pull my fingers through my hair before moving again. Stepping closer, I realize the body is a woman's. Brown boots are pulled over her jeans. The hood of her red coat hides her head. I close the distance and suck in a deep breath, unable to move.

Sarah's lifeless eyes stare into mine.

# Chapter 10

## *The Ice Princess*

"Dacia, wake up."

I opened my eyes to find Samantha standing on the ladder of my loft, shaking my shoulder. "I'm awake. I'm fine."

"You screamed."

"I …" I pictured Sarah's empty eyes. "I had a nightmare. I'm sorry I woke you up."

"So, are you ever gonna talk to me about these nightmares, or are you gonna just keep waking me up every night?"

I ran my hand through my hair. "I can't right now. I'm sorry."

"Fine." Samantha climbed down my ladder and up into her loft. "I need to get some sleep before I start failing my classes anyway."

ℵ

Morning's light warmed my skin but did little to stop the chill from last night's dream. I couldn't keep the images from playing back through my mind. I climbed out of my loft and grabbed my bathroom bag before slipping out the door.

I hoped a hot shower would wash away all traces of my latest nightmare. When I opened the door, the scent of bleach, perfume, and soap assaulted my nostrils. Cassandra stood in front of the sink dressed in a pink bathrobe, applying makeup. Seeing her there, I wanted to turn around and go back to my room, but I didn't want her to know she could get to me without even trying.

She caught my eye in the mirror as I walked by. "You sure you should be here without blondie?"

Ignoring her, I decided to use this opportunity to practice restraint, and if I wasn't able to control my powers, oh well. We were alone after all.

Cassandra, it seemed, didn't deal well with being ignored. "What is he doing with you anyway? Do you have some sort of spell on him?"

I locked the door and set my bag on the bench. I took out my soap, conditioner, and shampoo.

"Ooh, if I kissed him, would it break your hold on him?"

I turned the shower on to warm the water. *Don't listen to her. She doesn't know what she's talking about.*

"I don't know why they even allow people like you out in public."

Her voice clung to my skin and tore away my control.

"Your parents must be so ashamed and embarrassed by you."

The words cut through my barrier, lodging in my head, replaying over and over again. I pictured my parents' disgust every time my powers surfaced.

"I can almost imagine their surprise when they found out what a freak you are." A phony laugh followed her words.

My teeth chattered and goosebumps rose on my skin. I rubbed my arms, only managing to get colder.

"Poor mommy and daddy, I bet their first thought was they should have given you up for adoption."

I slid down the wall to the floor, trembling. My fingers and toes were numb.

"I'm surprised they didn't lock you in a cellar to keep you away from everyone."

The tips of my fingers turned blue. Nothing like this had ever happened to me before. I breathed onto my hands but felt no relief.

"I can't believe they let you out in public, but they were probably too excited to get rid of you to care what a menace you'd be. I can't really bl—"

A horrified scream stopped her incessant chatter.

Warmth reclaimed my body. Confused, I pulled myself off the floor and left the stall to see what I'd done. Cassandra stood in front of the sink, her hands frozen together under the faucet. The mirror in front of her was coated with a heavy frost. She fought to free her hands, but she couldn't budge them.

I struggled to keep the smile off my face. "Well, Cassandra, you can't say you didn't deserve that."

"You little witch." Unshed tears made her voice husky. "Fix this!"

"If you stop insulting me, I'm sure the ice will melt in a couple of minutes. If you continue to annoy me, God only knows how long you'll stand there." I took a lengthy shower. Then pulled on black sweat pants and a grey hoodie.

If Cassandra was still frozen to the sink, I wanted her to spend that time fretting about whether or not she would be okay. When I got out, she was gone and the sink was back to normal.

Humming, I walked back to my room, feeling good about the upcoming day.

I opened the door to find Samantha with her arms crossed, glaring at Cody. She only came up to his armpit, but even in her pink Tweety Bird pajamas, the look on her face could've stopped a grizzly.

Cody's hands were tucked in his jeans pockets, and his shoulders hunched forward.

"You need to explain to him"—she jabbed her finger toward Cody—"that Saturday mornings are for sleeping, especially if you're going to keep waking me up every night."

Cody threw his hands up. "It won't happen again."

I pushed the door closed and set my bathroom bag on the floor. "I'm sorry, Sam. I don't mean to wake you up."

"It's fine." Samantha's voice was gruff.

"Nightmares?" Cody asked at the same time.

"Later, Cody."

Samantha started back for her bed but turned back toward me and asked, "What was the huge grin for when you came in? Did you know *he* was here?"

A smile tugged at my lips, but I suppressed it. "Uh, no. I sorta froze Cassandra to the faucet."

"What?" Cody's eyes narrowed.

"You did what?" Samantha said at the same time.

I rocked from heel to toe. I should have realized Cody would be annoyed with me. "I tried to ignore her, but she went too far."

Samantha clasped her hand over her mouth, but the giggle escaped anyway. "I've got to see this. Is she still down there?"

Cody slowly shook his head before focusing his attention on the ground.

"No, she left before I finished showering." I let out a deep breath. "I'm sure I'll end up paying for it, but the look on her face … it just might have been worth it."

"Oh, that is too funny," Samantha said as she climbed into her loft.

Cody led me outside. "Dacia, you have to be careful. It's one thing when you're in a group and nobody knows who set the books on fire, but when you're alone with Cassandra, you have to get a grip."

I stopped, put my hands on my hips and glared up at him. "Don't you think I know that?"

"You're not acting like it," he answered, but I talked over him, not allowing his words to sink in.

"Don't you think I'm scared to death that somebody is going to take her seriously and I'll end up expelled or in some government lab somewhere?"

His expression softened a little. "Why do you let her get to you?"

"She knows all the right buttons to push." I kicked at the ground. "Somehow she knows all my insecurities, all my fears, and she won't stop until she gets some sort of reaction from me."

Cody's breath tickled my ear. "You can't let her win."

Goosebumps dotted my skin. I had to regain my composure before responding. "I know." I rested my hand on his arm. "I have to go see Sarah now. Do you want to come with me?"

"Yeah, and on the way, you can tell me about these nightmares you're having." He put his hand on the small of my back, leading me down the sidewalk.

"That's okay." I remembered Sarah's lifeless eyes staring up at me, and a chill ran over my skin. "They're just dreams."

He frowned at me but let it go.

When we arrived at Sarah's office, the receptionist wasn't at her desk. I thought about leaving, but I knew Sarah would want to know what happened this morning. Sarah didn't look surprised when she answered my knock. She led us to the couches and sat across from Cody and me while I told her my side of the story. When I finished, she paced in front of the windows.

"Cassandra's version was different," she finally said. "She, of course, didn't provoke you."

"She's been here?" Cody asked what I'd already guessed.

"She called me." Sarah continued pacing. Finally, she stopped and stared into my eyes. "You are putting me in a very difficult position."

I rubbed my arm while looking at the floor. "I know."

Cody stepped in front of me. "You can't blame Dacia." His voice rose steadily. "Cassandra can't keep egging her on."

I put my hand on Cody's arm. "She can blame me. It is my fault. I'm the abomination here."

"First off," Sarah shook her finger at me, "you are *not* an abomination. You have an amazing gift."

I opened my mouth to argue.

"Don't. Secondly, Cody, I know you feel the need to protect Dacia. You *don't* need to protect her from me."

"That's good to know," he said.

"I informed Cassandra that she couldn't continue making up such ludicrous stories. However, I'm not going to be able to hold her at bay forever." She resumed pacing. "You're going to have to learn control *soon*."

"I didn't mean to put you …"

"Enough said." Sarah held her hand up. "If you have some spare time today, you need to start training."

Cody turned from Sarah to me. "Why not now?"

Sarah looked at her watch. "I do have some time if you'd like."

I nodded.

"Since we met on Thursday, I've been going over my grandfather's journals."

"Not the prophecy." I shifted uncomfortably on the couch. "I don't think I can deal with that today."

"The prophecy is written in the journals, yes, but it also contains information on how I might help you."

"Oh. I'm sorry."

She grabbed a pen and notebook off the coffee table. "Do you have nightmares?"

"Yes," I whispered, "every night."

"She doesn't talk about them." Cody narrowed his eyes at me.

"Until last night, they weren't really anything." I placed my hand over Cody's. "I saw creepy, yellow eyes and heard screaming. If they didn't feel so real, I don't know if they'd even be scary."

Sarah's elbows rested on her knees. "What did you dream last night?"

A thousand butterflies sprang to life in my stomach. Their fluttering made my hands shake and my thoughts scatter. I opened my mouth but couldn't find the words. Sarah's teacup started dancing across the coffee table, and the knick-knacks on her shelf rattled.

"Dacia, breathe," Cody whispered in my ear while he rubbed my hand. "Everything's okay."

The butterflies settled one by one, giving control of my body back to me. I squeezed Cody's hand before running mine through my hair. "Sorry about that."

Sarah offered me a comforting smile. "That's perfectly fine. After all, it's why we're here."

I lowered my head so I couldn't see Sarah at all. "Last night, my dream started the same. I ran toward the scream, but this time I saw a body on the ground."

"Who was it?" Cody asked.

"I … I …" I wanted to lie to them, but what did it really matter? It was only a dream. I looked into Sarah's eyes. "It was you, Sarah."

The color drained from Sarah's face.

"I'm sorry." I wrapped my arms around my belly. "I didn't want to tell you, but it's only a dream. Right?"

"That depends on what you believe." Sarah's eyes were haunted. "For you, they are just dreams. However, I believe in the prophecy, so to me, they are premonitions."

"Premonitions? As in, I can see the future?" Nervous energy pushed me to my feet. I walked to the window and rested my forehead against the cool glass.

"How long have you been having these dreams?" Sarah asked.

"Since my first night here." My breath settled on the window, haloing the mountains in fog.

Cody crossed his arms over his chest. "Why didn't you tell me?"

"I don't know." I pulled my fingers through my hair. "I feel like … like I'm going to have an anxiety attack every time I think about talking about my nightmares."

"Is there more to your dream?" Sarah asked.

"After I found your body, something told me to run, hide. I did. I saw the monster's eyes through the fog. They looked right at me, without seeing me. Then I screamed. I had nowhere to run. I backed myself further into the corner. Right before I woke up, an enormous clawed hand reached in to grab me." The image of it made me tremble.

Sarah gestured toward the couch. "Whether you believe your dreams are premonitions or not, I think it's time to start training. Why don't you have a seat?"

Once I resumed my spot next to Cody, Sarah said, "I want you to relax. Close your eyes and picture yourself in a safe, comfortable place, somewhere you feel at ease. Focus on your breathing, and let all of the tension leave your body."

Taking long, slow breaths, I pictured myself sitting on a rock on the edge of a mountain lake. The reflection was so clear that if you took a picture, you wouldn't be able to tell which was the sky and which was the water.

"You should feel at ease." Sarah's voice blew in on a gentle wind.

The sun kissed my cheeks, and the breeze blew my hair back from my face. I felt completely at ease, like nothing could touch me here. Tension drained from my body. Gentle waves lapped at my feet.

All too soon, Sarah said, "It's time for you to return."

With a sigh, I opened my eyes, blinking several times as if awakening from a deep sleep. I stretched my arms out in front of me.

"Whenever Cassandra bothers you, I want you to picture yourself in that place. If you can do that, you may be able to control your powers."

"That would be nice."

"You're going to have to practice," Sarah said as we started for the door. "If this doesn't work for you, we'll try one of the other relaxation techniques."

ꕥ

Samantha frowned at us when we walked in. "So did you get lost?" She was sitting at the desk dressed in a red shirt and black leggings.

"No. After what happened this morning, Sarah thought I should start training right away."

"What does that entail?"

"Helping Dacia relax," Cody said.

"So … uh, I've been thinking." She looked down and tugged on her earlobe. "In all the books and movies, there's a point to prophecies."

"Yeah?" I coaxed her along.

"So what's the point? What are you supposed to stop or defeat or end or whatever? There must be something."

My head slumped forward. "Oh." I pictured the yellow eyes and monstrous, clawed hand from my nightmare. *That can't be real, can it?*

Cody set his hand on my shoulder. "Don't worry about it. It's not like you believe in it anyway."

"No, but Sarah does."

# Chapter 11

## *Uphill Battle*

Cassandra blocked the doorway to advanced algebra. "You're going to pay for what you did to me." She jammed her finger into my chest.

"Really, that's the best you can come up with?" I tapped my index finger against my chin. "It lacked content, and the intimidation factor … I'm not really feeling it." I pushed past her.

Hatred flashed through her eyes.

Cody and Samantha followed me in and sat on either side of me.

"What was that?" Cody asked.

I traced my fingers over the desktop, following the grooves in the wood. "I didn't sleep last night, and I'm sick of dealing with her crap."

Samantha patted my back. "It was. Awe. Some." Her voice lilted up at the end.

"I just wish she'd leave me alone." My hands hardened into fists as I watched Cassandra sit down with her entourage. "After what I did to her, wouldn't you think she'd be scared? Wouldn't you think she'd stay away from me?" I took deep breaths, but my fingers continued fusing together. Strength surged through my muscles, and I felt myself slipping away.

"I never understood why she had it out for you in the first place," Samantha answered.

Cody's eyebrows pulled together. "You okay?"

*Your parents must be so ashamed and embarrassed by you,* Cassandra's words echoed through my memory.

The part of me that fought to pull myself together warred with the part of myself I didn't want to admit existed—the part of me that wanted to see her suffer.

"Good morning," Professor Granite said as he walked into the room.

I concentrated on Professor Granite. His salt and pepper mullet suited his easygoing personality. His matching mustache wiggled like a wooly worm resting on his upper lip while he delivered his lecture to us. Warmth in his gray eyes belied his sternness. I had never been so happy to see a teacher before.

The hatred that had threatened to consume me slithered away, hiding in the darkest shadows within me until it could surface again.

I held myself together through the rest of class, but when he dismissed us, I grabbed my books and dashed out of the room without glancing in Cassandra's direction.

"Training for a race?" Cody asked when he caught up to me.

"I needed to get away from her. I don't want to lose control."

"Let's get lunch and eat in your room," he suggested.

ᘓ

I paced in Sarah's office. "I'm not sold on the idea of a prophecy, but I want to know what I am supposedly training for."

"I wasn't expecting this so soon," Sarah said.

I waved my arm in the air. "Well, Samantha pointed out last night that prophecies tend to involve more than just training."

"Yes, and this one is no exception."

My heart sank like the small jerk you feel when an elevator comes to a sudden stop. "I was afraid you would say that. So what is it?"

Sarah pinched the bridge of her nose. "Are you sure you want to know?"

"No." I plopped down on the couch across from her. "I really don't want to. I'd rather be oblivious, but I don't think that's a choice I have anymore."

"Will you excuse me for a moment?" she asked as she got up from the couch.

"Sure," I answered with a hard edge to my voice. *What am I supposed to think when she can't even answer a simple question?*

Sarah went to her office. After a few minutes, she emerged carrying two books. One of them was a battered relic. The cover was worn leather, and the binding was hanging on by a thread. The other seemed to be a newer version of the first book.

Sarah opened the newer journal. "This has been translated from Latin, so there's always a chance something is slightly off." She flipped through the pages. "Here it is. The chosen will emerge with powers unrivaled in this world. To fight a demon from the Abyss is the savior's onus. Fail and the world will perish. Succeed and win nine hundred ninety-nine years before the cycle begins anew." Sarah closed the book.

"A demon? Like a little gremlin? Or a devil?"

"No." She opened the older book. "This is the demon referred to as Nefarious." She handed the book to me.

A detailed drawing covered one page. A beast with scaly skin, massive, clawed hands, and bat-like wings held a flaming sword.

I threw the book down on the couch and sprung to my feet. "That's what I'm supposed to fight?" I pointed a shaking finger at the picture. "And how do you propose I kill something like that?" *I can't even deal with Cassandra. How am I supposed to deal with this?*

"You can't."

"Oh … well, thanks for the vote of confidence." I yanked up my jacket and started for the door.

“Dacia, stop.” Sarah’s voice shook. “That’s not what I mean.”

“I have no doubt. I can’t kill something like that.” My shoulders slumped. “I can’t even get Cassandra to leave me alone.”

Sarah gestured toward the couch. “Please, let me explain.”

I looked from her to the couch, wondering if I should listen to what she had to say or if I should turn and leave. *This can’t be real.* I ran my hand through my hair and walked to the couch, perching on the edge, ready to leave if it was too much. “Go ahead.”

“Demons are not from Earth. They’re from the Abyss and can only be destroyed there. Each demon is able to return to Earth every nine hundred ninety-nine years without being summoned here.”

“Okaaay.”

“Nefarious will return over and over again until he defeats the chosen one and conquers the world.”

I pulled my fingers through my hair. “No pressure then.” An uneasy laugh escaped my lips. “How am I supposed to do this?”

“You have to find a way to send him back to the Abyss.”

*Why did I think I needed to know this? It could have waited.* “So, the only way to end this cycle is to fail?”

“Unless somebody can figure out how to travel to the Abyss to kill him.” Sarah resumed pacing. “You, Dacia, are the chosen one the prophecy speaks of, and somebody with my bloodline has been the teacher for every savior. You must master your powers in order to prevail.”

"What if I don't believe in the prophecy?" I folded my arms over my chest. "What if I refuse to learn?"

"Well, it's hard to win if you don't try." She walked over and sat beside me. "I know this is a lot of pressure to put on you, and I am sorry for that."

I shrugged.

"I know you don't have to believe a word of what I've said, but I would like to keep training you in the meantime."

"I have to keep training," I told her. "I have to control my powers before I end up seriously hurting somebody."

"In that case, why don't you try to relax, like I showed you Saturday?"

I closed my eyes and tried to picture the mountain lake, but my mind whirred with information. Nine hundred ninety-nine years kept running through my mind. Unable to relax, I opened my eyes and asked, "If Nefarious hasn't been around for nine hundred ninety-nine years, how did the prophecy get handed down through your family without being distorted? You would think somebody would stretch the truth or quit believing in it."

Sarah picked up the newer journal. "This belonged to my grandfather. Before he passed away, he gave it to me. In it, he wrote about when his father first told him about the prophecy." She flipped through the pages of the journal, "He wrote, 'My father was a man of few words, never speaking unless he thought it was of the utmost importance. One cold December morning, he set me down and told me to pay attention because what he had to say was crucial. My father's revelation stunned me, but I knew he wouldn't tell me something this farfetched without believing in it unconditionally.' My grandfather carried that same conviction with him to the grave; he never once faltered in his beliefs." A look of nostalgia passed through Sarah's eyes.

"This book" —she held up the relic— "begins by telling the tale of a young man who defeated an evil monster. It describes the beast, speaks of its return and the chosen one who must face it. This book holds the prophecy." She held the book so the cover faced me.

"What's on the cover?" I asked.

She held the book closer to me. Embedded in the cover was a gold, diamond-shaped pendant with what looked like a cat's eye in the center. The eye was an almond-shaped sapphire with an onyx pupil. The gold around the outside edge of the pendant was smooth with diamonds on the four corners. The inside was rough with inscriptions that I couldn't read.

"This was worn by the last chosen one. In this journal, it is written that the pendant will give the savior extra strength to help them stand against Nefarious. When danger is near, the eye is supposed to glow."

"What does the writing mean?" I asked.

"Find courage within yourself—loosely translated. I'd like you to take it with you, to help protect you from Nefarious."

I reached out to it then pulled my hand back. I didn't share her beliefs and wasn't ready to be sucked into them. "No, I don't think so."

Sarah sighed. "I wish I could make you believe, but it is a choice you have to make on your own."

We sat in silence for a moment while I tried to process all this new information. Sarah's certainty and the evidence she had to back her beliefs surprised me. "Why nine hundred ninety-nine years?"

"There are nine hundred ninety-nine realms attached to the Abyss, and demons can't return to one until they've been to them all." She waved a hand above her head. "Well, unless of course, they are summoned."

"So how many years are left? Twenty? Thirty?"

Sarah swallowed hard, and my stomach dropped to my toes. Her voice was nearly a whisper, "At most a year."

"Out of nine hundred ninety-nine, I get less than a year to figure this out!" Heat fluttered across my skin, and beads of sweat formed on my forehead and neck. I laid my head back and covered my eyes with my arms. Breathing slow and steady, I tried to picture the mountain lake again.

"I'm sorry," Sarah's voice threatened to break my concentration. I held my finger up, hoping she would realize I needed some time.

Once I regained control, I asked, "So besides the journals and the pendant is there anything else that can help me? A magic sword that wields itself? Or something?"

One side of Sarah's mouth lifted into a smile. "Though it's probably not what you're looking for, there is a vase."

"A vase?" I held my hand out in front of me. "Here Nefarious. Have these nice flowers and run back home."

Sarah stacked the journals. "I have no idea what the vase is for, but it was handed down with the rest of the stuff."

"So where is it?" I looked around. A few vases sat on Sarah's shelves.

"In a safe. It's a priceless artifact."

I rubbed my neck, trying to ease the tension building there. “Is there more I should know?”

“When you’re ready.”

ꙮ

Fire.

Everywhere.

Flames leap across the tops of trees, devouring foliage. Crackling branches drop to the ground like missiles.

Smoke burns my eyes. The pungent taste gags me.

*Did I do this?*

I run, trying to stay ahead of the orange flames. *Orange flames?* I fall to my knees. Air catches in my throat. My head spins, and my pulse beats in my temples. I claw at my neck, trying to pull oxygen into my body.

Tortured screams break through the roar of the fire.

*Get up.*

Sweat drips into my eyes. The flames stretch forward, longing to embrace me. I pull myself to my feet and run through the trees. Breaking out of the forest, I come to a stop.

Phlox University is an inferno. Students run from the buildings, screaming, falling to the ground. Several don’t get up.

“Cody!” I run forward. “Samantha!”

Charred bodies litter the ground. Some writhe in agony. Some will never move again.

Fearing the worst, I run on. “Cody. Samantha.” My voice is ragged.

Tears spill from my eyes without bringing any relief to the burning. My vision blurs. I wipe my face with my shirt and run toward the flames. Smoke fills my lungs. I hunch over choking, trying to draw in air. I gasp and open my eyes.

*A dream. Thank God.*

I stared at the ceiling, refusing to close my eyes. The fear from my nightmare hadn't released me from its grasp.

*Is it possible that there's more to these nightmares? Could the prophecy be real?* I shook my head, unwilling to believe. *No. How could demons go unchecked in this day and age?*

# Chapter 12

## *Learning Control*

Dark bags made my eyes look dull and washed out my skin. I stood, wobbling unsteadily. I threw my arm out, balancing myself with the wall. *I need sleep.*

I glanced at my make-up bag. It wasn't part of my daily routine, but I decided I should go through the trouble of covering up my sleepless nights. By the time I finished, I no longer looked like a zombie.

Speech didn't start until 8:00, but at 7:30 I sat at my desk. I thought I would have a better chance of avoiding Cassandra.

Between solving algebra problems, I kept an eye on the door, not wanting to get blindsided by her. I was figuring for the value of x when cold chills crept over my body like a fever. Cassandra walked in the door and climbed the stairs deliberately, never taking her eyes from mine, until she stood before me, her friends at her back. In one swift movement, she threw my books to the floor.

With her face inches from mine, she said, "You messed with the wrong person."

"Me?" I pointed at myself. "I messed with the wrong person?" My voice didn't sound right. It came out high-pitched.

"You heard me."

"Yeah." I fought back my anger. "But you're delusional."

She slammed her fist on my desk. "Stay away from me."

I stood and looked down at Cassandra. Her eyes widened a fraction, and she took a step back. Bryce grabbed her arm, but she pulled away from him.

"We'd never see each other if you'd quit seeking me out." The chairs around me rattled nervously.

Bryce grabbed Cassandra's arm again, never taking his eyes off me. "I believe you, Cass. Come on before something else happens."

She let Bryce pull her away, leading her to her seat. I waited until they sat down to pick up my books.

Closing my eyes, I focused on breathing. Once my hands stopped shaking, I pictured myself sitting by the mountain lake. I leaned back and let the calm of nature quiet my anger.

ഌ

A few weeks after my lessons started, I knocked on Sarah's door.

"Hello, Dacia."

"Hey." I walked over to the couch and set my backpack on the floor.

Sarah squeezed my shoulder. "You look tired today. Is everything right?"

*Nothing's all right. I'm an eighteen-year-old who has to fight a demon. There's no way I'll win. What would be all right? I can't sleep at night, but who needs sleep?* "Yeah." I stifled a yawn. "I'm just trying to keep up on my studies and lessons with you. The teachers have been handing out a lot more homework lately."

She nodded. "Well, this is college. Assignments are to be expected." She sat across from me. "I think there is more to it than homework, though. Are you having more nightmares?"

I leaned back and covered my eyes with my arm. I lifted my other arm in a shrug.

She shook her head but didn't press me for more. "Are you ready to begin then?"

I nodded.

In a calm, soothing voice, she said, "Okay, Dacia, I want you to relax."

I let out a deep breath and tried to release my stress.

Even if I never learned how to control my powers, this made my lessons worthwhile. I pictured myself sitting on a rock on the edge of a mountain lake. Nothing could harm me here.

"Let yourself feel free and alive. You should be in the zone, somewhere between sleep and alertness." Sarah's voice was somewhere far off in the distance.

I was in a total state of relaxation, staring at the water in front of me. After quite some time, Sarah's voice blew in on a breeze. "You're doing well, Dacia. Now I want you to come back here."

When I opened my eyes, she said, "It seems like this relaxation technique is helping you."

"Yeah, I use it almost every day." I looked down at my feet. "Otherwise Cassandra would be in here complaining about me more often."

"Hmm." She stood and started pacing. "I guess we need to work on keeping you from getting overly emotional to begin with. We also need to work on focusing your energy."

"I thought you wanted me to suppress my energy?"

She stopped and looked down at me. "I want you to control your energy." Her hands were in constant motion while she talked. "When you intend to use your powers, though, you need to be able to. You need to know what will happen and when it will."

"Yeah," I nodded, "it'd be nice to be in control."

Sarah sat down. "I want you to imagine yourself sitting in Professor Granite's class. He's in the middle of his lecture, and you accidentally drop your pen to the floor. When you go to reach for it, Cassandra kicks it over to Alvin. She turns to you and snickers. Her eyes are fixed on you, just daring you to interrupt Granite's speech. Then she mouths the word 'FREAK'."

*I can almost imagine their surprise when they found out you were a freak.* The books on the shelves tremble.

"Alvin holds the pen out to you, but when you reach for it, Cassandra snatches it."

I fought to control my temper, and the books quieted down. *So far so good.*

Sarah tilted her head to the side and tapped her finger on her chin. "When class ends, you grab your stuff and hurry to leave. Halfway down the stairs, your books are knocked out of your hands. Cassandra points at you and laughs as she steps on your notebook. Pivoting her foot, several pages are ripped out."

The trembling of the books turned into more of a rumble. I opened my eyes just in time to see one flying toward Sarah. She dodged, narrowly escaping being hit by it, but another whacked her in the back of the head before falling to the ground with a thud.

"Oh, Sarah, I'm so sorry." The words gushed from my mouth. "Are you all right?"

She glanced around the room before answering me. "I'm fine." She rubbed her head. "I would suggest taking our lessons outside, but I'm afraid an uprooted tree might fly out of nowhere at me."

I knew she was saying it to lighten the mood, but it didn't hit me that way. Without meaning to, I glared at her.

"I'm sorry, Dacia. I shouldn't say stuff like that. I know it has to be hard for you to be different from everyone else. I imagine the kids in school haven't always been as nice to you as they could've been." Her eyes softened, and she sighed.

"No. They still aren't. Cody's the only person who accepted me. He stuck up for me so many times I lost count years ago." Lack of sleep wasn't a good partner for this conversation. My emotions were getting the best of me. I fought to hold back tears. "When I came here, I was so lucky to be given Samantha as a roommate. She's been great." I pulled my hand through my hair. "Thank God I didn't get stuck with Cassandra."

Merely the mention of her name made books start rumbling again. Before they had a chance to fly off the shelves, I took a couple deep breaths and tried to place myself on the edge of my mountain lake. When I heard Sarah breathe a sigh of relief, I realized it must have worked.

"I think you need a break. Why don't we pick up here next time?" Standing at the door, she said, "Try to get some rest."

I walked looking down, kicking at leaves on the sidewalk. *If I can't control myself when Sarah's describing situations to me, how am I going to do it in the real world? Why would the fates choose me to save the world?*

"You can't seriously believe in this," I whispered to myself. *Did I believe, or was I just sleep-deprived and frustrated?*

"Oh, look. The freak even talks to herself." Cassandra's voice sent chills up my spine. She stood, glaring at me with her hands on her hips. "In trouble again? Who'd you torment this time?"

*Just keep walking.* I didn't; I whipped around to find Cassandra with Vanessa, Alvin, and Bryce.

"Isn't it about time for her to expel you and get it over with?" Cassandra asked.

*Breathe.* "My business with Dean Aspen is none of yours."

"Evil triumphs when good people do nothing." Vanessa's voice was soft and sweet, unlike her words.

*Evil. They think I'm evil?* I took a step back like she had slapped my face. My control waned. I tried to picture the beautiful mountain scene, but I couldn't focus. Then I noticed something Cassandra and her friends hadn't, and some of my tension melted away.

Cassandra took a step toward me. "You hide behind your powers." Another step closer. "If I had your abilities, everyone would know it. I wouldn't cower back in the corner like a lost puppy-dog. I would command fear and respect." She took another step toward me and said, "I wouldn't use them to wreak havoc." She poked me in the arm. "I wouldn't be like you."

"You're so pathetic," Alvin said. "Power like yours should belong to someone worthy."

*How does this make any sense to them? They think I'm evil, but they would use the powers for control?* "What exactly do you think I'm doing with my powers?"

Cassandra stood with her nose inches from mine. Her eyes blazed. Any fear she had after having her hands frozen to the faucet was gone now. "We both know what you plan to do, and I won't let you hurt my friends."

*Hurt her friends? What in the world?*

"What's wrong, Dacia? Can't defend yourself in the open?" Her minty breath blew across my face.

A sly smile played on my lips. "Hi, Sa … Dean Aspen. How're you?"

"Nice try." Bryce snorted.

"I'm doing splendidly, Dacia." Sarah's voice was uncharacteristically stern. "These four aren't bothering you, are they?"

Cassandra pivoted to my side. Her expression became a mask of innocence.

"Not now," I said.

"Good. I wanted to talk to you more about that project. Why don't you keep me company for a bit?" Sarah put her hand on my shoulder and led me back toward the dorms.

I breathed a sigh of relief and glanced over my shoulder. The look on Cassandra's face was one of pure hatred. Before I turned back around, she mouthed, "I'll get you for this."

Sarah looked off into the distance and sighed. "Maybe Cody should meet you in my office after your lessons are finished."

I groaned.

"Not for your protection," Sarah explained. "But to keep you from hurting somebody … at least until you learn control."

I pulled my hand through my hair. "I'm sure Cody will do it."

The hesitation in my voice must have been obvious because Sarah said, "But?"

"But …" I rolled my neck from side to side. "I don't want him to be in danger because of me."

"I think if the two of you are together, they'll steer clear of you."

Kicking at the ground, I asked, "But what about when he's alone?"

"Their problem isn't with him." She shot me one of her sympathetic smiles. "After you kept those books from flying off the shelves, I'm surprised you had the energy to control your emotions."

I lowered my eyes. "I wouldn't have if I hadn't seen you come out of your office. Anger was building in me, and I knew it was only a matter of time. I tried to picture myself on the shore of my lake—" I looked up at her, hoping she'd understand "—but I couldn't do it."

"It doesn't matter how you controlled your anger." The look of pride on her face helped me feel better about myself. "It matters that you controlled it."

We walked along in silence. Sarah seemed lost in concentration. Wrinkles creased her forehead.

*With this scenery, why can't I relax? What is it about Cassandra and her friends that makes my anger spike?* I shook my head to clear it and looked around. The trees were sparse through here, leaving a clear view of the mountains. A rabbit hopped around a cedar tree. A gust of wind had me wrapping myself in my arms for warmth.

"I think you need to move on in your lessons," Sarah said. "We need to see what else you are capable of."

I stopped and turned to face her. "What makes you think I can do more?"

"While fire, ice, and telekinesis are good techniques to use against Cassandra and myself—" she rubbed her head to drive home her point "—I don't know how well they'll work against Nefarious."

The sound of his name made me cringe. "When do you think I'll have to face him?" My voice was quiet and unsteady.

"I don't know an exact date. My grandfather never told me how much time I would have to train you or when the prophecy would be fulfilled. I only know it will be sometime in the next year, but I don't know if it will be days, weeks, or months." Her voice was full of apprehension. "Who knows, maybe you're right and the prophecy is a bunch of malarkey." She laughed nervously.

"Well, uh—" I cleared my throat "—I, uh, I think I'm starting to believe in it."

Sarah simply looked at me.

I didn't intend to tell her everything, but it all came pouring out. "I've been having horrible dreams lately. I'm beginning to wonder if they are nightmares or if they are premonitions. All I know is it is nearly impossible for me to sleep at night. I haven't slept for more than an hour or two in a row in weeks. The only relaxation I get is when you help me picture myself somewhere peaceful in my lessons."

Sarah folded her arms across her chest, and her eyebrows furrowed. "Why did you lie?" I could tell by her voice she was wounded. "I thought you trusted me."

I felt a dull ache in my chest. "I do trust you." I shoved my hands in my pockets. "But my nightmares are so real. Every time I think about them, I relive them." I shuddered. "Anxiety builds up in my stomach, a knot forms in my throat, and I feel like I'm going to pass out. The air gets heavier. I can hardly breathe, and I relive the dream." I paused to catch my breath. "I don't like feeling that way." Tears stung my eyes. "I'm scared."

Her eyes softened, and she relaxed her stance. "Well, I can understand why you don't like feeling like that, but it always helps to have somebody to confide in. Wouldn't you agree?"

"Sometimes." I looked down at the ground and kicked a couple of rocks around. "Samantha has been putting up with my screams in the middle of the night for quite a while now, and I haven't even told her what my nightmares are about." I stared at the mountains, wishing I could disappear into them. "I'm afraid if I tell her I believe in the prophecy or that I'm dreaming about monsters, she will start thinking I'm a freak like everybody else does. I'm scared of what they'll think if I tell them I believe in the prophecy. This is probably the only thing I've ever kept from Cody."

"Dacia"—her voice sounded soft and comforting—"I think you need to give your friends credit. I know it's hard for you to open yourself up to people because you think it will give them the opportunity to hurt you." She put her hand on my shoulder. "However, Samantha and Cody are good kids who genuinely care about you and want to help you overcome your difficulties. You should let them into your world … all of it."

I knew she was right, but I had spent my life building up a protective barrier around myself. It was difficult to knock it down and let people in. "Maybe when I get back to my room, I'll have a nice long talk with Cody and Samantha. I could use them by my side through all this."

"Have you talked to anyone at all?" Sarah asked in her motherly tone.

I shook my head.

"Your parents don't know anything about this?"

I couldn't help but laugh before responding, "My parents would die if they found out people knew."

She shook her head. "I think you're underestimating them."

"No, I'm not." I crossed my arms over my chest. "They've spent my entire life denying I have powers. They convinced me that I had nothing to do with any of it. They worked hard to persuade me that everything was coincidental."

Sarah's eyes widened, and she shook her head. "I can't believe that. How could your parents be so blind? Your powers are obvious."

"Well, I uh … I don't think they're blind to them. I think they choose to ignore them because it's … well, it's hard for them to believe their child is a freak of nature."

"Oh, Dacia, I'm sorry."

"It's okay. I know you didn't mean anything by it. Besides, look how they'll feel when I save the world." I laughed in an attempt to remove some of the awkwardness that was in the air and, to my relief, Sarah joined in.

The rest of the journey back to my dorm was spent in silence. I couldn't help but think about the task ahead of me and wonder if I stood a chance. We reached the dorm in no time at all, and as I walked up the stairs to my room, I tried to decide if I really should have this conversation with Cody and Samantha or not.

# Chapter 13

## Coming Clean

The door squeaked when I opened it. The state of our dorm threw me off. Samantha's backpack seemed to have spewed its contents across the floor. I entered, careful not to step on anything.

Samantha turned from the computer. "Sorry about the mess." Her eyes were huge, and she talked faster than I'd ever heard her. "I've got a history report due, and I'm not done."

Knowing Samantha, she probably had at least three or four days until it had to be turned in. "How much caffeine have you had?"

"Too much I think." She spun her chair in circles. "The sugar probably didn't help either."

I couldn't help but laugh.

"How was your lesson?"

I told her about my run-in with Cassandra and her groupies.

"I don't know why you let her bother you so much." Samantha cocked her head to the side. "I'm sure it's hard for you, but you need to realize you are better than they are. Don't let yourself sink to their level."

I moved her things off Cookie Monster and sat. "I'm not better than anybody." I swiveled the chair from side to side to avoid her eyes. I didn't want her to see my insecurity. "I tell myself 'don't let them bother you, just ignore them', but I can't seem to accomplish that. Hopefully, with time."

"Yeah, I hope so, too." Samantha turned back to her homework. "I gotta get this done."

ꝏ

Cody arrived moments before the pizza did. The aroma filled the small dorm room. My stomach growled in anticipation of supper. I thought it would be better to wait until we had eaten to broach the subject of the prophecy.

"Have you decided yet, or still on the fence?" Cody asked me before eating half his slice in one bite.

*Decided. Decided what? Did he know I'd been thinking about the prophecy, trying to figure out if it could possibly be real?* "Uh … what?"

"Major." Cody pointed a second piece of pizza at me. "You said you might have a better idea after starting classes."

*Geesh, Dacia. You can be so stupid sometimes. I doubt he's given any thought to the prophecy.* "Fence," I answered.

"Part of me wants to be an English teacher. Part of me wants to be a writer, and an even bigger part of me has no clue what to do. How are you supposed to know what you want to be for the rest of your life? What if I change my mind?"

"I've always wanted to be a teacher." Samantha's voice had slowed down some, but it still sounded higher and faster than normal. "I don't think I'll change my mind, but who knows?"

"What're you gonna teach?" Cody asked.

"Kindergarten or first grade. I want to teach young impressionable kids. What about you?"

"History teacher and basketball coach."

"What happened to being a cop?" I asked.

"Not ready to give up basketball." He pointed at my pizza. "Gonna eat that?"

"Go ahead." I held my hands out palms up. "It looks like I'm the only one who can't figure out what to be when I grow up."

"So, how was your lesson?" Cody asked.

"I'm glad you asked. Sarah wanted me to see if you would walk back from them with me from now on. When it was over today, I ran into Cassandra and friends." I explained everything that had happened.

Anger flashed across Cody's face and his eyes narrowed. "What's her problem? She's been that way since the first day of classes, before you used your powers."

"I've been thinking."

"That's good." Cody gave me his typical response.

"Villains always have a title."

Cody looked at me like I was nuts.

"Nightshade sounds all menacing, but really it's just another way of saying potato or tomato, so I was thinking about calling Cassandra and her buddies the Rotten Tomatoes or the Potato Heads."

"I like it." Samantha bobbed her head up and down. "Potato Heads is perfect."

Cody set his hand on mine. My belly tingled in response. *You can't keep thinking about him like this.*

"I'll walk with you."

"What?" I asked.

"To your lessons." Cody's lips lifted into a lopsided grin. "I'll walk with you."

"Thanks." I sat there for a moment and took in a big gulp of air. "You guys are going to think I'm nuts. But, I need to talk to someone about this."

That got their attention. Their gazes held mine, and Cody asked, "What, Dacia?"

"I don't know where to begin," I couldn't help but pause. *How am I supposed to tell them I believe in a ludicrous prophecy?* I put my head in my hands.

Cody got up and sat on the arm of my chair. "You can tell me anything." He put his arm around my shoulders.

Samantha nodded in agreement.

*Just say it.* "I think the prophecy is real!" I winced as soon as I finished saying it, knowing full well they were going to erupt into hysterics, but they didn't.

Cody's arm slumped down on my shoulder a little bit, and they both stared at me. Samantha's mouth formed a perfect "o".

I waited for one of them to say something, anything at all, but they just sat there. “Hey, guys, snap out of it.”

Samantha responded first. “Sorry. That wasn’t what I expected to hear. I was under the impression you hadn’t considered believing it.”

I twisted my hands together. “For a long time, I didn’t, but, these never-ending nightmares are making me realize there is a possibility the prophecy could be real—maybe they are premonitions.” The thought terrified me. Sarah dead. The world on fire. If they were premonitions, the outlook was bleak.

“I wondered if you would ever tell me what your nightmares are about.” She picked up our pizza plates and threw them away. “Every time I wake you up, I expect you to say something, but you pass them off nonchalantly, like everyone wakes up screaming every night.”

“Nightmares? Still?” Cody asked. “Why haven’t you told me? If I have to, I’ll start sleeping here.” He pointed at the chair we were sitting on.

An uncontrollable laugh escaped me. I fought to stop, but that just made me laugh harder.

“You think I’m joking!”

“No. I was picturing Marcy checking in on us and finding you here. Dean Aspen would be able to hear her screams all the way over in her office.” The laughter that followed loosened some of the tension in my shoulders.

“Come on, Dacia,” Samantha said, “don’t get off the subject. Tell us about your dreams.”

A peculiar feeling enveloped me. My breathing became heavy and forced. I felt like a python had coiled itself around me in an attempt to squeeze the life out of me, stifling the scream that clawed its way up my throat. Panic consumed me as the invisible coils tightened. Then as quickly as the feeling came, it vanished. When the feeling went away, my muscles ached.

"You okay?" Cody pulled me against him.

I closed my eyes and let him hold me for longer than I should have. He felt warm and safe. "Yeah." I took a few deep breaths. "Every muscle in my body stiffened up. It was almost like when you're in a speeding car that slams on the brakes, and at the same time, I felt like the wind had been knocked out of me."

Their faces softened. "Are you sure you're all right?" Samantha asked. "If it's that difficult for you to tell us about your dreams or if you would rather not, we understand. You don't have to."

I thought about my newest dream. Charred bodies littering the ground. Screaming students burning alive. I couldn't talk about it. I couldn't believe that would happen.

"No." I looked into Samantha's doe eyes. "I told Cody and Sarah about my nightmare at a lesson. I should've told you a long time ago," I said, still fighting to regulate my breathing.

My mind whirred. I wanted somebody who had been through all of this to talk to, someone who could help me understand what was happening and who might be able to explain what I needed to do. I didn't know how to deal with this on my own.

Cody and Samantha watched me, making me feel even more uneasy. I knew they were worried about me. However, I didn't want them to treat me any differently, and I was afraid the more they witnessed stuff like this happening to me, the more they would want to stay away from me.

"It's okay." Cody's voice was soft and soothing.

I nodded. "Well, here goes." I told Samantha about my nightmares. When I got to the part about finding Sarah's body, I clutched the arms of the chair and forced the words out.

Samantha gasped and covered her mouth.

Cody pulled me closer. "It's not real, just a dream."

"That's the problem," I said, the panic apparent in my voice now. "I'm afraid it's more than a dream. I'm scared it's going to happen."

I hadn't planned to let them know how upset I was about the dreams, but now they did. Every time I thought about my nightmares they seemed even more real to me, and talking about them made them even more vivid.

I raked my hand through my hair and asked, "So do you guys think I'm a lunatic for believing in a prophecy?"

With narrowed eyes, Samantha asked, "How can you think we're so shallow?"

Before I could answer her, Cody moved his arm from around my shoulders and folded them over his chest. "You know I'm here no matter what."

"I'm sorry. I didn't mean to hurt your feelings. It's just … I think I'm harebrained for believing in it." My head fell into my hands, and I whispered, "I hope to God it's not true."

"Well," Samantha said, "I for one think it's about time."

My eyebrows pulled down. *I couldn't have heard her right, could I?* "What?"

"You have powers." She lifted her hands palms up. "Magic. Magic doesn't exist. Why would you have it if not to serve some purpose?"

Samantha was right. It was stupid for me to believe that my powers were a fluke. Obviously, they were given to me for a reason, but did it have to be to fight a demon? Couldn't there be another explanation? "What if I can't do it?"

Cody put his arm back around my shoulder, and the three of us sat in silence.

We were brought back into reality by a knock on the door. "What?" Samantha hollered.

"It's time for Cody to leave," responded the hushed voice of Marcy Cicada. "You do realize this is not a coed dorm, don't you?"

Cody responded, "You'd never let us forget."

"You better get going," Samantha said.

He gave me a quick hug before getting off the chair and walking to the door. "Don't forget we're here for you."

"Thanks." I felt chilled without him beside me.

"If you need me, I'll be here." He winked at us as he opened the door.

Standing in our doorway with her hands on her hips, Marcy scowled at us. It was funny to see her scolding Cody. Her head leaned as far back as it could go in her attempt to look him in the eyes. Her dirty blonde pigtails bounced up and down as she said, "I wish the three of you could learn to tell time. I can't believe how often I have to come down here and kick you out of their room. You could be a little more courteous and learn to leave on your own. By now, I'd think you would be old enough not to have a babysitter!"

"Oh, Marcy, if you weren't watching over us," Cody began, "you wouldn't know what to do with yourself." Before he shut the door, he leaned his head back in the room. "Sleep good. Sweet dreams."

# Chapter 14

## *Fairies And Unicorns*

Cody and I walked across campus. Birds sang. Couples walked hand in hand, several students tossed footballs or Frisbees, while others seemed content with enjoying the crisp mountain air. I wanted a life like that. Instead, I was being chaperoned to a lesson where I'd learn to defeat a demon … hopefully.

"Thanks for walking over here with Dacia," Sarah said to Cody as we walked in.

Cody smiled down at me. "No problem. I like to pretend I'm Dacia's knight-in-shining-armor."

"It's more like my knight-in-faded-denim." I chuckled.

"Yeah." He rubbed the back of his neck. "No armor." He turned toward the door. "When do you want me back?"

“It’ll be at least a couple hours,” Sarah responded.

“All right. Call if you need me sooner.” The door closed behind him.

“You know, Dacia, you’re lucky to have him as a friend.”

“Yeah, I’ve known that since we met. Sometimes I think he’s my guardian angel. There have been lots of times I wouldn’t have known what to do without him,” as I told her this, I looked at the door, hoping he’d come back to help me get through my lesson. I knew with him around I could do anything. “You know, I’m surprised he hasn’t gotten sick of me yet. He’s always coming to my rescue for one thing or another. One of these days, he’s going to decide I’m not worth the hassle.”

Sarah led the way over to the couches. “From what I’ve seen, I don’t think that will be an issue.” Her voice sounded amused.

We sat down, and she launched into the relaxation techniques without asking me any questions. I was surprised she didn’t ask if I had been having any more dreams, but maybe she figured after our conversation Thursday, I’d offer up any information without being asked.

I pictured myself sitting on the rock staring off at the reflection of the mountain. The only images in my mind were visions of utter tranquility. I was so in tune with the scene I smelled the scent of pine blowing on the wind. I heard the birds chirping and the rhythmic splashing of water on the rocks. Off in the distance, a fish jumped out of the lake. I looked up when I heard the splash but only saw ripples growing larger as they neared shore.

"You are completely relaxed now." Sarah's voice whispered on the wind. "Now I want you to pick up one of the rocks next to you. I want you to imagine this rock represents all of your ill will toward Cassandra. Throw it as far out in the water as you can."

I pictured myself hurling the rock through the air. As it landed in the water, I pictured Cassandra's face on it.

Sarah's voice blew in on the breeze again, "Now I want you to bring yourself back here."

I didn't want to leave and have to face reality again, but I pictured myself getting off the rock and going back to Sarah's office. Blinking back the light, I opened my eyes.

"Cassandra came to my office yesterday." Sarah resituated herself on the couch.

I narrowed my eyes and prepared to defend myself. I hadn't had any confrontations with her recently, and I wasn't about to accept blame for one. "What did she say now?"

"She told me all about her new boyfriend."

My head snapped back. *Why would I care about Cassandra and her boyfriend?* "Oh."

Sarah pulled the creases out of her slacks. "He's blond, tall and athletic. I can't help but wonder if it's Cody? Has he said anything?"

My stomach tightened, and my heartbeat quickened. *Cody and Cassandra? It wasn't possible, was it?* "No." My voice sounded shrill. "He hasn't."

She shrugged like it didn't matter one way or another. "You might want to ask him."

The room spun. Bile rose into my mouth. "Yeah, I'll do that." *He wouldn't do that to me. He's told her off for me before.*

"If the two of them are a couple, maybe she'll quit antagonizing you." She shrugged. "Cody wouldn't want the two of you fighting."

I took a deep breath and forced myself to stay calm. *Cody would never. This is a test. Just breathe.* There wasn't even a slight movement in the books.

"Wow, Dacia, you're doing so well!" The corner of her mouth lifted into a lopsided smile.

"Maybe—" I stood and walked over to the window "—but in the long run, what good will this do? I have no idea how to go about defeating something that isn't even human. I'm not sure why I was picked to fulfill the prophecy." I studied my shoes. "It should've been some gladiator type or macho man, not me." I turned to face her. I could feel the desperation in my eyes. "Look at me! How am I supposed to defeat a giant monster?"

"I know this is hard." Sarah walked toward me. "All I can do is tell you I will be here to help you. It's not much, but it's the best I can offer."

My mind filled with the vision of her dead body lying on the ground in front of me. "I …" I closed my eyes, and Phlox University erupted into flames. "I can't keep you, Samantha, and Cody safe. I can't do this on my own. I can't win." I held my head in my hands.

Sarah rubbed my shoulder. "Maybe your desire to protect those closest to you is why you were chosen to fulfill the prophecy. It seems to be one of your greatest strengths."

"I don't know." I sighed. "What if my dreams are premonitions?"

"They may or may not come true, but if something does happen to me, you need to remember why you're here, and you need to defeat Nefarious."

The somber air reminded me of a funeral. After my earlier victory, I didn't want to end my lesson like this. "One of the first times I came here you told me about creatures beyond my imagination. What were you talking about?"

A bark of laughter escaped from Sarah. "With everything you have been through, I'm surprised you remember that."

"Well, curiosity killed the cat."

"Satisfaction brought it back." Sarah led us over to the couches. "Have you ever noticed how some horses are so much more brilliant than others? They almost shimmer. Their luxurious manes and tails never seem to need brushed. They never have a speck of dirt on them. They are just a beautiful sight." A smile brightened her face. "And some dragonflies are enormous with shining, metallic-looking wings. They are so much more lustrous and beautiful than those you normally see."

I leaned forward in my seat, elbows on my knees. "Yes. I know what you are talking about. I've seen them before."

"Next time you see a horse or a dragonfly, look at it very carefully. If you stop and take notice, you might find yourself staring at a beautiful unicorn or a timid fairy. There are other magical creatures out there too, not all of them are good. Most of them have found a way to stay hidden from humans, but the disguises they wear can be seen through if you look carefully."

I didn't know what to say. I sat there for a while trying to let what she told me soak in. "Have you ever seen unicorns or fairies?" I heard the disbelief in my voice.

"Yes. I have. They are both truly magnificent." Her smile brightened her whole face. "I've also seen gnomes, gremlins, and sprites. I know it's not easy to accept, but these creatures exist."

My eyebrows rose.

"You need to remember what you are capable of before you decide this is unbelievable. Most have no idea anybody like you even exists."

"You're right." Heat crept onto my cheeks. "I guess I shouldn't doubt anything that seems farfetched without having all the facts first."

I stared into the fire transfixed. The coals danced from gray to orange to red and back again. "Sarah,"—I refused to make eye contact with her—"do you know anything else about Nefarious?"

She hesitated before saying, "You saw the picture. He's about 12' tall."

"You knew he was 12' tall when you showed me the picture?" *12' tall? I knew I'd be facing a monster, but I thought it would be a human-sized monster.* Fear coursed through my blood, threatening to spill out and wreak havoc. "And you didn't tell me?"

"I thought you realized."

The muscles in my jaw ached from clenching my teeth. "How would I?"

She stood up. "I'll be right back with the journal."

I closed my eyes and concentrated on my breathing until I heard her return.

"Here." She pointed at the drawing.

This time I realized the enormity of the demon. Standing beside it, less than half his size, a man shot lightning bolts from his hands at the monster. "Oh … I was so focused on Nefarious before, I didn't notice."

"That's perfectly understandable." She took the book back.

"Anything else?"

She crossed her legs, wrapping her hands around her knee. "I don't know if you're ready for this."

I rubbed my hand along the couch, watching the color of the fabric darken. Then I looked into Sarah's eyes and nodded. "I'm going to find out sooner or later."

"If you're sure you want to know." She sighed. "I guess it's my place to tell you."

"If you tell me what his powers are, I'll know what to expect. If you don't tell me, I'll imagine what they are." I threw my hands in the air. "Who knows, what I imagine might be a whole lot worse. And, well … if something happens to you, I'll never know."

"I suppose you make a good point." Sarah hesitated, taking in a deep breath. "He can cover his body in flames and …" She rubbed her hands down her legs.

"And?"

She cleared her throat. "And he has powers of his own."

I rubbed my hand over my mouth. "Of course he does."

"One of the things he does is try to find humans to stand in his fight against you. From some of the things my grandfather told me," she turned her eyes from mine, "I wouldn't be surprised if he tries to gain the loyalty of Cassandra and her friends."

I closed my eyes and exhaled deeply. "Go on."

"He also has the power of suggestion. In your dream, you said you heard a voice telling you 'to run, to hide.' That's the type of thing he can do. People with weak minds have no chance of defending themselves against this. He may tell you to flee from him or to run to him. If you have a strong will, you should be able to fight off the urge to do what he is telling you. If you don't …" she broke off in mid-sentence her face ashen.

I pulled my hand through my hair, already feeling defeated. "So fire, the thing I'm best at, won't do any good against him."

"I don't see how it could. Ice might have some effect, but I don't know how much." She sat next to me. "I'm sorry, Dacia. I hate to see you go through this. I wish I could take your place."

Cody walked in the door as I said, "I can't say it's something I want to do. But, at least I have good friends to try to help me through it." It wasn't how I felt, but I was trying to be optimistic.

"Especially me." He smiled. "You okay, Dean? You look pale."

"I'm fine, Cody," she said not managing to hide the stress in her voice. "I'm worried about Dacia, but I think she might have a little more strength than I've given her credit for."

"Yeah, she's pretty tough."

"Why don't you two get out of here and try to enjoy the rest of the day?" Sarah suggested.

"That sounds like a great idea," I said.

"I'll see you Tuesday, Dacia," Sarah said as Cody and I headed out the door. "Unless, of course, something happens before then that you think I should know about."

When we got out into the fresh air, Cody asked, "So, how was your lesson?"

"It went pretty well. I controlled my powers, and nothing even flew at Sarah." I threw my shoulders back and felt a wide grin spread across my face.

"Great!"

We walked on in silence for a while. "Sarah tried to use you against me in my lesson."

"Why?" Cody stopped walking and frowned down at me. "I'd never hurt you."

"I know you wouldn't." I patted his arm. "Sarah tried to make me believe you were Cassandra's boyfriend. She must think we're more than friends …" I looked away from him. *Why would she do this to me? I don't need to think about Cody as anything more than my friend.* "I guess she was trying to make me jealous."

Cody's face reddened, and he stared into the distance. He'd never asked me out, and I'd never expected him to. However, when Sarah mentioned him and Cassandra together, jealousy tore me up inside. I didn't like the thought of him dating anyone. Even though we weren't involved romantically, he was still *my* Cody, and as much as I wanted him to ask me out, I didn't want to ruin our friendship if things didn't work out either. *Why mess up a good thing?*

"Did it work?" Cody still hadn't looked at me.

"I held my own." I knew what he meant, but I wasn't about to admit it to him.

He raised a single questioning eyebrow.

*Time to change the subject.* "I asked her if she knows anything more about Nefarious than what she told me at our first meeting."

"And?"

"She told me Nefarious has the power to gain the allegiance of humans, so not only do I have to worry about defeating him, I might have to fight people, too." Saying it made my stomach sink.

Cody put his hand on my shoulder. "It'll be all right, Dacia. I know it doesn't seem like it, but things'll work out. Samantha and I will help you any way we can." His jaw set, and his eyes lit up like they were on fire. "You know I won't let anything or anyone hurt you."

"Yeah, I know you'll do your best to keep anything from happening to me." I slid my hand into his. Warmth spread from my fingertips up my arm. *Get a grip. Seriously.* "But I don't know if you'll be able to protect me this time, Cody."

We walked in silence for a while, both of us a little uneasy. "Sarah also told me unicorns, fairies, and other magical beasts exist. She told me she has seen some of them, too."

Cody cocked his head. "You believe her?"

"I don't know—" I paused thinking of what Sarah said "—but, how can I deny they're real when I believe in a fantasy that includes a horrific beast?"

"Touché." He squeezed my fingers. "I wouldn't mind seeing one."

"Me either," I said, still not sure if I should believe any of this stuff. A month ago all these things were the makings of fairy tales and childhood imaginations. Now I thought they might be true. Who knew what I'd believe next?

# Chapter 15

## *Flying High*

Samantha, Cody, and I hiked through the trees to Falcon Lake. Thick woods surrounded a path worn into the forest floor by hundreds of students through the years. Roots and rocks jutted up through the dirt. Low-hanging branches blocked the path.

"I really should be reading a book for English Lit." I pushed a branch out of the way. An orange leaf fell, drifting to the ground. "I have a book report to do, but I don't think I could concentrate on it today anyway."

"Sounds like you." Samantha tripped on a root. "I suppose it's due Friday, and you'll read the book and write the report Thursday."

"You're giving her too much credit, Sam." Cody chuckled. "It won't be done 'til class Friday."

"Well, for your information, the report is due Wednesday," I said in the haughtiest voice I could muster. "I guess that makes both of you wrong. You know I'll get it done. I always do."

"You'll finish Wednesday morning then," Cody said.

"I'm going to finish it before then just to prove the two of you wrong!"

Cody rubbed his chin. "Pay for dinner Friday if you finish before Wednesday."

He should've known better; I loved a challenge. This would be the perfect motivation to get me going.

After walking nearly a mile, we stepped from the path. Picnic areas scattered around Falcon Lake were shaded by century-old trees. A quaint little park, with swings, merry-go-rounds, and slides, was the highlight for children. It evoked memories of childhood, the laughter, and innocence of youth.

Leaving our stuff at a picnic table, we walked down to the shore. Like most glacial lakes in the mountains, the water was crystalline, and you could see every rock for about ten feet out. After that, the bottom dropped out, and the water darkened to navy. It was about two hundred twenty feet at its deepest.

We skipped a few rocks across the surface before playing Frisbee. Setting up in a triangle, I threw to Cody who threw to Samantha who time after time tossed the Frisbee over my head. After about fifteen minutes of chasing the Frisbee and being good-natured about it, I was getting frustrated.

"Samantha, I'm here. I'm five foot five inches tall, not seven feet. Please throw it to me!"

Her face flushed with embarrassment. “I’m sorry, Dacia. I’ve never been good at this.”

The next time she threw it to me, it was above my head again. Even though I knew there was no hope of catching it, I jumped.

The Frisbee hit my hand, and I closed my fingers around it. Samantha’s and Cody’s mouths hung open.

“What?” I stepped to throw the Frisbee, but my foot only touched air. I flung my arms out and plummeted back to earth.

Cody ran over, getting there the same time I landed on my butt. He lowered his hand to me. “Nice hang time!”

My eyes darted around, checking the area, hoping no one else had seen me. There was a couple holding hands, walking along the beach, but they were gazing into each other’s eyes and didn’t seem to be aware anyone else even existed. As far as I could tell, nobody had noticed. “Thank God there weren’t too many people around,” I said. “That would’ve been hard to explain.”

“How did you do that, Dacia?” Samantha asked, her mouth hanging open and her eyes widened.

“I was frustrated.” I wiped dirt off the back of my jeans. “I didn’t want to chase the Frisbee again. I leapt and all that emotion must have …” I pulled my fingers through red tangles. “I don’t know … given me a boost.”

Cody shrugged and acted like it was no big deal. “Wonder what else you can do.”

“I wish I knew how to make myself do these things instead of them just happening to me.”

“You’ll figure it out,” Samantha said.

"I've had powers all my life." I folded my arms over my chest, holding my insecurities in. "I haven't figured anything out."

Clouds rolled in and blocked the sun. Thunder rumbled in the distance, and I took a deep breath. I walked to a picnic table and sat. Instead of picturing my mountain scene, I looked at Falcon Lake. Wind blew waves across the water, crashing against the beach.

Cody sat next to me. He reached to put his hand on my shoulder, but I dodged it.

"I need a few minutes." I rubbed my hand over my face. "If you don't mind."

Cody's shoulders hunched, and his mouth twisted. He reminded me of a lost puppy dog. I always ran to him when I had problems, but now I was pushing him away.

"Uh, sure. I'll hang with Samantha."

I grabbed a bottle of water. I wanted a normal life. When I left Bittersweet, I thought I might find that here. Things were farther from normal here than they had ever been at home, and the end was nowhere in sight.

I watched people at the lake and tried to imagine what it would be like to be them. I wondered what it must be like to be the couple I had seen walking around the lake holding hands. They didn't appear to have a care in the world. They seemed happy to share each other's company. Another guy played fetch with his loyal dog. I longed to be like him, not thinking about the end of the world, simply enjoying myself. I knew there had to be difficult things for him to deal with in his life, but in my mind, my problems outweighed everybody else's.

The sky continued darkening. People grabbed their stuff, clearing the area. "Snap out of it," I said to myself. I needed to get control before we had to walk back in the rain. I leaned my elbows back on the table and gazed at the mountains. My troubles dissolved. The clouds drifted away.

Cody and Samantha sat with their heads bent together, whispering. They looked up and saw me watching them, so I waved them over.

"Well, what did you two decide?" I asked as they approached the table. "How are you going to make things better, or did you decide I'm a lost cause?"

Samantha smiled. "You know we decided a long time ago that you're a lost cause."

I forced myself to return her smile.

"Actually, we decided it's about dinner time, so do you want to eat here or go?" she asked.

"All we have here are snacks," I said.

Cody rubbed his stomach. "I could go for a bacon cheeseburger and fries."

Samantha went over to her bag and pulled out a pen and paper. "Why don't you two tell me what you want? I'll go back and order it while you get all of our stuff rounded up."

"That works," Cody said. "Bacon cheeseburger, lettuce, tomato, mayo and cheddar fries. Dacia?"

"I'll have the same, hold the mayo."

Samantha patted me on the back before heading up the trail.

Cody sat down beside me and took my hand in his. "You okay?"

"I'll be fine." I pulled my hair off my neck. "I'm sorry I sent you away. I needed a little space."

Cody stared into my eyes. I wondered what was going through his head, but I was afraid I wouldn't like what I found out. "Don't apologize. Sometimes you need space. Sometimes you need me."

"Thanks, Cody." I laid my head on his shoulder. "I have no idea what I'd do without you."

"You'd be lost." He rested his head on mine.

Having Cody hold me like this, my heart threatened to fly from its cage. "There's more truth to that than you realize."

"Let's sit by the water." Cody stood and reached for my hand. "It'll take a while for our food to get there."

We sat on the edge of the lake. Waves crashed against the rocky shore. It was nearing sunset, making the trees and water appear more intense.

Cody reached up and put his arm around my shoulders pulling me closer to him. "I've, uh, been thinking about Sarah using me and Cassandra to make you jealous."

I tilted my head and looked up at him. "Okay?"

He focused on the lake. "Thought about it. More than once."

"Cody, I never expected you to ask me out." My insides wobbled. *Had he really considered dating me?*

He cleared his throat. "You're my best friend. I don't want to lose you."

I slid my arm around his back. Sitting this way felt good … right. *You can't let him think it would work. He deserves better.* My heart stopped when I said, "Friendship's good."

Even with the glow from the setting sun warming his skin, I saw his face redden. I laid my head on his shoulder and stared at the clouds reflected on Falcon Lake. Dating Cody had been on my mind on and off again all day. Sitting with him like this, I wanted it more than I'd ever wanted anything else in my life.

"Are you ready to go back?" I looked at his profile. With the sun behind him, each of his eyelashes was highlighted. It was hard for me to remember why we shouldn't be together. "I imagine Samantha wonders what happened to us."

"Nah." Cody squeezed my arm. "Told her we needed to talk."

Shadows lengthened. The sunset was little more than an orange glow on the horizon and stars dotted the sky by the time we decided to leave. The trail was unlit.

"I guess I should've packed a flashlight," I said.

Cody and I held hands, helping guide each other through the woods. I strained my eyes to see the path. A couple shadows moved too quickly. I nudged Cody, and he bent down.

"What?" he whispered.

A cold tingle ran up my spine, twisting my stomach. Keeping my voice low, I said, "Somebody's hiding behind those trees."

He pulled me off the trail into dense timber. Our eyes adjusted well enough to see the trees, but we were insecure about our footing. Every now and then a twig snapped. We made it past the spot where I had seen the people hiding, but there was no sign of them.

We stood still, searching the darkness. My heart thudded against my ribs. If anyone was hiding in the trees, they'd be sure to hear it.

A branch snapped, and Cody's grip on my hand tightened. Somebody stood in the shadows in front of us. I took a step back and bumped into someone else. My heart jumped into my throat, blocking a scream.

In the darkness, I couldn't make out their faces.

"Nice of you to step off of the path where nobody can see you."

I recognized the voice as Bryce Sumac's.

"What do you want, Bryce?" Cody asked.

"We'll do the talking here." Alvin Leach's voice came from behind us.

"The freak here"—Bryce pointed at me—"needs to stay away from Cassandra. If she doesn't, she'll answer to us."

I tried to calm myself, not wanting anything else to happen today, but I didn't like being threatened. "I've been trying to stay away from her since I got here, so that won't be a problem on my part! Now, why don't you move out of the way?"

Bryce stuck his face right in front of mine. "We'll be keeping our eyes on you, Freak. You'd better watch your back." He pushed his fingers into my shoulder.

"Back away from her. Now." Cody's voice turned dark and dangerous, protective.

Bryce pulled back from me and punched Cody in the jaw. Cody, caught off guard, stumbled backward, catching himself before falling to the ground.

A familiar sensation burned in the pit of my stomach, and I knew I wouldn't be able to control myself much longer. This was why Cody and I couldn't be together. He would always be a target because of me. People feared anything different, and I couldn't let Cody live like this. Somehow, I needed to let him go.

Cody regained his bearings and pulled his fist back.

"Go ahead, Cody, hit him," Alvin hissed. "You can't get us both at the same time."

Cody turned his head to get a better look at Alvin and was lowering his fist when Bryce threw another punch at him. I clenched my fists and stepped forward.

Bryce's punch didn't land on Cody's face. It stopped about an inch away, and Bryce howled in pain.

Cody and I ran through the trees, stumbling and fighting our way back onto the path. We sprinted until the campus lights illuminated us. Bryce's screams followed us back to the dorms.

Panting, we stepped into the glow of the lamps. Even in the dim light, I saw the red mark on his cheek and felt horrible for not stopping Bryce's first punch.

"What'd you do to Bryce?" Cody asked.

Gasping for air, I answered, "I have no idea." I sucked in a breath, trying to ease the burning in my lungs. "I couldn't let him hit you again. He should've hit me."

"No." Cody's hands clenched at his sides.

"I'm the one he has a problem with."

"If he'd hit you, more than just his hand would hurt." Cody spoke with a fierceness I'd never heard from him. "I didn't hit him because I couldn't bear to see you get hurt. If you'd've gotten hit, all bets would've been off."

I put my hand on Cody's shoulder. "Stop worrying about me. I can handle myself."

"I'll never stop worrying about you." He grabbed my hand and led me to the dorm. "I know you can handle yourself, but I also know you'd never forgive yourself if you took it too far."

When Cody opened the door, Samantha said, "Where have you been? I thought something hap—" Her voice broke off when she turned around and saw us. "Cody, are you all right? You look like you've been in a fight."

"Fine and sort of." Cody summed everything up quickly, then said, "Let's eat!"

"That's all you're going to tell me?" Samantha sounded a little wounded about not getting the full story. "How did Dacia save you?"

"We're not sure." I looked out the window, wondering if they'd made it back to campus yet. "Bryce's hand stopped about an inch short of Cody's face. We didn't stick around to see what happened. We took off running and didn't stop until we were under the lights."

Cody folded his hands together and asked, "Can we eat now?"

"Yeah, the food's over here." With a hint of guilt in her voice, Samantha said, "It's been here for about fifteen minutes. I ate some of my fries while I waited for you." She rubbed her arms. "I guess I should've been there trying to save you. I just figured whatever Cody wanted to talk to you about took longer than he expected."

"Don't worry, Sam," Cody said with a mouth full of food. "You'd've never found us."

By the time we finished eating, it was nearly nine o'clock.

"I should leave before Marcy kicks me out," Cody said.

I pulled my hand through my hair. "Will you walk with me to Sarah's office tomorrow?" I wanted to leave Cody out of my problems, but I kept pulling him into them.

He turned to look at me. He might as well have had a question mark painted on his face. "Yeah, why?"

"I better talk to her about what happened tonight."

"Yeah, you should."

ꙮ

Cody and I sit on the beach at Falcon Lake. His arm is around my shoulders, and my head rests against his chest. It's nearing sunset. The clouds turn vibrant shades of pink, orange, and purple, and the reflection on the water mirrors the sky, not a single ripple disturbs the surface of the lake.

Silence surrounds us as we enjoy the view and each other's company. The wind picks up, and the serene reflection is cast aside by intense ripples moving across the surface.

A burst of cold air makes me shiver. Cody holds me tighter and rubs my arms. Just as quickly as the wind comes up, it is gone. An eerie feeling crawls along my spine. Something tells me to run. I try to shake off the sensation, but it increases until my resistance crumbles. I decide to get Cody up and leave, but he seems to be frozen in place. I can't even move his arm from my shoulder.

A wave crashes against the shore, drawing my attention. Yellow, glowing eyes stare at me through the water. I struggle to pull myself out from under Cody's arm. My legs flail, trying to pull my body free.

"Dacia, give up. You can't win." I hear a low, growling voice. Then a clawed hand the size of my body reaches up out of the water.

I kick harder but can't free myself. I feel a surge of relief when Cody moves. I turn toward him intent on making him leave, but instead of Cody, I peer into Bryce's pale green eyes.

"Look what you did to me." His hand is wrapped in bloody bandages, his fingers contorted. "I'll get even with you for this."

I struggle to get away, but Bryce pushes me toward the lake. I stumble backward. The icy water crashes against my legs. My feet slip out from under me, and I fall back. Nefarious closes me in his fist. His claws dig into me, pinning my arms to my sides.

I fight to free myself, but I'm no match for his strength. As he pulls me into the depths of Falcon Lake, I gasp for air. Water fills my lungs. My chest burns. I know I'm going to drown. My head spins. My legs thrash out. Everything goes dark.

Then I feel myself being pulled out of the water. As I near the surface, the light blinds me. I can't see who is lifting me.

Nefarious' claws tear through my shirt as he grabs at me.

My eyes adjust to the light. I look around to see who is saving me, but nobody is there. I'm flying.

Yellow eyes stare at me from under the surface of the water. A thick stream of ice flows from my hands, and in a matter of seconds, Falcon Lake is frozen solid. I hover above the water victorious.

A low, rumbling noise pierces the surface of the lake. It grows louder until the lake explodes. Shards of ice fly through the air. I twist and turn, dodging them. I roll to the side, but intense pain shoots through my face. My eyes water. Blood runs down my cheek and drips off my chin.

From the depths of Falcon Lake, Nefarious rises. His body is covered in bright red flames. He tips his head back and roars.

I feel small, insignificant.

# Chapter 16

## Dreams Do Come True

"Dacia, wake up." Samantha shook my arm. "It's just a dream."

I woke up startled, saturated with sweat. I turned to face Samantha, and she gasped.

Her mouth hung open, and her eyes widened with fear. "Dacia, what happened to you? You were asleep!"

I reached my hand up to my cheek; it was sticky with blood. "Oh, my God, Samantha, I dreamed I had been hit in the face by a shard of ice. How did it—" I swallowed over the lump forming in my throat "—how did it come true?"

"I'm calling Sarah." Her determined tone left no room for dispute.

“Call Cody, too.” My voice trembled. “He’ll never forgive you if you don’t.” I climbed out of my loft on shaky legs. “I’m going to go wash my face.”

Samantha turned the overhead lights on. My pillow was covered in blood. I fell back, grasping at my ladder. I clung to it, struggling to catch my breath. I felt a breeze on my back and reached behind me to find my pajama shirt shredded. I finished climbing down and sank into Cookie Monster.

I heard Samantha in the background, “Hello, Sarah, this is Samantha. I’m sorry to bother you so late, but Dacia just woke up from a nightmare, and her face is covered in blood.” Her voice wobbled. “Okay, I’ll tell her.”

Samantha walked over to me. “Dacia, you’re as white as a ghost. Are you going to be okay?”

“Look at my pillow.” My voice was cold and detached.

Samantha’s hand shot to her mouth. “Oh, Dacia, I can’t believe you bled that much! Sarah will be over here as soon as she can. Everything’s going to be fine.” She sounded like she was trying to convince herself as much as me.

“Please call Cody,” I said my voice still lifeless.

“Yeah, I’m sure he’ll come rushing right over here, too.” As she walked away, she mumbled, “I don’t know why the two of you aren’t dating.”

“We don’t want to ruin our friendship.” My voice sounded hollow, dazed.

“Did you ever think it might be worth the risk?”

“Yes”—I looked up at her—“way too often lately.” I stared down at my hands. The blood on my fingers reminded me I should be doing something about my face. “I think about it, but … but I don't know what to do about anything in my life right now." The thought of Cody coming over to comfort me made me feel better. I got up to go clean my face and heard Samantha gasp as I walked to the sink.

"I'm going to let Cody in." I held my fingers up in the Girl Scout salute. "I promise not to go anywhere else."

Samantha nodded. "Change your shirt first."

I pulled on a tank top and threw a hoodie on over that. Then I rushed down to the door closest to the men's dorm, holding the washrag against my cheek.

Cody rushed across the parking lot. He was dressed in thin pajama pants and his Bittersweet Lions hoodie. His hair stuck up at odd angles.

My hand slipped, sliding the rag lower. *You can't have him. He'll always be a target if he's with you.*

I held the door open and Cody rushed in.

His eyes were wide with fear. He came to an abrupt stop. "Samantha sounded like something awf—" Cody suddenly seemed wide awake. A muscle in his jaw ticked. He pulled the washcloth off my cheek. "Who did that to you?"

I put my hand over his mouth. "Another nightmare. But, I woke up with this. And my pajama shirt torn to shreds."

"How … how did that happen?" He reached his finger to my cheek but pulled away before touching it. "It's bleeding."

I brought the rag back up to it. "Good grief."

We jogged up the steps to the third floor. I held my finger over my lips. We'd almost made it to my room when Marcy stepped into the hallway.

"Cody Hawks! What are you doing here at this time of night?"

He pointed at me. "Dacia fell out of her loft, so Samantha called me to come get her and drive her to the doctor."

I removed the washrag again to show Marcy my cut.

"How did you fall out of your loft?" she asked like she was addressing a two-year-old.

"I went to climb down my ladder and didn't realize my foot was asleep. As soon as I put weight on it, I fell. Those things are dangerous, you know."

"Well, just get out of here before somebody else sees you," she instructed. She turned back into her room and slammed the door behind her.

"Good thinking," I said, turning toward my room. "Maybe I should get a ladder to lower from my window. Then you could climb in without Marcy finding out. Or maybe we could tie some sheets together and throw them down to you."

We opened my door to find Sarah and Samantha standing by my bunk, whispering.

"Let me see your face." Sarah hurried over to me.

"I'm not sure, but I think I'm going to need stitches." I removed the rag once again. "What do you think?"

"Oh, dear." Sarah gasped. "I think we should have you see the school nurse. You might at least need butterfly stitches. We'll have to think of something to tell everyone."

"Marcy jumped us in the hallway." Cody explained what he'd told her. "I think we should stick to that story."

"Yeah, I know how rumors spread, and it would be best to tell everyone the same thing," Sarah agreed. "Why don't we take you over to the nurse's office? I'll call her and let her know we're on our way. Then we can come back here, and you can tell us what happened. Is that okay with you, Dacia?"

I nodded, knowing full well there was no point in arguing with Sarah. Her face was set with determination.

"We're coming too," Cody informed us.

"There was no doubt in my mind," Sarah responded.

When we arrived at her office, Nancy Heron, the school nurse, was waiting for us. "Come in, come in," she said in a bubbly voice. She was a short, heavy-set woman in her mid-fifties. Her graying hair was tousled. She wore a flowery robe and a warm smile. "This is the second accident I've had this weekend."

"How is Bryce?" I asked.

"He'll live," she answered gruffly. "Now, let me have a look at your face."

I pulled the washrag down again.

"How did this happen, dear?"

"I went to step out of my loft. My foot was asleep, and I fell off the ladder." The lie tasted like curdled milk, but how could I tell her the truth?

"What did you cut yourself on?"

"I don't know." I didn't know why that mattered anyway.

"It's a clean cut. I think we can get by with butterfly stitches. I'll give you some bandages to wear over it for the next couple of days. I'm afraid it will scar. If you're lucky, it will be pretty thin and not too noticeable." She fixed me up. Then Cody, Samantha and I waited outside while Sarah talked to her.

"What a beautiful night." I waved my hand in an arch. "Look at all of the stars."

Millions of tiny twinkling lights dotted the sky. A thin crescent moon smiled down at us.

Out of the corner of my eye, I saw it. A silvery moth-like creature flittered through the air. "A fairy!"

The fairy turned toward me. Her eyes were wide and metallic blue. Silver hair flowed over her shoulders to her ankles. Her wings were silver and blue. She screeched something at me before vanishing into the night.

"Did you see it?" My voice was high-pitched, and I bounced up and down like a little kid.

"Right before she disappeared," Cody answered. "Holy crap."

"Why do the three of you look so excited?" Sarah asked when she came out.

"We saw a fairy!" Samantha answered, unable to contain her excitement. "She was beautiful."

Sarah's frown deepened, and a sad sigh escaped her lips. "It's been a long time since I've seen one. I wish I'd have come outside earlier."

"She wasn't what I expected," I said. "She looked like a moth, not a dragonfly."

"That was just an example." Sarah waved her hand in the air. "Think of fairies like birds. There are so many varieties."

She glanced wistfully over her shoulder before walking away. Following her, my eyes darted from side to side, hoping for another glimpse of the magical realm.

"How did you know it was Bryce?" Sarah released a deep breath. "Do I even want to know?"

Cody summarized our trip to Falcon Lake. When he finished, I added, "We were going to see you about it in the morning."

She folded her hands together, then released them. "Bryce's hand was badly bruised with four broken bones." Her voice hinted at disappointment. "Nurse Heron suspected it had been crushed, but he was very evasive when she questioned him."

*I crushed his hand.* I twisted my hoodie strings together. *What would happen if I tried to hurt somebody?* "I only meant to keep him from hitting Cody."

Cody put his hand on my shoulder and squeezed. "Maybe they'll back off now."

"No … probably not." I put my hand over his. "Now, I actually deserve their anger."

"Don't blame yourself," Sarah said. "Those boys shouldn't have hidden in the trees waiting to ambush you. Violence begets violence."

"If you wouldn't have stopped him, I'd have two bruised cheeks," Cody said.

Samantha added, "Who knows what else would've happened?"

"None of you understand what it's like to do this to somebody," I said. "If you had punched Bryce, you would've meant to"—I waved my hands in the air while explaining my position—"and you would've known what you were doing to him, how much force you inflicted. Don't get me wrong. I'm glad we got away from them. I'm glad you didn't get hit again. But, Bryce shouldn't have gotten hurt as badly as he did."

Cody shook his head. "What you don't understand, is if he hadn't gotten hurt that bad, he would've been able to catch us. Or, Alvin would've taken off after us. Then you might've gotten hurt."

I stopped walking. "I'm the one who should've been hurt!"

"Dacia, Cody knew what he was getting himself into," Samantha sighed. "He can't keep himself from trying to protect you. He cares about you too much."

"She's right," Cody admitted. "I wouldn't let anything bad happen to you if I could prevent it."

"I put him in that position," Sarah stated. "I'm the one who suggested he start walking to and from your lessons with you. Cody has been following my instructions."

I clenched my hand in the hair at the top of my head and stared at the stars. "Sarah, you had nothing to do with it. I'm the one who stayed at the lake with him until after dark." *How can I make them understand I don't want anybody to get hurt because of me?* I released my hair and took a deep breath. Quietly, I said, "I never should've let Cody put himself in that position."

"What?" Cody asked like that was the dumbest thing he'd ever heard. "You wanted to go with Samantha. I made you stay."

I didn't want to admit it, but Cody was right. I'd tried to leave a couple times, but I still felt like the whole thing was my fault. I felt like a terrible person for hurting Bryce. There was no way he could understand what had happened to him, and even though he was a rotten egg, I didn't think he deserved it.

When we got to my room, I went over to the refrigerator and pulled out a bottle of water. "Does anybody else want something to drink?"

I handed everyone water and sat down. I wanted all of us to be able to get some sleep tonight and knew that wouldn't happen until they heard about my dream. Even though I hated talking about my nightmares, I started right into this one, careful not to leave out any details. As I told them, I became uneasy. My pulse galloped, and I gripped the armrests of the chair in an attempt to keep from fleeing the room.

When I got to the part about freezing the lake, a chill came over me. Sarah, Samantha, and Cody looked from my face to my hands and then back to my face. Their expressions were a mixture of concern and horror. I couldn't stand for them to look at me like that. "What?"

Sarah spoke up first, "Dacia, why don't you try to calm down?"

"I'm fine," I said through clenched teeth. "Just stop looking at me like that!"

"It's, uh, hard to," Cody stammered. "You're sitting on a froz—a frozen chair."

Samantha nodded in agreement but didn't say anything.

"Wha …" I began to ask before looking down. I threw my hands up and jumped out of the chair.

"It's okay, Dacia," Sarah said in a calm, relaxing voice.

I looked down at the frozen blue chair and wondered how I could have turned it into an ice cube without even realizing it.

I pulled my hand through my hair, and a nervous laugh escaped my lips. "I guess that's why I felt so cold all of a sudden."

Before our eyes, the ice receded. The chair wasn't even wet. It was as if the ice had evaporated.

I bent over, hands on my knees. "I have to get a grip on my powers. This is getting ridiculous."

Cody rubbed my shoulder. His mouth was next to my ear, his words only for me. "You're okay. You don't have to talk to us anymore."

I squeezed his hand. "I'll finish." I sat on the edge of the chair and went on. *Stay calm.* "The nightmare was vivid and terrifying." My hands trembled. *Keep calm. You can do this.* "But waking up wounded … what am I supposed to think of that?"

Cody's lips were drawn into a deep frown. Samantha folded her arms over her chest and looked at the ground.

Sarah shook her head. "My grandfather never warned me about anything like this."

"I don't know if I'll be able to get any more sleep tonight—" I covered a yawn "—but you should try."

"Yes, you're right." Sarah stood. "You need to try to sleep, too."

"I'm a little scared to close my eyes." I stared off into space. "What if next time, it's more than just a cut?"

Sarah squeezed my shoulder. "I don't know what to tell you."

"Before you go, you should see this." Samantha held up my pajama shirt.

Sarah looked from the top to me, and Cody put his arm around my shoulders. It seemed that was becoming his favorite position. "You're going to be all right."

"I hope you're right, Cody."

"I assume that happened when Nefarious grabbed you," Sarah said.

I lifted one shoulder. "That's my guess."

She pinched the bridge of her nose. "I'm going to have to think about this." She turned to Cody. "Come on. Let's get out of here so these two can get some rest. It would be best if I went with you. That way Marcy won't be able to say anything."

Cody rubbed my head and stood up to leave. "See you both tomorrow."

"Goodnight." Samantha climbed into her loft.

"Goodnight." I grabbed my report, climbed into my loft, threw my bloody pillow on the floor and grabbed one off the end of my bed. I dimmed my light and started writing my report. Maybe I would actually get it done ahead of schedule.

Sometime in the wee hours of morning, my pen fell to the floor, and I drifted off to sleep. I woke up to the buzzing of my alarm clock.

Standing at the sink, I brushed my teeth. I looked in the mirror. Almost half of my face was covered by a bandage. I pulled it back and gasped. The butterfly stitches remained on my face, but there was no sign of an injury.

"Samantha. Wake up." Panic rose in my voice.

"What?" she responded with a yawn.

"Did Cody and Sarah come to our room last night?"

"What kind of question is that?" She rolled over, hugging her pillow. "Of course they came. We went over to the nurse's office. Don't you remember?"

"I thought I remembered, but when I looked at my face, I thought maybe I had dreamed the whole thing."

"Why?" She sat up. "What's wrong with your face?"

I walked over to her bed and showed her.

"Oh, my God!" Her hand covered her mouth. "If you run into the nurse, she'll never understand!"

"You're right. I figured I'd take the butterflies off and pretend nothing happened, but too many people saw me."

Samantha yawned. "At least Nurse Heron didn't think you needed stitches."

"Yeah, that would've been bad." I slung my backpack over my shoulder. "By the way, my report is done. It's sitting by Cookie Monster."

"All right, Cody's buying dinner Friday!" Samantha did a little dance.

I closed the door and let the mask of happiness slip off my face. Friday … it's only Monday. After last night's dream, I couldn't help but wonder what might happen before Friday got here.

# Chapter 17

## Crushing Weight Of Guilt

I trudged to speech class, not looking forward to sitting in a room with the Potato Heads without Cody or Samantha around for moral support. With my head down, I opened the door. I didn't want to see any of them, but I felt my eyes being pulled in their direction. All four sat in the upper corner of the auditorium-style seating. Bryce's right hand stuck out of a sling. His cast appeared bulky and uncomfortable. My gut wrenched, and guilt tipped my head forward.

I took a deep breath and slunk to my seat. The classroom was filled with noisy students. I tried to eavesdrop on one of the many conversations, but none held my attention. Instead, my eyes were drawn back to Bryce's hand. *How did I do that to him?* I wanted to apologize. I stood up, but as soon as they noticed me, I sat back down. Alvin narrowed his eyes at me and punched his hand.

I lowered my head. *This isn't good. Why can't he see it's better to stay away from me?*

Mrs. Mantis walked up to the podium. "Vanessa Badger, you're up."

Vanessa made eye contact with all the students as she recited her speech. When her eyes met mine, she glared, and I felt her hatred. She'd stood up for me when Cassandra dumped her cappuccino on my lap. Now she hated me as much as the others did.

Since I recited my speech in Friday's class, I stretched out and listened to the other students. Somehow I managed to keep my eyes open through all the speeches about the history of cartoons, the chores done on a farm, how cell phones work, and every other topic imaginable. Exhaustion weighed heavily on me, but I fought off the urge to snooze. I wouldn't allow myself to fall asleep in front of anybody. If I started screaming or something weird happened, even more students would think I was a freak.

As soon as class ended, I jumped out of my seat and ran down the stairs, squeezing past any students who stepped in front of me. This time I refused to give in and let my eyes be drawn to Bryce's hand. I darted out of the room and didn't slow down when the cool breeze hit my face.

*I should've taken Cody up on his offer to walk me to and from my classes today. I need to quit being so stubborn.*

Footsteps pounded against the ground behind me. I quickened my pace. So did they. My pulse ratcheted up another notch. I needed to get away. If I turned and saw Alvin or one of the others, I didn't know if I could control myself.

I searched for an escape, but I was in the middle of the courtyard. The footsteps closed in on me. Adrenaline rushed through my veins, urging me to run or fight. I couldn't fear confrontations forever. I needed to face them. I stopped and turned, my hands held in front of me ready to defend myself.

My jaw dropped.

"Cody Hawks, don't you ever do that again!" I couldn't believe Cody would walk up behind me without letting me know it was him. "I figured you were one of them. You're lucky I didn't hurt you!" The adrenaline spike left my arms and legs shaky.

He held his hands up in surrender and walked toward me. "Sorry. I needed to see if you were okay."

My heartbeat resumed its normal rhythm. "Did Samantha tell you about my face?"

"Yeah." He touched the bandage. "I don't get it."

"Me either." His touch made my stomach flutter. I pulled away from him. "Aren't you supposed to be in class?"

He looked down and kicked the dirt. "I was worried. You had class with your archenemies. I wanted to make sure you were safe."

"So, now they're my archenemies, are they?" I bumped my hip into him. "I always wanted to be a comic book superhero."

Cody laughed.

"It's very sweet of you, but you can't keep skipping your classes."

"Who says I'm skipping?" He jerked his head back and pointed at himself. "I'm fashionably late. There's a difference."

"You'd better get going." I nudged him. "I'm going to sit in the classroom and work on my speech assignment."

"You should work on your book report instead," he suggested. "Although, you could buy the food for a change."

"Oh, didn't I tell you?" I shot him a sly grin. "I got up early this morning and put the final touches on it, so I guess you're buying. Samantha's counting on it."

"I shouldn't bet against you." He shook his head, but his blue eyes held a smile. "It gives you the kick-in-the-butt you need." By this time, we arrived at my next classroom. Cody held the door open for me. "You can go alone from here. Be a good girl, and don't leave."

The speech I was working on was supposed to be another how-to speech. With the way things were going, I thought maybe I should give my speech on 'How to Intimidate Your Enemies and Worry Your Friends'. It took me twice as long to come up with a topic as it took me to write the speech.

I was putting the finishing touches on it when the other students started filing into the classroom. Cassandra and Bryce came in together. They steered clear of me, watching me as they passed by my desk. I wanted to lurch out at them to see if they'd jump. It took all the self-control I could muster not to.

Cody walked in the door a couple minutes later. He nodded toward them as he sat down, "They bother you?"

"No, I don't think Bryce will be a problem until his hand heals." I paused while thinking about it. "Alvin could be an issue if I run into him by myself. He seems to be holding a grudge. Hopefully, I won't have to worry about it, though." I rubbed my arm. "I don't want to hurt anybody else."

The classroom quieted down as Martha Basil entered the room. Mrs. Basil was a stern woman who was nearing sixty. She tolerated no talking in her class unless answering one of her many questions. Her hair was as white as the new-fallen snow, and her eyes were a faded shade of blue. She informed us on the first day that all we needed to do to pass her class was to turn in all our assignments and listen to her without interrupting.

When class ended, Cassandra and Bryce exited the classroom in the same fashion they had entered. I'd never thought of myself as intimidating, but if it kept them from bothering me, I could learn to live with it.

"After lunch, I'm walking you to your next class." Cody's voice had a hard edge. "No arguments."

"Fine."

His voice softened. "I'm worried about you, and I feel better knowing you're not alone."

"I've always wanted a bodyguard." I winked at him. "It might as well be you."

&

Oil Painting with Pete Quercus was without a doubt, my favorite class. Mr. Quercus was only a couple inches taller than me and very muscular. He wore his salt and pepper hair in a braid that nearly reached his waist. He looked like he belonged on a Harley, not teaching class, but boy could he paint.

I stood in front of my canvas. My brush flew across it. The scene was dark, eerie, not at all what I'd expected. I'd told Mr. Quercus I was going to paint mountains with a herd of wild horses running in front of them. I stepped back, and my brush fell to the floor with a thud. I'd painted my nightmare. Nefarious stared up at me from Falcon Lake.

"Interesting."

I jumped at the sound of Mr. Quercus' voice.

He rubbed his chin. "You've got a dark side."

I couldn't tear my eyes from the painting. "No … it's a nightmare." The room felt small, and the air thickened.

"It's not a nightmare." He rested his hand on my shoulder. "This is an excellent painting. You've got real talent."

"That's a scene from my nightmare."

His head tilted to the side. "Maybe now that you've painted it, it won't hold any power over you."

*If only.*

ꙮ

The next day, Cody knocked on my door fifteen minutes before Samantha and I had to leave for Advanced Algebra. "Your escort has arrived," he said, holding out his arm for me to take. "You ready, Samantha?"

"Yeah." She grabbed her backpack.

Alvin and Vanessa stood outside Kalmia Hall when we arrived. "So now you can't go anywhere without Cody," Alvin said.

Cody stepped forward, but I put my hand on his chest. "I don't recall either of you walking alone."

"It doesn't matter. We can wait." Vanessa's face twisted with anger. They turned and walked into the building, slamming the door in our faces.

"Wait? For what?" Samantha asked.

"Don't know," Cody answered before turning to me. "Don't go anywhere without me."

"I know, I know." I threw the door open and stomped to my seat. *Will I have to hurt all of them before this is over?*

I couldn't focus on algebra; my mind kept wandering to Alvin, Vanessa, Nefarious, and my afternoon lesson with Sarah. Off and on throughout the class, I looked around the room to find Alvin glaring at me. The expression on his face was one of extreme hatred. "He's going to try to get even with me," I whispered. "Why can't he just realize the same thing will happen to him?"

Cody put his hand over mine but said nothing.

When class ended, we crammed our things in our bags. I was thankful it was my only class for the day.

"Alvin was making me nervous in there," Samantha said when we stepped outside. "He kept shooting daggers at you."

"Noticed that," Cody said. "Don't even open your door without me around."

"Cody"—I put my hands on my hips—"I appreciate your concern, but I can't spend my life hiding from the Potato Heads."

"I know you can handle yourself. But I …" He rubbed the back of his neck. "I worry about you, and I'd never forgive myself if something happened to you, especially if I could've prevented it."

Samantha rolled her eyes and mouthed something I couldn't make out.

I turned back to Cody, my demeanor softened. "Thanks, but sometimes I'm going to be by myself. You can't keep that from happening, and chances are that if Alvin tries to attack me, he'll end up wishing we'd never met."

ꟷ

Sunlight caressed my skin. The autumn-leafed trees stood out against the cloudless sky. I longed to spend the afternoon outside enjoying myself but, even if I wasn't on my way to a lesson with Sarah, Cody wasn't about to let me forget my problems. He was acting like an overprotective guard dog.

As we walked to Sarah's office, his eyes darted from side to side. His body was tense, and his steps were quick and deliberate. I knew he worried about me and wanted to protect me, but I felt like meandering along. Instead, his hand pressed on the small of my back, forcing me to move at the same speed as him.

We arrived at Sarah's office in no time at all. "Hello," she said.

Cody stood with his hands on his hips, blocking the door. "Under no circumstances is Dacia to leave here on her own."

She looked from Cody to me then back again. "Why? What happened?"

"Alvin and Vanessa seem to be trying to figure out how to get even with me." I rolled my eyes. "They were waiting for me to show up to algebra and weren't very happy to see that I had an escort."

"Oh." Sarah shook her head. "I'll have a talk with them. I'll tell them to quit harassing you."

I ran my fingers through my hair. "I'd rather you didn't. They hate me enough as it is. I don't need them thinking I'm a tattle-tale too."

"While I can understand that," Sarah said, "I have to do something, and it'd be best if you didn't go out alone."

Cody nodded his agreement. "I'll walk with her."

"I'll be lucky to go to the bathroom by myself," I muttered.

"What was that, Dacia?" Sarah asked.

"Oh, I'm lucky somebody wants to watch out for me."

"Yes, you are." Her head bobbed up and down. "Cody, why don't you come back in about two hours? If we get done sooner, I'll give you a call."

"Sounds good," Cody said on his way out.

Sarah sat on the couch and grabbed her coffee cup. "Why don't we start by relaxing? You seem tense today."

"I'm frustrated." I plopped down on the couch harder than I planned. "I'd like to get out and enjoy myself, but I have to look over my shoulder everywhere I go. Cody's so nervous. I'm surprised he hasn't set up camp outside my door. He doesn't want me to move at all if he's not around." I leaned forward. "I'm afraid for Cody and Samantha, too."

"Why?"

"Guilt by association." I shrugged. "I wish Alvin and Vanessa would realize I had no control over what happened to Cassandra and Bryce. And the same will probably happen to them if they ambush me." I sat back and rubbed my hand over my face. "It's in their best interest to stay away from me."

"One of the things you'll learn as you go through life is that some people's egos can be very powerful. Deep down, I'm sure Alvin and Vanessa know they shouldn't mess with you, but they are too proud to back off." Sarah spun the cup in her palms. "Unfortunately, people don't always take the time to listen to that little voice in their heads."

"I wish they would."

Sarah lifted her lips in a sad smile and began my lesson. "Try to relax. Close your eyes. Now take deep, calming breaths. Let out all of your negative thoughts. I'm going to count backward from five to one. When I get to one, I want you to be sitting next to your mountain lake, 5 … 4 … 3 … 2 … 1."

My breathing slowed as I sat on the rocks, staring at the reflection of the mountains in the tranquil lake. A fish jumped up out of the water, and ripples made their way toward me, distorting the lake's mirror-like quality. Birds chirped in the distance, and for a moment, I was convinced I could smell the pine trees. I no longer felt the weight of the world bearing down on my shoulders. Serenity washed over my body.

Out of nowhere, I heard Sarah's voice, "Dacia, I want you to bring yourself back to my office. I'm going to count to five. When I reach five, I want you to find yourself sitting on my couch, 1 … 2 … 3 … 4 … 5."

I forced myself to come back and face reality once again.

"How do you feel now?"

"Much better, but I wish my little retreat was real." I rested my head against the back of the couch. "I wish I could get away from everything for a while. It seems like it has been forever since I enjoyed myself or even had a good laugh."

"I know this is hard on you. I wish it wasn't your fight." Her voice started out strong and steady but broke at the end. "But if you're going to do it, we need to get you trained. I think the next step is to figure out how to control your actions. When you set something on fire, I want you to know ahead of time that you were going to set it on fire and not freeze it or send it flailing through the air."

A snort of disbelief snuck out before I asked, "And, just how do you plan on doing that?"

She placed two ceramic bowls on the coffee table, and I noticed the table between us had none of its usual décor on it. "This"—she pointed at the dark blue striped bowl on the left—"has shredded paper in it. The other bowl"—she pointed at the burgundy striped one on the right—"contains water. I want you to picture yourself setting the paper on fire and freezing the water. Then I want you to send this ball"—she said as she set a red ball down between the bowls—"flying across the room."

I shook my head. "Do you really think it will work? Because, honestly, I think it would take a miracle."

She sat down and crossed her legs. "I think you can do anything you set your mind to. I know you don't have a lot of confidence, but you can do this."

Staring at the bowls, I asked, "Well, if all of your life you were told you were a freak, would you be full of confidence?"

I didn't give Sarah a chance to answer. "Until I met you and Samantha, Cody was the only person who ever believed in me. Everyone else, including my parents, has helped to remove any assurance that Cody was ever able to instill in me."

"I'm sorry for that, but I believe in you. I know you can do this," she told me with heartfelt conviction in her voice.

I looked at the bowls and let out a deep breath. "I'll do my best."

Sarah rubbed her hands together. "From everything you've told me, fire seems to be your go-to power."

I nodded my agreement.

"So, I want you to picture yourself lighting the paper on fire. Then I want you to do it. Take as much time as you need. Use all your concentration. You can do this." Confidence radiated from her smile.

I closed my eyes and pictured myself setting the paper on fire. Then opening my eyes, I struggled to accomplish my vision. I stared at the paper and imagined it on fire. Nothing, not even a tiny spark.

"Aaaaah! I can't do this!" I blew out a frustrated breath.

Sarah reached out as if to pat my hand, but I was too far away. "Relax. You're putting too much pressure on yourself. When you're ready, try one more time."

I concentrated on calming every muscle in my body. Then I took a deep breath and refocused my attention on the bowl. Flames shot from my fingertips, missing the bowl and landing on the floor next to Sarah. She set her mug down—sloshing coffee over the side—grabbed a fire extinguisher I hadn't noticed and put the flames out.

My hand shot up to my mouth. “I’m so sorry.”

“You did it! Good job.” She smiled down at the fire extinguisher. “As you can see, I anticipated difficulties.”

“Yeah, but …”

Sarah waved her hand in the air. “Let’s try it again, but this time why don’t you try to freeze the water. I think that will be a little less dangerous. I should’ve had you do that in the first place.”

Once again, I attempted to relax. I tried to picture myself freezing the water bowl, but something kept breaking my concentration. I resituated myself on the couch trying to get more comfortable. I took a couple deep breaths. Then I pictured ice flowing from my hands, hitting the water and freezing it solid. I opened my eyes to find that none of that had happened.

I slumped back and pulled my hand through my hair. “It didn’t work.”

“Don’t give up yet, Dacia.” Sarah leaned forward, folding her hands together. “The fire didn’t do what you wanted, but you were able to call upon it.”

I heard Sarah. I even understood what she said, but I felt far away. I searched through my memory for an indication that I had purposefully used my powers before, but I couldn’t come up with any. They seemed to be tied to strong emotions, nothing else.

Somehow I needed to figure out another way. I had to learn control.

Sitting up straight, I concentrated on the bowl. I imagined ice streaming from my fingertips. I thought about snowflakes drifting down from a dark, winter sky. I pictured icebergs, igloos, and glaciers, and still, nothing happened.

My hands fell to my lap, and I stared down at them. "I … can't."

Sarah came over and sat next to me. "You will never achieve anything if you don't believe you can."

I released a heavy sigh. "You're right … but I don't know how to make it happen." I turned my hands over in front of me, searching for a clue.

Sarah reached out and stopped them. "I don't think it comes from there." She looked into my eyes. "I imagine it comes from inside." She patted her chest before returning to her couch.

I didn't say anything. I just closed my eyes and visualized the bowl of water. I pulled from deep inside, imagining the water turning to ice. A shiver ran up my spine and down to my fingertips.

Smiling, I opened my eyes. The table was covered in a thick layer of frost, but the water in the bowl was still liquid. Disappointment pulled my shoulders down. "I thought I did it."

"No, but you're headed in the right direction." She stood up and asked, "Would you like something to drink before trying again?"

"Yeah, that'd be nice." While she went to get it, I got up and stared out the window at the mountains. Soon the ground would be covered in a thick blanket of snow and travel off campus would be next to impossible. My thoughts turned from travel to Nefarious. *How can I defeat him when I have no idea how to freeze a bowl of water?*

"You can't," a low, deep voice growled from the far corner of the room. "What makes you think you can stand against me? You are nothing but an insignificant little girl." Reflected in the window, I saw the familiar yellow eyes, but when I looked over my shoulder, nothing was there.

I slumped to the floor. With my back against the window, I stared across the room. My heartbeat pounded in my ears. *How could he be here, then not? Am I losing it?* With my arms wrapped around my knees, I rocked back and forth.

Sarah walked in a couple minutes later. "What's wrong, Dacia? You look like you've seen a ghost."

My voice shook when I explained what happened.

She squeezed my shoulder. "I can call Cody if you'd like to go."

"No, Sarah … the only chance I have to defeat Nefarious is to learn how to use my powers," I told her with more determination than I'd been able to muster to this point. "I need to get this right."

I took my place back on the couch and drank half of my water. "I'm going to try the ball this time." I closed my eyes and imagined myself throwing the red ball across the room and into the garbage can next to the door. Menacing yellow eyes appeared on the image of the ball. I sucked in a startled breath. My concentration faded, but I fought to keep control. If every time I saw those eyes appear I backed down, I would never be able to prevail. A force welled up inside my body. I pictured the ball hurtling through the air and heard it land in the trashcan on the other side of the room. I opened my eyes to find the ball missing from the coffee table. I spotted it rolling on the carpet a few feet away.

I rubbed my face. “I didn’t do any of them right.”

“But you used each of your powers.” Her smile was genuine. “With some practice, I have no doubt you will get this. It’s about time for Cody to arrive. Do you want to try again or do you want to call it quits for today?”

“Why don’t we try one more time?” I looked at the bowls. “I’d like to try ice again.”

“Okay, go whenever you’re ready.”

I thought about Cody, Samantha, and Sarah. They had faith in my ability to do this. I let their optimism replace the negativity I held within myself. Then I pictured ice streaming from my fingertips.

I opened my eyes just in time to see the stream of ice hit the water. An ice sculpture of a wave trying to flee the bowl sat between us on the coffee table. Tiny droplets froze in mid-air above the bowl and fell.

“Nicely done.” Sarah clapped.

“Holy cow—” I laughed “—but I didn’t mean to do it yet. I was trying to visualize it happening.” My words came out in an excited rush.

“I don’t know why it happened the way it did, but that was exactly what I wanted you to do,” Sarah said unable to hide the excitement in her voice. “I think you’ll get this if you practice a little.”

“How am I supposed to practice something when I have no idea how I’m doing it?” I rubbed my hands down my legs.

She shrugged. "Well, I guess the best thing would be for you to try to concentrate like you were just doing and see what happens."

I reached out and touched the ice. There was nothing about it that spoke of its creation. My fire was always blue, but this was just plain ice.

Sarah watched me fiddle with the ice. "This has been a very productive lesson. I didn't think you'd accomplish quite this much today. I'm impressed."

"I've still got a long way to go, but it's a start." I tilted my head to the side. "Cody's here."

As Cody walked in, Sarah looked at me. Her brow was furrowed, and I could see the question in her eyes before she asked, "How did you know that?"

"Uh … I don't know." It dawned on me he hadn't knocked, and I hadn't heard a car pull up or any other noise to give his arrival away. "I just sensed it."

"What did you sense?" Cody asked.

"Dacia informed me moments before your arrival that you were here. I just wondered how she knew," Sarah explained.

"Stranger things have happened," he said without a hint of surprise in his voice. He turned to me. "You ready, or you need longer?"

"I'm ready." I stood to leave. "I'll see you later, Sarah."

"Let me know if anything comes up," she said.

"I will."

When we were on the sidewalk, Cody asked, "So, how did things go today?"

"You know, they went pretty well." I gave him a quick recap of my lesson, leaving out the parts with Nefarious. I didn't want him to think I was becoming paranoid or hallucinating.

Cody nodded. "Cool. I'm not surprised."

"I know." I put my hand on Cody's bicep. "I think I'm beginning to gain some of that confidence in myself. Maybe if I can keep accidents from happening it will eventually grow into a full-blown case of self-esteem."

The days were getting shorter, so it was twilight when we left Sarah's office. Cody was on edge all the way back. He put his hand on the small of my back forcing me to hustle to keep up with his long strides. He was rigid and kept an eye out for anything out of the ordinary. His head tilted, listening for any unusual sounds. My spirits dropped when I realized this was how things would be until The Potato Heads gave up or I ended up hurting them.

"You know, Cody, maybe a confrontation would be good."

"What do you mean?" Cody stopped. "Are you nuts, Dacia?! I'm trying to protect you, and you want to battle it out with them. I don't understand you anymore!" His face reddened, and he stood there shaking his head.

In the most convincing tone I could muster, I told him my feelings, "Until we do, we are going to be on edge, waiting for somebody to jump out of the bushes. The only way they are going to leave us alone is if I do the same type of thing to them that I did to Bryce." As I told him this, another solution came to mind, "If I could get a few minutes alone with Bryce or Cassandra, maybe they could convince them to back off. Maybe they'd realize that nothing good can come from this."

"I don't know, but it's better than confronting them." We started walking toward the dorms again when Cody said, "Do you remember … Oh, never mind."

"What? You can ask me whatever it is."

He began again, but his voice was unsteady this time. "Do you remember telling me that Nefarious can control humans?"

"Yes, I do, and yes, I think it's safe to assume he's the puppet-master controlling them." I breathed deeply, letting the air back out slowly. "Thinking that's what leads me to believe I may need to hurt them in order to get them out from under his thumb."

He put his hand around my shoulders. I fought the desire to lean into him. With weak knees, I walked the rest of the way to the dorm.

For the first time in a long time, I had a good night's sleep. The only dream I remembered was one of Cassandra. With her hands froze together, she ran down the hallway screaming. Bryce, Alvin, and Vanessa ran after her, trying to figure out what was going on. I remembered being startled for a moment when I saw Bryce's eyes. They were yellow instead of green.

# Chapter 18

## Revenge

I woke up Wednesday to a thousand wings flapping in my stomach. Maybe Samantha and Cody were right and this was a bad idea, after all. *Who am I kidding? There's no way things can go well with Bryce and Cassandra. They're stubborn and proud. I have to try, though. Don't I?*

I dressed and got ready for class. Then I stood at the window, waiting for Cody to arrive, all the time wishing I didn't have to worry about walking by myself. I wanted all of this behind me. I longed for the day when I could look back on this and laugh about some of the things that had happened.

My reverie was interrupted by a knock on the door. I hadn't noticed Cody, but it was time for him to be here. I threw on my jacket and grabbed my backpack. An uneasy feeling came over me when I reached for the doorknob. I frowned. Was it just the confrontation or something else? I shook my head. "Quit being paranoid," I whispered, not wanting to wake Samantha.

I opened the door and instantly tried to shut it. The Potato Heads stood in the hallway. Cassandra and Vanessa pushed on the door with all their weight, making it impossible for me to close it. Bryce and Alvin reached through the opening, grabbed my arms and pulled me into the hallway. I opened my mouth to scream for help, and Vanessa shoved a rag in it.

"Keep quiet," Bryce ordered. "Don't try any of your hocus pocus crap, and this will be over with quickly." He nodded to the cast on his right hand. "I owe you."

My chest tightened. My lungs were suddenly unable to take air in. I scanned the hallway, searching for help. There were no signs of any other students. The one time I would have loved to see Marcy, she didn't come rushing out of her room. *Where is Cody anyway? Will he get here before I have to hurt them?*

Cassandra pushed my hair back from my ear, scratching my cheek with her fingernails. "Cody won't save you," she stage whispered. "We took care of him." Her eyes sparkled with excitement. "I think he'll be laid up for a few days!"

Unshed tears blurred my vision. A lump caught in my throat. *Oh, God, what did they do to him?* I lowered my head, defeated.

*No.* Now was not the time to give up. I needed to free myself and get to Cody. He needed me, and I couldn't let him down. I had no choice. I would have to use my powers—but could I?

Bryce and Alvin held my arms and dragged me down the hallway with Cassandra in the lead. Vanessa followed. We were almost to the stairs when panic struck me.

A bulletin board hung on the wall near the steps. I concentrated on it, visualizing it flying off the wall like a rocket and smashing into Bryce's injured hand. I felt the thrill of success when I heard Bryce whimper, but he didn't free my arm like I intended. I opened my eyes just in time to see Cassandra's fist flying toward my face.

Her punch landed squarely on my jaw and knocked my head backward. Blood trickled from the corner of my mouth. "Don't even think about trying anything else," she said through clenched teeth.

At the top of the stairs, Cassandra said, "This will do." She turned to face me. "Remember you brought this upon yourself. It's time for you to learn where your place is in the world."

She and Vanessa bent down and reached for my feet. I kicked out at them, but Bryce yanked my arm, pulling me off balance. The four of them lifted me into the air and swung me. My stomach lurched when they let go.

*How did I let them get the upper hand? Why did I care if I hurt them?* The muscles in my neck and jaw tightened. *Not today. Today I won't let them win.* I twisted in the air until my feet were under me, stopping myself before I hit the ground. Maybe I'd celebrate this victory later, but right now I only cared about finding Cody.

I flew to the top of the steps and hovered in front of my stunned attackers. Fear held them frozen in place.

I pulled the rag from my mouth and threw it at Vanessa's feet. My body trembled with rage and fear for Cody. "Where. Is. Cody?"

Bryce's eyes were cold and hard. A muscle in his jaw jumped. "Find him yourself."

Vanessa muttered something to Cassandra, and Alvin glanced around uneasily.

Anger and anxiety gathered together in the pit of my stomach. "That"—I pointed at Bryce's hand—"is just the beginning of what I can do to you."

"Whatever, freak." He spat at me.

At that moment, I no longer felt sorry for Bryce. I no longer cared if I hurt any of them. My fingers burned. I looked down to see a small fireball appear in the palm of my hand. It grew to the size of a tennis ball, and I asked again, "Where is Cody?"

The color drained from their faces. Vanessa clung to Alvin's arm, and Bryce stepped in front of Cassandra. A small, shaky voice came from Vanessa. "He's … uh …" She glanced at each of her friends, then pointed. "He's behind the bushes, against the building."

Just then, I could see him, like I was there. Unable to get up. Unable to move at all. He had a cut on his forehead. Both his eyes were swollen shut, and his leg was bent at an awkward angle.

My heart clenched, and the flame in my hand flickered. Before it completely fizzled out, I turned and flew down the stairs and outside.

I found Cody lying exactly as I had pictured him. I knelt down next to him. My vision blurred, whether from tears or rage, I didn't know.

Black clouds blocked out the sun's light. Lightning flashed, only to be immediately answered by the crash of thunder. *Not now.* I tried to stop the storm, but my emotions were too out of control.

Swallowing the lump in my throat, I whispered in a quivering voice, "Hey, Cody, I'm here. I'm going to help you." I ran my fingers through his hair while I tried to figure out how to get him to the nurse's station before the storm cut loose. "Do you think you can lean on me and try walking?"

He cringed and nodded his response. I wanted to hurt all of them for what they did to him. Hatred built inside me with every breath I took. I grabbed Cody around the waist and helped him to his feet. His eyes pinched shut as he tried to stand.

Fat raindrops fell around us. Somehow, I lifted Cody to his feet, and we walked to Nurse Heron's office. Rain fell behind us only occasionally hitting Cody or I. *Stay back* was a constant medley running through my head.

Cody's arm was draped over my shoulders. I held onto it with my right hand. My left arm was wrapped around his waist. His weight should've pulled me down, but it didn't inhibit me at all. *Maybe he's not injured as badly as I thought.*

A glance in his direction told me that wasn't the case. His head drooped forward. His shoulders were hunched, and his feet hovered above the ground.

I looked up to the heavens and said, "Thank you." Then I hurried to Nurse Heron's office, hoping my luck wouldn't run out. I opened the door and pulled Cody inside, lowering him to his feet. Thick sheets of rain poured down, splashing against my legs before I got the door shut.

"Oh, my!" Nurse Heron said. "What happened to him?"

Cody tried to answer but only winced in pain.

"I left my dorm and found him this way." *It's not a lie. It's just not the whole truth.* "Can I use your phone to call Sa—uh, Dean Aspen?"

"Yes, dear"—Nancy pointed—"it's over there. Help me get him back here first, though."

Nancy and I let Cody lean on us as we led him to the cot.

"I'll be right back," I whispered in Cody's ear after we got him situated. He grabbed my fingers and squeezed.

My hands shook so much; it took me three tries before I managed to dial the number to Sarah's office. She answered on the fourth ring. "Sarah…" My voice broke.

"Dacia, is that you? You sound terrible. What's wrong?"

"Cody's in Nurse Heron's office. Can you come?" I fought to hold my tears back. *Be strong*, I told myself. *Cody needs your strength.*

"Yes, Dacia, I'll be right there."

Nurse Heron closed the door to her examining room. I paced the floor, waiting for Sarah to arrive. The thunder and lightning diminished as my anger melted into worry, but rain pelted the roof, making it impossible to hear what was going on behind the door.

Sarah stepped into the office and set her umbrella down. "What happened? Is he okay? Are you okay? You're bleeding."

"Cassandra punched me." I forgot about that when I only gave Nurse Heron part of the truth. *I'm surprised she didn't mention it.* I told Sarah everything, swiping angrily at the tears that spilled.

"Oh, my." Sarah's face tightened. "Is Cody okay?"

"No, he looks awful." I slumped down in a chair and covered my face. "Nancy hasn't been out since I brought Cody over here. I … I—" I tried to keep from sobbing so I could talk to Sarah "—I don't know if he's going to be okay. I'm so scared, Sarah."

She patted my back. "I'll see if I can find out how he's doing." She knocked on the door and went inside.

I paced. I concentrated on my breathing, but nothing stopped the deluge.

After an eternity, Sarah came out. "Nancy cleaned Cody's wounds. She can't do anything else for him here, though. She called an ambulance to take him to the hospital in Althea." She put her hand on my shoulder and led me to the door. "Why don't you go in and see him? I'll let Nancy know it's all right."

What I saw of Cody's face looked somewhat better now that the blood had been cleaned off. An ice pack covered his eyes. I went over to the cot and laid my hand on his. I stared at his face realizing for the first time he also had two fat lips.

*I will get them back for this,* I vowed to myself.

"Dacia—" Cody struggled to talk "—thanks for helping me."

"Yeah," I said, trying my best to sound brave. "I just wish I could've stopped this from happening."

"You need to—" Cody shuddered.

I squeezed his hand. "Don't talk."

"Calm down … stop rain."

I looked out the window. "Yeah, it'd make it easier for the ambulance."

"I want you to—" he winced "—to come to the hospital with me."

"I'll follow the ambulance. I won't let you go alone."

"No, ride with me … I need you."

"I will if they'll let me, Cody, but I can't promise anything." I twined my fingers through his and rubbed his hand with my thumb. "Why don't you try to save your energy now? I'll stay right here with you."

The rain slowed but didn't stop. The dreary day matched my melancholy mood. Cody and I stayed silent until Nancy and two paramedics came in. The first one was over six feet tall, muscular, with red hair and eyes. "Ma'am, we'll need you to move," he said as he pushed by me. The name on his uniform was Trent.

The other one, Matt, was shorter and a little heavier. He had brown hair and green eyes. He looked at me and mouthed, "Sorry."

"Cody wants me to ride along with him," I said.

"Are you related?" Trent asked while checking Cody's pulse.

For Cody, I lied. "Yes, I'm his sister."

Nancy raised her eyebrows and cocked her head but didn't say anything.

"As soon as we get him in, you can climb in the ambulance," Matt said. They moved Cody from the cot to a stretcher while we talked.

I walked out into the main office. "Sarah, I'm riding along with Cody. He asked me to."

"I'll get Samantha, and we'll be down before too long."

"Samantha doesn't know about any of this. She's probably still asleep," I said, realizing for the first time I hadn't thought to call her. "She's going to be really upset with me."

"I'll let her know you didn't want to worry her until we knew how bad it was. She'll be all right." Sarah walked with me to the ambulance.

Trent made the ride to the hospital uncomfortable. He kept asking questions I didn't know the answers to—"What insurance do you have?" "What's your medical history?" "Does he have any allergies?"—and I didn't want to tell any more lies. We couldn't have arrived at the hospital soon enough. I waited outside while they took Cody into the emergency room.

# Chapter 19

## *Fruits Of Revenge*

While Trent relayed information to the emergency room doctors, Matt turned to me and said, "Your boyfriend's going to be okay with time."

He caught me off guard, but I managed to spit out, "He's not my boyfriend but thanks for letting me know." I smiled at him, grateful for the information. To this point, nobody had said anything to me about Cody's injuries.

"He might not be your boyfriend, but he's definitely not your brother." He shot me a knowing smile. "I don't know any sisters who look at their brothers the way you look at him."

"You're right," I admitted. "He's not my brother. He's my best friend. I'm sorry for lying."

"Don't be," he said. "I would've let you ride no matter what, but Trent's a stickler for the rules. It's a good thing you said you were his sister."

"Thanks."

"Yeah, take care. We need to get out of here." He waved.

Not knowing if I could go into the examining room, I went to the waiting area. I bought a bottle of water with a dollar I found stuffed into my jeans' pocket and paced the floor waiting for Sarah and Samantha to show up.

The second hand on the clock didn't move. It felt like hours had passed but mere minutes had gone by. I sat on the chair, waiting for somebody to tell me what was happening. My legs bounced up and down. *Why hasn't anybody come out yet?* Tap, tap, tap. *Matt said Cody'd be okay. Was he wrong? Did something happen?* I picked up a magazine, but the words blurred together.

Cassandra's voice echoed through my mind. *We took care of him.*

Hatred seeped into my heart. Its darkness spread through me. I jumped, scared by a clap of thunder. *They're going to pay for this.* Another flash of lightning followed by booming thunder.

I shook my head and ran my fingers through my hair. "I can't think like this," I whispered.

Samantha rushed in and threw her arms around me. "How's Cody doing?"

"He's pretty beat up"—I was on the verge of tears again—"but one of the paramedics told me he should be okay in time. I'm keeping my fingers crossed."

Sarah sat down beside me. "The storm's getting worse."

There was a question there that couldn't be asked in public. "I'm scared. Nobody's told me what's going on."

"The doctor hasn't come out?" Sarah asked.

"No, not yet." I nodded toward the examining rooms. "He went back with Cody ages ago."

"I'll see what I can find out." Sarah pressed her lips together and stalked off.

Samantha turned to me. "How are you holding up?"

Through clenched teeth, I answered, "I want to hurt all of them for what they did to Cody. I want to hear them beg me for mercy." My anger burned, hot and bright. The water bottle melted in my grasp. *So much for control.*

I closed my eyes to try to calm myself. When Sarah returned, I still hadn't found my happy place; my emotions were too overwhelming for me to conquer on my own.

"Sarah"—Samantha's voice shook—"Dacia needs your help. Her water is about to come to a boil."

"Dacia, I want you to relax. Take a deep breath," Sarah instructed as she placed her hands on my shoulders.

"I'm trying." There was so much tension built up inside that it wasn't as easy for me to let go as it had been in my lessons.

"Dacia, you need to relax. Breathe deep. Concentrate on the cleansing air you are inhaling. And exhale. Let all of your anger out with your breath. Now picture yourself sitting by your mountain lake."

Sarah's voice sounded like it was getting farther away. Before long, I found myself sitting on the rocks looking across the water at the mountains. The scene was as breathtaking as ever, and the cool air was invigorating. I felt a peaceful sensation wash my anger and hatred away.

"Okay, Dacia," Sarah interrupted my reverie. "I want you to open your eyes and find yourself back here with Samantha and me."

Blinking back the light, I opened my eyes. "Thank you." My water bottle was molded to my hand. I yanked it off and threw it in the trash.

"No problem, Dacia." Sarah sat in the chair next to me. "You've been through a lot today, and sometimes we all need a little help."

"I'm glad you're calm now," Samantha said. "But, I've got to know what the doctor said about Cody."

Sarah had our undivided attention. "Dr. Sequoia took Cody into x-ray as soon as he got here. Cody has two broken ribs. His leg isn't broken, but his knee is damaged. They won't know the extent until they run more tests. He may end up needing surgery."

Every word Sarah spoke felt like a punch in my gut. *This shouldn't have happened to him. The only thing they have against Cody is me. I should be lying in that bed.* I covered my mouth and forced myself to keep listening to her.

"Until it heals, he'll be on crutches. His nose is broken. They thought his jaw was broken, too, but it's not. He'll be swollen for a while. They're going to keep him in the hospital overnight and reevaluate in the morning. They want to make sure he doesn't have any injuries that were overlooked, and they're not sure how well he'll be able to eat. Right now, they're getting him a room. As soon as they do, you two can go visit him." She patted my leg. "I have to go make a couple of phone calls. I'll be back in a few minutes."

Tears streamed down my cheeks. Cody would be devastated by a knee injury. It wasn't right that he was broken and I'd escaped unharmed. I was the one they wanted to hurt.

"Dacia, he's going to be okay." Samantha rubbed my shoulder. "It's just a good thing you found him when you did and got him help right away."

Not trusting my voice, I nodded. *Get a hold of yourself.* I swiped at my eyes and stared at the floor. "What's going to happen?"

"Sarah said they'd be suspended for about a week …"

My head jerked up. "That's it!"

Samantha held her hand up. "You need to let me finish."

"Sorry."

"She's trying to get hold of the Board of Trustees to have a disciplinary hearing. Sarah can make recommendations, but she can't expel them."

The fiery inferno that had erupted inside me subsided. I pulled my hand through my hair. "I hope something happens to them. I'm not sure I'll be able to control myself after this."

Sarah returned fifteen minutes later and said Cody had been moved to room 355, and for the time being, he had no roommates.

The three of us went up to his room. The ride in the elevator amplified my fears. *What if I lose control again when I see him?* The doors opened, and I forced myself to walk down the hall. I stood, looking at his door.

"Dacia?" Samantha's voice was soft, comforting. "He's going to be okay. It'll take some time, but he'll get through this."

I put my hand on the door but couldn't force myself to open it.

"Let me," Sarah said. She pushed the door open and guided me in.

If I hadn't known it was Cody lying there, I wouldn't have recognized him. His skin was red and swollen with cuts and bruises covering his entire face. His eyes were tiny slits. An IV stuck out of his left hand. I walked over, sat on the edge of his bed, and put my hand on his. "How are you doing, Cody?"

"Sore," he whispered. "Glad you're here." It looked like it was an effort for him to open his mouth to talk.

"Samantha and Sarah are here too," I told him as they sat on the only two chairs in the room.

"Hey," he moaned. "Gave me pain pills, so I'll fall asleep. Sorry."

"Don't worry, Cody. You need your rest so you can get better," Samantha said.

Under the influence of the pain pills, Cody drifted off quickly.

Sarah looked down at her watch. "Oh, my, it's later than I thought. Do you girls want something for lunch?"

"I'm going to stay here." I patted the bed. "I don't want Cody to be alone."

"Just let me know what you want, and I'll pick it up for you."

"If you don't mind, I'd like to go with you," Samantha said. "Hospitals give me the creeps, so I'd like to get out for a little bit."

"That's fine, Samantha. So what would you like, Dacia?" Sarah turned to take my order.

"Oh, don't worry about bringing me anything," I said.

She gave me a curious look.

"I just realized I don't have my purse with me."

"No, don't worry. I'll get it for you. You need to eat something."

"I'll pay you back," I told her. "I'll have chicken tenders and fries from wherever you decide to go. Thanks."

Cody and I were left alone. I got up from the bed and looked out the window. The storm had subsided, and the view of the Snowfire Mountains was spectacular.

I sat in one of the chairs beside Cody's bed and held his right hand in both of mine. "Cody," I whispered, "I need you to get better. You're my guardian angel. I need you to watch over me." I laid my head down on my hand and sat there crying silent tears.

When the door opened, Cody's nurse, Tammy Cypress, walked in, her black ponytail bouncing from side to side. "Excuse me, Miss," she said as she walked to Cody's side. "I need to take his blood pressure and temperature." She lifted his hand, and her head jerked back as a gasp escaped her lips.

*Oh, no.* My heart sunk. "What's wrong?"

"Look at him."

I didn't want to pull my gaze away from her grey eyes. I was terrified of what I'd see.

"Look." She pointed at Cody.

His appearance shocked me. The bruise on his cheek was all but gone, and his eyes were only swollen about half as much as they had been.

"Wow. So what kind of wonder drug is he on?"

"Painkillers." She put the blood pressure cuff on his arm and mumbled, "Nobody heals this fast, even when they are on medicine."

As soon as she touched Cody with the stethoscope, he woke up. "Wow, that's cold."

"Sorry about that," Tammy said. "I didn't mean to wake you, but I have to take your vitals."

"It's okay." He turned to me. "Where are Samantha and Sarah?"

Tammy finished what she was doing and left.

"They went to get lunch." I realized that his eyes were half-open. "You can open your eyes! And you sound a lot better."

"Yeah, I feel better." He tried to sit straighter but cringed and stayed where he was. "Must be a wonder drug. It's good to see you, though."

I felt myself blush. "I'm glad you're better, but you still have quite a way to go." I tried to wipe the tears off my cheeks without him noticing what I was doing.

"What's wrong?" He reached up and wiped a tear off my cheek. His hand lingered on my face. "Why you crying?"

I closed my eyes and pressed my face against his hand before realizing what I was doing. "I'm worried about you. You looked really bad for a while."

"Yeah, I'm sure." He pulled his hand away. "Won't be able to take care of you while I'm on crutches."

"You shouldn't worry—"

Even through his pain and injuries, his expression softened. "I always worry about you. Somebody needs to."

"Not now you don't. Just rest, take care of yourself, and get better." I glanced down at his injured knee, hoping it would heal.

He nodded at his knee. "It'll be fine. If it's not, I'll deal." He twined his fingers with mine. "I'm glad you're okay. Didn't know if you'd be. Told me they were going to take care of you."

The door opened, bringing with it the smell of lunch.

"You look great!" Sarah and Samantha said in unison when they walked in and saw Cody's face.

Cody looked up at me, and I knew we'd be finishing this conversation later.

"Yeah, I know." His smile didn't look sincere. He was trying too hard. "Maybe I should be a model."

"Dr. Sequoia told me he could only give you painkillers," Sarah said. "I guess he must've decided to give you something else."

"No, that's all they have him on." I moved onto Cody's bed so they could sit. "The nurse was surprised by how good he looked for only being on pain pills."

Sarah handed out our lunches. Cody looked at mine with wide eyes. I expected him to start drooling like a half-starved puppy.

"You can have some if you think you can eat it." I held my bag out to him. "I'm sure you can handle the fries at least. You can try some chicken, too, if you'd like."

Cody ended up eating about half of my food with no trouble at all.

Once we finished, I asked, "So how did they do this to you?" Then realizing this would be a sore subject for someone as proud as Cody, I added, "You don't have to tell me now if you don't want to."

He closed his eyes and let out a long sigh. "They hid in the bushes." He stared out the window, but I saw the pain in his eyes.

*Guilt by association.* I pulled my trembling hand through my hair. *I knew this would happen. I should've made Sarah listen to me. I should've made her believe.*

"Bryce and Cassandra jumped out in front of me. Alvin and Vanessa behind. Bryce said he wanted revenge. Alvin bashed my knee with a bat." His hands clenched in his lap. His eyes focused somewhere outside. "He knocked me down. After that, they all started swinging. When they finished, Alvin held me up while Bryce threw a few more punches. They tossed me behind the bushes. I heard them say you were next, but I couldn't get up to warn you." He looked at me then. His eyes begged for understanding. He grabbed my hand and said, "I tried, but I guess I'm not your knight-in-shining-armor after all."

I hated them. Every molecule in me oozed loathing, and that made me hate them more. "You still are, Cody, but it was my turn to rescue you." I couldn't believe his main concern had been to protect me. Guilt pooled in my stomach, mixing with my hatred, threatening to erupt like a geyser.

The room darkened as black clouds filled the sky again.

"Dacia needs a minute," Sarah said.

Cody rubbed my arm. His touch sent tiny points of light into my body. They shone on the darkness consuming me. The light spread, and the storm clouds weakened.

"I'm glad you found me." Cody's voice was soothing. "But how did you carry me?"

"I, uh … didn't exactly … carry you. You sort of floated along beside me. I guess I can levitate things now, too."

"Thanks." He squeezed my hand. "So … what's going to happen?"

Sarah told Cody about contacting the board members. "The meeting will be later this week or early next week, as soon as everyone can meet."

Cody's eyes darkened, and he nodded.

"I've tried to get in touch with your parents. Nobody was home, so I called their work numbers. Your mom was in a meeting, and your dad is out of town on a business trip." She put her hand on his shoulder. "Give them a call."

"I will."

"Well, kids"—Sarah grabbed her purse—"I've got to get back to the school. Samantha, would you like to ride back with me and bring Dacia's truck back down here, or how would you guys like to handle this?"

"That'd be fine," Samantha said. "Are your keys in our room still?"

I nodded at her. "They're in my purse. Will you bring that back with you, too?"

"Sure thing—I'll be back in a bit."

"Take care of yourself, Cody," Sarah said. "I can come back tomorrow morning to see how you're doing and to talk to Dr. Sequoia if you'd like."

"We'll see how it goes," Cody said.

Sarah turned to me. "Don't stay too late, Dacia. You need your rest, too."

Once again, Cody and I were alone. As soon as the door shut, he turned to me and said, "Earlier you were going to say you should be laying here instead of me, but, Dacia, you're wrong."

"No, it shouldn't be you." I shook my head. "Bryce and Cassandra were injured because of me. You were an innocent bystander in all of it. If you hadn't been with me when Bryce jumped me, you wouldn't be here now."

"I'm not an innocent bystander!" His face reddened, and he winced. "I put myself into this position because I can't bear to see you go through this alone. We've been friends for too long."

I grabbed his hand. "Calm down, please."

We sat in silence for a while. When he looked more relaxed, I let go of his hand.

"Thanks for riding with me and staying all day. I know it's not fun."

"You'd do the same for me." I looked away from him. "I had to tell them I was your sister to ride along on the ambulance. Then when we got here, one of the paramedics told me that you, my boyfriend, were going to be okay. He said there was no way we were siblings."

"Oh, well, uh—while I was lying behind the bushes, I was thinking about that." He twined his fingers with mine. "I was, uh, I was thinking that … well, that, uh—" he cleared his throat and took a deep breath "—life's short. Maybe we should, uh, go ahead and get together if, uh, you want to."

My heart raced, and warmth spread throughout my body. *I should say no. He deserves better.*

"Dacia?" His voice was small.

*But I want this ... so bad.* "Yeah." I squeezed his hand. "Maybe we should."

He raised his bed to a sitting position, reached his hand over, caressed my cheek and said, "You really are a sight for sore eyes." Then he leaned his face in and kissed me.

My first kiss. My stomach dropped to my toes with a whoosh. His lips were soft as they gently parted mine. I was afraid to hurt him, but his hands spread over my back, pulling me closer. Sparks ignited in me, and I let out a soft moan of contentment. I wanted this feeling to last forever.

We sat there for a while not saying anything. Cody closed his eyes to rest again. I reached up and ran my fingers over his face. It looked better, but I wished the bruises and cuts would disappear.

As I ran my fingers through his hair, the marks on his face diminished. A mocking laugh escaped from my lips. *I'm going crazy.* I closed my eyes and shook my head before opening them again. His face did seem to be a lot better. I laid my head down on his chest and fell asleep.

When I woke up, I looked at the handsome, unmarred face of Cody. There was no evidence he had ever been injured—no swelling, no cuts, no bruises. I couldn't believe my eyes.

I must have gasped because Cody opened his eyes and asked, "What's wrong, Dacia?"

"Your face is, uh…" I waved my hand at it.

"Is beat up, I know," he sounded irritated. "Did you forget?"

"No, that's just it. It's not anymore."

"What do you mean?" he asked like I spoke a foreign language.

"I was running my fingers through your hair wishing that this hadn't happened to you, and all of your bruises and cuts began disappearing before my eyes. I thought I was seeing things. I fell asleep, and when I woke up … well, you look great. I don't know what else to say."

He sat quietly, staring at the wall. "Another power. I bet that's why your face healed so fast."

I rubbed my cheek. "I don't know. I figured it disappeared because there was no way it ever could've happened to begin with. I never considered any other options. Oh." I covered my mouth with my hand. "Maybe you'll get out of here today."

"That'd be nice. Sick of lying here—" he paused for a moment "—although, I'm enjoying the company."

"Yeah, the company's good. It's just too bad it took something like this to make us realize we should be together."

His hands were clasped behind his head. "I've thought about it since Falcon Lake. Sitting with you felt good, but you didn't seem interested." Oh, so gently, he reached out and traced a fingertip along my cheek.

Goosebumps rose on my arms. I finally didn't have to pull away when he got close. I could give in to my feelings and revel in his touch. "I've been thinking about it too much. Every time you hold my hand or touch me, but Cody—" My voice cracked.

"What?"

"You deserve so much better."

"Dac—"

"Things like this are going to keep happening. People are scared of me, and it's going to affect you." I lifted his arm over my shoulders and rested my head on his chest. Careful not to bump his IV, I took his other hand in mine.

"It's worth it," he mumbled into my hair.

All the clouds disappeared, and the room brightened. *This is how every minute of every day should be, spent with somebody you love.*

"Samantha'll be back soon," Cody said. "Do we tell her?"

I sat up. "I'll tell her on our way back to campus."

Thinking about telling Samantha brought a huge smile to my face. Cody and I together. For a moment, I didn't feel weighed down. I felt light and carefree.

Gravity couldn't contend with the feelings inside me. My body lifted off the bed. "Oh, crap." I hit the bed with a thump and stood up.

"What was that?"

Heat rushed into my cheeks. "Happiness." I took a step back from him.

He grabbed my hand before I could back any further away. His voice was soothing like someone talking to a frightened animal. “Don’t be embarrassed. I’d fly right now if I could.”

Samantha walked into the room carrying a flower arrangement. When she saw Cody, the vase slipped from her fingers, shattering into a thousand pieces. “Oh, wow, I guess you don’t need ‘Get Well’ flowers anymore. Do you?”

“No, Dacia has healing powers,” Cody said. “She’s the best doctor ever. Thanks, though. Was a nice thought.”

Looking at the mess on the floor, Samantha said, “I’ve got to find someone to clean this up. Will you come with me, Dacia?”

I didn’t want to be away from Cody, but I stood up. “Sure.”

As soon as we stepped out into the hallway, Samantha turned to me. “What’s with the smile? Something’s up.”

“Cody asked me to be his girlfriend. So, I guess we’re moving onto the next level in our relationship.” In my head, fireworks shot through the air, and I jumped up and down. “I was going to tell you on the way back to campus.”

“It’s about time. Everyone except the two of you knew you should get together.” Samantha hugged me.

“I’ve known it for a long time.” I ran my hand through my hair. “Seeing Cody this morning made me realize I care too much about him not to be with him. It would be impossible to just be friends feeling the way I do right now.”

“I’m so happy for you, but I need to find someone to clean up the mess I made.” She held the door open and waved for me to enter. “You can go back in with Lover Boy if you want.”

"Thanks." I smiled at her, turned around, and pranced back to Cody's side. "Samantha knows. She could tell something was up."

"What'd she say?"

"She said everyone but us has known for a long time that we should be together."

"Well, at least we know now." He grinned and pulled me toward him. I sat on the edge of his bed.

We thought nothing of it when the door opened again. Both of us figured Samantha returned. So imagine our surprise when a deep male voice boomed, "What is this mess?"

We turned to see Dr. Sequoia looking at the smashed vase and flowers scattered across the floor. It was the first time I had seen him. I was surprised by how young he looked; he couldn't have been any older than his mid-thirties with auburn hair and green eyes. He was slender and stood about six feet tall.

"Our friend is finding someone to clean it up," I said. "She was a bit stunned by Cody's quick recovery."

"She should be more careful. Somebody could get hurt." He still hadn't looked at Cody. "So what's this improvement?" He turned toward Cody. Cody's chart fell to the floor, and Dr. Sequoia's jaw dropped open. He stood, looking at Cody for what seemed an eternity. "How did this … when did … what's going on?"

"We don't know, doctor, but it's pretty amazing," Cody said. "I feel like a new man."

I reached down to pick up Cody's chart. "Now you know why my friend dropped the flowers."

"Yes, I guess I can understand. Even the gash on your face is gone." He looked over Cody searching for any trace of his injuries. He pressed on Cody's ribs. "Does that hurt at all?"

"No, sir."

"I can't imagine how you could've healed so fast. It doesn't make any sense." He flipped through Cody's chart and rubbed his jaw. "I'm taking you back to x-ray. I want to see new films."

I got the impression he wanted to see Cody's broken ribs so he would know he wasn't going crazy. In a way, I felt sorry for him. He would never know what happened here.

Cody shrugged. "Sure, Doc, but I feel fine."

Dr. Sequoia's chest puffed up as he inhaled. He slowly blew out his breath. "I'll send Nurse Cypress in with a wheelchair. We'll take some x-rays and see what's going on with you."

Samantha walked into the room as Dr. Sequoia was leaving. "Sorry about the mess." Her cheeks flushed pink. "It took me a while to find someone to clean it up."

He smiled uneasily at her. "Don't worry. If I'd had flowers, I'd be in the same predicament." His words were polite, but his voice was gruff.

"He dropped my chart instead," Cody said.

"The nurse will be in soon." Dr. Sequoia shut the door behind him.

Samantha hooked her thumb toward the door. "Is it just me or does he seem grumpy?"

"Confused," Cody said. "His bedside manner was much better this morning."

"I imagine." Samantha laughed. "He probably thinks he stepped into the Twilight Zone."

"Samantha and I can wait until you get back from x-ray. Then we should head back to campus." I rubbed my thumb under his eye. It was hard to believe it had been swollen shut only a few hours ago. "It might've been better for you if I'd waited to heal you until you were out of here."

"No." He said. "I hate hospitals. Now, hopefully, I'll be out tomorrow."

I twisted a lock of hair around my finger. "I know, but they'll want an explanation."

"If they need one"—Samantha shrugged—"they'll just have to settle for a miracle."

"It's not like you knew you were doing it," Cody said.

The janitor came in and cleaned up the flowers. As soon as he finished, Tammy came in and wheeled Cody away. *Six o'clock. I doubt we'll make it back before dark.*

"I'm so happy for you two!" Samantha said as soon as the door closed behind Cody. "You're perfect for each other!"

"Thanks." My cheeks hurt from smiling so much. "He's pretty great, and I don't have to hide anything from him. He already knows about my powers and isn't bothered by them. He's seen me at my worst, and I haven't scared him off yet."

"He adores you." She lifted her hand to her heart. "I've been able to tell from the first time I saw the two of you together. And, let's be honest. You've felt that way about him for a long time, too."

I nodded. "Let's just hope he still does after we've been dating for a while."

She rose up on her toes, bouncing up and down. “He will, Dacia.”

At 7:50, Tammy brought Cody back to the room. “My shift’s done in ten minutes,” she said. “I’ll be back at 8:00 in the morning.”

“Thanks.” Cody sounded irritated. He hopped out of the wheelchair and plopped down on the bed, crossed his arms tightly and glared at the door.

“Well …” Samantha said.

“They said they were taking me to x-ray. They poked and prodded me.” He threw his arms up. “They took tons of blood. I’m surprised they didn’t try to take samples of my brain tissue.”

“I’m sorry, Cody. I didn’t mean to put you through this.” Guilt twisted my stomach.

“It’s okay, Dacia. I’d rather be annoyed than feel like I did earlier. Besides now I can open my eyes and see you.” He grabbed my hand.

“Aaah, isn’t that sweet?” Samantha chortled. “I think I’m gonna puke.”

I rolled my eyes.

“What? Somebody’s got to tease the two of you.”

“Yeah, yeah, yeah,” Cody said. “Anyway, I’m no longer broken, but I’m missing a lot of the blood I came in with.” He massaged his temples. “Figured I’d already lost enough of that today.”

The image of Cody lying behind the bushes broken and bleeding flashed before my eyes. “Yeah, I’d have to agree with that.”

"I get to leave tomorrow."

Samantha went to the door. "I'm going to get out of here and let the two of you say goodbye. You don't need me standing around making you feel uncomfortable." As she reached for the doorknob, she turned to Cody and said, "I'd tell you to get some rest so you can get better, but I think that's been taken care of."

I sat on the bed and ran my fingers through Cody's hair. "I'm sorry this had to happen." He smelled like antiseptic. "I'd better go. Samantha's waiting on me. Don't forget to call your parents."

"Yeah." He sighed.

"They should be home by now."

His hands clenched and unclenched in his lap. "What do I say? I'm fine now."

"I don't know." I looked at the door, wanting to stay with Cody but knowing Samantha was waiting for me.

"You better go." His voice softened, and his eyes pleaded with me. "Watch your back until I can." He squeezed my hand. "I know you can take care of yourself. You did a better job than me, but I worry."

It felt good to have somebody care for me this much. "Thanks, Cody."

He reached up, brushing his hand over my cheek. Then he pulled my head down to his. His kiss lingered on my lips all the way back to campus.

# Chapter 20

## *Bad Choices*

"So tell me what happened, Dacia," Sarah said, as Samantha and I sat on the couch across from her.

I started explaining, but Samantha took over. While she talked, I thought back on my life. I couldn't remember ever being sick.

*That can't be right. Who's never been sick?* "When I was little—four or five maybe—I fell off my bike and scraped up my hands and knees. The next day I was fine. Mom and Dad never acted surprised or upset. I can't believe I never realized."

Sarah sat on the edge of her seat. "Were there other times?"

Heat flooded my cheeks. "When I set my house on fire—"

Samantha gasped. Sarah held her hand up, stopping Samantha.

"I didn't touch the flames, but the heat burned me. By the time the paramedic saw me, I was fine." I tucked a strand of hair behind my ear. "I breathed in so much smoke. I shouldn't have been okay."

The silence in the room was deafening. I willed them to understand that I didn't do it intentionally.

Samantha cleared her throat. "You set your house on fire?"

I rubbed my hand over my mouth and nodded. Looking down at my feet, I said, "My bedroom."

"Why?"

"Samantha." Sarah's voice was severe.

"Sorry," Samantha said, but it was obvious she needed to hear the whole story.

Raspberry carpet and pink walls filled my vision. A small nightlight shown on the beast in the corner. It snarled at me, sharp fangs jutted out of its snout. Long pointed ears flattened against its head as it crept forward. The half-human, half-dog creature growled.

I raised my hand. "Stop."

It stalked closer, and blue flames erupted from my fingers.

The beast exploded, and fire spread to my ceiling and walls.

I slumped forward with my head in my hands. I'd never told anybody about the fire, and I really didn't want to now. "I was six. My parents told me it was a dream. They said I must have had matches in my room." I shook my head. "I knew the fire came from me, but all this time …" My hand trembled when I raked it through my curls. "All this time, I believed the monster was a dream."

Samantha put her hand on my shoulder.

Sarah said, "I imagine the fire saved your life."

I looked at her through my fingers. "Maybe, but …" I lowered my head. "My brother died. He was two. The paramedics said he probably didn't even wake up."

Samantha gasped. "Oh, Dacia. I'm so sorry. I shouldn't have pushed."

I tried to remember Jonathan's laugh, but the only memory I had of him was Mom holding him in the hallway, begging God not to take him. "Cody doesn't even know this." I stared at the carpet until the strands blended together. "We moved to Bittersweet after that. My parents never forgave me, never trusted me again."

Sarah's voice was soft, comforting. "It wasn't your fault, Dacia."

I rubbed my hands over my face, refusing to look up at them. "My brother died because of me."

"Your brother died because a monster, most likely a demon, came into your room to kill you." Sarah stood and started pacing. "I can't help but wonder if Nefarious sent it so he wouldn't have to face you." She sat down again. "That thought gives me hope."

"Was that the first time you used your powers?" Samantha asked.

"I don't know if it was the first time, but it was the most devastating." I pulled my hand through my hair and sat up straight. "There were other times I got hurt, but I don't remember staying injured for long."

Sarah smoothed her grey slacks. "I can't think of a better ability for you to have."

"Yeah." I walked over to the window and stared out. It was dark, so I couldn't see anything but my own anguish. "I wish I would've known before Cody went to Nurse Heron's. I could've healed him before anybody knew he was hurt." My thoughts trailed back to Jonathan. *Could I have saved him?*

"You know now," Samantha said.

Sarah walked up behind me. "You did all you could, and Cody will be back tomorrow."

"I hope so. I feel better with him here."

ꙮ

I drive to the hospital hoping to bring Cody back to campus with me. I can't wait to see his face. I feel like I haven't seen him in ages. I enter his room grinning from ear to ear. I stop dead in my tracks and draw in a sudden breath. Cassandra and Bryce stand by the window.

"What are you doing here?" I demand.

"If you look around, you'll figure that out all by yourself." Bryce's voice drips disdain.

I turn to see Cody lying in his bed. "Oh, my God!" I wail as I hurry to his side.

Bryce and Cassandra fill the room with evil laughter. Cody's sheets are soaked in blood, his face unrecognizable. I reach for his hand to try to comfort him. Before I grab it, I realize his fingers are broken. I press the call button and pray for the nurse to answer. Tears stream down my face, and even though I don't think he can hear me, I try to hold back my sobs.

With a flood of relief, I hear a woman's voice crackle through the speaker, "What can I do for you?"

"Please send the doctor in." Somehow the words manage to escape my mouth.

"I'll have a nurse come in right away, and she'll decide if a doctor needs to see him."

While I wait, I look around the room and realize Bryce and Cassandra are gone. I pace, waiting for somebody to come help Cody. My patience dwindles, so I press the call button again.

"Don't you realize nobody is going to help you?" Nefarious growls into the speaker.

My heart sinks in my chest as I back away from the bed. "No, no, no." I sob. "Cody, please, I need you." I cry knowing this is the last time I will see him. I back myself into the corner and sink to the ground. Violent sobs send tremors through my body.

"No, no, no." I woke up, twisted in my blankets, my face soaked with tears. I closed my eyes and saw Cody's broken body. *What if he's hurt? What if he needs me?*

I climbed out of my loft, quietly grabbed my jacket and keys, and slipped out the door.

Stepping outside, the air was crisp, cool. I shoved my hands in my pockets and looked up. Even with the building lights, I could see millions of stars dotting the sky.

I meandered around campus with no destination in mind. I found myself standing in front of my truck. The faint scent of rotten eggs made me wrinkle my nose in distaste.

*What if Cody needs me?* I shook my head. *It was just a dream.* I turned. *But what if it wasn't.* I put my hand in my pocket and found my keys. *What if he's hurt? I could save him.*

I got in my truck and sat holding the key in front of the ignition. I wanted to see Cody to make sure there was nothing wrong with him, but I knew it was stupid of me to go. I also knew that if I didn't go and something had happened to him, I would never forgive myself.

Before I could change my mind, I threw my seatbelt on, shoved the key in the ignition, and drove out of the parking lot. Once I was off campus, I cranked the radio and rolled my windows down. The road was narrow, winding, and lined with trees. I kept a watchful eye on the ditches, hoping no deer or other animals would jump out in front of me.

The cold air invigorated me. My heart swelled. I was going to see Cody.

As I rounded a curve, my headlights reflected off an animal's eyes. I slowed down, waiting to see if it would jump out. When I arrived where I thought it should've been, I looked out the window but didn't see anything.

I stepped on the gas. The song changed, and I bobbed my head in time to the music. I wasn't worried about Cody anymore. Now I just wanted to see him, if only for a minute. *It's amazing how much can change in a day.*

The song ended and commercials started playing. I looked down to change the station. I turned my attention back to the road. My heart stopped. Yellow eyes stared at me. I slammed on the brakes and fishtailed. I fought for control.

Trees whizzed past me. I bounced down the hill, clenching the steering wheel. Adrenaline shot through my veins. "Stop," I yelled, hoping my powers would take over.

Nothing.

The airbag exploded in my face. The seatbelt jerked me back, and my truck stopped with a loud crash.

༄

When I opened my eyes, there was an orange glow on the horizon. In the dim light, I saw blood all over the inside of my truck. I stretched my arms and legs. *Nothing hurts.* I looked in the mirror. There were no cuts or bruises on my face, no marks of any kind. I doubted I would ever know what happened to me, but I was glad not to be injured.

I pushed on my door, but it was jammed. I crawled over to the passenger's seat and attempted to open that door. Finally, it gave way. I stood outside my truck, surveying the damage. *My poor truck.* The driver's side door had smashed into a tree.

"Well, I guess there's no sense standing here, staring," I murmured. I turned around and realized it was a small miracle I hadn't rolled down the hill. I stood at the bottom of a steep embankment. My tire tracks gouged the hillside, broken tree branches scattered along its path. I thanked God for keeping me safe before walking to the road.

*No wonder Nefarious showed up here. Nobody would've found me down there. But why did he leave me alive?* I stared down the hill and wondered how long my luck would hold out. I pulled my phone out of my pocket and glared at the No Service message on the screen.

I closed my eyes and breathed deeply. Thoughts of birds, butterflies, and planes filled my mind. I willed my body to fly, but my feet stayed on the ground. I pulled my hand through my hair. *I guess I'm walking.*

I was only a few miles from campus, at the most. The hike helped me clear my head, but I would have preferred driving my truck back.

Sleepy students made their way through the dorm halls to the showers. One girl's lips curled into a grimace. "What happened to you?"

"I wrecked my truck, but I'm all right." I walked the rest of the way back to my room with my head down. I opened the door to find Samantha pacing.

She stopped, hands on hips. "Where were you?" she demanded. "I woke up in the middle of the night, and you were gone."

"I'm sorry—"

"You should be!" I could hear the fear and anger in her voice and decided to let her get it all off her chest. "If something had happened to you, Cody would never forgive me. What were you thinking? And why are you covered in blood?" Her hand shot to her mouth. "Oh, my God, Dacia. What happened?"

"I'm sorry." My fingers caught on a blood-crusted strip of hair. "I had a nightmare."

"You always have nightmares."

"Yeah … but this one was Cody." My voice stuck in my throat. "I can't talk about it." I sat down. "I went for a walk and found myself standing by my truck."

"Your truck?" The tendons in her neck were taut. "You left!"

"I didn't plan to leave, but I was afraid something had really happened to Cody."

"Is"—she looked at my bloody clothes again—"is he okay?"

I shook my head and looked away. "I don't know. I saw Nefarious in the road and wrecked before I found out." Tears stung my eyes, but I couldn't cry. I couldn't think the worst. Cody had to be okay.

"Are you all right? Do you need to go to the hospital?"

"I'm fine. I passed out, and when I woke up, all my wounds were healed." I pulled my shirt away from me and looked at it. "I have no idea what happened to me."

"Why don't you call Cody?"

*That's what I should've done last night, but if I call him now … No. If the doctors have him out of the room, I'll think the worst.* "No, I'll go get him after I clean up." Visions from my dream entered my mind. I saw him lying lifeless in the hospital bed, his sheets covered in blood. *Please let him be okay, Lord. I can't live without him.*

I glanced over at Samantha, and the thought that kept replaying was that she would be next. So far in my dreams, I had managed to kill off my mentor and my boyfriend.

# Chapter 21

## *Love Is …*

I skipped my classes for the second day in a row. This time instead of spending the day at the hospital, I called a tow truck, the insurance company, and several body shops to find out which one would be the cheapest and fastest. When I got all of those things taken care of, I went to Cody's dorm and knocked on the door.

A shirtless Drew Crocus answered. He held the door and the frame, flexing his muscles. *Maybe I should introduce Samantha to him.*

"Hey, Dacia," he said. "Uh … Cody's not here. I heard a rumor that he got the crap beat out of him and is in the hospital." He pulled his hand through his auburn hair.

I cocked my head to the side. *What do I tell him?* "Well … yeah … he's in the hospital, but he didn't get beat up."

"Well, what happened then?" He blinked his amber eyes several times.

"You'll have to ask him. I came over here to get him a change of clothes and his spare key so I can pick him up." To speed things along, I said, “I was supposed to be there about fifteen minutes ago.”

Drew opened the door wider, lifting his arm a little for me to walk under. While I grabbed a change of clothes for Cody, Drew looked for Cody’s spare.

“I guess when he gets back, I’ll have to find out from him what’s going on.” Drew held the key out of my reach. “I wonder why Bryce told me he’d gotten beaten up.”

*Bryce. I should’ve known.* I fought to keep my voice under control. “Well, you know how rumors spread.”

“Yeah”—he stepped closer to me and grabbed a strand of my hair—“who knows what will be said about you being here with me when Cody’s not.”

*Yeah, definitely not for Samantha.* I moved toward him and grabbed the key. “Good point, thanks for the key.”

I hurried to Cody’s car. My hand shook when I turned the key in the ignition. I rested my head against the steering wheel and closed my eyes. *It’s going to be okay. Nothing’s going to happen.*

“Yeah, but what if Cody’s not okay?” I mumbled.

“Oh, just shut up.” I shifted the car into reverse and then drove to the hospital.

The elevator door opened. I pushed the button for the third floor and huddled in the back corner. When the doors opened, scenes from my nightmare brought my breath out in nervous, ragged gasps. I forced myself to move forward. I wanted to run down the stairs, get in Cody’s car and drive away. I didn’t.

Putting one foot in front of the other, I walked to Cody's room. Closing my eyes, I gathered my composure and knocked on the door as I pushed it open.

My heart leapt into my throat when I saw a silhouetted figure standing in front of the window.

He spun around and stood rigid. My eyes adjusted to the light. I stumbled back a step and grabbed the doorframe for support. *He's okay.* I covered my heart with my hand. *Of course, he's okay.*

His expression softened, and he walked over to me.

"Hey." My voice sounded rough. I cleared my throat. "How are you doing?"

"I thought you were another doctor wanting to run tests on me." Cody embraced me with an intensity that made me want to sink deeper into him.

I dropped his clothes on the ground and wrapped my arms around him. *He's here, and he's okay.* Relief brought tears to my eyes.

Cody stepped back, still holding onto me. He rested his forehead against mine. "What's wrong?" His fingers traced along my arm.

Tears rolled down my cheeks as I told him about my dream and the ride in my truck. I ended my story by saying, "I know that I shouldn't have gone out by myself, but I wanted to see you. I was so scared." I collapsed against his chest and cried into his hospital gown. He stood with one hand caressing my head and the other wrapped around my waist while uncontrollable sobs racked my body.

I gathered myself and backed away from him. My eyes felt swollen, and I was sure my face was red and splotchy. This wasn't how I wanted Cody to see me. "I'm sorry," I said. "I don't know what came over me."

Cody folded his arms over his chest. "Could be saving the world, finding me beaten, or wrecking your truck. Don't be sorry. There's nothing wrong with crying."

"There is when it's all you do …."

"You held up yesterday."

"I wanted to be strong for you." I reached for his hand. I didn't want to be this close without touching him. "I didn't want you to know how worried I was or how awful you looked."

"Probably why you needed to let it out today."

"Maybe."

He pulled me close and rested his head on mine. His touch comforted me, and I felt like all my broken pieces were fitting back together.

I tilted my head back to talk to him. Instead, our lips brushed. Cody sucked in a surprised breath. Then deepened the kiss. My muscles turned to liquid. I ran my fingers up his arms, feeling them flex under my touch.

The door creaked. I stepped back, but Cody didn't let go of me. Flames clawed up my neck onto my face and ears.

"Excuse me."

Cody's hands tightened on my waist. "My ride's here. No more tests." He looked down at me. "Let's go."

"As cute as I think you are in that gown, maybe you should change." I lifted the bag off the floor. "I brought some clothes."

He looked at himself, and a smile crept over his face. "Yeah … thanks." The nurse left the room, and Cody went to the bathroom to change.

A peaceful feeling came over me. Maybe things would be okay. I couldn't remember ever being this happy before.

"You ready?" Cody's voice brought me back to reality.

"Yeah."

"What were you thinking about?"

I shrugged.

"Must've been good. You had a sweet smile." He brushed a strand of hair off my forehead. "So what was it?"

"Nothing." Warmth spread up my neck and onto my cheeks.

"That wasn't nothing." He looked at me with puppy-dog eyes. "I thought couples weren't supposed to have secrets."

"I suppose you're right." I shot him my orneriest grin. "One of the paramedics who brought you in here yesterday was really cute." I looked around Cody like I was searching the halls. "I wonder if he's here today."

"Ouch, did you hear that?" He grabbed his chest. "That was my heart breaking."

I giggled and rolled my eyes at him. "Actually, I was thinking you made me pretty happy yesterday when you, uh, well, kinda sorta, well, umm, asked me to, uh, go out with you. I think you made me the happiest I've ever been."

His voice softened, and his eyes lit up. "Yeah, made me happy when you agreed. But, that doesn't mean you can make fun of my speech."

"Somebody has to. Might as well be me."

Since it was Cody's car and I didn't think I'd ever want to drive again, I told Cody to drive back. As we drove by, I pointed out where I wrecked my truck.

I strained to see down the hill, to catch a glimpse of it. The world stopped. I couldn't hear anything, feel anything, smell anything. When it started spinning again, my stomach dropped. All the air was sucked out of me. My hand went to my throat, and I gasped for breath.

"What's wrong? Are you okay?" Cody reached for my hand.

Tremors rumbled through my body, but at the touch of his hand, they quieted. I caught my breath and said, "If I hadn't healed, nobody would've found me for days."

"If I'd've known, I'd've been looking for you last night."

"Nobody knew where I was going." I rubbed my forehead. "Nobody would've found me."

He squeezed my hand. "I'm glad you're all right, but don't do that again. Don't go anywhere alone."

"I know." I hung my head. "It was stupid, but it's better for me to be alone than you … and maybe even Samantha."

The tendons in Cody's forearms stuck out as his grip tightened on the steering wheel. "That won't happen again."

When we arrived back at campus, Cody and I went to my room to see if Samantha was waiting for us. As soon as I opened the door, Samantha started venting. "Did Dacia tell you what she did last night?"

"She told me, and I let her have it." His lips twitched, threatening to expose his exaggeration.

"She told you?" Samantha's mouth hung open. "I can't believe she told you. She must've felt really guilty."

"Yes, I told him." My voice took on an indignant tone. "You do realize I'm standing here in the room with you, don't you?"

Samantha's hands dropped from her hips. "I can't believe she told you."

"Hello." I waved my hands in the air. "I'm right here. I figured he would find out when we left the hospital in his car instead of my truck."

"Oh, yeah"—she looked up out of the corner of her eyes—"I guess that might have made him wonder what was going on."

"Thanks for telling on me, though." I crossed my arms and tried to glare at her, but the smirk gave me away.

"Well, ladies, if you're done fighting, I'm starving." Cody rubbed his stomach. "Do either of you want to come along?"

Samantha and I looked at each other and smiled. "Of course we do," she said.

On the way to the lunchroom, I remembered that more than just the three of us knew about Cody being injured. "The Potato Heads might be confused by your speedy recovery if they're in the cafeteria."

"Well, maybe they'll back off," Cody said with a hard edge to his voice. "Half the school probably knows I went to the hospital, but I'm not going to hide until this blows over."

"I don't expect you to hide out or pretend like you're still injured. I just wanted to remind you before we walk into the cafeteria."

"I know." His lips pressed together and his forehead creased.

"We're going to have to come up with a story so we're all on the same page," I said as he opened the door. A glance around the room led me to believe they weren't in there. Cody must have come to the same conclusion because I heard him let out a relieved sigh.

"Maybe they won't be around until their hearing," Samantha said.

We grabbed our food and sat at an out-of-the-way table.

"Justin and Dan are coming over," Samantha whispered across the table.

Cody's lips tightened into a thin line, but by the time his buddies reached the table, he'd managed to stifle all outward appearance of tension. They nodded at each other in that way guys do.

Justin grabbed the back of a chair but didn't sit. His deep brown eyes swept over Cody. "I heard you were in the hospital." His black eyebrows pulled together, making creases on his forehead.

"Spent the night there." Cody sipped his drink.

I think he was trying to look nonchalant, but I noticed his hand shake. I rubbed his thigh.

He looked down at my hand. "Dacia just brought me back."

"What happened?" Dan asked. "Drew said Dacia stopped by this morning but didn't have too much to say. You look fine to me."

"Kidney stone," Cody answered. "You guys up for a game?"

Justin and Dan looked at each other and shrugged. "Sure … when?" Justin asked.

"3:30," Cody said.

*During my lesson then. I hope he's careful.*

"We'll get Drew and round up a couple of other guys. See you on the court." Justin turned and left.

"Later, Dacia … Samantha," Dan said. Even though he said my name first, he never looked at me. His hazel eyes lingered on Samantha. Her face grew redder by the second.

"See ya," I replied. I turned to Samantha and raised my eyebrow. She shook her head and nodded at Cody.

"Well, I guess I got outta that one … at least for now," Cody said. His shoulders relaxed, and he released a deep breath.

As soon as Samantha finished eating, she stood up. "Well, I'm going to get out of here. Be careful at your lesson, Dacia, and be careful playing basketball, Cody. Keep your eyes open."

"You too," he said.

"I will for real this time," I told her. When she was out of earshot, I turned to Cody. "Well, I guess she thought we should have some time alone."

"There's nothing wrong with that." He hooked his fingers under my chair, dragging me closer to him. My hands rested on the table. He reached up and placed his over mine. "In fact, I don't mind at all. Sam's great, but it's nice to have some time to ourselves. We haven't had a lot of that since we got out of high school."

"No, we haven't." In high school, we didn't have to worry about any of my friends hanging around since Cody was the only one I had, and his friends wouldn't come near me because they thought I was weird. "But I have to admit, it's nice to have a female friend for a change." I lifted his arm over my shoulders and snuggled up against his chest. He traced small circles on my skin.

# Chapter 22

## *Fire And Ice*

With Cody's arm over my shoulder and mine around his waist, we strolled to Sarah's office. Tension no longer lined Cody's face. His lightness surprised me. The Potato Heads should've learned to stay away from me and mine, but they seemed like old dogs to me.

My stomach tightened when we reached Cacomistle Hall. "She isn't going to be happy with me."

"Brought it on yourself." Cody ushered me inside.

I waved to Alicia and climbed the stairs. I stood in the hallway staring at Sarah's office door, trying to build up my courage. Taking a deep breath, I knocked and went inside. There was no sense in hiding. She'd eventually find out.

"Hello," Sarah said. "You look amazing, Cody. Maybe Dacia should think about medical school."

I cringed at the thought. "Maybe, but I don't like blood and gore."

"She'll be good at anything she does." Cody kissed my cheek. "Don't leave without me."

Blood rushed to my face.

"Cody"—Sarah pointed at the couch—"have a seat."

Cody sat beside me and pulled me against him. Even though I knew what Sarah had to say wouldn't be pleasant, I couldn't help the thrill of excitement that tickled my stomach.

The faint lines on Sarah's face deepened, showing her annoyance. "I suspended your attackers until next week."

"Right." Cody's voice was clipped.

"The Board of Trustees will meet Friday morning to decide on their punishment." She got up and walked behind the couch she'd been sitting on. "I have no control over the board. I can offer suggestions, but I cannot make the decision or contend it."

"What will you recommend?" I asked.

"Expulsion." Her face contorted, showing a side of her I hoped I never crossed. "They could've killed you both." She waved her arm in our direction. "Not that you can see that now."

Cody's grip on my arm tightened. "But …"

"But …" She sucked in a deep breath. Her shoulders slumped. "The board won't believe the extent of your injuries, and Cassandra's mother is one of the members."

The pulse in Cody's throat thrust furiously. Red mottled his skin. "They're going to get away with it." He pulled his arm out from behind me and leaned forward on his steepled hands.

"Most likely," she said. "You can file assault charges with the police, but I imagine, with no injuries, the results will be the same."

I rubbed his back. "They won't stop."

"No, probably not." Sarah looked weary.

"They'll attack Dacia next," Cody said.

Sarah focused on me. "Did you happen to mention to Cody what they did to you yesterday?"

He sat up straight, focusing on me like a sample under a microscope. "What happened? Why didn't you say anything?"

"Well, I, uh …" My fingers snagged on a knot in my hair. "With everything that happened, it kind of slipped my mind."

He cocked his head to the side and lifted his hands. "It's on your mind now."

When I told him, he closed his eyes and winced as if each word hurt him physically. His voice was tortured. "I should've been there to protect you." He turned away, rubbing his neck. "And since when can you control your powers like that?"

I put my hand on his knee. "I can't. Knowing you were hurt was the catalyst."

"You had quite a day yesterday," Sarah said. "Your control was very impressive."

I tilted my head to the side and shook it. "I didn't do so well at the hospital."

"What happened?" Cody asked.

“I nearly boiled a bottle of water, and I started several storms.”

He nodded. “Remember the storms.”

“Yes, but for the most part, you had outstanding control,” Sarah said.

“I need to get outta here,” Cody said. “I’ve got a game to get to. Be back around 5:00.”

I walked him to the door. “I know this is your line, but *please* be careful.”

He bent down and kissed me. “Promise. Later.”

When I walked back over to the couches, Sarah said, “It looks like there was a development in your relationship.”

My face felt like it was glowing. “Yeah. A lot of things happened yesterday. Some we still need to talk about.” I pulled my fingers through my hair. “I want you to find out from me how stupid I was last night. This might take a while.”

“What did you do, Dacia?” Sarah asked. I wasn’t sure if she was concerned for me or for who I might have hurt.

“I’ll get to that, but I’d like to start at the beginning.” I tried to get comfortable.

“Okay, go ahead whenever you’re ready.”

“Last night I had a new dream, a horrible nightmare actually. It was so real.” I swallowed the lump in my throat. “As soon as I saw Cody lying there, I knew he wouldn’t make it.” I looked down at the ground, trying to make the vision disappear. “I *needed* to see that he was all right.”

“Everything was okay, though. Wasn’t it?”

“I never made it there.”

“Why not? What happened?”

I told her what happened. "Cody went easy on me, but now it's your turn. So let me have it."

I expected Sarah to lay into me, but instead, she got up and walked into her office without saying a word. When she came back, she held the battered old journal from one of my first lessons. "I think it's time for you to have this." She handed me the amulet from the cover.

"I'd forgotten about that." *I shouldn't have been so stubborn about taking it before.*

She handed it to me.

"So this is supposed to protect me?"

"The journal says it will help you in your battle with Nefarious." She sat on the couch and rubbed her hands over the cover of the journal. "I should've insisted that you take it before, but I was afraid I'd scare you away."

I put the necklace on, and a warm sensation rushed through my body. My skin tingled, and the hair on the back of my neck stood up. "Whoa."

"What's wrong?"

"This chain does something. When I put it on, I felt like I got shocked."

"Well, next time you have a nightmare or you see Nefarious, see if the eye is glowing. That's the only way you will be able to tell if what the journal said is true or not. You're a strong young lady, but a little extra strength wouldn't hurt."

"I haven't been very strong the last couple of days."

"I think you're stronger than you believe. There are a lot of people who couldn't put up with what you go through every day, and maybe it's a good thing you don't realize your strengths. I'm sure it helps keep you from getting cocky."

I twirled the amulet around my fingers. "Well we wouldn't want a cocky hero, would we?"

"No, we wouldn't." Sarah rubbed her hands together. "What do you want to work on?"

"Aren't you going to put me in my place?"

"No"—she leaned back—"you know you shouldn't have gone off without telling someone." She fidgeted with her sleeve. "I'm pretty sure if I'd been in your shoes, I'd have done the same thing. I believe some of your dreams may be prophetic, but please be careful and don't take any unnecessary chances. I believe in fate, but why tempt it?"

I shook my head. "I can't believe that of the three of you, Samantha was the hardest on me."

Sarah raised a single eyebrow. "She found you gone. She worried about you while Cody and I slept."

"Yeah, that makes sense." *I'm going to have to be better about that. It's not fair to Samantha.*

"I imagine there will come a time when you have to go out on your own to fulfill the prophecy." Sarah lifted her hands palms up. "Samantha and Cody aren't going to like it."

I didn't want to talk about this anymore, so I said, "I need to work on my control. I tried to fly back to campus from the wreck, but I couldn't. I also need to figure out what I can do." I waved my arm around. "Maybe Cody's right and I can do anything I put my mind to, but I would like to know before my showdown with Nefarious."

"Maybe you should just start trying different things."

"Yeah." I thought about flying to catch the Frisbee and how I couldn't this morning. "Or maybe the powers will come when I need them."

"I think you'll be okay without relaxing today," Sarah said. "You seem to have yourself under control. What do you think?"

"I feel pretty good right now." I lifted my shoulders. "After yesterday, I'm more motivated than I have been. Let's go for it."

Sarah looked around the room for a moment. "Do you see the book over there with the green binding?" She pointed at it.

I nodded.

"I want you to move only that book from the shelf. Do you think you can do it?"

Rubbing my hands together, I said, "Bring it on."

With my jaw set in determination, I stared at the book and visualized it flying from the shelf. For quite some time, nothing happened. Then it began working its way free from the others. Once it was off the shelf, it flew through the air and landed on the couch next to Sarah.

"Wow! I guess I need to come up with something more difficult for you." Sarah threw several challenges at me. She had me stacking and unstacking books, juggling them, holding several books in the air while spinning her empty cup. She asked me to move around while doing all those things.

I conquered each trial. Confidence flowed through me. *Why today?*

"You're doing great, Dacia." Sarah's smile encouraged me to excel. "Now, I want you to make a fireball in your hand and then freeze it."

"You want me to what?"

"Just try it." She sat back like she was ready to watch a show. "Let's see what you can do."

I stood and screwed my face up in concentration. Staring at the palm of my hand, I visualized a fireball. A small, blue flame appeared above my fingers, steadily gaining in size. The smell of the smokeless fire reminded me of lying in the sun on a hot summer day.

"That in itself is impressive." Sarah stared at the fire in my hand. "Can you feel the heat from it? Does it burn at all?"

"It doesn't burn, but it warms me up." I pulled my hand out from under it hoping it would stay in mid-air. It flickered but didn't move. I watched it hover before trying to freeze it. A stream of ice flowed from my fingertips.

"That tingles when it happens," I told Sarah.

The ice flowed through the air wrapping itself around the ball of fire. The globe crashed to the couch but stayed in one piece. I picked it up. Peering through the frosted surface, I saw the flame and ice fighting against each other for control. In the end, the ice triumphed over the last spark. It looked like a glass paperweight. I tossed it to Sarah. She held it, mesmerized.

"I'm pretty sure you've figured out how to control your powers," she said, turning the ball in her hands. "What happened to Cody yesterday was terrible, but it seems to have given you the incentive you needed." The globe began to melt. "I'm going to throw this out before I'm sitting in a puddle." She stood and said, "While I'm up, think about what you would like to achieve next."

"Sure." *Holy cow. I just froze fire.* Never in my wildest imagination did I think I could do something like that.

Sarah walked back into the room carrying two bottles of water. "Have you thought of anything?" She handed me one of the waters.

"Thanks," I said, "but all I've thought since you left is *I froze fire.*"

"I have to admit I'm amazed, too. I figured it would take a few tries, maybe even another lesson or two."

"Now that I have more control of my powers—" I sat on the couch, suddenly worn out "—what's going to happen?" Fear crept into my voice, making my words quiver.

"I don't know." She edged forward. "Nothing I can remember. My grandfather's journal doesn't contain everything the relic does, but I don't know how to read Latin."

"Can I take the journals back with me? Something tells me I should look at them."

"I don't have a problem with that." She stood up. Looking over her shoulder at me, she said, "Promise me you'll be careful with them."

I yawned and closed my eyes. "I will. I know your grandfather's journal means a lot to you."

She walked across the room and into her office. A few moments later she appeared with the newer journal. She stacked the relic on top and handed them to me.

"Do you think I'll be able to do this?" I shook my head, trying to fight sleep.

Her head tilted to the side and her face softened. “I don’t know, Dacia, but you have a better chance now than you did a week ago.”

I set the journals on the coffee table and walked to the window. “One of the things I’m best at is creating fire, but I don’t think that will help since Nefarious is covered in flames. The only thing I think I’ll be able to use against him is ice, but I don’t know.” I rested my head against the window. “It doesn’t seem like enough.”

“It sounds like you’ve given this a lot of thought.”

I shrugged. “It’s hard not to think about when it consumes your dreams and most waking moments. In a way, I’d just like to get it over with, but I know I can’t beat him.” I walked toward the couches.

“Be patient,” Sarah advised. “I don’t think this is something you want to rush into. I can understand why you’d like to get it over with, but I can also see several reasons to hold it off for as long as possible.”

“I know. It’s not like I have a choice anyway.” I slumped back on the couch. “I have to wait for Nefarious to show up and hope I’m ready when he does.”

“I’ll do my best to have you ready when he comes.”

“Cody’s here.” A smile crept across my face.

“It’s nice to see you smile.” Sarah strode to the door, opening it just as Cody arrived. “Hello, Cody.”

“Guess I better get used to this,” Cody said with his hand still in the air, ready to knock. He tilted his head, and his eyebrows pinched together. “Yesterday, why didn’t you realize it wasn’t me at your door?”

"Uh, good question." I thought about it for a minute. "I don't know for sure. I was staring out the window, waiting for you to come, and I sort of spaced out. When they knocked on the door, I hesitated for a moment but opened it anyway."

"Don't sense me, don't open." Cody tucked his hands in his pockets like he needed to hide them.

"That's a good idea," Sarah agreed. "It never occurred to me to ask that."

I fought to keep my eyes open. *Why am I so tired?* "I'm not used to it yet. If I'd been sensing people's approach for the last five years, maybe I'd've thought about it, but I only sense Cody and only for the last couple of days."

"Just do me a favor and think about it." He walked over and put his hand on my shoulder. "So, how was the lesson?"

"She was very impressive today," Sarah answered.

Cody's voice filled with excitement. "Oh, really, what did you do, Dacia?"

"Would you like to see?" Without waiting for his response, I formed a fireball in the palm of my hand. Cody nodded, already mesmerized by the blue, green flames. The fireball grew in my palm to the size of a grapefruit. I pulled my hand out from under it and left it floating in midair.

Cody's eyes widened and he mouthed, "Wow."

"That's only the beginning," Sarah told him as she too stared into the flames.

Once again, I watched as the stream of ice shot from my fingertips engulfing the fire, fighting for dominance. This time when the globe of ice was completed, I kept it levitating in the air and floated it over to Cody.

He grabbed it, turning it in his hand while staring at it. “Saaa-weet!”

“Well, everybody has to be good at something,” I told him. “I can turn fire into ice. That should get me far in life. Don’t you think?”

“It just might,” Sarah murmured.

Pretending I didn’t hear her, I asked, “So when do we meet again?”

“Tomorrow afternoon.”

I stood to leave, and my legs gave out. I fell forward, catching myself on the arm of the couch.

“Dacia—” Cody grabbed my arm and helped me back onto the couch “—are you okay?”

A deep yawn kept me from answering right away. “I don’t know what’s wrong with me, but I’m exhausted.”

Sarah rubbed her chin. “I wonder if using your powers takes some kind of toll. You’ve used them a lot today.”

“And yesterday,” Cody added.

My chin fell forward. I shook my head and forced my eyes open. “Yesterday, when I was healing Cody, I fell asleep, so—” I yawned again “—it could’ve been sapping my strength.”

“Stay here until you’re ready to leave,” Sarah said. “I’ve got some work to do in my office.”

“Thanks.” Cody sat beside me. I laid my head on his shoulder. “You can sleep if you need to.”

“Maybe for a few minutes.”

An hour later, Cody and I left Sarah’s office hand in hand. Fluffy clouds dotted the sky. Dry leaves crunched underfoot. I looked at the mountains. *So close, yet still so far.* I wanted to get lost in them, far away from the Potato Heads and Nefarious.

"What's with the books?" Cody asked. "Sarah giving you homework?"

"Not exactly, one of them is Sarah's grandfather's journal. The other is an older journal written in Latin. While Sarah and I talked about them, I felt an overwhelming need to bring them back with me." My hands trembled. "Maybe I'll learn something about Nefarious from them. I don't know."

Cody put his arm around my shoulders and pulled me closer. "It'll work out. The sun always rises in the morning and always sets at night. Nothing is going to change that. I know you're worried, but you'll figure out a way."

"Thanks, but I don't think so." Even to me, my voice sounded a little dispirited.

"You need a break," Cody said. "Let's go to Falcon Lake."

I came to an abrupt halt. "Aren't you worried about getting jumped again?"

"Why? Are you?"

"Yeah. Suspension won't deter them. Fear of retribution might slow them down, but I wouldn't count on that either. Smashing Bryce's hand should've convinced them to back off. I don't want to spend my life in fear, but I don't want to be careless either." I paused and looked down at my feet. "I don't want you to get hurt again. I can't handle it."

"Don't worry about me."

"You don't understand, Cody." I clenched my fists. "I wanted to tear them apart." I looked away, not wanting him to see the hatred in my eyes. "I wanted them to beg for mercy.

That's why the water almost boiled. If I wouldn't have been so worried about you, I don't know what would've happened."

He stroked my cheek with the back of his hand. "I'm okay. If I get hurt again, you'll heal me."

"Not necessarily." I kicked at the ground. "One of these days, I'm going to fight a demon, and I might not walk away from the battle."

"If that happens, there isn't much hope for the rest of us." He grabbed my hand and pulled me forward. "Don't wanna be reckless, but wanna enjoy some time alone with you."

That thought was enough to persuade me. "Let's just watch our backs."

"We make a good team. I get their attention while you take care of them." He threw a couple quick punches. "Just need to come back before dark."

ꟾ

Sitting by the lake with Cody's arm around me, a calm serenity washed over me. I wondered what held us back from dating each other earlier. Our new relationship felt perfect. I peeked up at his face, and a creepy feeling possessed me.

My breath caught in my chest, and I staggered to my feet.

"What's wrong?" Cody asked, trying to come to my aid.

I couldn't help myself. I backed away from him, half expecting to look at him and see Bryce, expecting his eyes to be yellow.

"Dacia! Snap out of it!"

"I'm sorry, Cody." I ran toward the trail. His footsteps pounded against the ground behind me. He gained. Knowing I couldn't outrun him, I dropped to my knees and buried my face in my hands.

He gripped my shoulders. "Are you okay? Did I do something wrong?" He knelt on the ground beside me.

I didn't answer. He pulled me to a sitting position and wrapped his arms around me. "It's okay, Dacia," he whispered softly in my ear while combing his fingers through my hair.

"I'm … I'm, so, so sorry," I finally managed to say. As I regained my composure, my hysteria turned to embarrassment. "I'm sorry."

He dropped his hand from my face, and his body tensed. "Quit. Saying. That!" Softening his voice, he pleaded, "Please tell me what's going on. Let me in on what you're going through, but don't keep apologizing."

I took a deep breath and tried to still my trembling lip. "Do you remember the night I woke up with my face covered in blood? Of course, you do. What a stupid question," I mumbled to myself. "Anyway, that's how my dream started. We were sitting by Falcon Lake, nobody else around, just enjoying each other's company. I freaked out. I knew I would glance over at you and see Bryce sitting in your place. I just—" my words caught in my throat "—I just panicked."

He pulled me close and whispered in my ear, "Dacia, I'll always be here for you. I'd never hurt you."

"I know." I clutched the hair on the top of my head. "That's why I feel so bad."

"Don't. You're going through a lot. If I were in your shoes, I may've done the same. It was a scary night for all of us." He brushed his thumb along my cheek. "Can I kiss you now?"

I brought my lips to his in response. Cody pulled me onto his lap. His hands slid to the small of my back. Electricity sparked inside me. I wrapped my arms around his neck, pulling myself closer. His lips left mine, kissing a trail over my chin and along my neck to my collarbone. I nudged his head with my nose. He crushed his lips against mine, needing me as much as I needed him. The kiss softened. I laid my head against his shoulder.

"We should go." He kissed my temple. "It'll be dark soon."

Cody stood, pulling me to my feet. He retrieved Sarah's journals, and we walked back to campus. The sun hadn't set, but the trees blocked most of the light. I ignited a small fireball in my palm, hoping I wouldn't weaken myself too much by using more of my powers today.

An eerie feeling stole the breath from my lungs. Something big was going to happen. But what and when?

# Chapter 23

## *Lightning Crashes*

I sensed Cody's presence and opened the door. He stepped in, swinging me into his arms. My gasp made him chuckle, low and raspy.

"I missed you," he whispered. His lips skimmed across mine.

My heart did an unexpected flip. I slid my hands up his chest and wrapped my arms around his neck, pulling him closer to me. I doubted I would ever get used to Cody kissing me, but I hoped to spend a long time trying. I wanted him to hold me in his arms forever. I felt safe there, like nothing could go wrong as long as I was in Cody's embrace.

"Ready for class?" he asked.

"I'm ready, but I don't want to go."

"Me either, but we've already missed two days—"

"—so another won't hurt."

Cody snickered. "More along the lines of … so we need to go today."

"I knew you'd say that. That's why I'm dressed, my hair is combed and my teeth are brushed." I grabbed my backpack and left the room with Cody's arm around my shoulders.

His fingers brushed my neck, and he lifted up the necklace. "I noticed this yesterday, but where did it come from? It looks ancient."

I smacked his hand. "Because it is. Sarah gave it to me to help protect me from Nefarious."

We were almost to the Quartz Building when the cat's eye started glowing blue. "Cody—" I stopped and pointed at the amulet "*—look.*"

Cody spun in a circle, scanning the area for danger. "Why?"

*Nefarious here. No, no, no.* I doubled over. *I can't do this now. I'm not ready.*

Cody rubbed my back. His strength seemed to seep into my body. I straightened up, flipped my hair over my shoulder and continued to class.

As we got closer, I noticed the Potato Heads waiting outside. My eyes danced from them to Cody then back again. "What are they doing here? They're supposed to be suspended."

Cody moved his hand to my neck, massaging it. "Just breathe."

I poked him in the ribs. "Don't you get it?"

"What?"

I pointed at the Potato Heads then at the amulet. "They're here, and this is glowing."

Cody's eyes widened, and his head jerked back. "So they really are—"

"—under Nefarious' control." Even though I'd expected it, I hadn't wanted to believe it. I took a couple steps back. *It can't be. I can't do this.*

"Come on, Dacia." Cody held his hand out. "They can't do anything here."

I tucked the amulet under my sweater. It felt hot against my skin. I wrapped my arm around Cody, clenching his sweatshirt in my hand.

"Well, look who's here. It's the freak and gimpy," Alvin bellowed. "How ya feeling Cody?" The four of them laughed.

*How can they not see Cody's fine?*

Cody's arm tensed, but he replied in a steady voice, "I'm fine. Thanks for asking."

As we got closer, their laughter died one by one. The confused masks they wore almost brought a smile to my face, almost.

"You don't even have a bruise." Bryce's face scrunched up in confusion.

Cassandra's sails hung limply without the wind behind them. "I … I don't understand."

*Was that fear that flickered in her eyes?*

"You shouldn't even be out of the hospital yet." She looked at him then at her friends as if expecting an explanation.

"I'm a quick healer." Cody shrugged one shoulder like she wasn't worth the effort of a two-shoulder shrug. "Don't you have a hearing to attend?" He led me past them, his hand pressed against my lower back.

Once in the building, my breath leaked out like air escaping a balloon. "How did you handle that so well? They weren't even talking to me, and I wanted to punch them. It has to be eating at you."

"They're not worth it. They'll never change." He looked over his shoulder toward the door and shook his head. "If they think I'm afraid of them, they'll keep coming after me. If they think they're not bothering me, maybe they'll back off."

I sat at my desk. "I guess that's a good way to look at it, but if they're possessed, they won't stop until this is over."

"We can't give up." He pressed the back of my hand to his lips. "Be careful." Cody walked to the door.

"Cody—" I ran to him, grabbing his arm and jerking him back "—go out the back door."

His nod was nearly imperceptible. "Do. Not. Leave. Without. Me."

ꝏ

I relaxed. The wind whipped my hair around my face, blowing the smell of fresh pine my way, birds sang and fish jumped in the lake. *This is where I want to live after college.* Now all I had to do was go out and find this place. The only time I had ever been there was during my relaxation techniques. I didn't even know if this exact spot existed.

"Okay, Dacia," Sarah's voice blew in from across the lake. "I want you to find your way back here, rejuvenated and ready to begin."

I opened my eyes. "I love the relaxation part of my lessons. It's the only time I can let go. I get some sleep through the night, but not as much as I'd like." I twirled my hair between two fingers. "The premonition thing has me worried. Since last night, I've had the feeling something bad's going to happen. I can't shake it."

"It may be nothing." Sarah tried to sound optimistic, but I could tell she was concerned.

"As long as I'm telling you about my problems, the amulet glows around Cassandra and them."

Sarah's forehead scrunched up. Her eyebrows disappeared behind her hair. "I feared this would be the case." She pulled lint off her pants. "Unfortunately, their hearing went as I suspected."

"Crap." I sat there for a minute, pulling on the sleeve of my shirt and fidgeting nervously. "I don't think anything other than being hospitalized will get them to stay away from us."

She stood in front of me with her hands behind her back. "You're not thinking about putting them there, are you?"

"Oh, no, no I'm not." My eyes widened, and I shook my head. "Wednesday, I wanted revenge so bad I could taste it, but now that Cody's okay, I don't want to hurt anybody." I pulled my hand through my hair. "I was just pointing out that they're never going to back down. I will have to watch for them until after my fight with Nefarious."

She sat back down. "I've instructed your teachers to keep the four of them away from you, Cody, and Samantha."

I shot her a look that asked, *Do you really think that'll do any good?*

She closed her eyes and shook her head. The hopelessness in her action made my stomach plummet.

She studied me for a while before saying, "I'll be right back." She went into her office, and when she came out, she was carrying a football and a basketball. She sat down. "I want you to try to crush one of these. Try to recall the emotions you felt when Bryce and Alvin attacked Cody, and use that energy to smash one of the balls."

"Okay, I'll see what I can do." I sat upright, closed my eyes and concentrated on squashing the football. I could tell nothing was happening. I tried to draw on the guilt and fear I felt that night. I could hear some air expel from one of the balls. When I opened my eyes, the football was gripped by an invisible force. It looked like somebody was clutching it in mid-air.

"That was good, Dacia, but it lacked intensity," Sarah said as she watched the ball drop back onto the couch beside her.

A bright flash and a loud clap of thunder sounded outside. Both Sarah and I jumped. There had been no distant rumbling forewarning a storm, but one was upon us.

I looked out the windows at the ominous black clouds that had moved in. "Those aren't mine."

"Good to know." Sarah pointed to the basketball. "Imagine something happening to the ball." She shrugged. "Maybe whatever you imagine will happen."

"It's worth a try." Once again I straightened up, closed my eyes and let my imagination go to work. I pictured the basketball hovering in the air. Then another loud clap of thunder startled me.

"Oh, my God," Sarah exclaimed. I opened my eyes to see the charred remains of the basketball. "A bolt of lightning struck the ball. I can't believe you did that."

"You told me to imagine something." I twisted my mouth into a lopsided smile. "That loud clap of thunder made me think of lightning striking the ball."

"The electricity made the hair on the back of my neck stand on end, but that was all I felt. I would tell you to try again so you could watch, but I think conjuring lightning is something best suited for outdoors."

"Yeah," I agreed. "I just want to know what all I can do. I'm going to try to look through the journals this weekend to see if they give me any ideas. I think I would like to skip my lesson tomorrow, but if I need to, can I call you Sunday?"

"That'd be fine." Sarah nodded in agreement. "I think a day off would be good. Do you have something planned?"

"Tomorrow morning I plan to look at the journals. Then Samantha, Cody, and I are going to spend the rest of the day in Althea."

"Be careful in town, but try to have a good time." Then out of the blue, she asked, "What did you ever find out about your truck?"

"I should have it back late next week. The general consensus is that I was very lucky. I saw all of the blood on the airbag and seats, so I already knew that."

"Well, maybe it will keep you from going out by yourself," Sarah said.

"Yeah, it's a good deterrent."

"Cody should be here any minute," Sarah said, realizing how late it was. "Time flies when you're having fun, huh?"

"Yep." I glanced out the window at the monsoon. Rushing rivers flowed down the sidewalks. "I don't mind walking in the rain, but the way this is coming down, I'll drown before I get back."

"Look on the bright side. You shouldn't have to watch your back."

Cody showed up a few minutes later, sopping wet. He stood in the hallway to keep from dripping on Sarah's carpet. "Dacia, you ready?"

I stood up and threw my jacket on. "As ready as I'll ever be."

"Do you want an umbrella?" Sarah asked.

"No, it won't hold up in this wind." Cody shivered. "It's brutal."

She pointed at the fireplace. "Would you like to come in and get warmed up?"

"No." His words were distorted by the chattering of his teeth. "I'd like to get some dry clothes on. I'm freezing."

"Have a good weekend, Sarah," I said.

"You too, Dacia … be careful."

We stepped out into the pouring rain. *I don't want to get drenched.*

As soon as I thought it, it was like Cody and I stood inside a clear plastic bubble. The rain fell, but where we stood was as dry as could be. We started moving, and the bubble stayed around us, keeping us dry. Rain pummeled the ground around us, but where it hit the protective sphere, there was no sound.

"Cool. I could've used this on the way to pick you up." He went to throw his arm over my shoulders.

I dodged and smiled at him. "You're soaked."

"And, you should be." He laughed and grabbed me around the waist, pulling me into him.

I giggled and held onto him. I could handle being wet if it meant being closer to Cody. "Do you want to go to your room to get some dry clothes?"

"Nah, I dropped some off." He reached his hand out, and the bubble extended. "You're the best umbrella ever."

I ran ahead, but Cody caught up to me quickly, wrapping his arms around me and dragging me back against him. He put his head on top of mine and his feet outside of mine. "You're not getting away that easily." I heard the laughter in his voice and felt his chest vibrate against my back.

Without ever letting go, he stepped beside me. I laid my head against him. I wanted to slow down and enjoy this time alone with him, but he was still shivering.

We opened the door to find Samantha at the computer. Books and notebooks spread out across the desk. I couldn't help but think she needed to get out and enjoy herself instead of spending all her time studying.

"Jeez, Cody," Samantha said. "How did you get soaked? Dacia's hardly wet at all."

"I used him as an umbrella." I flexed my arm muscles and laughed.

"Unfortunately, Dacia wasn't with me on the way." He grabbed his clothes and went to change.

"What was that supposed to mean?" Samantha asked, looking at me like Cody spoke Greek.

"I didn't want to get rained on, so we didn't." I had no idea where all of these new powers were coming from, but I hoped something in the journals might help me understand what I was going through.

"That reminds me. When Cody dropped off his clothes he told me to ask what you did at your lesson yesterday."

I tilted my head. *Why was I so tired yesterday, but I'm not at all today? Shouldn't I be zapped from being an umbrella?*

"Uh … Dacia?"

"Sorry. I was thinking." I held my palm up. A small spark ignited, growing into a fireball.

Samantha couldn't tear her eyes away from the flames. "Awesome!" I heard her whisper. When ice began flowing from my fingertips, you could've heard a pin drop. "That is so cool!" she said as she watched the ice devour the flames.

When Cody knocked, my concentration was broken. The globe fell to the floor and shattered. "That was wicked," Samantha said before she opened the door.

Cody stepped in wearing dry blue jeans and a blue sweater that accentuated his eyes. I'd always liked the way he looked when he wore that sweater, but now that he was mine, I liked it even more. "Looking good." I wagged my eyebrows at him. Then I reached my arms behind his neck and pulled his mouth down on mine.

"This is not the time for kissing," Samantha said. "Dacia just showed me what she can do. It's amazing."

Cody pulled away and wrapped his arm around my shoulders, leading me to the chairs. "You weren't too tired?"

"No," I said. "I'm going to have to figure out my limitations."

"But first we need to get dinner ordered." Food was always on Cody's mind. Samantha and I were sure he had a hollow leg.

While we waited for our food, we sat and talked about the kinds of things college students should talk about.

"Why you going home?" Cody asked Samantha.

"I haven't been home for a while. Mom called me yesterday and asked if I remembered where I live, so I decided I should go visit them."

"Since I started college, my parents have turned into quite the social butterflies." My heart seemed to slow for a moment, and my stomach hardened. *Now that they don't have to worry about me burning down the house, they can get out more. I wonder if they even miss me.*

A serious expression came over Cody's face. "Glad Sarah couldn't get holda mine."

"You didn't call them?" I asked.

"I did, but I didn't tell them I was calling from the hospital."

"Won't they figure it out when they get the bill?" Samantha asked.

"Nah. Sarah told the hospital to bill the school since it happened here."

We spent the evening eating, playing video games, and enjoying ourselves. It was a nice change of pace. Marcy showed up right on time to kick Cody out of our room.

"Time for me to go." Cody pulled me to my feet. His hands slid up my neck, sending shivers through me. He tipped my head back and pressed his lips against mine.

I grabbed hold of his shirt and pulled him closer to me. "Don't leave," I whispered.

"I have to. Marcy won't go away until I do." His lips brushed mine. "Good night. Sleep tight," he said as he headed out the door.

# Chapter 24

## Ominous Feelings

"Dreams do come true," the deep, rumbling voice growls.

I lie on the ground trying to get up. My entire body aches, and blood drips off my chin. I try to stand, but Nefarious has beaten me down. I know I can't win this battle, but I can't give up either.

Off in the distance, I hear Cody calling my name. "Dacia, where are you? Dacia?"

*No!* I scream in the confines of my head.

I can't let Nefarious hurt Cody. Hearing his voice helps me find the strength to face the demon. I struggle to my feet. I stumble but catch myself.

Nefarious stands twelve feet tall. Four horns jut from his head. The two largest protrude from the top of his skull and another smaller one sticks out on each side. Fangs the size of my forearm fill his immense jaw. His crimson skin appears to be thick and hard. His legs are massive—the size of tree trunks. A spiked, jagged tail the length of his body slices through the air. His enormous, bat-like wings are tipped with sharp claws. In his right fist, he holds a sword that looks like a bolt of lightning, in his left, a flaming whip.

A scream rises in my throat, but I swallow it and advance on shaky legs.

He looks down at me like I am nothing more significant than an ant. Hatred fills his snake-like eyes, and for a moment, I am paralyzed by fear.

A rumbling voice in my head says, "Run away. You cannot defeat me, insignificant human."

And I agree with him wholeheartedly. *How can I defeat such a beast?*

"You cannot!" the voice rings out as if he has been reading my thoughts. "Surrender to me."

My legs tremble, wanting to heed his command. "No." My voice is weak, scared. *I can't hand the world over to him. I have to fight for it, no matter what.* "I won't give up!" I sound strong, determined.

Once again the voice echoes in my head, "Give up, and I'll spare him. If you insist on this battle, I'll kill him right in front of you."

I gasp. *No, not Cody.*

"Everyone you love will perish if you continue this fight."

"Nothing will happen to them if I stop you," I yell at him.

"Dacia?" Cody's voice is closer.

An evil laugh erupts from Nefarious, and I know I have to do something. Now!

A lightning bolt shoots from my fingertips. It sizzles as it's absorbed into Nefarious' body.

"So, you have chosen your fate." He growls and cracks his whip.

It flies through the air at me. I jump up and soar above it. The flames scorch my shoes, and the air smells of burnt rubber. Once again Nefarious cracks his whip, but this time it doesn't come near me. I turn to follow its path. I hear Cody scream. He writhes in agony, entangled in the fiery whip.

"No!" A stream of ice flows from my fingertips, freezing the flames. I levitate a rock, hurling it toward the whip. It makes contact, and ice dances through the air in an impromptu storm as the whip shatters.

"Cody," I call out as I run to him. His body is covered in burns. I kneel down and place my hands on his face. "Please, Cody, please."

Nefarious' steps shake the ground as he approaches. I need to turn to fight him, but I can't leave Cody like this. I have to make sure he'll be okay. I hold him a little longer. I can't see his wounds healing, but his breathing evens out. "I'll be back," I tell him as I turn to face the demon.

He's close enough to strike me with his sword. My heart pounds against my chest, sending waves of panic through my body. I fight to calm myself, to get a grip.

A fireball flies toward me. Ice flows from my hands. The fire sizzles, melting its way toward me. Water droplets fall to the ground. The flames diminish, but the ice isn't enough to stop them. I turn to the side and brace myself for impact. The fire hits my arm, and my scream shatters the still night air.

"Dacia, wake up!" Samantha shook my shoulders. Her eyes were wide, her face flushed.

"I'm fine." I reached over to turn on my light. "It was just another nightmare, a new one."

Samantha gasped. "Oh my God."

"What's wrong?" I asked with a catch in my throat.

"Your chin is bleeding."

I sat up, and Samantha's face paled.

"What?"

She pointed a shaky finger. "Your arm."

Blackened skin covered my left arm. I touched it gently. Nothing. I pressed harder. "I can't feel anything."

"Stop." She pulled my hand away. "Just stop."

"I'm sorry, Sam. I'm the worst roommate ever." I stared at the charred skin. "I'm sorry I keep waking you up. You must get sick of it."

"Luckily, I took mostly afternoon classes." She smiled with her mouth only. "I get some good sleep in after you leave."

"I need to get cleaned up." I pulled the covers back and waited for her to go down the ladder. "Why don't you try to go back to sleep?"

She waited for me at the bottom, hands on hips. "Use the sink here."

"No." I grabbed my bathroom bag and a change of clothes. "I'm gonna rinse off in the shower."

Samantha widened her stance and crossed her arms. "Do not go anywhere else."

"I promise."

I rinsed off, changed into uncharred pajamas, then stared at my reflection. The cut on my chin was barely noticeable, but I was bruised and burned all over.

As I stood there trying to decide how to save the world, the familiar uneasy feeling returned to the pit of my stomach. I doubled over thinking I might throw up. When the nausea released me, I hurried back to my room, no longer wanting to be alone. I closed the door and turned the lock. I stared at it, waiting for Nefarious or some other force to knock it down and attack me.

"Get a grip," I said out loud to myself.

"If you want me to." Arms wrapped around my waist.

With my hand keeping my heart from escaping my chest, I turned to face Cody. "Don't ever do that again!"

"Sorry. " He fought to hide his smile. His eyes traveled from my face to my arm, and his expression turned serious. "You okay?"

"A little spooked." I nodded at my arm. "I can't feel that yet. I hope it heals without me feeling it."

"Spooked?"

I nodded. "What are you doing here anyway?"

"Samantha thought you might wander off, so she called me."

I glanced at her bed. She was sleeping or pretending to.

"I'm going to sleep in Cookie Monster, unless you want to talk." He raised his eyebrow in a challenge. "Actually, I plan to sleep in one of these chairs 'til this is over."

"You can't stay here! What about Marcy?"

He put his finger over my lips. "Quiet, and she'll never know."

I thought about biting his finger.

"It's one o'clock. If she knew I came in, she'd've kicked me out."

"Fine. I'm going to bed."

He pulled me close to him and kissed me before sitting in the chair.

I climbed into bed on unsteady legs. Darkness shadowed my thoughts. Shallow breaths and a racing heart left me lightheaded.

I wondered if it was time for me to face Nefarious. I'd never seen him so clearly before. Maybe this was a sign my wait neared its end.

I drifted in and out of a tortured sleep. At three-thirty, I woke panicked. Knowing whatever I feared had finally happened.

# Chapter 25

## *Second Chances*

My arm burned and throbbed. I bit my lip and tried to fight the pain. *I guess it's healing.* I climbed out of bed and got dressed, careful not to make a sound. I blinked back tears when I pulled my jacket over my arm. I didn't want Samantha or Cody to wake up and keep me from leaving. It would've been nice to have them with me, but I knew they would try to talk me into staying. And, something told me there was no time to waste.

I hurried through the hall and down the stairs. Opening the door, I hesitated, intimidated by the thick blanket of fog. I reached behind my back for the doorknob. I knew I should go back to my room and go to sleep, but I let the handle slide out of my grip.

I couldn't shake the need to do this. It gnawed at my insides, leaving me no choice but to follow through. I pulled the collar of my jacket up, snuggled into it for warmth, and mustered the courage to continue toward the commons.

Streetlights brightened the fog around them, but the light that reached the ground was so diffused that objects in front of me were merely shadows. I walked forward in what I hoped was the right direction. The fog disoriented me, making it impossible to tell where I was. Everything had a dream-like distortion to it.

My footsteps were deafening in the eerie silence. Nothing moved. There wasn't a cricket chirping, an owl hooting, nothing.

My ears were tuned to listen for any noise out of the ordinary. As my imagination took over, my heart thumped against my chest, trying to free itself from my ribs. The hair on my neck stood on end. A chill rippled along my skin and left goosebumps in its wake.

The shadows created by the mist and fog surrounded me. I kept looking over my shoulder, but if anything was there, I didn't see it.

"Dacia, stop scaring yourself," I said out loud in an attempt to penetrate the silence and dispel the fear that overwhelmed me. *They're just shadows, nothing more. No one is following me. No one is going to jump out and grab me because no one in their right mind would be out on a night like this.* I hated walking by myself in the dark, and tonight my normal fears were amplified thanks to the nagging feeling that compelled me to keep moving.

A terrified scream pierced the still night air.

*I'm too late.* The realization sent an icy spear of dread through my stomach. *No.*

I ran to the commotion. *Please be okay. Please be okay. Please.*

Light illuminated the ground in front of me. I stopped and took in my surroundings. With slow, deliberate steps, I moved forward. My eyes darted from side to side. On my left, a fire escape ran down Quartz Building. On my right, one clung to Primrose Hall and disappeared behind two huge dumpsters that stood alongside the building.

In front of me, I saw a crumpled body lying on the ground. My heart jumped into my throat, stopping my breath. Without seeing her face, I knew it was Sarah. I sprinted to her body and rolled her over. Her blank eyes stared straight up.

"Oh, please don't be dead." I choked back a sob and felt for a pulse. Finding none, I began CPR. I hoped that combined with my powers, it would be enough to bring her back. I squatted, keeping on my toes in case I needed to dart away.

The darkness closed in around me.

My mind raced, a thousand thoughts running through it at once: "Run. Give up. Don't listen. You're stronger than that. Stay calm. You can't win. You'll never defeat me. What will you do without your teacher? You're an insignificant fool."

Nefarious was nearby. I felt his presence even though I couldn't see him. The urge to run—like I had in my dream—nearly overwhelmed me, but in my dream, I didn't know I had the ability to heal. Now that I knew, I hoped I wasn't too late to help Sarah.

I stared down at her lifeless face and thought I saw her eye move. I watched more carefully. Nothing … no movement. *No, don't die.* Then she gasped for air. My heart leaped, but I couldn't relax yet.

"Sarah, I know you're hurt and you need to rest, but now is not the time. We have to get out of here as quickly as possible." Fear crept into my voice. "We're being watched. Nefarious is close."

She nodded in understanding, and I helped her to her feet, levitating her like I had done with Cody.

"Go to my office." Pain made her voice raw. "It's closer."

"Give me your keys."

As I led her off, I heard Nefarious' evil laughter, then the familiar growling voice, "Give up, Dacia. You cannot win."

I looked over my shoulder and saw him shrouded in fog. I ran all of the way to Sarah's office. I didn't want to see if the Nefarious in my dream was the reality, but I couldn't help but wonder why he didn't stop me.

I laid Sarah on one of the overstuffed couches. Then I called my room.

Cody answered on the first ring. Panic filled his voice.

"Cody, what's wrong?"

"Where are you?" He didn't wait for an answer. "Are you okay?"

"I'm fine."

"I woke up and you were gone. Why?" Desperation clung to his voice. "Samantha and I looked, but in this fog, you can't see anything. Where are you?"

“I’m in Sarah’s office.” I fought to keep my eyes open. Exhaustion from using my powers threatened to overcome me. “I need sleep. I’ll tell you and Sam—” I yawned “—all about it over breakfast.”

“We’ll be there in a few minutes,” Cody said right before I heard the dial tone.

I called my room again, but nobody answered. *Please, Cody, pick up the phone. It’s not safe out there tonight.* I let out a heavy sigh, hung up and looked at Sarah. “Nefarious is still out there. I have to find them before he does.”

“You didn’t think they would stay behind. Did you?” Sarah’s voice was so quiet, I had to strain to hear her.

“No.” I started for the door and clutched my arm. Searing pain radiated through it, burning, scorching. I tugged my jacket off. The once blackened skin was bright red and blistered. The touch of the air was like a thousand needles stabbing my arm.

Darkness crept over the edges of my vision, and my legs wobbled. I reached for the couch to steady myself.

“Dacia, are you okay?” Sarah asked as I fell to the floor.

Sleep welcomed me into its arms, embracing me like it hadn’t done in days. I never heard the door open, never heard Cody and Samantha enter the room. I don’t think I moved for the rest of the night. And dreams did not dare to disrupt my slumber.

I woke up Saturday morning with the sun shining on my face. I yawned and stretched like a cat, then realized I was on the couch.

“Morning, sleepyhead,” Cody said.

"Hey." I combed my fingers through my hair, trying to pull the tangles out of it. As I did, I noticed my arm was completely healed. *Thank God.* "When did you get here?"

"About five minutes after your call," Cody said.

"Thanks for waiting up for us." Samantha's voice held barely contained anger.

"I'm sorry." My heart sank. "I collapsed."

"We could've used some sleep. But between your nightmares and sneaking off, we didn't get much rest," Samantha grumbled. Heavy, black bags weighed down her red-rimmed eyes.

"I'm sorry. I couldn't help it. I literally collapsed."

"That explains you lying on the floor," Cody said.

"Did either of you sleep?" Guilt welled in me for what I'd put my friends through.

Cody patted the couch. "With my head right here, so I'd know if you moved."

I lowered my gaze to the floor. *I had to leave. Sarah would be dead if I'd stayed.*

"I tried to sleep in the chair." The sharp edge of Samantha's voice had dulled slightly. "Here—" she tossed me the amulet "—you left this hanging on your bed."

I turned it over in my hands. *I wonder if it would've helped me at all last night.*

I looked around the room and realized Sarah wasn't lying on the couch opposite me. "Where's Sarah?"

"Went to get breakfast." Cody sat on the couch, putting his arm around my shoulders and pulling me to his side.

I looked out the window. The fog had cleared, and the sky was the blue you only find in the mountains. "Did she tell you about last night?"

"No. When we got here, she could barely keep her eyes open. Her face was really pale. She looked sick." Samantha paced the room, stopping with her hands on her hips. "I want to know what would make you consider going out on your own in the middle of the night after what happened last time."

"That uneasy feeling I've had lately made me get out of bed. I knew I had to leave the room, and I knew you two would try to talk me out of it." A chill ran up my spine. "I didn't want to go out on my own. Believe me, I was scared to death, but it was something I *had* to do. And I had to do it immediately."

We sat in silence. Samantha's annoyance began to turn into curiosity. Sarah stepped through the door. "Breakfast is here," she announced. "Dacia, I see you finally woke up."

"Yeah, I actually slept pretty well after passing out."

"That's good to hear. Cody, would you mind clearing the coffee table? We'll eat there." She carried the donuts, coffee, and milk over to it. "Why don't you all have a seat, and we'll talk about last night. I want to start with Dacia's dream."

I launched into my story. "I saw Nefarious."

"In your dream?" Cody asked.

"Yes." *And through the fog.*

Samantha's voice shook when she asked, "What was he like?"

*Massive. Horrible. Unbeatable.* His reptilian eyes appeared in my head. *Why did he let me go?* The rest of him painted in around them with deft brush strokes—claws, horns, tail, fangs, wings—until the image was complete. My throat closed, and I gasped for air. I panicked, making it even harder to breathe.

"Dacia," Sarah said, "relax. I want you to find yourself in front of the mountain lake. Picture yourself sitting there, staring out at the tranquil reflection. Feel the cool mountain breeze blow through your hair."

My muscles relaxed. My breathing returned to normal as I found myself staring across the lake at the mountains. I wanted to stay there forever, far away from the stress and worries of my real life, but when Sarah called me back to reality, I went.

"Are you okay, Dacia?" Samantha asked.

"Yeah, for now." I rested my elbows on my knees and stared at my hands while I described Nefarious to them. "When I was in his presence, I felt pure evil and hatred. Thoughts raced through my mind." I paused. "No not thoughts, suggestions. When I turned and saw him, all hope fled. There's no way I can defeat him. He's more evil … more monstrous than I ever imagined he would be." My voice sounded small and hopeless.

Cody wrapped his arms around me and lifted me onto his lap. "Don't give up yet."

He was trying to be supportive, but he hadn't seen Nefarious. He didn't know how ferocious he was. It was easy for the three of them to tell me things would be okay, but I knew better.

"It's too late." Then without giving them a chance to respond, I started telling them about my dream. My voice raced and my heart pounded out of control the whole time, but

I wanted to get it over with. "When Samantha woke me up, my chin was bleeding and my arm was burned beyond recognition."

Sarah nodded like this all made perfect sense. "Let's move on to the rest of the night's events from Dacia's perspective. How did you find me?"

"For the last couple of days, I've known something bad was going to happen."

"We know." Samantha's leg tapped against the ground in a staccato beat.

"Last night it happened. I didn't have time to spare, so I left without waking you." I told them everything. Then I looked Sarah in the eyes and said, "What were you doing out alone at that time of night?"

"You sound like my mother." Sarah laughed at me. "Nancy Heron called and told me Cassandra was hurt. I went out to check on her. The fog was awful. I couldn't see at all."

"Yeah, we went out to look for Dacia," Samantha said.

Cody cleared his throat. "Do you think Nefarious brought the fog with him?"

Sarah covered her mouth with a finger while rubbing her chin. "It's a definite possibility."

"It kept him hidden," I said. "You left to check on Cassandra. Then what?"

"Suddenly, in front of me, I saw the yellow eyes that Dacia's described so many times. I keep rewinding the events in my mind, but I don't know what happened. One minute I stared into those eyes. The next, I was lying face down on the ground. The air was torn from my lungs, and everything faded into nothingness. I heard laughter in my mind. It was strange …

like a thought. Around me was silence, but in my head was this laughter followed by a voice telling me Dacia would be next, that she couldn't survive without her mentor. Then he said, 'The world will, at last, be mine.' There was more laughter, then nothing. I think I died."

Samantha's hand shot up to her chest. "Oh, my God."

Cody held me tighter against him, rubbing my arm.

"The next thing I remember Dacia told me we had to get out of there. We came back here, and Dacia collapsed."

"Have you talked to Nancy?" I asked.

"Yes, I called her last night after you fell asleep and told her I would come by in the morning because of the fog. So I went there before getting breakfast."

"We wondered what was taking so long," Samantha said.

"Cassandra had to have several stitches in her leg, but she'll be fine. She wouldn't tell Nancy what happened to her," Sarah said.

I stuffed my hands in my hoodie pocket and weaved my fingers together. "My guess is Nefarious used her as a pawn to get you out in the open."

"Yeah, I thought about that." Sarah rubbed her hands down her legs. "But there's no way to prove it."

"You're in good spirits for somebody who was killed by a demon," Cody said. "Why aren't you scared to death?"

"I faced evil and walked away from it. What else is there to be afraid of?" she asked. "Now, I noticed nobody has eaten anything. We must keep our strength up. Cody, you and Samantha need to be strong enough to help Dacia when she needs you, and Dacia, you need to keep your strength up so you can fight."

We ate our breakfast in silence. I couldn't help but think about last night. *If Nefarious can get Sarah to venture out alone in the middle of the night and kill her, when will he send for the rest of us? How will we be lured to our dooms? And will I be able to save Samantha and Cody when he calls on them?*

# Chapter 26

## *Fresh Air*

With our nerves shot, Cody drove Samantha and me to Althea. The ride to town was quiet. As we drove past the spot where I wrecked my truck, Cody reached over and took hold of my hand. He looked at me, and I saw everything he wanted to say in his eyes. His lips turned up to form a comforting smile. I felt like I should say something but didn't know what.

Cody pulled onto the main street and found a parking spot. He turned off the engine and asked, "Where to?"

After each of us had said, 'I don't know. What do you want to do?' once or twice, we decided on Putt-Putt. We stepped out of Cody's car and walked down the street.

Mountain View Putt-Putt was three blocks down and two over. None of us had been there before, so we were taken in by its landscaping. There was no concrete in the complex. The flagstone walkways sat in beds of mulch. Mountain wildflowers nestled beside every boulder. Most holes had a waterfall or pond beside them. The "greens" were a tan color that blended well with the landscape design.

Despite the setting, I didn't play very well. I either hit a hole-in-one, two or took the maximum seven-stroke score for each hole. Samantha ended up with a score near mine. Instead of playing opposite extremes, she averaged a 3 or 4 on every hole. Cody beat us both by ten strokes. We did manage to relieve some stress, though; after all, laughter is the best medicine. When we finished, we decided on The Avalanche for lunch.

While there, we kept our conversation away from any discussion about what had happened to Sarah. It wasn't something that should be overheard by the general public, but it was all I could think about. *What if I hadn't gotten to her when I did? Would she have died?* "I need to quit dwelling on this," I mumbled to myself. *I did get there in time so the 'what ifs' don't matter.* I glanced up to see Cody and Samantha staring at me. *They probably think I'm losing it.*

"Just don't argue with yourself," Cody said to me before shoving his mouth full of fries.

Samantha pointed her fork at him. "Actually, you don't have to worry about her until she loses an argument with herself."

My lunch looked delicious, but I couldn't eat. I couldn't shake the feeling my battle with Nefarious would be upon me soon, and I wasn't ready for it.

Cody placed his hand on top of mine. I looked at it, then into his eyes. Their depths filled with concern.

"You need to eat," he said.

"I know, but I can't." I glanced at the Fettuccine Alfredo on my plate, then looked away. The thought of eating made me gag.

Cody didn't press the issue. He asked the waitress for a box. "Now what?"

"I, uh, think I'm ready to go back," Samantha answered. "I'm a little on edge."

"Back to campus, it is then." Cody grabbed my food, then took my hand.

When Cody dropped us off at the door, I didn't argue, but I also didn't take my eyes off him until he stood next to me. He walked Samantha and me back to our room before going to his for a while.

"Please be careful, and call me when you get there." I grabbed his hand, not wanting him to leave.

"I will." He pulled me closer to him, holding my face in his hands. "I'll be fine."

My pulse ratcheted. "Don't go."

His hands dropped to my shoulders, then trailed down my arms, coming to a rest at my waist.

I twined my arms around his neck and pulled his mouth down on mine.

Cody pulled away. "I'll be back before you know it."

I watched him walk down the hallway. *Please let him be okay.* I closed the door and waited by the phone. When it rang a few minutes later, relief washed over me. I answered it, and Cody said, "I made it. See you later, okay?"

"Yeah, thanks for calling."

"No problem. I love you, Dacia. Please, don't leave."

A smile spread across my face. My heart raced, and time stood still. *He loves me.* I wanted to shout it to the world. "I love you, too," I said before hanging up.

My body thrummed with energy. I grabbed Samantha and spun in a circle. Laughter filled the room.

"What was that about?" she asked.

"He said he loves me!"

She squealed with excitement and hugged me.

I wanted her to share my happiness. "So … Dan?"

Samantha's face glowed. "What about him?"

"That's what I'm asking."

She played with the hem of her shirt. "Have you seen his smile? Wow!" She bit her lip. "But I don't think he's interested."

My eyebrow lifted on its own. "Really? He couldn't take his eyes off you the other day."

The smile that brightened her face rivaled the sun.

"I bet Cody could get you together."

She kicked her toe against the ground. "Not now."

"Oh … why?"

"I don't want to keep secrets."

I pinched my nose. *She shouldn't have to miss out on dating because she got stuck with me as a roommate.* "Maybe, when all of this is over, we can go on a double date."

"I'd like that," she said with a dreamy look in her brown eyes.

ℵ

Seated in Cookie Monster, I opened the ancient journal, careful not to tear the pages, and flipped through it. Even though it was written in a language I couldn't understand, I felt compelled to look at it. Throughout the journal were pencil sketches. Flipping through the pages, a drawing caught my attention. My fingers wouldn't work when I tried to turn back to it.

*Calm down.*

When I got to the page I wanted to see, I found myself staring at the drawing Sarah had shown me of Nefarious.

Taking a closer look at the picture, I noticed lightning bolts shooting through the air at him from the fingertips of a young man. As I studied the drawing, I realized the words made sense to me. I turned the book over to make sure it was the one written in Latin. Scratching my forehead, I thought, *Well, stranger things have happened.*

Below the picture was the caption, "The lightning was at best a deterrent. Nefarious continued charging. I feared there would be no stopping him. I feared for my life and for the lives of those I love. How could I defeat such a horrible monster?"

"I've been wondering that myself," I responded to the book.

Focusing on the drawing, I wondered if this was something he had dreamed or if it had happened to him. It reminded me of the dream I had when Nefarious attacked Cody. *Could the same dreams that haunted him be haunting me?*

I flipped through the previous pages and found several drawings of the evil eyes. Under one of them was written, "The monster's eyes focused on me. Thoughts filled my mind. I fought the urge to flee." I turned a few more pages and decided beyond the shadow of a doubt that these were sketches of his dreams. The drawing on one of the pages showed him under water. His eyes opened wide with terror. Behind him, the clawed hands of Nefarious reached for him, the same hands that pulled me into the depths of Falcon Lake. I stared down at the sketch and wondered how I would learn anything from this journal.

I decided to turn to the back to see if there was anything in it about the final battle between Nefarious and this savior. As I turned to the last pages, they crumbled in my hand, leaving little more than dust on the back cover. A sense of hopelessness swept over me.

*I guess this means I have to figure out my own way to defeat him.*

Feeling like all was lost, I laid the journal on the floor and got up. I needed to get out. I needed to clear my mind. I needed to come up with a game plan.

"Samantha, would you go for a walk with me?" I hated asking her, but I knew neither she nor Cody wanted me out on my own.

"Where to?"

I twisted my hair around my fingers. "I don't know. I could use some fresh air. Maybe we could find a bench to sit on."

"Okay … sure." She grabbed a book, and we left.

When we stepped outside, the slight breeze rejuvenated me, clearing some of the cobwebs from my head. Somehow I had to figure out how to defeat Nefarious and sitting in a stuffy room didn't seem to help.

We made our way to a bench in the courtyard and sat. Samantha opened her book while I focused my attention on the mountains. The beauty of them always inspired me. I could spend hours gazing at them. I thought if I was in a place I loved, lightning might strike, and maybe I would get an idea that would help me win.

I lost track of time, staring off in the distance without anything on my mind. It reminded me of when Sarah had me imagine my happy place.

An arm dropped around my shoulders, bringing a smile to my lips. I turned to glance at Cody but found myself looking into pale green eyes.

"Hello, ladies."

I tried to get out from under Bryce's arm, but his grip tightened on me.

"Don't fight me, Dacia. It's not worth it." His voice was resolute. He sat on the bench between Samantha and me.

Samantha's face paled, and she edged down the bench.

"What do you want? Why can't you guys just leave me alone?" My voice rose as a sense of uncertainty engulfed me.

"What? I came over here, put my arm around you and didn't do anything to harm you." His smile was hard, cruel. "You were so out of it, if I'd have wanted to hurt you, it would've been cake."

His eyes flashed dangerously, and I knew he was right. I'd been stupid—totally unaware of my surroundings. He could've hit me on the back of the head with a baseball bat instead of sitting beside me, wrapping his arm around my shoulders.

"By the way, where's your guard dog?"

"If I remember right"—I looked pointedly at his hand—"I don't need one."

"Good thing." Bryce snorted. "He's more like a Chihuahua, isn't he?" Before I had the chance to say anything, he added, "Don't tell him, but I think you protect him more than he protects you. It was pretty easy to bring him down when he was alone, not much of a man if you ask me." He shook his head, and his voice filled with disgust. "I can handle a lot of things, but I would hate to have to depend on a girl for protection. What a wimp!"

My stomach tightened as anger welled up inside me. "You should watch what you say."

"That's exactly what I mean! He's not even here, and you're protecting him."

Samantha opened her mouth, but I shook my head. I wanted Bryce's attention to stay focused on me, not her. In a sugary-sweet voice, I asked, "So why didn't you try to hurt me, and why are you sitting here with me?" I let my eyes get big. "Did you miss me?"

Hatred flashed across his face, and I knew there wouldn't be too many cordial visits between us. "I want to know what you did to Cassandra."

"I …" This was not what I expected. "I don't know what you're talking about. The last time I saw her was before class yesterday … with you."

His grip tightened on my shoulder. "If you don't tell me what you did, you won't ever be able to go anywhere without looking over your shoulder."

Dumbfounded, I shook my head in disbelief. *Did he think I'd been able to since I came to school here?* "Every time I step out of my dorm room, I have to watch my back, so that's not much of a threat." My voice rose. Students walking by stared in our direction, but I continued. "You can bully me all you want, but I didn't do anything to her. As far as I can tell, there are a lot of things wrong with her, but I imagine she's been that way since birth. It's nothing I did." I focused all my attention on him. He flinched and jerked his head back. *He's scared of me.* The realization gave me power.

"If you didn't do anything to her, then why has she been lying in bed since then, staring at the ceiling, not moving?"

I looked at my fingernails like I was bored with this conversation. "Laziness."

"It's like she's in a … a trance or a coma or something …" His voice trailed off. "It had to be you."

"I swear to you, it wasn't." Even though I hadn't intended to do anything to her, in the back of my mind, I wondered if somehow I did. I still didn't know what all my capabilities were. *Was it me? Could I have done that to her without even being near her? Maybe I stopped Cassandra in one of my many dreams, but at the same time stopped her in reality.*

*No.* I shook my head. She was the reason Sarah went out last night. "The only way I'd hurt any of you is in self-defense. I don't want to hurt anybody."

The muscles tightened in his neck. "Do you really think I believe you?"

"Why don't you?" I clenched my jaw and tried to contain my frustration. When I talked again, my voice had softened. "I've had so many opportunities to hurt all of you, but even in self-defense, I didn't do anything when you threw me down the stairs."

"Only because you were so worried about your precious guard dog."

Heat burned my stomach, saturating my veins. "I could've killed all of you right then. It wouldn't have taken me any longer to get to Cody. I didn't have to extinguish the fireball." I held my head in my hand, trying to fight down my anger. "What did I ever do to any of you, anyway?"

"You came to school here. Isn't that enough?" His mouth curled up on one side. "Don't you realize what a menace you are? You're an abomination. People like you shouldn't exist."

My hands clenched into tight fists, but somehow, I managed to hold my temper at bay.

"You're nothing but a FREAK!"

Anger boiled in my stomach. Through gritted teeth, I said, "If I were you, I'd leave now."

"Cassandra knew before she even met you that you would try to hurt all of us. She warned us all the first day she saw you here." Confusion clouded his eyes. He took his hand off my arm and rubbed his neck with it. "I don't know why you didn't hurt us when you had the chance, but I know somebody needs to stop you." He stood.

"What do you mean 'she knew'?" I asked. *How could she know about me?*

"She just knew. She had dreams about meeting you. She knows what you're trying to do. She knew you would try to stop anyone who got in your way, and she wanted to stop you first."

"I'm not trying to do anything," I yelled at him. "I just want to graduate from college and not be bothered by anyone in the meantime."

"Yeah … uh, huh. I'm sure that's what you want." He backed away from me. "Just stay away from us, or you'll wish you would have."

I didn't move until he was out of sight. The last thing I wanted to do was take my eyes off him. I still believed he was intimidated by me, but there was no way I would intentionally turn my back on him.

I had so many questions racing through my head. *Did Nefarious have his grasp on Cassandra before we even met? Did he cause her dreams? Is that why she's hated me all along? What do they think I'm trying to do anyway?*

"That was tense." Samantha scooted back over.

"Yeah." I searched the area to make sure none of the Potato Heads were near. "I'm sorry about hushing you, but I thought it would be best to keep his attention on me."

She nodded and stood. "I realized what you were doing, but I don't think I matter to him."

*If they can use you to hurt me, they'll do it.* We walked back to our room in silence.

Cody stood rigid in front of our door, arms folded over his chest. His blue eyes darkened with anger and concern. "I thought we had an understanding." Cody's words forced their way past clenched teeth, cold, raw and fierce.

"I didn't go anywhere on my own." I used both hands to direct his attention to Samantha.

Samantha came to a stop in front of him. "Let me in, Cody." She put her hand on his arm, and his posture loosened fractionally.

"Where. Have. You. Been?"

"Not here." She pointed at the open doors lining the hallway.

He stepped to the side, and Samantha unlocked the door. "Come on in."

As soon as the door shut, he asked, "What happened?"

I cleared my throat and tried to decide what to say. "I just had an … uh, interesting chat with Bryce."

His chest heaved, his nostrils flared, and his eyes sliced into mine. His tone changed to one of pure hatred when he asked, "What'd the little weasel want?"

I summarized, not wanting Cody to get any more worked up than he already was.

"And he let you walk away? He didn't try to hurt you?" Cody asked.

"Actually," Samantha said, "Bryce walked away. We waited 'til he was gone to come back."

My two closest friends were in the room with me, but I'd never felt so alone. *Cassandra's a nasty person who's being controlled by a demon, but if I can do this to her without meaning to, what else can I do?*

"Dacia—" Cody grabbed my hand "—tell me what you're thinking."

"I, uh …" I pulled my hand through my hair and slid down the wall to the floor.

Cody knelt in front of me. Worry softened his eyes.

I reached up and put my hand on his cheek. He leaned into it. He smelled like cold, fresh mountain air. I wanted him to hold me and take all my problems away, but he wanted to hear my thoughts.

"Please, Dacia."

"What if I did it?"

"Did what?"

"Put Cassandra in a coma."

Samantha answered, "Then you should do it to the other three so they leave you alone until this is over."

"Sounds reasonable," Cody said.

"There's just one thing I don't understand," Samantha said.

"What?" Cody asked.

"Cassandra went to Nancy Heron last night because she cut her leg. If she's in a trance or whatever, how did she get there? And, how did she get hurt in the first place?"

I wrapped my arms around my legs and rocked back and forth before answering. "I wondered that, but I didn't want to be the one to tell Bryce she'd been out." I pulled myself to my feet. “What I’d like to know is why the amulet didn’t heat up when Bryce came over.”

“It can’t be a coincidence that it did before,” Samantha said.

“No.” I leaned my head on my knees. “But all four of them were there that day.”

# Chapter 27

## *Things That Go Bump In The Night*

I lay in bed and stared at the ceiling. I tried to visualize my mountain getaway, but every time I closed my eyes, a wave of dizziness crashed over me. I climbed out of my loft and pulled on a hoodie. Then I looked at Cody asleep in Big Bird.

*He looks peaceful. Should I wake him? If I don't, he'll be angry.* "Cody—" I put my hand on his arm, and he jerked awake.

"You okay?" His voice sounded groggy, but his eyes were alert.

"Fine." I finger-combed my hair. "I can't sleep. I'm going to walk the hallway and see if I can clear my head."

He reached for his shoes. His hand stopped mid-air. "I can't go with you." He rubbed his face. "Promise you'll be careful."

I knelt in front of him and put my hands on his knees. He leaned his forehead against mine. My stomach tingled the way it did only around Cody. *Maybe I should stay here with him.* I closed my eyes, and my head spun.

"I promise," I whispered.

He lowered his mouth to mine. The kiss was tender, sweet.

He walked me to the door, his voice rough. "You have fifteen minutes. After that, I'm coming after you. I don't care if I get caught."

I squeezed his hand.

"Clock's ticking."

I ran down the steps to the main floor. I walked two laps around the commons, then sat down and closed my eyes. Dizziness made my stomach roll. The smell of sulfur amplified my queasiness.

I grabbed my amulet—it was cool to the touch—and looked outside. I still had five minutes. *I need to go outside.* The compulsion pulled me to the door.

The chilly mountain air refreshed me. I walked for a little bit before stopping to look up at the sky. Gazing at the multitude of stars, I felt at peace for the first time since I talked to Bryce. I asked myself, "How do I even know if what Bryce said was true? Why should I believe him?"

"Why wouldn't you believe me?" Bryce's voice came from behind me.

Before I could turn around, I was hit in the back of the head. Sharp pain pulled the air from my lungs. I fell to my hands and knees.

"Did you think I was lying to you?" Bryce asked.

I never had the chance to answer. He hit me again, and this time everything went black.

Pain sliced through my head. I squeezed my eyelids tighter, fighting against the pounding in my skull. My wrists burned. I lifted them but, instead of moving, they throbbed.

I opened my eyes, and a blinding light forced them shut. I turned my head away from the source and pulled them open. The pain in my head screamed at me.

Earth and water mixed together, making the room smell damp and old, like a cellar. I blinked until my eyes adjusted and my vision cleared.

My hands and feet were bound to a wooden chair in the middle of what seemed to be a large room. Blood dripped from ropes pulled too tightly. The rest of the room was covered in shadows. Every few seconds, water dripped.

*Where am I and why?*

I tried to use my powers to free myself. When nothing happened, I closed my eyes and concentrated on fire. My hands warmed slightly, but that was all. The throbbing in my head increased each time I tried.

Light flickered and shadows crept closer. Water drops took on a life of their own.

"What do you want from me?" I screamed. My voice echoed through the darkness.

*Be strong.* I pictured my lake, but it wasn't peaceful. A storm raged. Water crashed against the rocks.

I jerked my eyes open. My heart pounded against my chest so hard I thought it might break my ribs. I hung my head. *Why was I chosen? How can I be a hero when I can't even free myself?* I felt inadequate, hollow, broken.

The silence was interrupted by a low, rumbling noise that shook the ground. Panic spread through my body. I thought I heard the noise again, but I wasn't sure. It was hard to tell over the beating of my heart. Another rumbling sound, and this time I knew it wasn't me. The amulet warmed my skin, and the ground shook with fury. *Nefarious.* I had to free myself, and I had to do it now.

With every step he took, my fear intensified. I shook and couldn't think straight.

*What's going to happen when he finds me sitting here, tied to this stupid chair?*

My stomach twisted and convulsed. My breath came out in ragged gasps that tore at my lungs and throat.

*Pull yourself together or he'll kill you!*

I tried to yank my hands free, but the ropes cut into my wrists. The night Bryce and Alvin ambushed Cody and I came to mind. The only way I could've smashed Bryce's hand was with pure brute strength. I poured all of my energy and concentration into freeing my arms and legs. After a few seconds, the ropes gave way. They flew through the air along with slivers of wood from the chair. I turned my back to the light and in desperation searched for a way out.

I stood in shock, staring at the walls of the room. The dripping wasn't a faucet. I was in a cave. Stalactites hung from the ceilings, and stalagmites shot up from the floors. I knew there were caves in the Snowfire Mountains, but I had never been in one and didn't even know where one could be found.

The rumbling grew louder, snapping me out of my stupor. I didn't want to face Nefarious here. I wouldn't stand a chance. I searched for a way out and spotted one across the cavern.

My only chance was to sneak out the very opening Nefarious would enter.

The narrow, twisted pathway gradually ascended. Stalactites and stalagmites dotted the path. I stepped into it and realized it didn't offer many places to hide. Thunderous steps advanced toward me. *I have to try.*

I ran forward. The amulet burned my skin. The path curved. Nefarious was close enough I could hear him breathe. *He's going to find me and kill me.* Fear gripped my body. My insides froze, then shattered into a million jagged pieces that stabbed me every time I took a breath.

A large crack ran down one of the walls. I ran to it and squeezed myself as deep into it as possible. A stalagmite helped conceal me. I pulled my hood over my face and cowered.

Sulfurous stench filled the air. I fought the desire to cough. My only hope was to go unnoticed until Nefarious passed me.

I crouched as low as I could and prayed. *Dear, God, I know I'm not the best person in the world, but if you help me out of here, I will try to be better. Please help me find a way out of this. Please, please, Lord.* The prayer kept repeating through my mind while I waited for Nefarious to walk past.

Silence. *Look. See if he's gone.* I inched forward but stopped. The sulfur smell burned my nose.

He sniffed, a predator scenting its prey.

Fear marched up my spine like an army of ants. *Run.* My legs longed to follow the command. I gritted my teeth and fought the compulsion.

My heart stopped when Nefarious said, "I can smell your fear." His voice gave me the impression of boulders crashing.

A braver person might have challenged Nefarious, but I wanted to live to see another day. I crouched down, burying myself in shadows.

"You are worthless! Come to me now, and your death will be fast. Spare yourself the pain and suffering."

The impulse to get up and run to him pulled me to my feet. *No! Don't let him have control.*

"Your will is strong, but your fear is stronger." Nefarious roared. "Coward! If you will not surrender, stand and fight me!"

Nefarious' whip cracked, sizzling as it flew through the air. I jumped out, preparing to defend myself. *You idiot!*

Nefarious turned toward me from further down the path than I'd expected. I ran up the trail, knowing he'd catch up. *Think, Dacia, think.*

The whip cracked again. I turned to avoid it, but it wrapped mercilessly around my ankle. Flames ripped the flesh from my leg. A scream tore from my chest, pulling all the air from my lungs. My head wobbled to the side, and darkness threatened to pull me into its grasp. Nefarious dragged me toward him. The dream version of him was a softer, subtler rendition than what stood before me. Flames flickered on his scales like a campfire that burned down to coals.

The rock floor gouged my back. I held my head up to try to keep from hurting it any more than it already was. As Nefarious pulled me closer to him, I shot a stream of ice at the whip, but before it hit, Nefarious swung it out of the ice flow's path.

"You'll have to do better than that," the low voice rumbled.

Only a few feet remained between Nefarious and me. With all the strength I could muster, I shot a steady flow of ice from both hands. This time I wouldn't miss my target. Ice filled the entire width of the trail and covered everything in its path, forming a wall between the two of us. A cool sensation soothed my ankle. I slammed my foot down on the ground as hard as I could, cringing. Shards of ice flew through the air as I freed myself.

He roared and slammed into the ice. Cracks spiderwebbed across the surface.

I rolled onto my stomach and lifted onto my hands and knees. I pulled myself to a standing position. My right foot touched the ground, and I fell forward. Struggling, I mustered up the concentration to get myself in the air. Hovering a few inches above the ground, I flew through the cave with a speed I didn't know I possessed. I went around the next curve and heard the ice wall explode.

A deafening roar echoed throughout the cavern, shaking the cave walls. Small rocks broke loose. As they tumbled to the ground, larger chunks crashed down. I raced to get out of the cave before Nefarious caught up to me and before being crushed by falling rocks.

A beam of light bounced off the wall in front of me. The exit! *I'm going to make it.* Fresh air never smelled sweeter.

I flew toward the entrance. The rocky ground had patches of snow scattered here and there. Short pine trees bent at strange angles to survive the wind and cold.

Boulders crashed down. I spun through the air, dodging them. *I made it out.* I lifted my eyes to heaven. *Thank you.*

A pika chirped a warning. I looked over my shoulder, and my heart dropped to my toes, pulling all hope with it. Nefarious hadn't been trapped in the rockslide. Out in the open, he spread his wings and targeted me.

*Think, think, think.* I flew faster. *He won't stop. Where can I go? What can I do?*

Nefarious lunged forward and seized my right leg. His claws ripped through burnt flesh. Bile rose in my throat as pain clouded my sight. Darkness touched the edges of my vision. *No!* I struggled to escape Nefarious' grasp. *I can't let it end this way.*

He pulled me closer. Fallen rocks littered the ground at the entrance to the cave. I levitated the largest one, hurling it through the air at his skull. It struck him with enough force for me to free my leg from his claws. He threw his head back and let out a ferocious roar. Flames erupted, engulfing his body.

Trying to figure out how to escape, I hurtled rock after rock through the air at him. Enraging him even more.

"Petty, worthless human." He stepped toward me as a wall of flames rose behind me. The heat brought me to a stop. I was trapped between the hideous monster and the flames. I looked around but saw no way out.

Nefarious pulled out his flaming sword and took a step closer to me. The blade sliced through the air, foretelling the end. I gazed down the hillside at Phlox University and longed to be in my dorm room with Samantha and Cody. I closed my eyes and sank to the ground. Flames grazed my neck.

# Chapter 28

## *Home Sweet Home*

"Dacia"—Cody's voice was like the growl of a grizzly bear—"where've you been? How did you get here?"

I peeled my eyelids apart. *Cody?* I glanced at my surroundings. Furniture and homework replaced the trees and bushes. *How?*

I crouched on the floor, not the rocky ground. A sob raced up my throat, rushing out before I could stop it. I slumped against the door, and tremors shook my body. I fought to steady them, but they only deepened.

Cody sat and wrapped his arms around me. His breath hitched when his fingers touched my back. "You're here. You're okay." His words caressed my ear.

I stared at nothing. Terror clung to me. My heart pounded in my temples. *Nefarious lifted his sword. Flames. He stepped forward. Burning. Pain. I couldn't move. Whistling as the sword cut through the air. Fire on my neck.* Again and again, the vision replayed. I closed my eyes, and the image intensified. A scream lodged in my throat. *Fire. Blood. Pain.*

Cody held me tighter, rubbing my arm, whispering in my ear.

*It can't be real. Monsters aren't real.*

"Please say something … anything." Cody's touch eventually stopped the trembling. He slid one arm under my legs and lifted. "Oh, my God, Dacia—" he nearly dropped me "—what happened to your leg?"

I looked at it as if through another's eyes. Mutilated flesh. Muscles. Bone. Blood. So much blood. Crimson stained my blackened skin and muscles. The room spun. Then nothing.

Pinpricks of light broke through my eyelids. *Was it all a dream?*

Fuzzy fabric massaged my fingertips. *Not my bed.* I pulled in a deep breath and opened my eyes. I sat in Cookie Monster with Cody kneeling on the floor beside me. Samantha, her eyes red-rimmed and scared, sat in Big Bird. My injured leg was propped up, covered with a towel and I couldn't feel it.

"Sarah's on her way over." Cody's voice was hoarse, strained.

I nodded. *This can't be real.*

I reached for my leg, and pain tore across my back. The room lurched into a nauseating spin. Sweat dotted my temples.

I put my hands on either side of my leg, gripping it, fighting the pain. My fingers tingled. Healing energy flowed into my leg, but it drew on my strength. My breath shallowed, and my vision blurred.

Startled by the knock on the door, I grabbed Cody's hand and clenched his fingers.

He rubbed his thumb over the back of my hand. "Dacia, it's okay."

"Watch your step," Samantha said as she let Sarah in.

Sarah glanced at the floor and, without a word, stepped over the blood. She sat across from me, and the three of them looked at me the way a child would watch over an injured pet.

Cody pulled the bloodstained towel back, showing Sarah my leg. Her face gave away nothing, but her eyes dilated with fear.

"The back of her shirt is shredded and bloody." Cody covered my leg again. "She hasn't said a word."

Even for me, my voice was hard to decipher. "I know … you want me to … tell you what … happened … but I'm … still trying … to figure it out … myself."

"Dacia," Sarah said, "I think you are in shock. Would you like to go see Nancy or go to the hospital?"

"Uh … no. Bad idea." I gave her a look that said she was stupid. I didn't mean to, but I was in no condition to filter my reactions.

"Think about it," she suggested.

"No, if it heals right away, how am I supposed to explain it? The doctors will think they're going crazy if they see two miraculous recoveries in such a short time."

"I'm just trying to help you," she said. "Why don't we get you cleaned up?"

A loud noise. *Rocks falling. Flames. Pain. Blood.*

I jumped and jerked my head around. My heart blocked my throat.

"Dacia"—Cody sounded like he was trying to calm a wild animal—"it was just a door. You're okay." His face was a blank mask, but I saw despair in his eyes.

I looked down at my lap and began my story. "I keep waiting to wake up. This has to be a nightmare." I felt lifeless, like a zombie sitting there.

When I told them about being tangled in Nefarious' whip, I jerked my leg back. I could feel the whip coiled around it, the blazing pain. I clenched my jaw and held my screams inside. *It's not real this time.* My fingers dug into the arm of the chair. *Breathe.*

"Take your time, Dacia," Cody whispered in my ear. "It's okay."

Sarah reached forward. "You're here with us. You'll be all right."

I looked Sarah in the eyes and said, "No, I won't. I can't beat Nefarious. I won't get out alive again."

For once, nobody told me about their unending faith in me.

I continued my story. I needed to get it over with. Using my powers had taken its toll on my body, and exhaustion made it hard to talk.

My chest tightened when I thought about Nefarious' sword slicing through the air. Sweat beaded at my temples and above my lip. My stomach heaved.

Samantha found her voice, "Dacia, you're white as a ghost. Are you going to be okay? Can I get you something?"

I shook my head and closed my eyes. *You'll feel better as soon as you're done with your story. Might as well get it over with.*

They stared at me. Their eyes filled with so much compassion. I wiped the sweat from my face and tried to finish. "He pulled his sword, and he, uh—" I took a deep breath "—he swung it at me. It was like a scene straight out of a movie. The sword moved in slow motion, and the rest of the world moved at its usual pace. I looked down at campus and thought how much I would like to be here. I was about to die, but then I was here." I held my hand up with my thumb and forefinger barely spread apart. "I was this close to death."

Cody sat down on the arm of the chair and pulled me to him. His hand traced circles on my arm. His eyes filled with tears.

My voice was somber. "So, when am I going to wake up?"

The three of them just looked at me.

"All my past dreams seemed so realistic, so today, I kept expecting to wake up. When the whip wrapped around my leg and I didn't, part of me knew it wasn't a dream, but the other part of me prayed it was." I stared at nothing. "I don't—" A lump formed in my throat. I closed my eyes and leaned my head back. Somehow I needed to figure out how to quit being so emotional. I needed courage to defeat Nefarious.

"Dacia, take all the time you need. We understand how difficult this is for you," Samantha said. "With all you've gone through, you have plenty of reasons to cry or scream or throw a temper tantrum or whatever you need to do. Somehow you have to relieve some of your frustration."

"I can't go around crying all the time." I swiped at my eyes. "What am I supposed to do, drown Nefarious in a river of tears? If you were watching a movie and the hero had a meltdown every other scene, wouldn't you think, 'What a wuss!'?"

"This isn't a movie." Cody's hand dwarfed mine, warm and reassuring. "This is your life. No one is paying you to play a part. You were thrown into it and have every right to get upset."

"He's right," Samantha agreed. "I don't know how you deal with this at all. You're so much stronger than you think. Give yourself a little credit."

I looked over at Sarah, waiting for her to speak her mind. She'd been quiet through this whole thing; it wasn't like her. When she didn't say anything, I said, "What I wanted to say earlier is Nefarious is *huge* and *strong* and *fast* and … pure *evil*. I guess that's the best way to describe him. The hero in the diary tried to use lightning against him. I tried ice." I pushed up my sweatshirt sleeve, then pulled it back down. "I'm, uh, pretty sure fire won't work against him. After a few rocks hit him in the head, they didn't seem to bother him. I'm out of ideas, and I think … well, I … I think I'm about out of time, too." The last words rushed out of my mouth, tumbling over each other in their hurry.

Sarah patted my good knee. "I don't know how you will defeat Nefarious, but you have proven you can hold your own."

"How do—"

She held her hand up. Her voice took on a no-nonsense tone. "Please, let me finish. You made it out alive, injured but alive. You found a new power, and if need be, you can teleport out of danger again. I know you're frustrated and discouraged, but it will get better. Now, I would like to see your leg." She stood and eased the towel from it.

Clear fluid oozed out of charred flesh. Two gouges ran from my knee to my ankle, exposing muscle and bone. My stomach rolled, but I couldn't look away. "It's not healing." I tugged my hand through crimson curls. "I healed the two of you faster than I'm healing myself."

Sarah sat again. "Your injury is severe."

I crossed my arms and glared at her. "Oh, I'm sorry if I'm being unrealistic. After all, you were dead," I snapped. "Something tells me no matter how mangled my leg is, dead is worse."

Sarah shook her head and shot me a disapproving look that any other day would've made me feel guilty. "Maybe it's a little harder to repair flesh and muscles that have been burned and sliced apart than it is to make somebody breathe or start the heart pumping again. Hmm—" she rubbed her chin "—it seems to me even doctors, at times, have more trouble with that. I've never seen stitches come out the same day they went in, but I have seen people receive mouth-to-mouth resuscitation and be fine after just a short time."

"Cody's cuts healed quickly," I reminded her. "I'm sure Dr. Sequoia will attest to that."

Sarah glanced at Cody and tilted her head. Her eyes held an apology. "Cody's injuries were serious. However, his cuts did not tear through muscle and weren't clear to the bone. Yours were also caused by a demon. That, in my opinion, could very well be a significant factor."

I had to admit she was right, but patience wasn't a virtue of mine. I wanted to be better *now*.

"How's your head?" Samantha asked.

I reached up and felt it. Both bumps were gone. "It seems to be fine."

"Maybe Sarah's right about the demon thing then." Samantha shrugged. "I suppose it's possible his magic counteracts yours somehow."

"Maybe not magic," Cody said. "Maybe venom or something."

"I just hope it heals soon." I looked down at my hands. "I hope I'm making the right decision about the doctor." A tear slid out of my eye.

Cody brushed it off my cheek. "We all hope so."

Sarah stood. "Let's get this bandaged."

"We can take care of it," Samantha said. "You should get back before it gets dark. Dacia won't be able to save you tonight."

"Are you sure?" Sarah asked.

"Yeah. Oh, and I'll be sleeping there." Cody pointed at Big Bird. His voice left no room for argument. "Hope you don't mind."

"For the record, Cody, you cannot be in the girls' dorm after ten at night." She shook her finger at him. "Unofficially, I think it's a great idea. We all need to watch out for each other."

Cody relaxed his stance. "Want me to walk you back?"

"Thank you. No," Sarah said. "I'll be fine." She stopped just before the door. "I forgot about this." She pointed at the floor. "Do you want help cleaning the blood?"

"No," Samantha answered. "You need to get going. Me and Cody will take care of it. Right, Cody?"

"No, I'll do it." I fought to hold a yawn in, but it pushed my jaws apart. "It's my blood, not yours."

"Dacia, you'll sit there 'til your leg heals," Cody ordered. "We'll take care of you. You have to let us."

Sarah looked me in the eyes and said, "Get some rest."

I tilted my head back, closed my eyes and tried to heal my injuries. I needed to be better before Nefarious' next attack.

# Chapter 29

## *Plagued By Nightmares*

The light from the exit shines in front of me. With a newfound sense of determination, I fly outside. I turn to see if Nefarious is behind me. His claws rip through my burnt flesh like a hot knife through butter, and he pulls me toward him.

Just outside the cave, hiding behind some bushes, I see her. The unmistakable coal-black hair of Cassandra glistens in the sun.

I jerked my leg up and gripped the arms of the chair. My knuckles whitened as I tried to fight off the pain.

"Dacia, breathe." Cody pried my fingers up and squeezed my hand. With his other hand, he brushed the hair off my face. "You're going to hyperventilate."

Shallow breaths dimmed my eyesight.

"Just a nightmare."

"Not your nightmares. Your nightmares are dangerous … life-threatening nightmares."

"What's your point?"

"Don't pass it off as just a nightmare." His fingers gently stroked my cheek, calming me. "They're a big deal."

"She was there," I muttered.

"Who?"

It took me a second to process his question. *Of course, he doesn't know. Nightmare.* I shook my head, silently reprimanding myself for being stupid. "Cassandra. I can't believe she just watched him try to kill me."

"What?"

"She hid behind the bushes. I didn't notice when it happened, but in my dream, I saw her as plain as day. Everything Nefarious or I said or did was exactly the way I remember it, down to the last detail. I probably saw her, but it didn't connect." I closed my eyes and focused on that image. "I'm sure she was there, though."

Cody rubbed the back of his neck. "Not good."

"Where's Samantha?"

He looked at the door. "Washing. We got covered in blood."

*They shouldn't have to take care of me. I'm supposed to be the strong one. I should take care of them.* I threw the blanket to the side and gasped.

"What's wrong?" Cody asked.

The lump in my throat kept me from answering. I nodded at my leg. The bandages were soaked in blood. I should've known. I got injured in a dream. Of course, the wound reopened.

Rocking back on his heels, Cody said, "I'll get something to stop the bleeding."

"Just use the blanket." I leaned my head back and closed my eyes. "It's probably covered already."

He grabbed it and looked at his bloody hand. "Yeah. Bandages off or blanket on top of them?"

"Just cover it. I'll take the bandages off when it stops bleeding."

Cody put pressure on my leg, and I inhaled sharply.

"Sorry." His eyes pinched together in an expression more pained than mine.

"I know, but it hurts like hell," I told him through clenched teeth.

After a few minutes of unbelievable pain, Cody released the pressure. The room spun, and darkness pulled me under.

ഇ

The crisp morning air combined with my walk invigorates me. After three days, it's great to walk without a limp. I close my eyes and lift my face to the sun. *Who knows how much longer I have to enjoy the simple things.*

I continue sauntering to the library. A sudden bout of nausea stops me. My stomach cramps, and I double over in pain. I feel like I've been kicked in the gut. I stay there—bent over, grasping my stomach and trying not to throw up.

Then I hear Nefarious' familiar growl. "You won't get away from me next time. Your worst nightmares will seem like nothing compared to the torture you and your friends will endure." His evil laughter echoes across campus.

When his voice trails off, his fiery whip flies through the air. Terrified, I try to run, but my leg won't hold my weight. I fall to the ground with a thud and roll to the side. The whip strikes the pavement next to my head.

"Dacia."

I opened my eyes to a dark room. Cody stood above me. His hair was tousled. "You okay?"

"What time is it?" My voice sounded scratchy.

"It's, uh, 2:33 Monday morning." He knelt beside me. "Are. You. Okay?"

"Nefarious threatened to get to me through my friends."

Samantha jerked upright in bed and switched on her lamp. "Us?"

I nodded. "He said because I got away, he wouldn't go easy on me or my friends." I stared down at my trembling hands. "I'm sorry."

Samantha's initial shock wore off. "Not all your dreams come true."

"Yeah … maybe."

Cody cupped my chin in his hand and turned my face toward him. "Are you hurt?"

I shook my head. "Nothing new."

Relief erased stress and fear on his face.

"Do you need anything?" Samantha asked.

My face heated up, and I imagined a wave of red covering my freckles.

Cody's head tilted to the side. "What?"

I turned away. "Glacier."

Cody climbed my loft ladder, grabbed my white teddy bear and handed her to me. "You're so cute when you're embarrassed."

I snuggled with Glacier, hoping she could stop the nightmares.

ꕥ

The pink glow of dawn filled the room. I rubbed sleep out of my eyes and stretched. Pain shot through my leg, stealing the air from my lungs.

*Heal already.* I focused all my energy on my leg. A cooling sensation traveled down my wound, fighting the burn. My shoulders slumped, and my eyelids drooped. *Why?* I stopped trying to heal myself. *Why does it take all my energy?*

"Hey, Dacia"— Cody's voice was rough from sleep— "how long've you been awake?"

"A few minutes."

"How's your leg?"

"It hurts." *As bad as it did yesterday.* "Can you help me up? I'm scared to try it on my own."

"Yeah, sure."

Cody put his hands on my waist, and I pressed down on the arms of the chair. As soon as my right leg touched the floor, excruciating pain shot through it. I fell against Cody so hard he had to brace himself to keep from falling.

"You okay?" he asked when he regained balance.

I gulped down huge breaths of air, trying to conquer the pain. "Sure." Leaning on Cody, I made it down the hall. He sat in the stairwell, out of sight, while I hobbled into the bathroom.

I stood under the shower, clinging to the wall for support. Piercing pain sliced through my leg with each bead of water that touched it. Blood and tears mixed with the spray washing down the drain.

"You idiot," I mumbled as I finished. *How long is it going to take to get used to these new powers?* I raised a couple inches off the ground and hovered while drying off. I dressed in a graphic tee and shorts, then pulled on a baggy pair of pajama pants to cover my leg and wrapped my hair in a towel. Dropping closer to the ground, I floated into the hall. Cody jumped up and hurried over to me.

"Hey … you're not limping." He looked at my feet then back into my eyes. "Your leg better?"

"No." I rose up to eye level with him.

"Oh. Why didn't you do that before?" He rubbed his neck hard enough to loosen knots. "Not that I minded holding you."

"I hate to break it to you." I lowered myself before anybody caught me hovering. "You're dating an idiot." I rested my head on his shoulder while we walked back. "But I didn't mind leaning on you either."

Cody stepped into my room just as a door opened down the hallway. He looked out through the peephole. "That was close," he whispered. "Marcy is patrolling."

I pulled the towel down around my shoulders and patted my hair with it. “Don’t be surprised if she stops by and asks if you’re here.”

A couple of seconds later there was a knock on my door. Cody vaulted into my loft and hid himself the best he could.

I took my time getting to the door. “Oh, hi, Marcy. What’s up?” I tried to keep my voice nonchalant.

She stood on her toes, trying to peek around me. “Cody’s not in here, is he?”

“No.”

“I could’ve sworn I heard him in the hall.”

I held my finger to my lips. “I just got back from showering, and Samantha’s still in bed. I’d appreciate it if you didn’t wake her. She gets grumpy when she doesn’t get enough sleep.”

Marcy spun around and hurried back to her room, mumbling the entire way.

Cody climbed out of my loft. “How did you know?”

I laughed quietly. “Marcy doesn’t patrol the halls, and the only rule she has ever seemed to care about is the hours guys can’t be in here.”

“Maybe because she’s never been on a date,” he suggested.

“Now, be nice.” I smacked his arm. “She’s just doing her job. Besides, I’m not sure I’ve been on a date yet—” I rubbed my chin thoughtfully “—or do you call sitting in my room eating pizza a date?”

His cheeks turned red. “What about putt-putt?”

Making my tone as serious as I could, I said, “If that counts, I have to call this relationship off.”

“Wha—”

"If those were dates, you're two-timing me." He looked confused. "You did pay for Samantha to come along, didn't you?"

"Yeah," he answered, "but, they should count."

"No, a date would just be the two of us." Walking my fingers up his chest, I added, "Me and you … alone."

"Okay." He put his hand over mine, flattening it over his heart. "Next Saturday dinner and a movie, just us."

I fanned my face with my hand. "Why, Cody Hawks, are you asking me out? That would be delightful."

Cody grabbed a strand of my hair. "I like the wet hair look." His eyes darkened, and he eliminated the thin strip of air that had separated us. His body pressed against mine. He brought his mouth down.

And I gasped. His leg touched mine. Black spots dotted my vision.

He kept his hands on my waist but stepped back. "I wasn't thinking. I'm s—"

I put my hand over his mouth and swallowed my pain. "I know. Help me out of these"—I tugged at my pajama bottoms—"so I can sit."

Cody's eyes dilated. I half expected drool to drip from his open mouth.

"I have shorts on." I pushed his chin up.

"Yeah … right." Cody eased them over my injury. Then he helped me sit in Cookie Monster.

His eyes ran the length of my leg. "Looks better."

"Just because I got more blood cleaned off it." I tried to keep the emotion out of my voice.

Cody looked at the door then back at me, seemingly torn in two. “I should go to class.”

“I’m not.” I pulled my hair into a ponytail. “I’m going through the journals. There’s got to be something helpful in them.”

“Promise you won’t leave?”

I crossed my heart. “I won’t. I don’t plan on doing anything stupid until my leg heals. Then, hopefully, after that, I still won’t do anything stupid.”

Cody leaned down and kissed me. I twisted my hands in his shirt and drew him closer. For the first time since Nefarious attacked me, I wasn’t thinking about my leg or pain or dying. Shivers of pleasure shot through me. He pulled away before I was ready for him to and went out the door.

I opened the ancient journal and flipped through the book, staring at an undecipherable language. I turned to the page with the young man shooting lightning bolts at Nefarious and couldn’t read it. I looked at the ceiling, then back at the page.

*Why could I read it before?* Maybe it had to do with my frame of mind.

Out of the corner of my eye, I saw my bathroom bag sitting by the door. A gold chain spilled over the side of it, and I wondered if that was what was missing. I concentrated on the amulet and wished for it to come to me. It shook, knocking the bag over. The chain tangled in the handles and dragged the bag. It made too much noise, so I gave up.

About an hour after Cody left, my boredom was interrupted by a knock. “Let me in.” Cody’s voice was rushed. “Please.”

Samantha sat straight up in bed. "What was that?" she asked, still half asleep.

"Cody's back," I said. The distance from where I sat to the door seemed insurmountable on my own. I pressed my hands down on the arms of the chair.

"Oh, Dacia"—Samantha climbed down—"don't get up." She tried to hold in a yawn. "How's your leg?" She opened the door.

"Not good," I said.

Cody hurried in. "Thanks. There are a lot more girls in the hall at this time."

Samantha scrambled back into her loft. "Skipping class?"

I nodded before realizing her eyes were closed. "Yeah."

Cody stood back from me. His expression was guarded.

"What?" I asked.

"You told Samantha your leg isn't good. Because of me?"

"Because I was attacked by a demon from the Abyss." I shook my head. "Can you help me with it?"

Cody wrapped my leg. "Need anything before I leave?"

I pointed at my bag. "The amulet."

He brought it to me, then held my eyes with his. "Stay here."

Samantha climbed out of her loft. "I'm giving up on sleep for now. I'll be back." She grabbed her bathroom bag. "Don't leave."

"I don't have much choice. I couldn't even get the door."

# Chapter 30

## *Hero's Journal*

*Will the amulet make a difference?* I breathed deeply, opened the journal and peeked at it through squinted eyes. The gibberish morphed into comprehensible words.

I flipped through the pages and found something about the vase Sarah had described to me in one of our earlier lessons. "The carafe seems to possess magical powers. I filled it with water before my journey. After drinking out of it for three days, it appears as if not one drop has spilled forth from it. My instincts tell me it is intended to serve another purpose. However, for what it is designed, I am uncertain."

I searched the journal three more times and couldn't find any other mention of it. Maybe he found its purpose and wrote about it on one of the destroyed pages, or maybe he never came up with another use for it. *I need to see the vase.* Maybe it was nothing more than a bottomless canteen, but if that was the case, when Sarah brought it over, it should still be filled to the brim with water.

"Hey, Dacia," Samantha said.

The journal flew through the air, my hands shook, and my heart raced. Somehow, I managed to stifle a startled scream. *Flames. Pain. Blood.*

"Are you okay?" She hurried over to me, picking up the journal on her way.

"You scared the crap out of me!" I clutched my hand to my chest, trying to steady my breathing. "As soon as my heart stops pounding, I'll be fine."

"Sorry." She handed the journal to me. "I figured you wondered what happened to me. I was gone longer than I planned."

"I figured you bumped into someone. Maybe … Dan," I added to hide my fear.

She grinned, and it lit up her whole face. "No, I saw Vanessa leave, so I took off after her to find out what's going on with Cassandra."

My heart turned to lead and plummeted. "Samantha, you shouldn't have." Now I knew how they felt when I took off on my own. "You could've been hurt."

She rolled her eyes as if to say, *Hey pot, meet kettle.*

"I told her Bryce confronted you about Cassandra. She looked a little surprised, but then she told me to mind my own business."

"Sounds about right."

She sat across from me and leaned in conspiratorially. "I told her Bryce seemed pretty upset about it and that I hoped Cassandra would be fine. At first, she just looked at me. Then she admitted they're all concerned about her. None of them have seen her move for several days." Her voice rose excitedly. "This is the interesting part. Even though they haven't seen her move, Sunday morning when they checked on her, she was dressed, and her shoes were muddy. Saturday night when they left her, she had pajamas on."

I looked at my mummified leg. No words were able to filter from my brain to my mouth. *How could she? She was there. She watched while Nefarious tried to kill me.*

"Well," Samantha prodded, "aren't you going to say anything?"

I shook my head in disbelief. "I'm processing."

"Vanessa told me I can hang out with them whenever I want." She cringed and gave me a half smile. "I think I'll pass. After what they did to you and Cody, I don't want anything to do with them. Anyway, since I was trying to get information from her, I told her that'd be nice."

"Wow." I pulled my hand through my hair. "How is she getting in and out without being noticed?"

"Probably the same way Cody is."

"Yeah." I bit my cheek to keep from grinning stupidly at the mention of Cody's name. "If Nefarious is controlling her, why is she in a trance throughout the day?" I knew Samantha couldn't answer my questions, but I thought maybe asking them out loud would help me come up with some answers. I wasn't having a lot of luck with it on my own. "I wonder if they know her leg is cut."

"I doubt it. I think, with everything else she told me, she would have mentioned that."

Warmth flared in me, sending tiny sparks throughout my body. My mouth spread into a slow grin. "Cody'll be here soon." I pulled on my lip with my teeth. *When did I turn into that girl?* "He needs a key."

Samantha stood at the door and looked out the peephole. A few seconds later, she opened it.

Cody's fist was in the air, ready to knock. "Hi. Leaving?"

"No, opening the door for you."

Understanding flickered across his face as he walked over to me. "Any better?"

"About the same." I shrugged. "I don't know how it looks."

He focused on me so intently, I wondered if he could see through to my soul. "I thought it'd be better."

"Yeah …" I didn't want to think about my leg or why it wouldn't get better. Every time I did, I wondered if I'd still be sitting here when Nefarious came for me. Some hero I'd turned out to be. "I need to talk to Sarah."

Samantha pointed at herself then Cody. "Why don't we get lunch while you call her?"

Cody brought me the phone before leaving.

I called Sarah, and after going through the customary small talk, I said, "I need to see the vase."

"Did you find something?" she asked.

"No"—my shoulders hunched forward—"but something tells me it's important."

"I'll bring it to your lesson tomorrow."

After I hung up, I flipped through the journal, but it couldn't hold my attention. My mind wandered to Cassandra. I needed to figure out what was going on with her, what role she played in this mess. *But how?*

# Chapter 31

## *When The Voices In Your Head Aren't Yours*

The new-fallen snow glistens in the sunlight as if fairies had sprinkled glitter across the ground. For a moment, I wonder if they played a part in the beauty that surrounds me. The once bare trees are stunning in their new coats. It's a winter wonderland, and a smile tugs at my lips.

As I cross the wooden bridge, an eerie feeling makes the hairs on my neck stand at attention. The amulet warms against my skin. Just as I turn back, the all too familiar voice echoes through my head, "Surrender!"

My breath rasps in my throat. The thud of my heart beats painfully against my ribs. My head swims. I take a deep breath to fight off my panic.

Once my dizziness fades, I search the trees for a glimpse of Nefarious.

A warm breeze blows my hair back, and a loud "whoop, whoop" sounds above me. I look up to find Nefarious soaring through the air. His monstrous wings flap, swirling the snow around me. Pulling his wings back, he dives like an eagle. I throw my arms up in front of me and long for protection. He ricochets backward as if he flew into a wall. The force from the impact knocks me to the ground. I jump to my feet and run toward the dorms.

Nefarious roars. "Your powers have developed. It is time for you to die!"

I look over my shoulder and see him lift off. On foot, I'm no match for his speed. He'll be upon me any minute. I come to a dead stop, close my eyes and will myself back to the dorm. Nothing happens. I hear the "whoop, whoop" of his wings, followed by the sound of his whip cracking. The thought of being entangled brings tears to my eyes. I long to sit in my room. When it doesn't happen, I fly into the air. The whip hits the pavement with a loud crack.

I turn to see a fireball hurling through the air. I dodge out of its path. As soon as it flies by me, I turn and shoot ice at it. The fire gives way to ice and crashes to the ground, shattering into a million pieces. I turn back to Nefarious and continue the flow of ice from my hands.

He swerves through the air to keep from being hit. Another fireball flies toward me. I nick it with the spray of ice, but it isn't enough to stop it. I dart to the side. Flames kiss my arm, igniting my sleeve, as the fiery sphere soars past me. I throw my coat to the ground and pat out the flames on my shirt, careful not to touch my singed arm. There's no time for pain, so without giving my burning arm a second thought, I search the skies for Nefarious. He flies toward me with another fireball speeding ahead of him. I can't dodge this one. I hold my arms in front of me and will it to stop. As the heat from the flames reaches my body, I scream.

"Dacia, wake up." Cody shook my shoulders. "You're having a nightmare."

I opened my eyes and yelled, "Let go of me!"

Cody dropped my arms and looked at me like I'd slapped his face. Without saying a word, he backed away.

"I'm sorry, Cody." I lifted the blanket to show him. The sleeve of my favorite sweatshirt was gone, and my arm was burned from my shoulder to my wrist.

"Sorry." His expression said he'd take my pain if he could. "You screamed. I wanted to wake you before anything happened."

I pulled a trembling hand through my hair. "I didn't mean to yell at you."

Samantha's alarm clock buzzed. She smacked it and rolled to a sitting position. "I thought—" a deep yawn silenced her "—I thought I'd get to go back to sleep. You okay, Dacia?"

"Been better," I answered. "I'm skipping again today."

She looked down at me through heavy eyes. "Your grades are going to plummet."

"Probably." Anger bubbled up inside me, not at her but at the situation. I'd worked hard to get good grades. I held my hands up like two sides of a scale. "Good grades." I tipped my hands. "Save the world."

Cody patted my knee. "If anybody can do both, it's you."

I rolled my eyes. Right now I couldn't even get up on my own. "Help me down the hall?"

"No problem."

I put my weight on Cody as he helped me out of the chair. I lifted myself so my feet were just above the ground. We passed a few people in the hall. Most of them just looked away as we went by. Right now, I was glad for my lack of friends. I didn't need a bunch of people asking me questions.

Marcy returned to her room as we passed it. She shot Cody a nasty look and said, "Make sure you're out of here on time tonight. I have a test in the morning and don't want to be up all night because you can't read a clock."

"According to my watch—" he glanced at his wrist like he had one "—it's a little early for you to start harassing me, so back off."

Marcy stepped inside her room and slammed the door before Cody could say anything else.

He looked at me and shrugged. "It's a little early, isn't it?"

"Yeah, but I'm the sarcastic one." I pointed at myself. "You can't take that away from me. It's all I've got. Now everyone who doesn't already is going to start thinking I'm a bad influence on you."

He bowed his head, pretending to be upset. "I'll do better."

I sat in Cookie Monster while Samantha and Cody got ready for class. *Tuesday. I should be getting ready for algebra instead of sitting around waiting for my leg to heal.* I didn't like the idea of Samantha and Cody going to class with the Potato Heads without me to keep an eye on them.

My eyes widened. *Of course. I can check on Cassandra during algebra.* I glanced between Cody and Samantha. *No. You can't wander off again. What if you get hurt?*

Cody rested his hand on my shoulder. "You'll be okay?"

I could feel the guilt in my eyes. I hoped Cody didn't notice it. "Bored but fine."

Cody's head jerked back. "I know that look. Don't do it. Whatever it is. Please don't do it."

"You're not going to like it." I combed my fingers through my hair. "I thought about checking on Cassandra."

He clenched his jaw. "Why?" He fought to keep his voice even. "What would possess you?"

How could I make them understand? I needed to know what was happening with Cassandra. Was Nefarious controlling her? Leaving her body drained when he relinquished his power over her. Or had I unknowingly done something to her? Was that why I couldn't heal myself?

I lowered my chin to my chest. "I … I need to figure out what's happening with her."

"You could get hurt. Again." Cody's voice rose, and his posture stiffened. "We wouldn't have known where you went. We wouldn't know where to look for you! Why do you keep putting us through this? Why can't you just tell us what you're up to?"

Tears welled in my eyes. "I'm sorry." I swallowed hard. "I won't go."

"Dacia," Samantha said in a voice calmer than Cody's, "we don't want to see you get hurt again. We understand you need to figure out what's going on, but you have to trust us."

"If it's that important, let's go after class," Cody suggested.

I shook my head. "The reason I was planning to go while you're in class is because they're all in there."

"Okay." He turned to Samantha. "Feel like playing hooky?"

"I, uh, I'd rather go to class."

"Oh, come on. Where's your spirit of adventure?" As soon as the words escaped from my mouth, I regretted them.

All friendliness disappeared from her voice. "My spirit of adventure disappeared a long time ago and, when you came back here the other day with your leg nearly ripped off, I lost even more of it. I expected you to lose some of yours, too."

Cody tilted his head to the side and nodded. "Good point."

I clamped my mouth shut, not wanting to say anything else I'd regret.

Samantha put her hand on Cody's arm. "Keep her safe, and watch out for yourself. I'll see you two at lunch."

Cody sat across from me in Big Bird. He leaned forward with his elbows resting on his knees. "What's your plan?"

Heat rose to my cheeks. "I, uh, kinda don't have one. I was winging this."

"Any ideas at all?"

I lifted a shoulder in response. "I suppose we should wait until class starts. Hopefully, Bryce, Vanessa, and Alvin go today. I'll knock on her door. If no one answers, I'll try to figure out how to get in. Otherwise, I'll make up a story about thinking it was someone else's room."

"That's your plan?" Without waiting for me to respond, he leaned back in his chair, his arms crossed over his chest.

The next fifteen minutes seemed to last seven or eight hours. Silence pressed down on me, weighing on my shoulders. Without saying a word, Cody got up and reached his hand down to help me. I balanced myself on my left leg until I could lift myself off the ground.

As we walked down the hallway, I wondered what Cody was thinking. I couldn't remember him ever being so quiet for so long. *If I knew what he was thinking, maybe I could put his mind at ease.*

"What am I doing?" Cody asked. "Dacia's going to get herself killed, and I volunteered to go along for the ride—good thinking."

"What did you say?" My voice had a hard edge to it.

"I didn't say anything."

"Oh." After a moment's pause, I realized I'd read his mind. I should've stopped, but I didn't. "I thought you said something to the effect of me getting myself killed and you volunteering to come along."

Cody stopped. "How? I didn't say that out loud."

"Well, you must've. Otherwise, I suppose I'd have a hard time hearing you, wouldn't I?" *What's wrong with me? Why am I acting like this?*

"You read my mind … didn't you?"

I stared at my feet. I had to stop antagonizing Cody before I made him regret dating me. I didn't mean to cause him grief.

"I don't know; I thought I heard you say it … I don't know what's up and what's down anymore. You were so quiet. I wondered what you were thinking, and you started talking. At first, I thought it was a coincidence." I lifted my hand but let it fall to my side without touching him. "Please don't hate me. I couldn't bear that."

He reached over and held my face in both his hands. As he wiped a tear from the corner of my eye with his thumb, he said, "I love you too much to ever hate you." He rested his forehead on mine. "Sure you want to do this?"

I put my hands on his. "I need to."

He tipped his head slightly, then started walking toward Cassandra's room.

I watched him walk away. When would I realize he cared for me? What would it take? I had never been loved so unconditionally before. My parents were unable to accept me for who I was. My powers embarrassed them, and they even tried to deny I had them. Cody knew more about me than any ten people put together and loved me anyway.

"Dacia—" Cody glanced over his shoulder "—snap out of it."

"Sorry." I caught up to him. "I was just thinking."

Cody wrapped his arm around my shoulders, and I drew strength from his contact. "No. You were spaced out."

We stopped in front of Cassandra's door. Cody watched me, waiting for me to make a move. I lifted my hand to the door and wondered if Cody was right. *Am I making a huge mistake?* I wiped my palms on my jeans and knocked before I could talk myself out of it.

No answer. I knocked again.

When Cassandra didn't come to the door, Cody asked, "Now what?"

"I'm working on it." I closed my eyes and pictured myself walking through the door. When I opened them again, the door shimmered. I stood half in, half out of Cassandra's room. I hurried through, afraid I'd get stuck if I didn't keep going.

"You okay?" Cody asked.

A dim blue light illuminated Cassandra's room. "Yeah … why wouldn't I be?"

His voice filled with awe. "You walked through the door … like it wasn't there."

My heart raced, and the room closed in around me. Even though I was hovering, my leg ached like it held all my weight. I wanted to scream and run out of the room. Instead, I forced myself to take deep, calming breaths.

When I regained control, I surveyed her room. It wasn't set up like mine. Instead of two lofts, there was a bed on the floor. A small round table sat in the middle of the room with two plastic chairs pulled up to it. A TV hung on the wall in the corner. No desks, no comfy chairs. It appeared cold and seemed to suit her.

It dawned on me there were no lights on. I pulled the amulet out from under my sweatshirt. The sapphire eye brightened the room. *Crap.*

Cassandra lay on the bed. Her eyes were wide open, staring at the ceiling. *Why did I need to see her?* The blue light blazed. *Time to go.*

I looked out the peephole. Cody waited alone in the hall. As I grabbed the doorknob, I heard her move. I turned around to find Cassandra standing behind me. She appeared zombie-like, her face expressionless and pale. Her outstretched arms reached for my neck. I moved to the side. "There's no hope for you, Dacia. My lord will take his rightful place in history. You will be destroyed." She followed me around the room.

I backed into a chair and sent it crashing to the floor.

Cody knocked on the door. "Are you okay?"

"I will be." I moved around the room, staying out of Cassandra's reach. Holding my arms out in front of me, I said, "Stop." If I could stop a fireball, I should be able to stop her. She stood in front of me, arms outstretched, still trying to march forward but held back by an invisible force. "Why are you following me? What do you want?"

"I want you dead." Her lifeless voice sent chills up my spine. "We all want you dead."

The hairs on my arms tingled. My power weakened. My chest tightened, and the air was sucked out of my body. My lungs ached, and everything spun out of focus. I moved toward the door. I couldn't allow myself to pass out in here. It would be the end of me.

The doorknob hit the middle of my spine, catching me off guard. I lost all focus. Unable to hold her back, Cassandra moved toward me. I willed myself through the door. As Cassandra reached for my throat, I fell to the floor.

Cody stood above me. "Dacia."

I couldn't answer. I laid flat on my back, gasping for air. Cody lifted me into his arms. I felt like a limp rag doll as he carried me down the hall to my room. I looked up into his eyes before everything went black.

# Chapter 32

## Hard Lesson To Learn

I woke up, sitting in Cookie Monster. Sarah, Cody, and Samantha stood around me.

"She's awake," Sarah said with a sigh of relief. "Are you okay?"

I nodded, and the movement left me dizzy and weak.

Cody dropped to his knees. His eyes glistened with tears. "Don't ever do that again. I thought you were dying."

I cupped his cheek in my hand.

"What happened in there?" Samantha asked.

"I don't know," a froggy voice answered.

Cody turned to Samantha. "Get her water. Please."

I drank half the bottle then I told them about Cassandra.

"Did she know what she was doing?" Sarah asked.

Cody's eyes sliced into hers. "What difference does it make?"

Sarah returned his angry stare. "I want to know what's going on with her. She's not going to classes, and her friends think she's comatose."

I rubbed my hand over my face. I didn't want to talk, but this wasn't going to go away on its own. "Bryce is a grade "A" jerk, but the amulet hasn't shown any signs of life when I've seen him by himself. With Cassandra, it brightened her entire room."

"Thank you, Dacia," Sarah said. "I'm trying to get a handle on everything. You need to remember this is a new experience for me, too."

"Sorry," Cody said. "I'm edgy and overprotective."

"I understand," Sarah told him. "However, you need to realize I'm not the enemy."

Samantha rubbed her arms. "What did you mean when you said you felt like you were being strangled? Was she strangling you?"

"No. I felt like the air was being squeezed from my lungs, but Cassandra didn't lay a hand on me. The edges of my vision went black, and I panicked. That made things worse."

Samantha's shoulder dropped, and she tilted her head. "I wonder why Cassandra was able to make you quit breathing. Do you suppose she has some of Nefarious' powers?"

"I don't know." *Cassandra with Nefarious' powers. How would I deal with that? Hopefully, she'll stay in bed until I figure something out.* "Nefarious hasn't ever made me quit breathing.

I'm just not sure. Maybe I had an anxiety attack or something." I held my head. "I wish I knew what was going on."

"I think Samantha's onto something here." Sarah tapped her finger against her chin. "There have been times when you started to tell us about your dreams, and you said you felt like the wind was knocked out of you. Was that the same feeling?"

"Yeah but more intense."

"Maybe she does then," Cody added.

"Maybe. I don't need this. " I raked my fingers through my hair. "New subject. I'm going to try to make it to your office for my lesson this afternoon. You've been over here a lot, and there are more people over here to—"

"Yeah, I know what you mean," Sarah agreed. "If you can't make it, let me know, and please have Cody walk with you. Try to get some rest before our lesson," Sarah said as she walked to the door. "You need your strength."

ꕥ

At two-thirty, Cody and I left for Sarah's office. The fresh air and sunlight did nothing to improve my mood. I hovered just above the ground, moving my feet to imitate walking. Hiding my powers from most of the world weighed on me. When I stepped into Sarah's office and didn't have to pretend anymore, relief flooded through me.

Sarah led us to the couches. "I'm waiting for a call. Have a seat, and I'll be out in a couple of minutes."

"Sure," Cody said.

The vase sat in the middle of the coffee table. It belonged in a museum behind thick glass. I'd never seen anything so exquisite before. The gold vase stood eight inches tall. The bottom was bulbous with an emblem similar to the amulet I wore. Instead of a sapphire eye, this one held an emerald. Rubies and diamonds encrusted the slender neck. At the top of the neck, there was a diamond-shaped onyx with tiny crystals encircling the edges of it. In the center of the onyx was a large round emerald.

I reached to pick up the vase but hesitated when I noticed a leather pouch beside it. "I wonder what that is."

"To carry the vase," Cody suggested.

"Could be." I picked up the vase. Optimism spread through me, washing away my doubt. I no longer felt like the end of the world was upon me. The feeling was gone almost as quickly as it settled over me, but it left me more at ease.

"You're smiling." Cody trailed his fingers over my lips. "Why?"

I closed my eyes at his touch, savoring his gentleness. "I don't know. When I picked this up, things didn't seem so hopeless. It's almost like this vase has a spirit of its own, a very noble spirit. I know that sounds stupid, but I don't think somebody evil could touch it."

"Most things said in this room sound stupid but have a lot of truth to them." Cody lifted his hands. "I don't think I'll ever say something sounds stupid again."

"Yeah, I know what you mean." I returned my attention to the vase.

"What does it say?" Cody asked, pointing at the emblem's inscription.

"Hope lives even in the darkest realms."

"It's very intricate isn't it?" Sarah said as she walked into the room. "I only wish I knew what it was for."

"Me too," I agreed.

"It made you smile," Cody said. "The last few days you've been miserable. It was nice to see you smile again."

"You don't strike me as the type to be won over by pretty objects," Sarah said.

"No, not really." I stuck my hands in my hoodie. "When I picked it up, I felt like maybe every cloud does have a silver lining … I guess I just need to search a little harder to find this one."

Sarah sat down with her elbow resting on the arm of the couch, her thumb against her cheek and her forefinger against her chin. "That's a good outlook."

Remembering what I read in the journal, I took out the stopper to find the vase empty. There wasn't a single drop of water in it. "Well, it obviously has some other purpose," I said out loud to looks of confusion. "Oh, uh, there's no water in it, so it isn't a bottomless flask like the journal said."

"Interesting." Sarah's eyebrows pinched together. "Hopefully, we can figure something out."

"Maybe it was a bottomless flask because the hero needed it to be," Cody suggested. "You've been down, so it gave you hope."

Sarah tapped her finger on her cheek. "That's an interesting theory. It's possible it transforms into what's needed at the time.

However, if you didn't know its properties changed, you might just toss it aside."

"Right now, I just need it to give me the answers to help me end this." I held the vase, wondering what purpose it served. "Can I take this with me? I'd like to see if I can figure it out."

"Don't let other people see it. I like to believe people are good and honest, but I could see that sprouting legs and walking off. I'm sure it's worth a pretty penny."

"No problem." I put the vase back on the table. "But, I think it's worth two or three pretty pennies or more than I will make in my entire lifetime."

Sarah turned her attention to Cody. "Are you staying?"

"I'd like him to," I answered at the same time he said, "Yeah."

He threw his arm over the seat.

I lifted my leg onto the couch and leaned against Cody. I looked out the window. "I think I'm going to have to face Nefarious soon."

"What makes you say that?" Sarah asked.

"Gut feeling. I think I can hold my own against him for a while, but in the end, he will win. I'm more powerful than I was, but …" I didn't want them to know how discouraged I was, but I had to tell them what I thought. "I don't know how to stop him. I barely know enough to keep myself alive. Nefarious knows several ways to kill me. I just can't quite figure out why he hasn't yet. It's like he's playing cat and mouse with me. One of these days, he'll pounce. And wham!" I slammed my hands together. "Everything will be over." An awkward silence filled the room.

Cody squeezed my fingers. In that single action, I could feel his fear for me, his desire to take me away from all of this, to save me.

Sarah smoothed her tan slacks. “I believe Nefarious had to let your powers develop before fighting you.”

“Why?” I sat up straight, pulling my hand from Cody’s.

“I believe he has to fight a worthy opponent in order to rule the world. He could have killed you before, but it wouldn’t have fulfilled the prophecy.”

Anger burned in my stomach, setting fire to my limbs. Sparks flickered on my fingertips. I clenched my hands and fought to calm my emotions. I swallowed over the lump in my throat. “Why did you let me learn? Why didn’t you just leave me alone?”

Sarah held her hands up like she was surrendering. “I can see where this doesn’t make a lot of sense.”

“It doesn’t make a lot of sense? It doesn’t make any sense!” My voice rose, and I feared for everyone in the building.

Cody’s hand covered my wrist. His thumb traced a path on the back of my hand.

When my breathing slowed, Sarah said, “If I’d left you alone, he would’ve killed you and taken his chances with whatever came next. It’s not like there are very many people out there who could challenge him. I wanted you to have a chance.”

“A chance?” It didn’t sound like Sarah had much confidence in me either.

“I should have said something to you earlier. I’m sorry.”

“Yeah.” I let a breath out through clenched teeth.

Cody continued tracing circles on my hand. "If Nefarious attacked before, you'd've died. Training was for the best."

"Whatever." I fought back tears. I felt like they were trying to sacrifice me, and I didn't want to play the part of the lamb. Sarah shouldn't have kept this from me. It should've been my choice.

"I'm sorry, Dacia." Sarah ran her hand over her face. "I should've told you."

"You think?"

"I didn't. You already thought I was nuts when I told you about the prophecy. If I'd have told you then, you wouldn't have come back into my office ever again."

"Maybe I shouldn't have!" The books on her shelves rattled nervously. "I'm sorry that I don't like being sacrificed!"

Sarah stood in front of me. "I am not sacrificing you! I'm trying to help you save your life and the lives of everyone else on this miserable planet. If you can't see that, I'm sorry! I wanted you to stand against Nefarious and fight, not cower in some corner while he destroyed you. I guess I assumed you would want a chance."

The room filled with the silence left when words were spoken that shouldn't have been. Silence that makes you want to apologize but whispers in your ear all the reasons you shouldn't. I looked at my lap trying to avoid eye contact with Sarah. She stood in front of me with her arms folded, staring at me. I knew she was right, and that just made me madder.

Cody's words about now or never played through my mind. I swallowed my pride and said, "Sorry."

"Me too," she said.

ꝏ

I snuggled against Cody. Earlier today, I felt like his contact gave me strength. I didn't tell him what I planned because I didn't want to get his hopes up. I rested my head on his chest and focused all my energy on my leg. My skin tingled, and the burning sensation dulled.

Cody fought against a yawn, holding it in until it erupted from within him. "Sorry. I'm really tired suddenly."

"I think that might be my fault." I moved away from him. "I thought you might be able to help me heal."

"Then use me." He pulled me down.

"No, I didn't know it would hurt you."

Samantha flipped through the channels, not finding anything worth watching. "What if you used some of his energy, then tried to use some of mine?"

"I already used some of his." I scooted further away from Cody. "We'll see how he's doing in the morning."

Samantha stopped on the local news. "A winter storm is approaching," the weatherman predicted. "We could see up to twenty inches of snow in some areas over a two day period."

My heart dropped, landing with a painful thud. I was running out of time.

"We'll have more on this as the storm approaches. Stay tuned to Channel 5 for 'The Most Accurate Weather in the Area'."

"Awesome! I love snow," Cody said.

The blood drained from my face. "No, no, no," I whispered.

"Are you okay?" Samantha asked.

I shook my head. "I'm terrified." I looked into her eyes trying to convey the extent of my fear. "All of my nightmares have been snowy lately." I squeezed Cody's hand.

He pulled out of my grip and wiggled his fingers.

"Sorry," I said. "I'm not ready, and I have no idea what to do."

Samantha set the remote down. "Well, if this storm hits before next weekend, I doubt I'll be going home. I know it's not much, but I can offer you moral support."

"Yeah." We sat in silence for a moment. "Let's not dwell on this right now; it's not like weathermen are always right. Pick out a movie so we can get our minds on something else. Something funny would be nice."

The movie wouldn't work for me, but Cody and Samantha didn't need to worry about Nefarious.

Samantha and Cody argued over which movie to watch before settling on *The Princess Bride*. As soon as our supper arrived, we turned it on. I couldn't get into the movie or do more than pick at the food, but I tried. There was no reason to let them see how upset I was. About halfway through the movie, I drifted off into a tortured sleep. Either Nefarious or Cassandra waited for me around every corner. No matter what I did I couldn't get away from them.

I wasn't ready.

# Chapter 33

## Optimism And Pessimism

Wednesday morning, I awoke free from pain. I slid my feet to the ground and stood, favoring my injured leg. I allowed my full weight to fall onto it. Tight skin caused a little discomfort. My lips broke into a grin. *Yes!*

The insurmountable space between Cookie Monster and the door no longer felt oppressive. I took one tentative step after another until confident my leg wouldn't give out. Then I grabbed my bathroom bag and marched to the door.

"Where you going?" Cody stood and stretched. His shirt lifted, revealing his abs.

Heat shot through me. "To check out my leg. I think it finally healed! Look at me. I'm standing here." I used both hands to emphasize my position. "I walked here!"

"That's great, Dacia." Cody put his hands on my shoulders. "Please come right back."

"I will." I strode down the hall, my steps lightened by relief. The closer I got to the bathroom, the heavier my steps became. *What will it look like? Will I ever be able to wear shorts again?*

I sat on a bench with my hand above my leg. My fingers shook. I unwound the bandage, peeking at my leg through squinted eyes.

When the wrapping fell off, I sucked in a deep breath of air and opened my eyes. The jagged scar ran from my knee to my ankle, angry and red. I'd never be able to show it, never be able to explain what had happened. The violent scar belonged to a victim of war, not a college kid.

*At least the pain is gone.* I swiped at my eyes.

Water pelted my skin. Steam rose in the air, but I shivered. My stomach dropped, and bile rose in my throat.

*Three or four days.* I stepped out of the shower and wrapped myself in the towel. If my dreams were predictions, I only had three or four days before I fought Nefarious. *I need more time.*

I dressed and went back to my room.

"Well?" Cody asked.

I covered my lips with a finger, then pointed at Samantha sleeping in her bed. "Let's go somewhere else to talk."

He grabbed my hand and led me outside.

Normally, the crisp mountain air rejuvenated me, but today it sent my spirits even lower. "I'm going to class. I'm sick of sitting around with nothing on my mind but Nefarious."

"You're leg's better then?"

I pulled my pant leg up and showed him the hideous scar. I gave him points for not cringing.

His eyes traveled over my leg then met mine. "Wow." He squeezed my hand. "I thought it'd be worse."

"Worse?" I shook my head. "I'll never be able to let anyone see it."

"Why?" He pulled me to a bench and sat, wrapping his arm around me. "Yesterday, it was gruesome. Today it's a scar. Maybe tomorrow it'll be a memory."

I threw my legs over his and laid my head on his chest. I could always count on Cody to see the positive side. Maybe he'd be right. "How are you feeling? Did I take too much?"

"Fine." He traced my ear with his finger. "I slept like a log." His other hand ran down my side and collided with the pouch hooked on my belt. "Did you figure it out?"

"No, but I think I should keep it with me. It has to serve some purpose. But if it's not with me, I won't have it when I need it."

"Makes sense." He drew his finger down my neck, then lifted my chin. "Everything okay? You seem down. I thought you'd be happy since your leg's better."

"I was ecstatic. It felt great to walk around on my own but, when I was in the shower, I thought about my dream with Nefarious. In it, my leg was healed." My chin trembled. "I don't want it to be better before this weekend."

"You don't know it's this weekend." He brushed his thumb along my jaw. "You know it snowed and your leg had healed. You don't know if it's this weekend or next year."

My skin tingled along the path his fingers traced. "You're right. I'm not sure it's this weekend." *But I know it is.*

"Let's leave."

"What?"

Cody dropped his hand, and my skin chilled. "Let's go away before the storm hits."

I sat up. "And lead Nefarious to our homes and families." I dropped my head. "No. I can't take that chance."

Cody held me close. His hand traveled the length of my spine, up, then down, soothing, comforting. "I know you can't see it, but it'll work out."

"I know what the light at the end of the tunnel is, Cody. It's the pearly gates, and I'm not ready to see them yet." My tone left no room for argument.

"Have a little faith."

"I do. If I didn't, how would I find myself standing at the pearly gates when this is all said and done? You don't end up there without faith," I explained as I pulled away from him.

He stood up. "Please don't give up."

"I won't." I wrapped my arm around his waist, needing him closer. "But the odds are against me."

"Still going to class?"

"Yeah, I should." I inhaled deeply and straightened my shoulders. "I better keep my grades up in case you're right."

ꕥ

Even though Cody didn't have Speech with me, he insisted on walking me to my seat. The amulet warmed against my skin. *Why?* I glanced at Bryce, Alvin, and Vanessa. *Who else is possessed?*

"Watch your back." Bryce's voice sounded more like a plea than a threat.

I stared over my shoulder at him, wondering if it'd been my imagination.

Pain shot through my leg. I felt Nefarious' fiery whip tightening, burning my flesh. I clutched Cody's jacket and limped to my chair.

Cody knelt beside me and asked, "You okay?"

I sucked in an unsteady breath. "My leg feels like it's on fire again."

"I'll understand if you need to leave."

I shook my head. "No, I'm okay. I just hope it's not injured again. I don't think I can handle that." The pain subsided, and I breathed easier. "Nefarious must be controlling one of them." I lifted the chain so he knew what I meant.

Cody rubbed his forehead. "They're all possessed."

"Go to your class, Cody." I squeezed his shoulder. "I'll be fine."

When class ended, Cody stood by the door. He walked to my seat, helped me up, put his hand in the middle of my back and guided me past Bryce, Vanessa and Alvin.

I narrowed my eyes at him. "You skipped class."

He looked down at his hands and nodded. "I was worried." He tugged on one of my curls. "I didn't like the looks they gave you."

He walked with me to my next classroom. English Literature didn't start for over an hour, but it eased Cody's mind knowing I didn't have to walk here on my own.

"I'm late." Cody gave me a quick peck. "Stay here."

"I know you've heard it before, but I will."

I sat in the empty classroom and pulled out my English paper. My eyelids pulled closed. I shook my head and focused on my homework.

The lights flicker, once, twice, then die. The amulet scorches my skin, flaring too brightly for one of the Potato Heads. This is no ordinary power failure.

My heart strives to free itself from my chest. Out of the corner of my eye, I see them. Yellow eyes pierce the darkness.

"Leave me alone!"

He answers with menacing laughter.

I attempt to stand, but my arms and legs are bound to the chair. *How?* I struggle to free myself, but the harder I fight, the tighter the ropes become. I slump back. "What do you want from me?"

"Death."

I feel his words like a blow.

The ground shakes with every step Nefarious takes.

I fight to free myself, calling upon my powers. Nothing. *Please ... please, don't let him find me,* I silently pray. *Please help me out of this.* Closing my eyes I picture myself in my room.

When I open my eyes, I see an empty desk. I wiggle my fingers, nothing. *Awesome!*

His eyes reflect what little light is in the room. I watch them as he moves closer. I want to dart across the room and take cover, but I fight to stay where I am. *You're safe here. He can't see you. Don't move. Don't make a sound.*

He stands right in front of me, a ferocious roar tears from his jaws. "I know you're here. I can smell your cowardice!"

I'm afraid to breathe for fear he'll hear me.

Nefarious pushes the desks out of his way. They fly across the room and crash to the floor. He swats the chair in front of me, and the force from his massive claws cutting through the air knocks my head backward. I gasp. Another swipe and my chair flies across the room. My head collides with the wall, and everything goes black.

"Dacia," somebody in the distance called. "Dacia," the voice said again, a little closer this time. I fought to open my eyes, but they rolled back. "Dacia."

*Cody.* He grasped my shoulders and shook. The fog in my mind dispersed.

"Dacia, please wake up." Emotion choked his voice.

Sharp pain sliced through my head when I tore my eyelids apart. I squinted against the light. Everything blurred. I blinked, trying to pull things into focus. I rose up, and the room spun. I lay back, fighting off the dizziness.

Whispers joined together, becoming undecipherable. I opened my mouth to ask Cody what was going on, but cotton stuck my tongue to my teeth.

Cody swept me up and carried me toward the door. I lay limp, my head tilted way back and my arms dangling. I kept my eyes open as he carried me out. Desks were scattered helter-skelter throughout the room.

As we walked past Bryce, I heard him say, "I warned you." He rubbed his hand down his face. "I wish you'd have listened."

Cody tensed, but he kept going without acknowledging Bryce's presence.

I slipped in and out of consciousness, waking up when Cody knocked on my door.

"Just a minute," Samantha said.

"I can't wait, Sam." Cody's voice sounded frantic. "*Hurry!*"

"Just hold your horses, Cody," Samantha said. "I was still sleeping. You have a …" Her voice trailed off when she opened the door and saw Cody holding my limp body in his arms.

"I know I have a key"—his voice was hard—"but I couldn't reach it." He carried me in and placed me on the floor. "Please call Sarah, and tell her to hurry."

"No problem," Samantha said before everything went black again.

# Chapter 34

## *Washing My Hair*

Distant voices drifted across the room. I strained to open my eyelids. Sarah, Samantha, and Cody huddled by the computer, whispering.

I lay on the floor, haphazardly covered by a blanket. My head rested on a pillow. The smell of blood filled my nostrils.

I licked my lips and tried to get some moisture in my mouth. Then in a gravelly voice, I asked, "Wha … happed … to … me?" The words were hard to form, and even though I had a hard time hearing them, they heard me.

Cody rushed over. "Dacia." His voice trembled. "Thank God."

In the same raspy voice, I said, "Wa'er."

Samantha responded, “Sure, I’ll get it.” She pulled a bottle out of the fridge and brought it to me.

I pulled myself up onto my elbows. They wobbled, unable to hold my weight, and I fell back.

Cody’s hand cradled my head. He brought the bottle to my lips, but water poured down my chin onto my shirt as if I’d become a helpless child.

“Sorry.” Cody’s cheeks flushed. “I didn’t—”

“Iss kay,” I mumbled. Dark patches filled my vision, and I fought to maintain consciousness.

“Let’s try sitting her up in one of the chairs,” Sarah said.

Once again, Cody lifted me into his arms like a fragile doll. He sat down in Cookie Monster and held me on his lap. His hand ran up my arm, and I wondered if he was trying to soothe me or himself.

“Take my energy.” Cody’s words tickled my ear. “Heal yourself.”

“Can’t.” I couldn’t focus enough to use my powers. “Might hurt you.”

“Please, Dacia.” His eyes glistened.

“Would you like to try another drink?” Sarah asked.

I nodded.

Sarah held the bottle to my lips, and I ended up with more in my mouth than on my clothes. The water helped clear my head somewhat. Details were fuzzy, but this morning’s events swam into focus.

“You had us pretty scared.” Samantha’s voice was tight.

“Dacia”—Sarah’s voice softened—“do you know what happened?”

I touched the back of my head. Blood stuck my hair together, but I didn't feel a cut or scab. I looked to where I'd been lying. Blood soaked the pillow I'd been laying on. My heart dropped to my stomach. *How am I going to survive?*

"More water first."

Sarah moved to help me, but I stuck my hand up.

"I'll do it."

She handed me the bottle, and with shaking hands, I held it to my mouth.

I stared at the bloody pillow. "I promised Cody I'd wait for him, and I did. I was working on my homework when the power went out."

"Dacia, dear," Sarah said, "the power didn't go out on campus today."

"Whatever," I said. "The lights were out in …" my voice trailed off as it dawned on me what had most likely happened. "Oh … a dream."

"That makes sense," Cody said.

"Why?" I asked.

"Chairs and desks were thrown everywhere, like a tornado hit." He squirmed. "I thought you left until I saw blood splattered on the wall."

I rubbed my hand along his side, a reminder I was okay.

"You wouldn't wake up. You didn't move." He brushed his hand across his eyes. "I carried you here, but you lost consciousness again. Samantha and I didn't think you were breathing …" His voice trailed off, and he wiped his eyes again. "I thought I lost you." He squeezed me against him.

"I'm here." My words were only for him.

"I can't …" He shook his head. "I can't lose you."

*You might.*

"It had to be a dream. If it wasn't, Nefarious would've ki—" his voice broke, and he cleared his throat "—finished you off."

I wrapped my arms around him. "I'm okay." *For now.* While I told them about my dream, Cody held me. Eventually, his hands quit shaking.

"That's all I remember. I don't remember Cody carrying me or any of that … maybe with time. I would much rather remember my knight-in-shining-armor coming to my rescue than the horrific beast trying to kill me."

"That's understandable," Sarah said.

"How are you feeling now, Dacia?" Samantha asked.

I rubbed my hand over my forehead. "Stronger than when I first woke up. I think I might even be able to move on my own now."

"Great," Sarah said. "We didn't know how your body would handle any new injuries—if you would heal right away or if it would be more like your leg."

"I think my leg took longer to heal because that actually happened to me, so since my leg is getting better … if that is the case … I think my head will heal faster."

"Take my strength." Cody's words sounded demanding, but his voice held a plea.

I cupped his cheek. "No. I'm getting better on my own." I wrinkled my nose. "I need to wash my hair. The smell is making me nauseous."

"I can help you with your hair if you need me to," Samantha said.

Sarah glanced at her watch. "If you're helping her, I'll excuse myself."

After Sarah left, I said, "I think I'll wash it here in our sink. That way I don't have to walk down the hall like this. I'm sure I've been the subject of enough conversations for one day."

"Yeah." Cody rubbed his neck. "People were talking before I made it to the door."

"Bryce was there, wasn't he?" I asked.

"Yeah," Cody said. "Why?"

"I think I remember him saying something when you carried me out." I tried to focus my thoughts and remember what he said. "When you made that comment about people talking, it started to come back to me."

Cody's eyes turned cold. "He said he warned you to watch your back."

"But why?"

"He wanted to gloat," Cody said.

"Gloat about what? He didn't make me fall asleep or give me nightmares. It doesn't make sense." I tried to figure out what he meant. When I saw the looks on Cody's and Samantha's faces, I added, "My head's still foggy. I'm probably not thinking right." The last thing I wanted right now was to get into an argument with them. "Help me up, please."

Cody stood with me in his arms and slowly lowered me to the ground. My legs wobbled. Even with him holding onto me, I almost fell twice when my knees buckled.

Samantha washed my hair for me while I clung to the sink. When she was lathering my hair for the third time, she said, "Oh, I forgot. The body shop called. Your truck will be ready for you to pick up tomorrow."

"Thanks." I never expected to get it back. I didn't think anybody would be willing to drive me to pick it up for fear that I would take off in it again.

When Cody helped me back to my chair, I thought I remembered something else. "Did you say something about having a key to my room?"

"Yeah."

"When did you get one?"

"Right after we talked about it. Sarah told Samantha to have one made right away. She thought it was a good idea."

"Well, you almost got to use it."

"I'm going to take a shower." Samantha looked at the clock. "I should be able to make it to Writing."

Cody left soon after, wanting to change out of his bloodstained clothes. I sat in Cookie Monster and stared at the blank TV screen.

*Is Bryce possessed?* I closed my eyes and pictured Cody carrying me past Bryce. *Was the amulet glowing?*

# Chapter 35

## Back To Class

"Dacia." Cody shook my shoulder. "You're late."

I pulled the blanket over my head. For the first time since Saturday, I slept in my bed. I didn't remember dreaming, and I wasn't ready to get up yet.

"Skipping class?"

"You should go," Samantha said. "You missed Tuesday."

"Just five more minutes."

"If you're going, you need to get up," Cody said. "Class starts in twenty minutes."

Grudgingly, I pulled the blanket back and sat up. Even though I felt better, I still had Cody help me out of the loft.

On the way to algebra, Cody said, "Althea after class? We can eat lunch. Then I'll take you to pick up your truck."

I jerked my head back and stopped walking. "Really? You want to take me to get my truck?"

"Yeah, that's what he said," Samantha answered. "I can drive one of them if you don't want to."

"Oh, wow. I, uh"—I pulled my fingers through my hair—"I didn't think anybody would want me to have it. I thought you'd be scared I'd take off again."

Cody shrugged. "Well, if you don't want it—"

"No. I want it." I hitched my backpack up onto my shoulder. "I didn't think I'd ever see my baby again."

"What do you mean by that?" Samantha asked.

"I didn't think you guys would take me to pick it up until after the prophecy's taken care of—" I fidgeted with the straps "—and I don't think I'll be around after that."

Cody closed his eyes and pulled his hand down his face. "Please, stop talking like that."

"Sorry, Cody. I'm trying to prepare you." I kicked at the ground. "I'm not going to win."

Samantha stood with her hands on her hips. "Dacia, Cody's right. You have to stop thinking like that, or you won't walk away from this. You need to have faith in yourself. Instead of giving up, maybe you should do something to figure out how to defeat him."

"Like what?" I threw my hands up in the air. "I've been going to lessons, reading the journals over and over again, and trying to figure out what to do, what the vase is for. What else am I supposed to do?" I yanked a shaking hand through my hair. "If you have any ideas, I'd love to hear them."

"Why don't we search some mythology books?" She tugged on her bottom lip. "There may be a solution buried in one. Now that we've seen fairies and know of the existence of other magical creatures, I wonder if some of those books are nonfiction."

"It's worth a try." I lifted my shoulder. "When we get back from Althea, maybe we could go to the library."

"I have class this afternoon," Samantha said. "But after …"

"I'll go with you." Cody rubbed my neck. "Maybe something will give you hope. I hate seeing you so defeated."

The idea of finding something to help me raised my spirits. *Amazing what a little hope can do.*

My leg bounced up and down all through class. *I get my truck back.* I squeezed Cody's knee, bringing an amused smile to his face.

The amulet warmed my skin, but I didn't spare the Potato Heads a glance. *Hope lives even in the darkest realms.* I don't know why the inscription from the vase ran through my thoughts. *But this is going to take more than hope.*

When class ended, the three of us piled into Cody's car. "The Avalanche first," Cody said. "After we eat, we'll get your truck. Then we won't have two vehicles the whole time. Okay?"

"Fine by me," I told them. "How about you, Sam?"

"Yeah, sounds good. Cody's driving. He's the boss. Besides, when hasn't he wanted food first?"

"Ouch." He covered his heart with his hand and winced. "Be nice."

We laughed and joked most of the way to Althea, but when Cody drove past the scene of my wreck, I grabbed the dash. *Yellow eyes in the road. Spinning out of control. Bouncing down the hill. Crashing into the tree. Darkness.* I gasped. Terror fisted in my throat, blocking the air. I bent over, clutching my neck and sucking in breaths.

"Dacia"—Samantha's voice was high and fast—"are you okay?"

The car came to a stop, and Cody slammed it into park. He rubbed my back. "Breathe." His voice was soft, soothing. "You're okay."

I kept my head bowed. "It seems like an eternity ago, but when we drove by, it felt like it was happening again."

Cody's hand slid down my arm. "Okay now?"

I nodded and sat up, staring out the window. "You can go." *Why hadn't Nefarious killed me that night? Did he plan to torment me forever?*

Cody parked on the street in front of The Avalanche. He held my hand as we walked in. We sat in a booth. I snuggled up to Cody, and Samantha sat across from us.

I ordered a chicken sandwich and fries, Cody ordered a steak dinner, and Samantha was a good girl and ordered a Caesar Salad. We tried to keep the conversation light. For the most part, it worked. A couple times thoughts of Nefarious slipped into my mind, but I pushed them away.

When we finished, we went to Sycamore's Auto Repair. I felt like a kid at Christmastime when I saw my truck sitting in the parking lot. It looked so nice with its fresh coat of wax. As soon as Cody came to a stop, I hopped out.

I peered in the window. *An orange glow on the horizon. Blood on the steering wheel and dash.* I shook my head, but the image stayed.

I handed Samantha my keys. "Will you drive it back?"

"Are you sure, Dacia?" Her eyebrows furrowed in confusion.

"Yeah, I don't want to drive right now."

"But you were so excited."

I sighed. "I know. I'm afraid to drive it. Too many things have happened lately." I ran my hand over the hood, wondering if I'd ever feel like driving it again. "At least it'll be back on campus in case I need it."

"Are you sure you don't want to drive it? I'll ride back with you."

"Why not?" Cody hooked his thumbs in his belt loops. "Cowboy up. Don't get behind the wheel, and you never will."

I snatched my keys from Samantha and climbed in. *I drove the day I wrecked my truck. Don't they remember?* I clenched my hands on the wheel, waiting for Samantha. Tears welled up in my eyes, but I refused to cry.

Cody leaned through the window. "I'll follow you. Be careful."

I nodded, and as soon as Samantha got in, I eased onto Main Street.

"Are you okay, Dacia?"

"Not really." I clamped my jaw shut and willed the tears out of my voice. "You guys don't understand. I'm not afraid of driving. I'm afraid of driving while Nefarious is hunting me and while he's still haunting my dreams. I never know when he'll show up … like he did last time I drove my truck."

"Why didn't you just say that?"

"I tried to." I loosened my grip on the steering wheel, flexing my fingers. "But it's not easy to constantly vocalize your fears, you know. Most people keep them hidden from everyone else. Every day, I have to tell someone I'm afraid of something."

"I'm sorry, Dacia." The lines around her eyes deepened. "If you want me to drive the rest of the way, just pull over, and I will."

"No, I'm already driving. If I pull over, Cody will think something's wrong."

A thick pine forest surrounded the winding road. My eyes darted from side to side. I expected Nefarious to strike. *Can I keep Samantha safe if he does?* I turned the radio up to drown out my thoughts.

When I pulled into the parking lot, I pried my fingers off the steering wheel. Blood flowed into them, bringing with it a tingling sensation.

Cody parked next to me. When we got out, he said, "You did fine."

Samantha didn't give me a chance to comment. "Cody, Dacia isn't afraid of driving. She's afraid of driving with Nefarious on the loose. And if we were in her position, we would be, too." She turned to me. "Now I've got to get to class, but I'll help you research later."

"Okay, thanks."

"Sorry." Cody grabbed my hand. "I thought you were scared."

"Don't worry about it. It's water under the bridge." I didn't want to dwell on it or be upset about it. Right now I needed my friends on my side. I didn't need them to be scared to say things to me. "Should we go to the library now?"

"Yeah, let's see what we can find."

We sat at a table in the corner. Stacks of mythology books surrounded us. We started with some that didn't seem too unrealistic, flipping through the pages, hoping for a miracle.

Samantha joined us after her class. "Find anything?"

"No," both Cody and I replied.

At 9:50, I slammed shut the last of the books in my stack. "In all of the books I have looked through, I haven't found anything helpful about defeating demons, but I learned tons about jinni, some fascinating stuff actually. I also read about unicorns, Pegasus, manticores, and oodles of other creatures. Either nobody has ever defeated a balor demon without a magical sword or nobody has recorded it."

"I didn't find anything in any of these books either." Cody waved his hand at a stack on the floor beside him. "What about you, Sam?"

"Nothing. I've gone cross-eyed from staring at these." She gathered books. "We should get going."

Cody sat quietly for a moment. "The last champion defeated Nefarious, so it had to have been recorded."

"Right," I agreed.

"You'd think one of his friends would've written something about him, made him into a hero or a god. You'd think they'd have tried to immortalize him somehow," Samantha said, finishing Cody's thought.

"Maybe a ballad," Cody said.

I stacked my books on a cart. "Nefarious probably destroyed his friends. He's tried to get mine, and this isn't over yet."

"Don't remind me." Samantha shuddered. "He's tried with Cody and Sarah … I keep wondering when it will be my turn."

ଌ

A thick blanket of snow covers the ground. As I walk to my painting class, a chill tiptoes up my spine. Every noise I hear, every shadow I pass fills me with a sense of dread. Adrenaline pulses through my veins. I'm ready to run at a moment's notice.

*It's just your imagination.*

But my gut says it's more than that, worse than that.

When I arrive at the bridge, I hesitate. *Don't be an idiot, Dacia. It was just a stupid dream.* I want to turn back but convince myself I need to face my fears.

I take a deep breath and step onto the bridge. When I'm halfway across, I see the ground on the other side. Tears well in my eyes at the sight of the melted snow. I turn and sprint.

"Surrender!" Nefarious roars, and I know what happens next.

Everything takes place just like in my dream: the force field, the crack of Nefarious' whip and the fireball.

The ball of flames whizzes toward me. There's no way for me to stop it. I close my eyes and will myself back to my room.

When I opened them again, I lay in bed. The amulet was dimming.

# Chapter 36

## *A Little Faith*

When Cody and I stepped into the speech room, heads turned in our direction. Hushed voices filled the room like a silent scream. Since several of the students in here were also in my English Literature class, the topic was obvious: Wednesday's incident.

*Why didn't I skip?* Lowering my head, I walked to my desk. I wasn't in the mood to deal with people.

"You okay?" Cody asked.

"Fine." The word came out angrier than intended. I grabbed his hand. "Just hurry back after your class. If I'm alone, it'll be easier for everyone to pester me."

"I will." He brushed a kiss across my lips—sending heat flaring through me—and left.

I did my best to ignore the other students, but after class, a couple of girls I didn't know came up to me. One with earrings that could double as fishing lures asked, "What happened Wednesday?"

"Yeah," the other said in a high-pitched voice, "weird things always happen to you."

I wanted to tell them to mind their own business and leave me alone. Instead, I took a deep breath. "I don't know what happened. I was studying, the power went out, and the next thing I remember Cody carried me out of the room."

"Wow," the first one said. Her earrings bobbed, drawing my attention. "There was blood all over. I'm surprised you're here today."

Cody walked in and flashed them a charming grin. "Excuse us. We have to get to class." He grabbed my elbow and led me out.

We walked outside, and Cody backed me up against the building. "If you want to skip, we can." He braced his hands against the building, one on either side of my shoulders. "Maybe by Monday, Wednesday will be forgotten."

I put my palms on his chest. He closed his eyes and sucked in a breath. "That's the best thing I've heard in a long time." I stepped closer, and he folded me into his arms. "I haven't set anybody's books on fire for a while, and that's the last thing I need today."

Cody slipped his arm around my waist and turned me toward the dorms. "You know, it's a beautiful day, one of the last ones for a while. You wanna go to the lake?"

Tension released from my shoulders. "A change of scenery would be nice."

We turned onto the path toward Falcon Lake. If the storm came as predicted, today might be my last day to spend with Cody like this. "Could you do me a favor?"

"Anything."

"Let's not talk about the weather today."

He squeezed my hand in his. "Sure, Dacia."

Falcon Lake was all but deserted when we got there. Cody and I strolled along in comfortable silence, enjoying each other's company. When we walked past the playground, I said, "Let's swing. I haven't done that for so long."

While my swing swayed from side to side, I stared at the mountains beyond the lake. Most of the trees had lost their leaves. The scent of pine filled my nose when the breeze blew. "I love it here. The mountains are so peaceful, beautiful."

"Yeah, they are." Cody jumped off his swing and reached his hand down to me.

I let him help me up, even though I wasn't ready to leave. Once I was standing, he wrapped his arm around my waist and walked me to Sarah's office for my lesson.

"Hello, Dacia, Cody." She turned her back on us and walked to the couches. "How are you doing today?"

"Better after skipping," I answered.

"Skipping?" She turned back, her eyes scanning me. "You're not injured again, are you?"

"No." I tugged my hand through red curls. "I wasn't coping, so Cody took me to Falcon Lake."

Her lips pinched together. “It was a beautiful day for it, but your studies need to be a priority.”

*A priority? A demon’s going to kill me in a couple days. Who cares about my grades?*

Cody traced a pattern on my arm.

*He knows what I’m thinking.*

“Have a seat.” Sarah pointed at the couch.

“Well … actually, we were thinking about going to the library.” I told her about Samantha’s theory.

“Are there more books?”

“Yes, tons,” Cody said.

“Maybe your time would be better spent there. I can arrange for the library to stay open late for you. ” Sarah smoothed the creases in her slacks. “Are you okay, Dacia?”

With my head in my hands, I said, “I don’t think it was supposed to be me. I don’t know what I’m doing.”

Sarah set her jaw. “This is a battle you can win.”

“I—”

She stuck her hand up. “Let me say what I have to say. Nefarious is evil, cruel, and monstrous. You are good, compassionate, and loyal. Perfect to defeat him. Who better to stop him than his exact opposite? Where he has hate, you have love. Where he has arrogance, you have humbleness. You just need a little faith.”

I looked down at my shoes. “I’m trying.”

On our way to the library, Cody asked, “Do you ever think about how fate brought you here … where Sarah could help you?”

"Not for a while"—I shook my head—"but I guess someone was watching out for me. If I hadn't met Sarah, I doubt I would've lasted this long. Maybe you and Sarah are right. Maybe I just need some faith." My lips parted slightly. *Could I have been put here to meet Sarah? Does that mean I have a chance of beating Nefarious?* My spirits lifted, but at the same time, my chest tightened. *Can I live up to their expectations?*

Cody put his arm around my shoulders and held me close to his side. "A little faith would do you a lot of good."

ᘓ

As the evening wore on, the sky darkened and the wind howled. I pushed my book forward and laid my head on the table. A great, gaping hole opened inside me, hollowing me out, leaving me empty.

We'd searched through books for four hours and had nothing to show for it. About halfway through, Samantha put her books down and searched the internet. "There's quite a bit about killing balor demons in games, but none of it is helpful in the real world unless you can find a magical sword."

"No magical swords. Just an amulet and a vase." I picked up my books and put them on the cart. "I'm done."

Cody pulled my fingers into his on the way out. His thumb caressed my hand, but the hollowness grew.

The wind tore through my jacket, nipping at my skin. Leaves blew across the sidewalks, and the bare trees added to the eerie feeling that held me in its clutches.

The warmth of our room did nothing to dispel the cold that had settled inside me. I wrapped a blanket around my shoulders and looked out the window. Wind rattled the frames, sneaking in through tiny cracks.

Something moved under the trees, just out of reach of the streetlights. An ominous prickle slid down my spine.

Cody put his hands on my shoulders. "You okay? You haven't eaten, and you've barely said a word."

"Something's out there." I pointed, and my finger shook.

He wrapped his arms around me and rested his chin on the top of my head. "I don't see anything."

My eyes blurred, forcing me to blink. "I'm scared."

"I know." He turned me around, lifting my chin so our eyes met. "It's going to work out."

I could see that he believed it. *I wish I did.*

ꕥ

Whatever I had spotted in the shadows is still there. I can't see it, but I can feel its presence, watching, waiting.

I climb out of my loft, change into my clothes and walk into the hall. Just as I shut the door, I hear Samantha say, "Dacia?"

I don't care. I'm on a mission.

Our door closes, someone runs down the hall. "Dacia, please don't go anywhere alone," Samantha begs.

I throw my hand up. "You're with me." I hustle down the stairs. "Something's been watching our window all night. I just want to scare it off."

"Come back to our room. We're safe there."

"I can't. I have to make it leave."

"Fine, I'll go out with you. But then, please come back in."

"I will. I'm just going to throw something at it to see if it will go away." I open the door and pull several rocks out of the landscape. One-by-one I throw them into the darkness. There's no movement, so I grab a few more. The amulet warms against my skin, and Samantha screams. I jerk my head up. Nefarious.

"Get inside!" I say.

Nefarious' whip flies through the air, wrapping around Samantha's legs. He tugs her toward him.

"Dacia! Help me!" Samantha's terrified screams tear through me.

"She can't help you," the evil voice growls. "She can't even help herself."

"Let go of her! It's me you want!"

His laughter echoes, covering Samantha's cries for help. "I want death. Destruction. Menace. Chaos."

I throw the rocks down and charge after him. A stream of ice flows from my fingertips as I rush to save Samantha.

Nefarious erupts into an inferno. Red flames leap from his skin. He pulls Samantha from the ground and holds her in his blazing hands.

Samantha screams. The sound fills all the hollow places in my body, ricocheting through me, tearing me apart. The silence that follows shatters my soul.

"No!" I feel like my heart's been ripped from my chest.

"You delivered her to me. Only two left, then I'll take care of you." He soars into the night leaving Samantha's lifeless body behind.

I run over and fall to the ground beside her. Hoping to save her life like I had Sarah's, I grab her blistered hand and will her to live, to heal.

*If I'd stayed in our room, she'd be fine. I'm destroying the people I love most.*

"Samantha," I cry, "please wake up. Don't leave me." I close my eyes and pray for her to pull through.

"Dacia," Samantha says.

I open my eyes. Samantha still lies lifeless in my arms.

"Dacia, wake up!"

I opened my eyes and threw my arms around Samantha. "Thank God."

Cody looked up, his eyes shadowed by fear.

"I thought you were dead, Samantha."

"Not dead—" she yawned "—just trying to sleep. Are you okay?"

"I'm fine, but if I leave in the middle of the night, don't follow me!"

"Why?"

"Because I don't want you to die."

# Chapter 37

## The Time Has Come

Thick, heavy clouds rolled over the mountains, swaddling the sky in darkness. Wind whipped through the trees. Branches creaked and groaned. Leaves dropped to the ground, where they whirled and danced across campus, piling against buildings. Cold air crept into my room, whining through the windowsills.

A tight fist clamped down on my heart. *It's coming. I'm not ready.* My breath came in harsh, shallow gasps. Standing on shaky legs, I clutched my chest with one hand and braced myself against the wall with the other.

A knock on the door sent my heart racing. I searched for a way out. The desire to flee overwhelmed me.

"Dacia." Cody's voice morphed into Nefarious'.

The room shrunk around me until I felt like a caged animal. I pressed myself into the corner and sank to the floor, wrapping my arms around my knees. The room closed in, suffocating me.

The door opened. I pushed further into the corner, closed my eyes and covered my ears. *I can't do this. I can't even breathe.*

Arms wrapped around me, and I struck out at them. My eyes opened with a jolt. Cody knelt in front of me, holding my wrists.

"Breathe, Dacia." His voice sounded distant. "Breathe." He repeated the words over and over.

I focused on his voice, on breathing. The room returned to its normal size. Everything sharpened, losing the blurry edges.

Cody lifted his hand to my cheek. "Better?"

I pointed at Samantha still sleeping and put a finger over my lips. I stood up, and my legs felt shaky and weak. I grabbed my coat and struggled to put my arms in the sleeves. Cody took it from me and held it out. I pulled it around me, trying to disappear into it.

In the hall, Cody moved in front of me, his eyes softened with worry.

He needed an answer. *I can't do this right now.* I shrugged and shook my head.

He wrapped his arm around my shoulders and led me outside.

Crisp, cool air caressed my skin and sent a shiver down my neck. I pulled my coat tighter around me. *So much for yesterday's warmth.* The cold seeped into my body, filling the void left behind by my nightmare.

Cody pulled me tightly against his side and rubbed my arm. “What do you want to do after your lesson?”

“I should read the journal or look through more books.” I snuggled against him for warmth. “I’m running out of time, and I don’t know how to win.”

“Maybe it won’t snow.”

*It will.* I shoved my hand into my pocket. “Maybe.” *Nefarious is going to end this. Soon.*

I sat on the couch in Sarah’s office, wondering why I’d bothered showing up. Sarah couldn’t teach me anything else. She was just as lost as me. Neither of us had any ideas to help me defeat Nefarious. The longer I sat there, the more I felt on the verge of another panic attack.

By the time Cody and I left, I couldn’t remember anything Sarah had said. I clutched Cody’s hand and debated borrowing some of his strength.

*You delivered her to me. Only two left, then I’ll take care of you.* The words reverberated against my skull, growing louder with each repetition. *Will he follow through?*

“Dacia.” Cody stopped walking and waved his hand in front of my face. “You’re out of it. Are you okay?”

“Yeah … no … I guess.” I pulled my hand through my hair.

“If I’m supposed to choose, I choose no.” Cody tucked a stray curl behind my ear. “You don’t seem okay. I can’t help you if you don’t tell me what’s going on.”

I hesitated.

“You don’t have to … but, I want to help.” He moved his hands to my shoulders. “Please let me in.”

"Last night's dream is freaking me out." I grabbed hold of Cody's arms for support. "Nefarious killed Samantha and told me he's going after you and Sarah before coming for me. I can't do this. I can't lose you guys!" Tears flooded my eyes, and my lips quivered. I buried my head in his chest.

Cody wrapped his arms around me while I tried to control my trembling. He whispered over and over again in my ear, "It's going to be okay. Everything's going to be all right. Dacia, I love you."

His voice comforted me. I took my gloves off and lifted my hands to his neck. Looking into his blue eyes, I said, "I need to take some of your strength … not too much. Can I?"

He pressed his hands down on mine. "Take it. Take it all."

I pulled his mouth down on mine, and while he kissed me, I siphoned his strength. The kiss warmed me, and his life force energized me.

With his arm wrapped around my shoulders, we went back to the dorm.

"Hello," Cody said to Samantha when we walked in. "How you doing?"

"All right, I guess." Her voice shook.

"I'm sorry about last night," I said.

"It's not your fault."

I grabbed the journal and a blanket then sat down in Cookie Monster.

"Why are you looking at that again?" Samantha asked. "You've gone through it a hundred times."

"Well, maybe it's gonna take a hundred and one." My voice had a hard edge. I closed my eyes and reminded myself I shouldn't take this out on my friends. "I have to find some way to beat Nefarious, and I don't have any other ideas."

Samantha's smile was apologetic. "I don't think you're going to find any answers in there."

"Then what do you suggest? I'm out of time and hope."

Cody rubbed my shoulders. "Why are you so sure it's this weekend?"

"Before Nefarious killed Sarah, I had an ominous feeling."

"Yeah?" Samantha said.

"I have it again now. With every passing moment, I'm more convinced something's going to happen in the next couple of days."

"Let's hope you're wrong," Cody said.

ꝏ

Snowflakes spun through the air. Leaping and dancing as they billowed across the sky. Coating the ground, collecting in piles. Before blowing up into the air again, drifting across the sidewalks and roads.

My heart sank further with each flake that floated to the ground. Tiny, crystallized reminders that I didn't know how to defeat Nefarious.

I pulled my boots on, then walked to the door. I reached for my coat. *What are you doing?* I jerked my hand back and tucked it into my pocket. *You can't go out there.* I sat in Cookie Monster and focused on Cody. He looked peaceful in sleep. The lines of tension no longer marred his face.

I took my boots off. *What had I been thinking? Why would I go out in this storm?* I tugged my hand through my hair. I couldn't deny the pull to leave.

I knelt by Cody's chair. "Cody." My voice was soft.

He jolted awake. "What?"

"I—" I looked up at the ceiling "—I want to go outside. It's all I can think about. I don't know if I can keep fighting it."

He reached for me, and I climbed onto his lap, curling into his arms like a child. He brushed my hair back and gently rocked the chair.

"Dacia, I want you to take my strength … all you can." His voice was sure and steady. "Take it all."

I shook my head against his chest. "I can't."

"You have to." Cody traced his hand down my arm. "If tonight's the night, take whatever you can so you can make it back to me."

My resolve cracked. "What if I hurt you … take too much?"

"You won't."

I slipped my hand under his shirt.

A startled gasp escaped his lips. He squeezed my shoulder, pulling me closer to him.

His skin was cool and soft. I ran my hand over his abs and around to his back. I slipped my other hand under his shirt. "You're sure?"

His voice was husky. "Please."

I pulled Cody's strength into me. His eyelids drooped, and I yanked my hands away.

"No, Dacia." He held my hand against his face. "You need it more than me."

When Cody fell asleep, I lowered my hand and snuggled against him. The urge to go outside tugged at me, but this time the call was easier to ignore.

The storm raged. Howling winds rattled the window. The longing to go outside became incessant. I put earbuds in and cranked the music. The desire to leave didn't lessen. It tugged at my limbs, pulling me toward the door. When I didn't heed it, I felt its draw intensify.

*Why not go?*

I shook my head, fighting the hold on me.

*Just one step. Just outside the door. Just one.*

I pulled my boots on, then grabbed my coat on the way out the door.

*Just a breath of fresh air, and I'll go back.*

I stood outside. Snowflakes stuck to my eyelashes and accumulated in my hair. The relentless call urged me to take another step, then another. *This way. One more.*

Wind-tossed the snow through the air, lifting it from the ground and covering my tracks. I spun in a circle. The dorms disappeared behind a billowing curtain.

*How did I get so far? I only took a couple steps.*

The amulet warmed against my skin. *No, no, no. This can't be happening.* I stumbled through the knee-deep snow.

"Lovely night for a stroll." Cassandra's voice was the same monotone as last time I'd seen her.

"Yes," I said, hoping I could figure something out. "I love the snow."

"I just love that you're out here alone." She lunged, catching me off guard. She drove her shoulder into my chest.

I hit the ground and gasped.

"My Lord will reward me for bringing you to him." She wrapped her hands around my neck.

The air fled from my lungs, and my body weakened.

"You look scared. You should be. This time you won't get away."

Darkness engulfed me.

I woke up dizzy and weak. Cassandra held my feet and dragged me. Snow piled on top of my body. The winds carried it away only to replace it moments later. My coat filled with snow, and my back numbed. But that was nothing compared to the icy dread that filled me.

"No, Cassandra, please … please don't take me there again." My voice hitched. I kicked, but my legs didn't respond. Spots danced before my eyes. *Breathe.* "How?"

Cassandra turned and kicked me in the knee. "Enough."

I tried to grab my knee, but my arms trailed through the snow, unmoving. Tears slid down my cheeks, leaving icy trails.

I strained my ears, listening for the sound of anyone approaching but heard nothing. As Cassandra dragged me through the snow, I remembered that after waking up from my dream last night I told Samantha not to follow me if she saw me leave the room and wondered if that was part of Nefarious' plan.

"Nobody is going to save you this time, Dacia," Cassandra said. "It's over!"

*She's right. I need to save myself.* I called on all my strength, then sent it at Cassandra's hands.

She glanced at me and laughed. "Your powers are useless."

I closed my eyes and pictured Cody sleeping in Big Bird, his blond hair sticking up every which way, his face peaceful, stubble covering his chin and cheeks. I willed myself into that scene.

My eyes opened to find the cave entrance looming in front of us. "Please, Cassandra."

She kicked me, harder this time, then brought her finger to her lips. "Quiet."

Torches hung at the mouth of the cave and lit the path. Cassandra stepped inside, leaving the storm behind us.

Rocks littered the trail, digging into my back and head, chipping away at my icy flesh. Cassandra dragged me deeper into the mountain than I'd been before.

Warmth spread across my back, sticking my shirt to my shoulder blades. *Too much blood.* My eyelids drooped, and the cavern spun. *At least death will come quickly.*

Cassandra stopped in a large cavern where torches hung from the rock walls casting long, creepy shadows. She dropped my legs and knelt down beside me.

"My Lord will be here for you soon. It should've ended last time you were here. This time, you won't be so lucky." She grabbed me under my arms, lifted me into a sitting position and pulled me over to a stalagmite, where she tied me to the rock pillar.

"What's this?" she asked, pulling the pouch off my jeans. Without giving it a second thought, she tossed it aside, then left. Absolute darkness filled the cavern.

Blood dripped from my head and back. My eyes grew heavy. I blinked, and lights appeared at the corner of my vision, drifting ever closer. They landed on me.

Tiny silver-haired fairies covered my body, bringing a surge of happiness with them. Strength returned to my limbs.

"Thank you," I said.

One flew in front of my eyes. In a screechy voice, she said, "Evil must not prevail."

I stared into tiny purple eyes. "I know, but how can I win?"

"The power is within you." The fairies scattered, leaving the room in utter darkness.

I held the rope and filled my palm with flames. Singed strands fell to the ground. I lifted my hand and willed the fire to burn brighter.

The vase reflected light back to me. I walked to it and reached down. The amulet burned my skin. *Grab the vase and teleport back to Cody.* I threw the fireball across the room. "No, this ends tonight. One way or another."

I pulled the glowing amulet from under my shirt. The exit beckoned me. I turned my back on it and walked deeper into the mountain. The passage sloped down. Scree cluttered the path, making the footing treacherous.

The ground trembled, and rocks slid in front of me. The amulet brightened further.

I positioned myself in the shadows and tucked the amulet inside my shirt. I waited for Nefarious to approach, hoping to benefit from a surprise attack.

Tremors started in my hands and spread throughout my body. I bit my cheek, holding in a scream. Thoughts poured into my head. *Run. Find help. Surrender. Show yourself.*

Shivers ran up my spine. The cavern wasn't too far away. I could make it.

*No!* Sweat beaded on my forehead as I resisted the urge to flee. The suggestions weren't mine. Nefarious planted them in my head because he wanted me to show myself.

The passageway lit up. Nefarious smoldered like the embers of a dying fire, flickering from red to orange to black.

I stayed hidden, waiting for a clear shot at him. *You can do this.* I jumped out.

A stream of ice flowed from my fingertips. I ran backward up the path. Nefarious roared and threw a fireball at me. A stalagmite stood to my left. Without knowing what was on the other side, I ran straight through it, narrowly avoiding the flames.

"Fight me!" Nefarious demanded.

I pictured myself standing further up the path and was transported there. I shot two lightning bolts at Nefarious. They hit him in his chest, sending him stumbling backward. While he fought to regain his balance, I covered the pathway in a thin sheet of ice and teleported further away.

Positioning myself in the shadows, I waited for Nefarious. The earth shook, and I fell to the ground. Nefarious roared, and

I realized he had slipped on the ice and fallen. I scrambled to my feet.

I positioned myself to strike. I counted to five and jumped out. A lightning bolt shot from each of my hands. As they struck him, I covered the trail in ice and teleported.

I didn't make it as far as intended. My breath came out in ragged gasps. Black dotted my vision. *I can't keep this up. I don't even know if it's working.* I closed my eyes and breathed in, filling my lungs completely before exhaling.

I sprang forward, and a stream of ice flowed from both hands. It sizzled and steam filled the air.

Nefarious threw his head back and roared.

I clasped my hands over my ears and lowered my head.

A fireball burst through the air. I threw my hands out. Ice collided with the flames, fighting for dominance.

The frost-covered inferno struck me in the chest and shattered, knocking me to the ground. Flames engulfed my coat. By the time I extinguished them, Nefarious closed the gap.

He lifted me into the air. "Your friends are next." He threw me at the cavern wall.

I flew toward Nefarious, lessening the impact. Then I scrambled to my feet and ran.

"Stand and fight!" Nefarious roared.

The familiar crack of his whip tightened my muscles. The fiery whip struck me in the middle of the back. I screamed as I fell to my knees. The whip raced through the air again. I rolled to the side, but the whip entangled my right leg just below the knee.

The cave reeked of burnt flesh. My burnt flesh. Bile rose into my throat, and I heaved.

Nefarious dragged me toward him. Rocks gouged my legs and arms. I rolled onto my back and shot ice at my leg.

"Give up. It's over." Rocks fell from the ceiling in reply.

"I know," I whispered.

I pictured the stalagmite Cassandra had tied me to and teleported into that cavern. The room spun out of focus and breathing took all my concentration. My eyes closed, and my body numbed. The sounds in the cavern faded.

*Am I dying? Can I die?*

The spinning slowed enough for me to assess my injuries. Where the whip had wrapped around my leg, the flesh was torn away, exposing my muscles, and in some places, it had burned down to the bones.

*Not again.*

The palms of my hands were covered with blood. I pulled my coat off and ripped scorched pieces of cloth from it to use as bandages, then wrapped my leg. My back throbbed, but I could only guess how bad it was.

I had a little time to heal before Nefarious found me, but if I didn't come up with a plan, this wouldn't end well for me or the rest of the world.

*Lord, I know I haven't always done things your way. I know I'm not perfect, but please protect my friends when I'm no longer here. And, please don't make me suffer too much.*

I dragged myself to the vase. I picked it up, but I wasn't filled with hope like the first time I'd seen it. This time, determination fired through my body.

*I can do this.*

I yanked on the stopper, but slickened with blood, it wouldn't budge. I wrapped my shirt around it and, wincing in pain, managed to pull it out.

Purple smoke streamed from the opening. Mesmerized, I watched as it spun through the air, filling the ceiling of the cavern. When the smoke stopped undulating, my heart sank. I stared at it floating above the ground.

*How's that supposed to help me?*

The cavern spun around me. I closed my eyes and rested my head on the cool rocks. My back convulsed, and pain sucked the air out of my lungs.

A soft trilling sound forced my eyes open. Purple light pulsated through the opening of the vase.

*Purple light. Purple light?* I'd seen something like this before. *Where?*

*The library books.* I sat up, fighting my pain, pushing it back. My heart lightened. *Can that be the answer? Can I still end this?*

The ground shook. *Time's up.*

As Nefarious approached the cavern, I focused on the smoke, willing it to morph into two giant hands. They hovered above the entrance.

"Dacia," Nefarious growled. "Your suffering isn't over yet. You will beg for mercy before the end." Nefarious stood outside the entrance of the cavern. "Don't hide. Come. Fight me."

I cowered behind the rock, not ready to give up my life yet.

Voices screamed inside my head. *Run, Dacia, run. Get up. Get out of here while you can. Fight. Coward. Fool. Run!*

"No!" My voice bounced from wall to wall.

Nefarious snarled and charged toward me.

I hovered in the air and mimed the actions I wanted the hands to duplicate. I slammed my fist down, and the smoke pummeled Nefarious, knocking him to the ground. Sparks flew from his smoldering flesh. A howl filled the cavern.

He clambered to his feet. Flames ignited over his body, flaring up, leaping across his hide.

I reached for Nefarious, and my back spasmed. Pain rippled through my body. I gasped for breath, choking on the air before it could fill my lungs.

"Magic weakens you." Nefarious pulled his sword from his scabbard and sliced through one of the hands. The smoke reformed behind him.

*Flames. Pain. Blood.* My heart raced. Spots danced in front of my eyes, and my ears rang. *Nefarious' blade biting my neck.*

*I should have died.*

Nefarious stepped forward. His sword sliced through the air. Flames trailed behind it.

*Snap out of it!* Air filled my lungs and sound returned.

*Give up.*

*Why am I fighting?* I lowered my hands. *There's no way I can win.*

*Come to me.*

I flew toward Nefarious.

He lifted his clawed hand and threw a ball of flames at me.

*Fight!* I flew to the side. The fireball singed my arm.

I grabbed Nefarious with both smoky hands and yanked, dragging him to the ground. I jerked my hands back.

Nefarious thrashed, fighting to free himself, roaring, and growling.

I pulled him toward the mouth of the vase. The smoke retracted, taking Nefarious with it.

The stopper lay on the ground. With the last of my strength, I picked it up and shoved it into the bottle, sealing Nefarious inside. The emerald eye on the vase cast an eerie green glow through the cavern.

The amulet dimmed. *Is it over?* I stared at the vase—waiting for Nefarious to erupt from it—until my eyelids grew too heavy to stay open.

*Cody.* I pictured him offering me his strength, his eyes full of love.

My breaths shallowed. My pain dulled.

# Chapter 38

## *Not All Wounds Heal*

Sunlight poured into the room, blinding me. I forced my eyes open and found myself lying on one of Sarah's couches. *How did I get here? Was it all a dream?*

I pressed my hand down on the couch and pushed up. My body groaned in protest, and I fell back to the couch. Bandages wrapped my body, hands, arms, and leg. I looked like a mummy.

*Not a dream then.*

Cody sat on the floor asleep. His head was propped on the couch beside me. Sarah and Samantha slept, sitting on the couch across from me. The eye on the vase glowed at me from the coffee table.

I cleared my throat. "Hmm, hmm."

Three sets of eyes popped open. "Dacia," they all said at once.

Their voices sent warmth racing through my veins. In the cave, I didn't think I'd ever see any of them again. "Hey." I smiled. "How did I get here?"

All three of them started talking at once. Samantha stood and said, "I thought I got to tell the story."

"Yeah," Cody said.

"Sorry." Sarah waved her hand through the air. "Go ahead."

"I woke up, and you were gone." Samantha sat and folded her hands in her lap. "Cody wouldn't wake up, so I called Sarah."

"I knew I took too much." I ran my fingers through his hair. "Why did you let me?"

His blue eyes held mine, radiating warmth and love. "You needed it."

"We searched for you, but snow covered any trail you might have left. We looked everywhere, but we had no idea where to find you." Samantha waved her hands through the air.

I found myself wondering if she would be able to talk if her hands were tied behind her back.

"We went back to our room and found you lying on the floor, clutching the vase."

"But how?" I asked.

Sarah pulled on her sleeves, straightening her blouse. "We can only assume you teleported there after whatever happened."

"So"—Samantha pointed at the vase—"what we've been wondering is: Why is the eye glowing, and is it over?"

I lifted my hand to pull it through my hair, but the bandage prevented it. "It's over." I told them everything that happened. "Nefarious could've killed me. Seeing me suffer …" I swallowed and stared out the window, not seeing anything. "Things should've ended differently."

Cody moved from the floor to the couch. He lifted me onto his lap softly—like a bubble he was afraid to pop.

I winced when his arm touched my back, then snuggled into him, breathing him in. Cold, fresh mountain air. I kissed his neck before remembering we weren't alone. Heat rushed onto my cheeks.

A soft chuckle escaped from Cody's lips.

"Nefarious is in the vase?" Samantha asked. "Like a jinni?"

"I never would've thought of it if you hadn't suggested looking at mythology books."

Sarah's maternal instincts kicked in. "You've been out of it for about two days. Are you hungry? Can we get anything for you?"

"Two days?" I repeated. "What day … what time is it?"

"It's Tuesday morning." Samantha looked at her watch. "And, it's just about eight o'clock."

"Wow." I slumped back against Cody. "Has anything happened around here?"

"Cassandra woke up," Cody said.

"Is she back to her loveable old self?"

Samantha rubbed her forehead. "Vanessa said Cassandra doesn't remember anything. She felt like she'd gone to sleep and was just waking up the next morning. I guess she's having a hard time believing she missed out on so much time."

"Yeah, I can understand that. I can't believe it's Tuesday." I stared out the window at the snow. "I wonder why Cassandra was so much worse than the others."

Sarah picked up her mug, cradling it as if for warmth. "Mind you, this is all speculation, but here's what I think. According to Bryce, Cassandra had dreams about you before the two of you met. That leads me to believe she'd been under Nefarious' control for quite some time." She set the mug down and crossed her legs. "Bryce would follow Cassandra to the ends of the earth. Alvin and Vanessa aren't leaders. So, Cassandra's the only one he needed to possess to gain the allegiance of them all."

"Either Alvin or Vanessa or both were possessed." I fiddled with the chain around my neck. "The amulet glowed around them when Cassandra wasn't there but not around Bryce."

"That makes Bryce worse," Cody said. "He knew what he was doing."

"And he did it anyway," Samantha finished.

"Do you want anything?" Sarah asked again.

"I'm a little hungry." I pulled at the bandages on my right hand. "I imagine Cody's starving."

"He hasn't eaten since we got you back," Samantha said.

I stopped fidgeting and stared at him. "Why not?"

He looked into my eyes, his gaze tortured. "I thought we'd lost you. I didn't think you'd wake up."

"I'm going to be okay." I put my hand on his arm. "But you still owe me a date."

ꙮ

My wounds healed completely with the help of Cody's strength—he insisted. No blemishes marred my skin, nothing to show I'd nearly lost my life fighting a demon. From time to time, my leg burned just under the skin. It was probably my imagination working overtime, but it brought with it painful memories that would never heal.

I never saw the fairies after that fateful night. I wanted to tell them how grateful I was for their help, but something told me they already knew.

# Chapter 39

## There Be Dragons

I soar high above the ground, riding a pegasus.

Clouds paint the sky: pink, purple, orange, and yellow.

We are one, flying through the clouds, diving toward the ground. My laughter fills the heavens.

The pegasus tenses. His ears prick up. He banks hard to the right, nearly throwing me. A fireball flies through the air beside us.

A giant beast flies straight at us. Smoke billows from its nostrils.

Fear clenches my heart.

A dragon.

A massive, fire-breathing dragon. Its scales are black as night, its eyes fiery-red, hate-filled orbs.

Another wave of flames shoots from the beast's jaws. The pegasus dives, dipping and weaving through the sky.

The dragon twists with a grace that belies its size. Streams of flame fly at us in relentless pursuit.

The pegasus rolls to the side, and fire shoots straight at us. I hold my hands out in front of me and command the flames to extinguish.

The blaze kisses my arms and the pegasus' wings. Unable to fly, it plummets toward the ground.

Just before smashing into the earth, I woke up. My heart pummeled my chest. I sat up and turned my light on. My arms were burned, my pajamas charred.

*How can this be? I defeated Nefarious. The prophecy is fulfilled. Was this just a dream? Are the burns a coincidence? Or is another battle waiting around the corner for me?*

I climbed out of my loft and changed pajamas. Since Samantha was at her parents' house and Cody had gone back to sleeping in his room after I defeated Nefarious, I decided there was no reason to tell them. Finals were closing in on us, and I didn't want to add to their stress. *What they don't know won't hurt them.* I hoped.

## ***The End***

If you enjoyed this book, please leave a review. Feedback from you, the readers, matters to me. Plus, reviews buoy my spirits and stoke the fires of creativity.

# Acknowledgments

Writing a book takes a village. The words flow from one person, but the ideas are bounced off others. The villagers give advice on plot, on edits, on making the writing flow better. Some ideas are well received others are ignored, but it's part of the process.

I'd like to thank the multitude of people who have helped me along this journey. First, my husband, Jeff, the best thing to have ever happened to me was falling in love with him. Second, my kids, Jami and Jesse, for encouraging me and being my biggest fans. Third, my parents, Jim and Vicki, for always supporting me.

I'd like to thank all the critters at Critique Circle who helped me improve my writing: Kathryn Sparrow, Stone Jeffers, Travis Sullivan, Nadine Ducca, and Astrea Taylor. There were many more who weren't mentioned because I couldn't contact them to get their real names. I'd also like to thank all the other people who helped me along the way: Marva Mitchell, Berni Stevens, Cheryl Gage, Tammy King, Eileen Sharp, Linda Hirscher (RIP), Curtis A. Cooper, and Peggylou Beazley.

A special thank you to the 2016 Chicago Cubs for winning the World Series in my lifetime. Do it again!

And, last but not least, thanks to all the people at 20BooksTo50K® for the wonderful information and the encouragement. Without them, I'd feel even more lost in this self-publishing wilderness.

If you liked this story, you can join my mailing list.
Drop by my website MandiOyster.com
or if you have any comments,
shoot me a note at mandi@mandioyster.com.
I am always happy to hear from people who've read my work.
I try to answer every email I receive.

If you liked the story, please write a short review for me.
I greatly appreciate any kind words, even one or two
sentences go a long way. The number of reviews a
book receives improves how well a book does.

Facebook – https://www.facebook.com/MandiOysterAuthor
Instagram: https://www.instagram.com/mandioyster/
My web page – MandiOyster.com

The Story Continues in …

# Dacia Wolf and the Dragon Lord

Book 2